KISS OF FIRE

Bianca looked up at him, a teasing glint in her eye. "Who are you, really?" she asked. "Who *are* you, Larkin?"

His strong hands clasped her waist, so tiny that they could almost span it. His green eyes gleamed as bright as the emerald earrings she'd worn to the fiesta. "I'm a man being driven crazy for your kisses," he murmured into her ear. "You can't know what you're doing to me, Bianca."

"Kiss me, Larkin," she whispered. "Kiss me the way you did in the garden!"

"Do you know what you're doing?" he asked in a husky voice.

"Perhaps I don't, but I know I want you to kiss me," she declared.

His lips captured hers in a long, lingering kiss and their bodies pressed urgently close to each other. The flames of passion soared as Bianca gave herself up to the wild, tantalizing sensations he was arousing in her. His kiss was a kiss of flaming fire!

Outside the barn, a loud clap of thunder exploded and the sharp flashing streaks of lightning lit up the barn, but Bianca and Larkin did not notice, for they were too engulfed in the explosion of their own passion. Larkin swept her up in his strong arms and carried her gently to a pile of clean, sweet-smelling hay. Reason had left him completely; he was ruled by his reckless desire.

His lips clung to hers, wanting more and more . . .

WANDA OWEN

TEXAS MAGIC

ZEBRA BOOKS
KENSINGTON PUBLISHING CORP.

This book is dedicated to my beautiful little granddaughter, Sandy, who presented me with my first great-grandson, Eric.

ZEBRA BOOKS

are published by

Kensington Publishing Corp.
475 Park Avenue South
New York, NY 10016

First printing: September, 1992

Printed in the United States of America

Part One

Bianca's Homecoming

One

The spraying mist of the fountain had a cooling effect on this hot summer Texas day as it had for many a summer now. Mark Kane sat on the bench, waving a fond farewell to his feisty granddaughter as she went toward the iron gate of the courtyard to leave. With her golden blond hair bouncing around her shoulders as she walked, he could have imagined her to be Amanda; time was standing still. But she was not Amanda; she was Bianca Moreno. She had not inherited Amanda's beautiful blue eyes—eyes that had reminded Mark of the fieldflowers in his pastureland. Bianca had the blackest eyes he'd ever seen, inherited from her father, Tony Moreno.

Mark sat there, thinking how he wished his sweet Jenny could have lived to know this granddaughter of theirs. Dear God, how he wished she had!

So much had changed around the Circle K Ranch over the last twenty years, Mark thought as he sat by the fountain where he and Jenny had spent so many serene moments.

The cantankerous old rancher didn't like it worth a damn that he could no longer straddle a horse and ride over the Texas countryside he loved with a deep passion. Sitting in a rocking chair most of the day didn't set well with a man like Mark Kane. The one bright spot in his life was his grand-daughter.

Like all grandparents, he wanted to tell himself that she

was like his people, but she wasn't. Neither could he say that she was a Moreno. Bianca was like neither of them; just·herself.

She adored her Grandfather Kane, for he never tried to bridle her as the rest of her family did. Her other champion was her great-grandfather, Estaban Moreno.

Perhaps the reason the two elderly gentlemen were so understanding of her was that they could recall the years when her own parents were Bianca's age and were as daring and reckless as she was now. Neither of them tried to deny that she was a wild and reckless young person, but her father had been the same in his youth. The beautiful Amanda Kane had been just as stubborn and willful as her daughter Bianca was now. Perhaps this was what made Bianca so special to Mark Kane and old Estaban Moreno.

Mark yearned to relive those glorious times! Though there had been heartache and pain, there were also heights of happiness.

It was a better time than this uneventful existence. The Texas countryside had calmed over the last twenty years and the ranchers were not met with the challenges he had faced running his Circle K Ranch.

Kane missed those rough, rugged days!

On her huge red stallion, Bianca had ridden at a fast gallop back to her parents' ranch. Nothing made her feel more stimulated than to spur Rojo over the countryside with the breeze blowing her long blond hair away from her face.

Those long golden tresses of hers and her flashing, excited black eyes were enough to make her a beautiful vision. One of Señor Moreno's hired hands found himself mesmerized by the sight of her galloping up to the corral. He tilted his flat-crowned hat back on his head so he could get a better view of her sitting in the saddle as she slowed Rojo's pace. Like most of the men who worked at the Moreno Ranch, Rick Larkin had heard the gossip about the reckless escapades of the señorita. She was nothing like her brother, the mild-mannered Estaban Moreno.

None of the hired hands had anything good to say about Señor Moreno's son with his highhanded, snobbish ways, and they were glad that his visits to the ranch were few and far between.

Rick Larkin had yet to encounter him, for he'd only been at the Moreno Ranch for six weeks. When he'd first hired on, the young señorita had been attending Stonebrooke's School for Young Ladies back East.

Larkin had to admit that after he first laid eyes on the beautiful Bianca, she was enough to urge him to hang around the Moreno Ranch longer than he'd originally planned to do. A good-looking woman always caught his eye, and there was no denying that she was a most unusual beauty with those flashing black eyes, long golden hair, and her light-tawny complexion. Most girls with blond hair were fair-skinned, but not Bianca. It had to be the blend of her fair-skinned mother and her father, Tony Moreno, that had produced such a lovely girl.

What Rick Larkin did not realize was that the Morenos' daughter had an eye for a good-looking fellow. Rick Larkin was no ordinary hired ranch hand, Bianca had decided the first time she'd spied him swaggering around the corrals. She had appraised the way his pants molded to his firm, muscled hips and thighs. She'd noticed how his trim waist expanded into a broad chest, and she'd seen the curly ringlets of hair on his chest when he left the buttons of his shirt unfastened.

There was also a cocky air about him as he moved that told her he was a very self-assured man, and Bianca liked that. She liked the way his sandy hair tickled the collar of his shirt

9

and the devious glint in his eyes as he'd looked her way. He was a man who challenged and dared a woman to get to know him better.

He was that handsome, rugged type of man that Bianca found intriguing. What she could not know was that her own mother had felt exactly as she did the first time she encountered the man who at that time called himself Tony Branigan and not Tony Moreno. But at her tender age of sixteen, Bianca had not been told about her mother's own reckless life and her tempestuous love affair with Tony.

Often, Amanda relived her own young life as she watched her daughter blossoming into such a beauty. More and more she and Tony were feeling concern over Bianca's recklessness.

Her own father and Grandfather Estaban certainly did not help them with their constant doting ways, but Amanda could see why the two elderly gentlemen were completely beguiled by her Bianca. She was a little enchantress and she always had been.

All the years of just being Tony's wife and the patroness of Rancho Río had been a serene time for Amanda. They'd been blessed with two children — Estaban, who they'd named for Tony's beloved grandfather, and Bianca Alvarado, named for the aunt of Tony's who'd played such an important role in their lives and love affair some twenty years ago.

But she was wondering if all the peace and serenity was about to come to an end now that her vivacious, energetic Bianca had returned to the ranch after three years away at finishing school.

Amanda could not help thinking that she herself had posed the same problems and concerns when she returned from the eastern boarding school. Her mother and father must surely have felt very much the way she was feeling right now.

Her son Estaban was a quiet young man who reminded Amanda of her older brother, Jeff, but Bianca was as stubborn and headstrong as she had been at her age. Coupled with that daring, adventuresome nature Bianca had inherited from her father, Tony, it was going to be an interesting time in their lives.

At least Bianca had not fallen head over heels in love with any of the handsome young suitors who'd been beating a path to their door since the news had spread over the countryside like wildfire that she was back in Gonzales County.

Her brother Jeff and his wife Mona were having a fiesta this Friday night to welcome Bianca back home. The Big D Ranch would host a multitude of neighbors and friends for the occasion. Amanda was hoping that her father would be able to share the evening with all his family.

It broke her heart to see how his huge, rugged body had been reduced to such an impaired state over the last two years. She was just grateful that Jeff had taken over the running of the Circle K along with his own ranch.

But Bianca insisted that her grandfather attend the fiesta. Giving that infectious laugh of hers, when they were dining that evening, she told her parents, "Grandpa told me this afternoon that hell or high water would not stop him from going to that fiesta Friday evening!" Her black onyx eyes twinkled brightly. Tony glanced over at his wife and grinned. He knew that Mark Kane meant exactly what he'd said. He also knew that Bianca was the apple of old Mark's eyes.

A devilish tease, Bianca asked her brother, Estaban, "And who will you bring, Estaban? Is it to be Lita Morales?"

"No, Bianca!" he replied indignantly. "I'm escorting Carolina Rivera."

"Oh, Estaban!" his sister sighed. "Carolina is not half as pretty as Lita."

"Pretty is not everything, Bianca," Estaban pointed out.

Even though Estaban was a few years older and several inches taller, he had never been able to intimidate his sister.

Neither Amanda nor Tony ever concerned themselves that Bianca would not hold her own with Estaban.

But privately, Tony Moreno had to agree with his young daughter that the little Morales girl was far more beautiful than Carolina. If he was in Estaban's place there was no question in his mind which young lady he would have invited to the fiesta.

Years ago, the golden-haired Amanda Kane with her flashing blue eyes was the most beautiful girl in Gonzales County and he had been determined that she would be his. And she had been — for twenty-odd years.

Estaban shot back at his sister, "And who is going to take you, Bianca?"

Tossing her head to the side as she forked at her beefsteak, she shrugged her shoulders and replied, "It could be Emilo or Armando. I've not decided."

"You mean that you've got both of them dangling until the very last minute? The fiesta is just a few days away. *Madre de Dios,* Bianca!"

"What? I might not accept either of their invitations and go with Julio." She took a bite of her steak and ignored her brother as he sat there shaking his head. Tony and Amanda could hardly restrain their amused laughter as they exchanged glances.

Later, when they were alone enjoying a leisurely stroll in their courtyard garden, Tony took his wife's hand. "It is quite a family we have, eh *querida?*" he lovingly told her.

"Oh, yes, it is that! Poor Estaban — she perplexes him so. It will never change. I remember when they were little and she drove him crazy with all her little acts of mischief."

Tony chuckled. "And she'd look up at us with those twinkling black eyes of hers and it would be impossible to be too harsh on her. At least, it was for me!"

Amanda laughed. "Tony Moreno, I found out very quickly

12

that for all that rugged, indomitable air of yours that you had a sweet, mellow nature."

He squeezed her closer to him and confessed, "But you conquered me, *querida*. For you, I can be very sweet and mellow. And the only other female drawing this from me is our beautiful Bianca."

Amanda gave him a loving smile. He still had the capacity to flame a passion in her that spread like a Texas wildfire to consume her completely.

Jeff Kane recognized the huge red stallion with his niece in the saddle as they approached his corral. Rojo was a handsome beast and he would have bought the horse if Tony had not seen him first. Bianca had loved horses from the moment she was able to toddle around the corrals with her father and she was riding her own little pony almost as soon as she was walking.

He recalled how concerned he and his wife Mona had been when they had seen that small minx at the Rancho Río astride the pony that Tony had purchased for her. But his sister Amanda had assured them that she would be fine, and she *had* been.

Jeff stood there by the corral fence and watched her gallop up with her long hair flowing away from her face and her eyes so alive and sparkling. Some dude was going to marry her and take her away from Rancho Río before very long.

She threw her hand up to wave to him and called out, "Tío Jeff! Good morning to you!"

"And a good morning to you, honey. You are one hell of a sight for these old eyes to behold!"

By now she was up to the fence and leaping off Rojo. "You're not old, Tío Jeff."

His hand went out to take hers as she scampered up the

13

railing to fling her leg over the top railing and leap down to the ground.

"And what brings you to the Big D? Is it just to see your uncle, eh?"

"Of course. I was taking my usual morning ride and somehow, I just found myself coming in this direction." She grinned up at him as he guided her across the corral so they could go to the house and sit down on the side veranda.

"Your aunt's going to be sorry she missed you, but she and Rosa went to town to get some things for the fiesta," Jeff told her as they crossed the ground between the corral and the house.

"I think Tía Mona is the sweetest woman. I appreciate her going to all this trouble for me. I — I can't wait for Friday night. I'm getting so excited, Tío Jeff!" she declared.

"Well, I would expect you to be excited. A fiesta always excited me, I can tell you," he confessed to her.

Her pretty face took on a solemn look. "I — I just can't decide who I wish to have as my escort, Tío Jeff. Do I have to have a particular fellow?"

"Don't know any rules that demand that, little one. If you can't make up that pretty head of yours because you probably have a half dozen eager to escort you, then come with your parents. I've no doubt that several gentlemen are going to be swarming around you all evening," Jeff Kane laughed.

"You just helped me make up my mind, Tío Jeff. I shall tell Emilo, Julio, and Armando I will be coming alone and I'll accept none of their requests to be my escort," she declared firmly.

Jeff Kane threw back his head and roared with laughter. "Oh, Bianca! I can tell you someone who'd be very honored to be your escort to the fiesta. He is a gent worthy of a beauty as you."

Jeff had gained her curiosity. She stared up at him for a

14

moment before she inquired as to who this man was.

"Your grandfather Kane, honey," he told her.

A slow smile broke on her face as she flung her arms around her uncle's neck to plant a kiss on his cheek. "Oh, Tío Jeff! I shall ride over to the Circle K and tell him. How smart you are! Of course, he should be the one!"

How happy that would make the old man, Jeff thought. It could be the last happy memory he'd have, and Jeff knew the special place Bianca had always held in his father's heart. Never had he resented this, though, because he knew what Mark Kane felt when he looked at Bianca. He saw yester-years and his young daughter, Amanda.

As different as they were, Amanda so fair with her golden hair and blue eyes and Bianca with her black eyes and tawny complexion, they were so alike in temperament and their ways.

Bianca told her uncle goodbye and made her departure from the Big D Ranch to head for the Circle K to see her grandfather.

So often she had ridden this trail between the three different ranches in Gonzales County that she swore Rojo could get her there even if she wasn't in charge of the reins.

As wild as the wind that blew over the Texas countryside, she and Rojo galloped over the rolling land. Her wide-brimmed, flat-crowned black hat was resting on her back. Riding sidesaddle was not for Bianca! She made a magnificent sight in her black twill divided skirt, which allowed her to straddle the big red stallion. The soft sheer black tunic she had on clung to her curvy body.

At two different points on the rolling countryside, two men were taking in the glorious sight of her. One man was hunting a stray bull who'd roamed away from the herd from Rancho Río at some point between the Circle K and Rancho Río. He was just about to give up on spotting the missing

15

bull and was taking a moment to rest and wipe the sweat from his brow before putting his hat back on. Suddenly, his eyes spotted the sight of Señorita Bianca. Rick Larkin's green eyes watched her riding toward the Circle K Ranch and he was mesmerized.

The other man was in the cluster of trees when he spied her riding over the countryside. But he had been stalking Bianca for days. From the first moment he'd seen her at Rancho Río, he was fired by desire to have her. But that would probably have been all it would have ever amounted to if Señor Moreno had not fired him a couple of weeks ago.

What else could the daughter of a wealthy rancher ever be but a fantasy to a common hired Mexican worker like Miguel Ortega. But now he would have his revenge on the father of this pretty señorita. Señor Moreno would not be happy that he had had his way with that precious daughter of his.

That would be Miguel's satisfaction before he drifted out of Gonzales County. And this was the moment. Without hesitation, he spurred his horse into a fast gallop, riding out of the grove of trees where he'd been waiting to see which trail she'd take.

Across the way, Rick Larkin's sharp eyes saw the Mexican riding out of the grove and guiding his pinto toward Bianca. Although the broad-brimmed sombrero shaded his face, Rick was certain that he recognized the man as a hired hand he'd seen around the ranch. He also knew that he was up to no good.

A moment later he saw him catch up with Bianca and reach over to grab the reins of her horse and she began to fight and struggle with him.

Immediately, Rick urged his horse to move in that direction. The Mexican was leading the red stallion out of the open country toward the wooded area close by. And it wasn't hard to figure out what was on the man's mind.

The fool had to be *loco* to try such insanity with Señor Moreno's daughter, Rick thought as he galloped faster. He admired the mighty battle the señorita was giving him as she swung out her arms trying to hit him as he held her horse at a close rein.

Bianca saw the evil gleam in the man's black eyes and she knew what his intentions were. As reluctant as she was to desert Rojo, she had her life to think about. She flung her leg over the front of the saddle and leaped to the ground. As soon as her feet hit the ground she immediately began to run as fast as she could.

She welcomed the sight of Rick Larkin galloping up to her. In one mighty sweep of his strong, powerful hands, she found herself lifted from the ground and swung up behind him.

"Hold tight, *chiquita*. We're going after that bastard," Larkin declared as he urged his horse to move again.

Her arms circled his waist as she held on tight and she felt the tenseness in his firm, muscled body as her body pressed against him. An excited, titillating sensation sparked within her. She had never known this wild, wonderful feeling before when she'd been around other men.

Now she knew why Rick Larkin had whetted her interest!

Two

Miguel Ortega knew a rider was pursuing him, and he dropped the reins of Bianca's horse to weave through the dense woods at a faster pace. But the rider still gained on him.

Larkin only slacked his pace long enough for Bianca to swing off his horse once she spotted Rojo. Rick yelled at her to mount up and ride to the ranch. "I'll tend to him," he told her as he left her behind and rode on.

By the time Bianca had ridden up the drive to the corral, she had decided that she was going to wait for Larkin. She had to give him the thanks he deserved.

She'd hardly had time to turn Rojo over to the young Mexican lad who worked around the corral and walk back out of the barn when she spied him astride his own horse guiding the Mexican's horse. Larkin had obviously subdued the man and tied his wrists with a leather strap to bring him back to the ranch.

Larkin grinned as he asked Bianca to get her father. The Mexican's eyes were cast down to the ground, for Miguel Ortega knew that he was probably never going to be leaving Gonzales County once Señor Moreno was finished with him.

She found her mother and father sitting out on the patio

that overlooked the courtyard garden. She quickly explained to them what had happened.

"I thank God for Larkin," she explained. "He saved me, sent me on home on Rojo, and went after this man. He's waiting for you now to turn him over to you, Father."

A deep, angry frown etched Tony Moreno's face as he leaped out of the chair to march across the courtyard. Amanda found herself left on the patio alone, for Bianca was trotting directly behind her father.

She smiled, watching the two of them leave the courtyard, and shook her head as she thought to herself that Tony and she would have many a restless night of worry over a daughter who was so beautiful.

Dear God, she prayed that she would be as wise as her own mother had been!

Rick Larkin had heard that Señor Tony Moreno was a man to be admired and respected before he'd hired on at the Rancho Río, but now he knew it to be true. He saw him marching toward the corral with Bianca almost running to keep up with him and thought him a most imposing figure of a man. Larkin was thinking to himself that he wouldn't want to get him riled at him.

He approached Larkin and Miguel sitting on their horses with Miguel's wrists tied and bound. "I thank you, Larkin," he said with sincerity, "for what you did for my daughter and we will talk later."

His fierce eyes then darted toward Miguel. "Miguel," he said gruffly, "if I followed my desires I'd string you up to that oak over there and let you swing, but I'll do you a favor and turn you over to Sheriff Duncan. I like to think I'm a law-abiding Texan now."

The señor's horse was brought to him and he took full

charge of taking his prisoner in tow. Justice would prevail one way or the other as far as Tony Moreno was concerned.

Larkin found himself politely dismissed, and Bianca stood watching her father ride away. Both of them were harboring similar thoughts as they observed the two departing men. Larkin was hoping he could one day be such a rare man as the señor; Bianca was thinking that it was a man like her father, with all his strength and power, who would capture and conquer her restless heart.

Larkin's green eyes met with her dark eyes. For one long moment neither of them spoke. Larkin finally broke the silence. "He's a remarkable man. I could have taken Miguel in for him."

"But he would not have allowed that. My father is a very proud man, Larkin."

"I know, *chiquita*. That is why I admire him so much." He grinned down at her. He did not wish to tell her the many other reasons he felt as he did about Señor Moreno. The time would come for that later. "You are all right, I trust?"

"I am fine, Larkin. I do thank you for what you did for me," she told him.

His eyes danced over her in a way that made Bianca feel as if he was slowly and sensuously baring her. It was as if he knew her innermost thoughts. She was more than convinced as she told him goodbye that this man was no ordinary hired ranch hand. There was a certain air and finesse about him that told her there was much more to Rick Larkin. It made her very curious.

A sly smile came to her face as she entered the courtyard garden. She wished that she could dance with him at the fiesta, strong arms holding her tight. He was far more exciting than Emilo, Armando, or Julio!

When she went inside, her mother was anxious to know

where Tony was. After Bianca had explained, she started to go upstairs to her room, calling over her shoulder, "I'll see you at dinner, Mother. Is Estaban going to be with us tonight?"

"No, dear—he's dining with Carolina and her parents this evening."

Bianca laughed. "Estaban had better watch out or that Carolina will be getting him to the church."

Amanda just smiled, knowing that Carolina's parents were overjoyed about Esteban asking to escort their daughter to the fiesta Friday evening. There might be a hint of truth in Bianca's statement.

An hour later, Tony returned home and climbed the stairway knowing that he would find his wife in their bedroom refreshing herself before their dinner hour as was her custom.

He went to the dressing table where Amanda sat on the stool brushing out her long blond hair, which was just beginning to streak with some silver.

He looked in the mirror and his black eyes met with hers. "That sonofabitch was going to take his pleasure with Bianca. Damn! If he'd managed to carry out his intentions, I swear, Amanda, I would have killed him!"

"Well, he didn't, thanks to Larkin," Amanda told him, patting his hand resting on her shoulder.

"Yes, I want to have a talk with Larkin tomorrow. I've had my eye on him for the last few days. I like him. Guess you could say I'm curious about him. Not just the ordinary hired hand. Can't tell you what I mean 'cause I don't know myself just yet." Tony smiled at her, leaving her at the dressing table while he changed into a clean white shirt.

As the two of them descended the stairs, Amanda remarked to him that the incident had not seemed to upset Bianca.

"I almost wish that it had—just a little so she'd be more cautious in the future," Tony commented.

Amanda understood exactly what he meant. She was also thinking as they strolled into the parlor to join Bianca that she was glad Estaban was not home tonight, for he would have given her a brotherly admonishment as he did so often about her riding alone over the countryside.

Late that evening when Estaban had returned to the hacienda he met his father coming out of his study.

Tony told his son what had happened to his sister that afternoon. Estaban accompanied him up the steps. "Bianca scares me, Father," Estaban told his father. "She—she is so reckless, and that is dangerous for a woman. She thinks that I'm just a nagging older brother, but it's only because I love her."

"A girl as beautiful as she is can prove to be a target for all the wrong kind of men," he observed. "The little minx is so bold that I fear one day she'll get herself into something she can't talk herself out of."

Tony had to agree with Estaban. They reached the second landing and Tony told his son good night as Estaban went to his room across the hall from his parents' bedroom.

Sharing the bunkhouse with the other men at the ranch did not appeal to Larkin. He liked all the fellows, but he also liked his own privacy. It was impossible to have that in a bunkhouse.

He was not in the mood to join in the nightly card games, so he'd roamed around the grounds and puffed on five or six cigarettes. He had allowed his eyes to glance toward the two-story, red-tiled hacienda. Bianca Moreno was somewhere within those walls.

He was remembering the way her soft body felt pressed against his back as she rode behind him for that brief moment this afternoon and it stirred a blazing flame of desire in him. There was a lot of fire and spirit in that girl. Larkin knew she could spell danger for him.

Usually he could keep a cool, level head, but Bianca Moreno with her golden hair and flashing black eyes was such a bewitching creature he found her hard to dismiss.

But everything told him that he should!

Three

Giving the incident no thought, Bianca got up and dressed in her riding garments. She intended to ride over to the Circle K Ranch this morning as she'd planned to do yesterday.

As soon as she ate one of the cook's cinnamon rolls and gulped down a cup of black coffee, she rushed out to the barn to get Rojo saddled up.

The cook, Selina, gathered up her empty cup and shook her head as she smiled, for it seemed to her that Señorita Bianca was always in a rush to be off somewhere. Señora Amanda's children were such a different pair. Señor Estaban moved in such an unhurried, dignified way, but not the little señorita.

Rancho Río had not been the same since Bianca had returned from the East. But Selina couldn't get angry when her kitchen was invaded by Bianca at various times of the day as the girl helped herself to the pastries she'd baked for the evening meal or the next morning's breakfast. How could she, when Bianca, that winning smile on her face and the piece of a pastry clutched in her hand, would declare that she was the best cook in the whole world and those twinkling black eyes would be looking at her.

Still munching on the last bite of the cinnamon roll, Bianca dashed into the barn, stopping short when she saw her father by one of the stalls talking to Rick Larkin.

Both of the two tall men quit talking to gaze in her direction. "Well, *niña* — good morning," her father addressed her. Larkin just stood there letting his green eyes survey the delightful sight of her in the burgundy riding skirt and pink voile blouse. She did not wear her hat this morning but had braided her hair in one long thick braid hanging down her back.

"Good morning, Father, and good morning to you, Larkin," she mumbled as she swallowed the last bite of the roll.

"And what are you in such a hurry about, Bianca?" Tony inquired of his daughter.

"I'm going to see Grandfather Kane. I wish to invite him to be my escort to the fiesta Friday night."

Immediately, she mellowed Tony Moreno, who had been prepared to forbid her from going out this morning. But he was so impressed by her thoughtful gesture, and he knew how happy and proud Mark would be, that he could hardly refuse her.

"That is very nice of you, Bianca, to be so thoughtful of your grandfather, and I shall allow you to ride to the Circle K — but only if Larkin rides with you. Is that agreeable with you, Larkin?" he asked, turning in Rick's direction.

"You're the boss, señor. I'll be glad to accompany Señorita Bianca to her grandfather's."

"Then it is settled," Tony firmly declared as he turned to leave the barn. Bianca and Rick found themselves left alone in the barn.

"Well, shall we get Rojo saddled up for the ride to the

Circle K?" Larkin asked her, knowing that she resented not being allowed to ride out alone.

"Yes—yes, I guess so," she mumbled as she watched her father going out the barn door.

His own horse was ready for him to mount, so he led Rojo outside the barn and assisted Bianca up. Larkin took pride in his own fine stallion Raven, with his black coat and mane.

Both the horses were fine-looking specimens of horse-flesh and both of them had the same kind of fire and spirit. Rick allowed Bianca to take the lead, thinking that this might soothe her resentment about him tagging along with her.

He quickly found that she liked to go at a fast pace, but Larkin never doubted that Raven could outrun Rojo if he wanted to allow it to be otherwise.

Bianca's black eyes darted over to him and she gave him a smile as she abruptly pulled up on the reins to slow Rojo's pace. She gave the horse's neck an affectionate pat and brushed her hand down its mane. Only his mane and tail were black. The rest of his coat was a rich reddish-brown color.

After Bianca complimented Larkin on Raven, she asked him how long he'd had the horse and if he had found him in Gonzales County.

"Nope. Got Raven over in Guadalupe County."

"So that's where you're from then?" Her curious nature was hoping to learn more about this man who'd rescued her yesterday and whose good looks had caught her attention since she'd arrived back at the ranch.

"Nope. I'm not from Guadalupe County. Just bought Raven over there." But before she could pursue the subject further, Rick pointed out that they were approaching the Circle K.

The ride had been so brief, Bianca was thinking, and she had not minded Larkin's company at all.

"I have no intentions of telling Grandfather about yesterday, but that old fox will be questioning why you are with me. I've got to think of some reason before we get there," she declared.

"Whatever you say I'll go along with, but you better think up something fast, señorita," he urged.

"I'm thinking. I'm thinking," she muttered, for the house was now in view. She said nothing more to him as they rode up to the hitching post to bring their horses to a halt.

He was curious to know what kind of tale she was going to tell her grandfather. Before he could get to her side to help her off Rojo she'd already leaped down to the ground.

"Better warn you, Larkin, that my grandfather can be a very blunt, gruff man. It galls him fiercely that he can't ride over to the Circle K or do the things he always did."

Rick grinned. "Guess I'd be cantankerous, too, if I was in his shoes."

She gave out a soft giggle. "Guess I would be, too." She took the lead as they went from the hitching post into the grounds surrounding the two-story house.

He was sitting in the courtyard garden by the fountain as Bianca had suspected, enjoying the sunshine as it glowed through the thick branches of the trees. He spied Bianca's golden head before he took notice of the tall figure trailing behind her. He wondered who this hombre was with his granddaughter.

"Good morning, Grandfather!" she called out to him as she walked up to the fountain. Bending down to plant a

27

kiss on his wrinkled cheek, she teased him about his whiskers pricking her face.

"Guess I'd better give myself a shave before Friday then," Mark grinned up at her.

"Guess you sure better do that, for I've something to talk to you about concerning the fiesta, Grandfather. But first let me introduce you to Rick Larkin."

Rick stepped up to give him a handshake. "Good to meet you. I've heard about Mark Kane often."

"Well, I'm glad to meet you, Larkin. Are you with Tony over there at the Rancho Río or are you new to the county?"

"I'm working at the ranch. Hired on a few weeks ago," Rick told him. Kane's keen eyes were carefully surveying him as he spoke and the old rancher was favorably impressed with his good manners.

The other thing that struck Kane was that Tony Moreno would not have allowed his daughter to associate with a mere hired hand around his ranch.

"Sit down, you two, and I'll have some refreshments brought out to you."

"Oh, no Grandfather Kane. I can't stay long, and Larkin has got to go to Tío Jeff's on some business for father. But I did want to ride over here this morning since I didn't get to come yesterday to ask you to escort me to the fiesta. Would you, Grandfather?"

For a moment Mark Kane could not speak. "You—you want me, Bianca?" he finally said.

"I want only you, and remember the fiesta is to celebrate my returning home," she declared with an impish twinkle in her eyes. Rick Larkin thought that she could charm the horns off a billy goat if she wished to.

Mark's wrinkled hand reached out to take hers and his voice cracked with emotion when he told her, "I'd be the

28

damnedest proud man in the whole state of Texas to escort you, honey."

All of them broke out with laughter. A short time later, Bianca and Larkin took their leave from the Circle K Ranch. She thought she had explained Larkin's presence very convincingly.

He would never know that Larkin was not riding on over to the Big D Ranch as she'd told him.

As Larkin helped Bianca up on Rojo, he thought about all the tales he'd heard about her being so wild and reckless. Today he'd seen a young lady who'd made an old man very happy, and he thought it had been sweet of her to ask the old fellow to escort her to the fiesta.

Their ride back toward Rancho Río was at a slower pace. Bianca allowed Rick to take the lead and she stayed at the pace he set. She noticed that he was not as talkative as he had been earlier. "You're awfully quiet. Did Grandfather do that to you? I thought you two got along just fine," she remarked.

"I'm sorry, señorita. I liked your grandfather, as a matter of fact. And he certainly has a fond spot in his heart for you." A smile finally broke on his face. A man could lose his heart to her very quickly, he realized.

"Well, I feel the same way about him. I'm so pleased it made him happy that I asked him to escort me to the fiesta."

Larkin suddenly pulled up on the reins. "Who would not be happy to take you to a fiesta?" As soon as the words were out, he realized how impulsively he'd spoken.

A pleased smile came to her face. "And does that include you, Larkin?" she coyly asked him.

His green eyes danced over her face for a second before he gave her his answer. "Yes, *chiquita*—that *does* include me." Immediately, he spurred Raven to move before he forgot himself completely and did something really rash—like reaching over and kissing those inviting lips that were tempting him so.

Maybe he should never have come to Gonzales County! But then he had not expected to meet such a devastating beauty like Bianca Moreno. In the past, he could take his pleasures with beautiful ladies and leave them without ever looking back.

But he knew that would never be the case if he ever made love to Bianca. She would haunt him the rest of his life!

Four

After Bianca and Rick Larkin left the Circle K Ranch Kane ordered his housekeeper to see to the airing and pressing of his best black coat and pants.

"Give that black hat a good brushing, Estella, 'cause I'm escorting my granddaughter to the fiesta," he boasted.

The señor had not seemed this alive and cheerful in a long time. Estella's eyes warmed with happiness for him. "Ah, señor, I will see that you are the grandest gentleman there. You and Señorita Bianca will make a most handsome pair."

Estella felt it was the passing of his dear wife Jenny that had devastated Mark Kane. While his daughter and son, Jeff, were very solicitous of their father and there were now the visits of Bianca to look forward to, they could not compensate for the absence of his devoted wife.

And to complicate matters, when his horse got spooked and threw him a few years ago, his leg and hip had never been the same.

Sometimes Estella wondered if it would have been better for the señor if he had gone to live with Jeff over at the Big D or if he would go to Rancho Río to live with his daughter, Amanda. But Mark Kane was not about to leave this house as long as he lived.

Estella knew that his son Jeff had approached him to come live with him and Mona. He'd even offered to buy the Circle K Ranch and combine it with the Big D Ranch. Over the years, Jeff had become a prosperous rancher in his own right. But Mark Kane had indignantly declared that the Circle K would never be sold. "Someone with Kane blood in their veins will one day inherit the Circle K and carry on after me."

Estella had never seen him so irate as he was that day, but she knew Jeff had not meant to offend him. He just did not realize how intense the old man was about wanting the Circle K Ranch to go on long after he was dead and gone. Never could he have accepted that his grand ranch would become known as part of the Big D and Jeff realized that when he'd left the ranch. Never had he mentioned it again to his father.

Tony Moreno had a keener understanding of the depth of passion a man could feel about his land and knew it was similar to what a man felt for his woman—a pride and a depth of love that demanded he protect it with his life if need be. He had never dared to make a suggestion like Jeff's, but he also knew that Jeff Kane had more than he could handle and had seen things deteriorating around the Circle K Ranch.

He had not discussed his feelings with Amanda yet, but he felt if he could just find the right kind of man to take charge of the ranch for old Mark, Jeff could be relieved of responsibility he could not handle.

But family harmony was very important to Moreno and he did not wish to get on bad terms with his brother-in-law. In another month, he would have the solution. He was sure of it.

"I've got to figure out a way to get all the people we're going to be taking to the fiesta over to Jeff's," Tony told Amanda the next morning as they enjoyed their breakfast on the veranda.

Amanda immediately thought of a very simple plan to save all the ladies' full gowns from being crushed and allow ample room for everyone. "It would probably heighten Father's pleasure to arrive alone with his granddaughter. Have a driver and buggy go by the Circle K to pick him up. That way he and Bianca can arrive separate from the rest of the family. He would love that!"

Tony bent over to plant a kiss on her cheek. "Now, why didn't I think of that?" He grinned, then left his wife to go to the barn and corrals in hopes of finding Larkin. He was going to appoint him to be the driver of the buggy taking Mark Kane and Bianca to the Big D.

He found him in a stall checking out one of the fine Thoroughbreds Tony had recently purchased. Tony asked him if something was wrong with the horse.

"Not sure, but I just noticed some swelling around that joint of his leg. Would you know if this horse has been ridden hard in the last day or two, señor? To my knowledge, he hasn't except for running in the corral," Rick Larkin told him, patting the horse's mane as he prepared to come out of the stall.

"I can't figure out anyone riding him. Bianca rides no horse except Rojo, and Estaban usually goes around the country in a buggy, as does my wife. None of the hired men ride my Thoroughbreds."

Tony told him to keep a very special eye on the horse. He also told him about his assignment for the night of the fiesta. Larkin was more than willing to accept. He would be going to the fiesta after all. He would not be allowed to join the group, but he could certainly stand in the shadows and observe the beautiful Bianca during the evening. That would be a hell of a lot more exciting than playing cards in the bunkhouse.

"I'll be happy to drive them, señor," Larkin told his boss. "Señor Kane is a remarkable gentleman and it was my pleasure to meet him."

"He certainly is. I admired him long before I married his daughter, and I still do."

Tony did not mention to his wife or his daughter who would be driving Bianca over to the Circle K Ranch to pick up her grandfather. But he did inform them of the general arrangement, and Bianca thought his idea was wonderful.

Amanda was just hoping her father would be having one of his better days tomorrow so he might enjoy himself.

The lamps dimmed early that night at the Rancho Río because all of them knew the next twenty-four hours would be busy ones.

Bianca had shrugged aside the idea of wearing the white organdy or the cream silk gown her mother had suggested for the fiesta. She wanted to wear a gown of brilliant color, so she had picked the emerald-green lace lined with the same shade of taffeta. It had a scooped neckline and short puffed sleeves. The fitted bodice had a basque waistline that displayed the sensuous curves of her figure.

On her dainty ears, she wore the teardrop emerald earrings her grandfather Estaban had given to her on her sixteenth birthday. She wasn't sure how she wanted to wear her long hair. To look sophisticated she could have piled it atop her head in a multitude of soft curls, but she did not wish to look sophisticated tonight. Neither did she want to look so casual as she did when her long golden tresses just flowed around her shoulders.

Finally, she tried pulling the sides of her hair up to make a crown of curls and allowed the back to flow down her back in soft curls. Her lovely face was enhanced with her hair pulled back, and Bianca was quite pleased by the reflection in her mirror.

When Amanda came to her daughter's room and saw the beautiful vision she made in the emerald-green gown, she had to admit that she'd made the right choice. Perhaps the white organdy would have been the perfect choice for her, with her fair skin and blue eyes, but for her tawny-skinned Bianca, vibrant colors were more flattering.

"You are breathtaking, Bianca! I don't think I've ever seen you look so lovely," Amanda told her daughter.

"Why, thank you, Mother, and may I say you look absolutely stunning in that blue gown," Bianca told her. She'd always wished she had her mother's lovely blue eyes. Tonight, Amanda had piled her silvery blond hair atop her head and placed a jeweled comb at the back.

On her ears she wore her favorite sapphire earrings, which matched her blue gown perfectly.

"Father will have to keep an eye on you tonight, you look so beautiful," Bianca teased her. But Amanda laughed and declared that she would be the one watching her husband, 'for he looked so very handsome.

"We will be leaving shortly, Bianca, so that we can pick up Carolina. I shall see you shortly at the fiesta, dear," Amanda told her as she turned to leave the room.

"Yes, mother." Bianca turned her attention back to the mirror to be sure her hair was in place and her gown hung just right before she left the room.

With a dab of toilet water at her throat and behind her ears, she started for the door to leave her room. No sooner had she reached the bottom of the stairs and entered the parlor to wait for the driver to bring the buggy to the front entrance, the servant girl, Nita, came into the parlor to announce that he was there.

Bianca had seen that darkness was quickly coming to the countryside. By the time they arrived at Tío Jeff's house it would be dark. But his courtyard garden would be glowing with lanterns hung from the branches of the trees and torches would be placed generously around the gardens to give a festive air.

She walked out the door holding up the skirt of her dress when her black eyes glanced toward the buggy to spot the devilishly handsome Larkin sitting there with a grin on his face. Instantly he leaped down to assist her into the buggy. He looked dashing in his black pants and a soft silk black shirt. Around his neck was tied a bright scarlet kerchief.

If she was stunned by the sight of him and the

knowledge that he was going to be her driver, Larkin was as mesmerized by the sight of *her*. She took his breath away. Dear God, he'd never seen a more beautiful girl in his life and he didn't figure he probably ever would.

As he walked up to her and she looked up into his eyes she thought that they were as brilliant as the emeralds on her ears. She tried being flippant in hopes of hiding the effect he was having on her as he took her hand to help her into the buggy. "Well, Larkin—I didn't know that you would be our driver tonight," she'd told him, praying her voice wasn't trembling.

"Nor did I know, either, señorita—until yesterday," he told her as he walked around to get in the driver's seat.

He immediately had the buggy rolling down the long drive. With his back turned to her and those devastating green eyes not piercing her, she had time to gain control of herself as they traveled toward the Circle K. But Larkin was an experienced man where ladies were concerned and almost ten years older than Bianca, so he sensed instinctively that she was feeling something akin to his own reaction. He saw it when he looked in those black, curious eyes of hers and watched the fluttering of her thick black lashes.

For a few moments they traveled in silence, but Larkin could not resist the urge to tell her how beautiful she looked, for he knew that it was probably going to be the only moment they were going to be alone. "You are very beautiful this evening, señorita," he finally said.

"Thank you, Larkin, and I must say you look very handsome yourself." She gave him a soft smile. More than ever she was convinced that he was more than a ranch hand.

With a crooked grin on his face, he replied, "And I thank you, señorita. But may I be so bold as to ask why you always call me Larkin instead of Rick?"

With a tilt of her head and a smile on her face, she declared, "I guess because Larkin seems right for you."

He made no comment, but gave her a nod of his head as though he understood and accepted her explanation. He found it very interesting that she would feel that way, for the truth was, his first name was Larkin and not his last name. Until the day his mother had died she had always called him Lark.

Once again he was questioning if he should have come to Gonzales County. Would it have been better if he had forgotten a lot of things and allowed the past to be dead forever?

The Circle K Ranch was straight ahead and the sun was down and a glorious Texas twilight was engulfing the countryside. It was a perfect night for a fiesta with a light gentle breeze cooling the effect of the hot summer day.

As soon as Larkin brought the buggy to a halt, he leaped down to go to the front entrance, but Mark Kane was already coming out the door with the assistance of his cane and the hefty support of Estella. Kane introduced his housekeeper to him, and Larkin was amazed that he had remembered his name.

"I'll take it from here, Estella," Larkin told her.

"Nice to meet you, señor," she told him, turning Kane over to the powerfully built Larkin. She watched how effortlessly he led Señor Kane to the buggy. This was the type of man Señor Kane needed to have around if he wished to remain here at the Circle K, Estella thought.

Kane was well aware of the power and strength of the young man supporting him as he went toward the buggy to join his beautiful granddaughter.

Mark Kane was suddenly thinking to himself that he was not ready to die. He had to stick around this Texas countryside to see what life was going to deal his granddaughter. He was also thinking that if he had a strong hombre like Larkin working for him, he would not have to be confined to that damned chair. This strong man could help him into the saddle of his horse. He was already having visions of riding over his beloved Texas countryside one more time.

He had some talking to do with his son-in-law, Tony, Kane was thinking. Larkin might just be the answer.

Five

A fiesta was a time for the Texas ranchers and their friends to celebrate some special occasion, such as a wedding or the birth of a baby or the wedding plans of a young couple. This particular fiesta was to celebrate Bianca's return from the East.

For the occasion long tables were laden with delicious food and after the feasting there would be music for dancing. All the ladies were colorfully gowned in their pretty frocks, and the gentlemen wore their best attire.

After Larkin had assisted Mark into the courtyard and left him in the care of his son Jeff, he turned to leave. Old Mark was about to make a protest, but his daughter-in-law Mona suddenly appeared and he was caught up in a beehive of people rushing over to greet him and his pretty granddaughter and didn't notice Larkin as he made his way back to attend to the buggy.

It did not take long for Julio Lopez to spot Bianca arriving in the courtyard, and the handsome young Mexican left the group of young friends he'd been talking with.

As far as Julio was concerned all the other señoritas

paled in comparison and he was determined to spend some time with her. He approached Bianca and her grandfather and politely asked if he might get them something to drink.

"Mona is bringing me something, young man," Mark Kane told him, "but there's no reason you can't take Bianca over to the refreshment table." He urged his granddaughter to join the young man. That fruit punch was not his idea of a refreshing drink, nor did he want any of the wine being offered by the servants carrying trays around the garden. He wanted whiskey and branch water and Mona was going to fetch it for him. Kane was very fond of his daughter-in-law and he figured Jeff was a lucky son of a gun to have married her.

Bianca did not protest as she took Julio's arm to go over to where the long tables were placed along the long patio. "You look so beautiful this evening, Bianca, and I must tell you I was devastated that you turned me down as your escort," Julio declared to her. It did ease the pain that she was strolling along with him now, her hand holding his arm, but he was searching the vast courtyard to find a place where they might go after they helped themselves to the punch to be alone. His black eyes finally saw a bench in a secluded spot, and he guided her to it.

Bianca confessed to Julio that she was ready to drink some punch and sit down for a while.

"I've got a dance or two coming tonight, Bianca," he declared.

"Of course you do Julio," she promised him as she surveyed the people in the gardens. Her Tía Mona always had such grand affairs and she could not have asked for a more perfect evening. The breeze was a calm one and the sky was ablaze with twinkling stars and a bright full moon.

Just when Julio was feeling confident that the spot he'd picked was secluded enough for him to have a few private words with the beautiful Bianca, Emilo and Armando came rushing up to greet her.

"You devil, Julio—you can't take Bianca away from us this evening. Isn't that right, Emilo?" Armando taunted his disgruntled friend.

"That's exactly right," Emilo declared, turning his attention to Bianca. He and Armando sunk right down on the thick carpet of grass by her feet.

After many admiring words from the three young men Bianca finally had to tell them that it was time she moved back into the courtyard where she had guests yet to meet and greet.

Emilo gave out a dejected sigh and she laughed. "Now, Emilo—don't be selfish. After all, I can't insult my tía Mona by spending all the time with the three of you."

Reluctantly, the three young men allowed her to lead them back to the refreshment table where the guests were beginning to fill their plates with all the delectable foods Mona's servants had been preparing for days.

Mona had instructed her servant, Rosa, to serve plates of food to the drivers out at the buggies, as well as drinks. Larkin wasted no time digging into the mountain of food piled on his plate, for he'd had an ache in his gut as he'd stood by the buggy and smelled the enticing aroma of the food just a short distance away.

He ate every slice of the juicy beef and barbecued

42

pork and could have devoured another thick slice of that fresh-baked bread if he hadn't restrained himself. Bianca's aunt certainly knew how to put on a spread. He found that the other drivers were agreeing with him, for they ate just as heartily.

When the music began to echo out through the darkness one of the drivers declared to Larkin that he would like to be dancing with one of the pretty señoritas.

Larkin just smiled, but he had to admit to himself that for sure he would like to have a dance with the beautiful Bianca.

Mark Kane knew there might never be another such night like this, so he was going to enjoy himself to the fullest. He had talked and visited with all his old friends for the last two hours and had eaten heartily. He had also drunk his whiskey and branch water with enthusiasm.

When the dancing began, he cussed the fact that he could not whirl his granddaughter around the plank dance floor like the young men who were constantly asking her to dance. When Tony asked Bianca for a dance, Amanda came over to sit with her father. "It's a grand night, isn't it, Poppa?" she remarked, putting her arm around his shoulder.

"A wonderful night, Amanda. Just wish Jenny could be here," he murmured softly.

When the music stopped, Tony came over to join his wife and father-in-law. Amanda told him how fine he had danced with his daughter and asked where she had gone.

He confessed she had disappeared after the dance was over. In his own lighthearted, gay mood, Tony invited his wife to dance with him and they left Mark.

Bianca had slipped through the darkness of the garden courtyard and out the iron gate. She spotted Larkin's tall figure immediately as he leaned against the buggy taking puffs on his cigarette and he recognized her instantly as she came walking in that feisty way of hers. He broke away from the buggy and, tossing the cigarette to the ground, he hastily joined her before she could come any closer.

"Señorita, you should not be out here," he declared.

"I came for you, Larkin. I want to dance with you before the evening is over." Her bold black eyes looked directly up at him and he inhaled the intoxicating fragrance of her standing so close to him.

"I can't do that, *chiquita*. You know that," he protested.

"I do *not* know that. The fiesta is for me and it is my wish to dance with you. Come on," she insisted, her hand taking his arm. He felt her give a mighty tug on his arm.

"I'll dance with you in the courtyard in the shadows but not on the dance floor, *chiquita*," he said firmly.

"Oh, all right, Larkin. Come on. The music is starting."

Bianca had not been in his strong arms for a few seconds before she realized that he was a magnificent dancer. As he guided her around the grounds, she looked up at him, questioning the mystery surrounding this intriguing man.

It was almost agony to Larkin to hold her so close and not want to kiss her. The heat of his body invaded her as he held her and they danced under the stars. Bianca was wishing that the music would go on and on, but all too soon it ended.

Larkin knew instinctively that she was feeling exactly as he was feeling right then and she did not want to be released from his arms. God knows, he didn't want to take his arm away from her tiny waist!

When she tilted her head back and he looked down at her face and those half-parted lips murmuring his name, he could not resist bending down to kiss her.

When his sensuous lips finally released hers, he urged her in a husky voice, "Get back where you belong, *chiquita,* and I will do the same. I—I thank you for the dance."

Suddenly his tall figure was swallowed up in the darkness and she was there alone. She could not have told anyone about the remaining hour of the fiesta, for she was in a daze from the effects of Larkin's kiss. No man had ever kissed her like that and she knew that her restless heart would not be satisfied with just one kiss. She'd felt the power and force of his firm, muscled body as he'd pressed against her and this, too, was an exciting sensation she'd never before experienced.

Slowly, she sauntered back to the crowd of people in the courtyard after Larkin returned to go back to his station at the buggy.

Her brother Estaban had just finished dancing with Carolina and observed his lovely sister as she moved amid the guests. He had never seen her looking so radiant as she did tonight.

45

For all her reckless ways he was very proud of her tonight. He watched her go over to sit by their grandfather and noticed that she politely turned down dancing with Emilo, Armando, and Julio, telling them she wished to share the rest of the evening with her grandfather.

A very smug look came to old Mark Kane's face as she sat holding his hand, her toe tapping out the lively tempo of the music being played.

Bianca could not know it, but she had given her grandfather the will to live. He was determined to stick around for a few more years just to see the overwhelming impact Bianca was going to have on the lives of the Moreno and Kane family.

Six

Bianca had assumed that she would be returning home in the buggy with Larkin and her grandfather and she was disappointed when her parents told her that she would ride in the buggy with them. She told her grandfather good night as Larkin and her father helped Mark into his buggy.

Darkness concealed her pout as she sat beside her father in the driver's seat while her mother, Carolina, and Estaban rode in the back. Knowing how late fiestas lasted, Carolina's parents had given their permission for her to be the overnight guest of the Moreno family.

Tony was very aware of his daughter's quiet mood as they traveled homeward, but he just assumed she was weary. She certainly had a reason, for he'd seen her dancing from the moment the music had began.

Larkin certainly did not find his passenger silent. Old Mark was very talkative all the way home. Larkin commented that everyone had enjoyed themselves. "Your daughter-in-law sure served some good food," Rick told him.

"Yes, Mona is a very gracious hostess."

The two of them continued to talk as Rick helped him to the house, where Estella was waiting for them.

She'd been concerned about Señor Kane as the hour had grown so late and he'd not arrived back home. She was afraid he might be overtaxing himself, but that concern was eased when he got to the door and seemed in such high spirits.

"Well, señor, I don't have to ask if you had yourself a good time," she smiled and glanced over at Larkin.

"Had myself a hell of a time." Now that Estella was there to help him, he thanked Larkin and told him he'd be looking forward to seeing him again very soon.

Larkin went back to the buggy to head for Rancho Río. He wished Bianca was driving through the late starlit night with him. But then, he amended his thoughts, maybe it was best for both of them that Tony Moreno had taken her with them.

He had noticed her dark eyes glance over at him for one fleeting second as she'd kissed her grandfather good night. Moreno was no fool and he knew his daughter was a beautiful little temptress. He couldn't fault him for being protective of her, Larkin had to admit.

Bianca had not lingered in the parlor with the rest of the family, but had excused herself, saying she needed sleep. But it was hardly sleep she was thinking about. She just did not intend to listen to Carolina's prattling tonight. She could do her chattering to Esteban, Bianca decided as she left them in the parlor.

Tony laughed. "I think our Bianca has had a very full night."

"Well, *querido,* I think we all have had a big night. I feel like Bianca does, so I'm going to show Carolina to her room. You are probably ready to retire, too, aren't you, dear?" Amanda asked Carolina.

"Yes, I guess so," she stammered. "It was a glorious evening, Estaban," she added.

Amanda led her down the hallway of the second floor to the guest bedroom on the same side of the hall as Bianca's bedroom.

She made Carolina comfortable and lit the lamps, then met her son coming up to his room. He bid her a goodnight and bent down to kiss her on the cheek.

She told him to rest well as she prepared to go back downstairs to join her husband in the parlor where she knew he was having a nightcap.

She sank down into the overstuffed chair and they spoke about the grand evening they'd just shared. It was nice to have this quiet moment before they retired, Amanda thought.

"Dear Lord, I pray Estaban doesn't become serious about that girl! I don't think she ever quits talking. I'd bet she even talks in her sleep!"

Tony threw his head back and roared with laughter, for he had to agree with his wife. Estaban was such a mild-mannered young man Tony figured that his wife had nothing to worry about. He suspected that Estaban wished he had invited Lita Morales tonight instead of Carolina.

Together, the two of them left the parlor to seek the comfort of their own bed.

Bianca had lain restlessly awake in her bed for the

49

longest time last night. She had thought about the fiesta and everything that had happened there. There was no question that the most exciting thing was dancing in the dark with Rick Larkin and the torrid kiss he gave her in the secluded courtyard.

She had anticipated sharing a brief moment with him after they'd left her grandfather at the Circle K and was a little vexed at her father for having her come home with them.

Had Larkin been as disappointed as she'd been, she'd wondered?

Bianca knew that there would be another time and place when Larkin's kisses would capture her lips again. As sure as that big moon was shining just outside her window she knew that his arms would hold her. She wanted to experience again those sensations he'd stirred within her.

It was Rick Larkin's handsome face and green eyes she envisioned as she fell to sleep.

When Bianca finally crawled out of her bed late the next morning, she moved lazily around her room in no great hurry to go downstairs. Maybe Estaban would have left to take Carolina home. She hoped so!

That silly giggle of hers wore on Bianca's nerves, and if she was not giggling then she was chatterboxing like a magpie. God forbid that she'd end up in the family, Bianca thought to herself as she finished fastening the front of her bodice. This morning she wished to let her hair fall loose and free.

When she had nothing left to do in her room she finally went out the door and down the hall. She saw one of the servant girls coming out of the guest bedroom down from hers. "Is Señorita Carolina gone, Cola?" she inquired of the servant.

Sí, señorita. She left Rancho Río a couple of hours ago."

Bianca bit her tongue. She'd wanted to say that was good, but she merely smiled as she quickly whirled around to go to the stairs. When she got downstairs she rushed out to the veranda. She found her mother there. Obviously, she been out to pick a basket of flowers, for she wore her wide-brimmed straw hat and cotton gloves, and the basket was filled with the giant zinnias and snapdragons in an array of colors.

"Oh, they're beautiful, Mother," she exclaimed.

Amanda turned around from the table, where she was standing cutting off some of the leaves and stems. "Aren't they! Have you had your breakfast yet, dear?"

When Bianca told her that she hadn't, Amanda suggested that she have Cola serve her outside. "Besides, I am ready for a cup of coffee myself. It's been hours since your father and I shared breakfast with Estaban and Carolina before they left."

"I heard she was gone, thank God!" Bianca declared as she went over to sit down while her mother went to summon Cola.

When she returned, Bianca asked of her father's whereabouts and Amanda told her that he'd left a moment ago. "He wanted to have a talk with Rick Larkin." Amanda sat down at the table and removed her cotton gloves.

"Larkin?" Bianca was curious about this.

"Yes, dear, Rick Larkin," Amanda repeated. Bianca didn't get the chance to pursue it any further, for

51

Cola appeared with a plate of food and a carafe of coffee for the two of them. The tempting plate of food drew her immediate attention, for she was famished after sleeping so late.

As soon as she had finished eating she found herself wondering if it was possible that her father might have seen Larkin kissing her last night. Was that why he'd had her ride back home with them instead of going with her grandfather and Larkin?

Dear Lord, she prayed that he hadn't! But she did not have to fret too long, for shortly Tony was coming through the courtyard gate to join them on the veranda and his mood seemed too cheerful for her misconduct to have been his reason for the talk with Larkin.

Soon they were all lightheartedly discussing and laughing about Carolina Estrada's very busy mouth. Amanda had to confess that she was a little surprised that Estaban had left with Carolina so early this morning.

"Knowing Estaban I would have expected that he would not have gotten started until after lunch," she remarked.

"Estaban did not wish to be bothered with her all morning, I'd say," Bianca grinned.

Tony could not resist laughing. "Oh, Bianca—I gather you don't enjoy Carolina's company." It touched him that as much as she and Estaban squabbled, they still knew each other so very well. He had already decided that Estaban was eager to have the girl out of his hair after having spent the evening with her last night.

It was at that moment they saw Estaban coming

52

through the gate. He'd heard the laughter of his family as he'd approached the courtyard.

He had a much happier expression on his face as he joined them now that he was rid of that silly girl!

Seven

Rachel Estrada saw the young couple arriving at the Estrada Ranch in the Moreno buggy and she was astonished by the early hour. It was not yet midday. She knew how late the fiesta must have lasted and she'd thought that it was very considerate of Amanda Moreno to suggest to her that Carolina stay overnight.

There was no denying that she her husband welcomed young Estaban as a suitor. Not only was he a very handsome young man but the Moreno family was highly respected and very wealthy. So she had high expectations that Estaban was surely attracted by Carolina for him to invite her to the fiesta at the Kanes. Had her husband not been ailing they also would have attended the grand fiesta last night and she was devastated because they could not.

She heard the servant open the door and voices at the door and she waited anxiously in the parlor for them. She figured she could observe their faces and tell if they had enjoyed their time together last night.

Carolina came slowly into the parlor to greet her mother. Rachel stood up with a frown on her face and a sharp tone to her voice. "Where is Estaban?" she questioned.

"Oh, he's gone. Said he didn't have time to come in

because he had to go on over to his grandfather's ranch," she casually remarked. Carolina was still slightly dazed by the hasty departure from the Rancho Río and feeling the need for more sleep.

An uneasy expression came to Rachel's face when she dared to ask Carolina if she had had a good time.

Carolina told her it was a wonderful fiesta.

"And how do you like Estaban Moreno, Carolina?"

"Oh, he's very nice, Mother, and so is his family."

"And Estaban—did he seem to like you, dear?"

Carolina knew exactly what her mother was curious to know and she hardly knew how to answer her.

"I guess he liked me, Mother. He invited me to the fiesta, didn't he?" Carolina pointed out to her. She had found him much more sober and reserved this morning than he'd been last night at the fiesta.

Rachel saw that she was getting nowhere with her daughter and becoming more irritated by Carolina's evasive replies. "Well, dear—I've got to go and see about your father." Getting up out of the chair, she left the room feeling very let down about any prospects of a union between her daughter and Estaban Moreno. He was such a well-mannered young man that she would have expected him to come into the parlor to greet her when he brought Carolina back home. She had to conclude that her daughter had not favorably impressed him last night and that was why he'd brought her back home so early.

But Rachel had to admit that her youngest daughter was not as beautiful as her daughter Elena. Young men were constantly coming to court Elena. She knew she had to tell her husband that Carolina was back home and that Estaban would probably not be beating a path to their door.

Manuel Estrada was sitting propped up in bed when his wife came into their bedroom. He wasn't in the best of moods with the miserable cold plaguing him and ·Rachel's news certainly did not please him.

"Carolina probably chatterboxed too much for the young man. From what I've seen of him he's a very serious young fellow—not at all like that sister of his."

"Nor is our Carolina like Elena, Manuel," Rachel made a point of declaring to her husband. Right now, she was out of patience with her youngest daughter, for she had been given the opportunity of making herself a fine catch of a young man for her husband. Rachel was convinced that she had done something to spoil it.

Rachel went about the chores of trying to make her husband comfortable by propping and fluffing up his pillows. Before she left the room she asked if there was anything she could bring him.

"Just to be rid of this cold is all I need," he mumbled in a gruff tone.

Rachel sought the solitude of her sitting room and her needlepoint, which was always a release for any agitated mood she might be in right now.

When Estaban joined his family on the veranda, Bianca was the first one to greet him. Tony and Amanda had to marvel at the way she could even bewitch her older brother. She did not mention the episode with Carolina, which she expected had been an ordeal for Estaban. Instead, she invited him to go for

56

a ride with her after he had lunch. "Nothing prevents a brother and sister from having a pleasant Saturday afternoon ride, does it?" She smiled a most charming smile.

"I guess it doesn't, Bianca." He grinned down at her.

"I'll go up and change while you have lunch with Mother and Father."

"And what about you? Aren't you going to have lunch?" Estaban wanted to know.

She giggled. "I've just finished a late breakfast."

All three Morenos exchanged smiles as the free-spirited miss dashed from the veranda.

Tony Moreno thought that Bianca had to be one of the greatest joys of his life. He also thought of the time when he was about Estaban's age and had just met the beautiful fair-haired Amanda Kane. She had been just as beguiling as his own daughter was now.

Amanda was thinking of the time she was Bianca's age and was just as anxious to know of life and loving when she had met the handsome Tony Moreno. She knew that Bianca would do exactly as she wished regardless of what her family thought. There was a time when her own father, being an Anglo-American, had not had any use for Mexicans. Of course, that had all changed after she'd married Tony. Only two Mexicans had drawn old Mark's respect back then and those were Jenny's housekeeper, Consuela, and her husband, Juan. But over the years, old Mark had had to mellow, for his beloved granddaughter and grandson were part Mexican with Tony's blood flowing in their veins.

As Estaban watched his sister's lively step, he had

the fleeting thought of the grand old lady, Bianca Alvarado, Tony's aunt, who'd originally owned the Rancho Río. She had left the vast acres to Tony when she died. It was for her that his sister had been named. He had been named to honor his father's grandfather, Estaban Moreno.

With a smile on his face he told his parents, "You know, I used to think that the very dignified Bianca Alvarado would have been displeased by her namesake, but now I think that she might have been a little like our Bianca when she was a young lady." Brotherly pride reflected in his voice as he spoke of how proud he was of Bianca the night before. "She was the most beautiful lady there besides you, Mother. I've come to the conclusion that I am going to be very hard to please as a man for the lady I choose. I have such a magnificent mother and such a little charmer as a sister that I find myself being very critical of most women," Estaban confessed.

"You will find such a lady, Estaban," Tony assured him. "The moment you see her you will know it, as it was when I first saw your mother. She will look like no other woman you have ever seen and she will impress you with such an intensity that you will know. Remember what I've said to you today, for one of these days you will be telling me that I am right."

"I shall remember, Father." Estaban had the utmost faith in anything his father told him.

A short time later, Bianca joined them, and she and Estaban left to go for their ride. Tony and Amanda were left on the veranda alone. He reached over to cover his wife's hand as he told her, *"Querida,* I love you so deeply and completely, for you gave me the world. A man could not have had a more beautiful daughter and a finer son than the ones you gave me, *mi vida."*

"Oh, Tony Moreno—you and that silken tongue of yours! Is it any wonder I lost all my senses when you talked like this to me years ago."

He gave her a devious grin. "I was a real devil, wasn't I?"

"You were, Tony, and you still are, but that's what makes me love you so much. So don't you ever stop being the Tony Moreno I fell in love with," she declared as she reached over the table to meet his lips in a kiss.

Estaban had shared a pleasant jaunt with his younger sister. He had enjoyed the time with her much more than that he had spent with silly Carolina Estrada. Bianca had been right. He should have invited Lita Morales to the fiesta instead of Carolina. But he had no intentions of ever calling on her again or escorting her anywhere.

He and Bianca had stopped by the river to rest their horses for a while before they started back to the ranch. It gave them the opportunity to talk, and Estaban realized that there was a very serious side to that vivacious little sister of his!

"What do you want out of life, Estaban?" she'd asked him.

"I guess I want to be the son Tony Moreno will be proud of. I'd never want to disappoint him or Mother," he told her. He had to admit that he was taken by surprise by her very sober mood.

"What's important, Estaban, is for you to be proud of yourself. You have to live your own way of life. I am probably not going to be like Mother and you might not be like Father, but the important thing is that you and I will be happy with our lives."

"Is this how you feel, Bianca?"

"Absolutely! You have surely suspected by now that I won't live by anyone's rules other than my own," she declared.

For the first time Estaban felt he understood his sister and he also knew why Grandfather Kane found her so special. She *was* special!

When she took his hand in hers and looked up at him with those big black eyes of hers and spoke with such sincerity, Estaban was very affected and also impressed. "Oh, Estaban, you just be yourself. You just be Estaban Moreno — not Tony Moreno. I know that this is what Father would tell you."

Was she only seventeen? he wondered. She spoke with such wisdom and authority.

"I'll do just that, Bianca," he declared, an easy smile coming to his face.

Estaban knew that he was always going to think about this summer afternoon he'd spent with his sister. She might be young, but she had changed the whole course of his thinking.

As they rode back to Rancho Río, she had no inkling of the tremendous burden he'd been struggling with to do as he wanted and pursue his law practice in San Antonio instead of remaining here at Rancho Río as he felt his father wanted him to do.

Bianca had been unaware that she had swept away the guilt he had been harboring within himself and

60

that he now felt he could do what he truly wanted to do and not feel guilty.

Forever he knew he was going to be grateful to Bianca. Never again would he consider her to be a frivolous little sister.

Eight

Everything seemed to have changed after that summer afternoon Estaban and Bianca went out for their ride. Their parents were very aware of it, for the siblings no longer battled with each other when they gathered in the elegant dining room for the evening meals. Both parents were very aware of the camaraderie between Bianca and Estaban and whatever had happened, Tony and Amanda welcomed it.

Tony Moreno felt in high spirits, for he had approached Rick Larkin about the possibility of his becoming a foreman over at the Circle K Ranch. Rick was very flattered by the offer and never doubted for a minute that he could take over the Circle K. Mark Kane was his kind of man.

When Moreno had first approached him, he had confessed to Larkin that he did not wish to offend his brother-in-law, Jeff Kane. "But the truth is, he has more than he can manage. Between the Big D and the Circle K we're talking about a lot of acres and many head of cattle."

Tony made a point of telling Larkin that he had yet to discuss the matter with his brother-in-law. "I figured I'd best find out if you were interested before I said anything to Jeff. Of course, there is Mark Kane to talk with as well."

"I understand, señor," Larkin told him.

"I'll get back with you then after I've had a talk with the two of them," Tony had told him.

Larkin gave him a nod of his head and turned back to go into the barn to check on the Thoroughbred's leg.

This was a happening that Larkin had not expected to come his way. The rest of the afternoon as he worked around the barn and exercised two of the other Thoroughbreds around the corral, he found his head whirling with conflicting thoughts. He could not pursue his original reason for coming to Gonzales County if he allowed the people at Rancho Río to affect him as they were doing.

The Moreno family was getting under his skin and his emotions were getting more and more involved. It was more than just Bianca. He genuinely liked and admired Tony Moreno and old Mark Kane.

Strangely, it was at the Big D Ranch he'd first sought to work. Jeff Kane had told him then that he did not need any more hands. He also sensed that Jeff had not recalled meeting him the night of the fiesta.

What an irony it would be if he did end up as the foreman of the Circle K Ranch, considering what his plans for coming here were.

But when those plans were made he could not know that so many things would make a fortune of money not worth the sacrifice he'd pay. He recalled sitting by his mother's deathbed and how she'd urged him to go get the money that rightfully belonged to him. He

63

promised her that he would do it.

It had been easy for him to reason that if the money did belong to him, then he should have it. That was what his mother had told him. And his mother had never given him wrong advice.

Hell, he'd been poor all his life! As far back as he could recall, he and his mother had lived at the boardinghouse where she worked in return for their room and board and a small salary. From the time he was nine years old, he had always found some way to make a little money, by sweeping out saloons or working in the livery. Often, there were little chores that Mrs. Carlton, who owned the boardinghouse, would pay to do.

There was never a day he'd not had a square meal or a bed to sleep in.

He never thought too much about not having a father around, for there were several young boys who lived with their widowed mothers. His mother had always told him his father had been killed in a gunfight, but as he got older he began to question her story.

Finally, her green eyes had misted with tears and she confessed, "Lark, we were never married. I—I was just a saloon girl and he was the son of a wealthy rancher over in Gonzales County." She admitted to her son that the last time he'd come to Guadalupe County to see her she had told him that she was pregnant.

"And he didn't offer to marry you knowing that?" Rick had asked her.

"He said he couldn't because he was in some kind of trouble and might have to leave Gonzales County hastily. But he did tell me that he'd buried a lot of money on his pa's ranch, and if he didn't come back he wanted me to know about it. He even left me a map showing exactly where it was buried and I've kept it safe all these years knowing that one of these days you would grow up."

Larkin remembered that particular day as though it was yesterday and he recalled how he'd told his mother that he was almost grown.

Another five years would pass. By the time he was eighteen he'd found a good friend and an employer when Fred Compton took him on as a hand on his ranch, so he no longer lived at the boardinghouse. But every time he came into town he went by the boardinghouse to give his mother a part of the salary he earned working for Compton.

He could recall when he'd bought his first fine leather boots and a felt hat like the one Fred Compton wore. Compton took a special interest in the young man and appreciated his keen mind and willingness to work hard. Rick learned a lot about running a ranch during that first year.

By the time he'd been working at the ranch for almost three years, it became his obsession to own a fine Thoroughbred like the one Fred rode. He saved all his salary except for the portion he gave to his mother.

When his mother was taken ill and he went to the boardinghouse to see her, Linda Miller knew it was time that she turned the map over to her son. She revealed that he would find the fortune waiting for him at the Big D Ranch in Gonzales County. "You were Derek Lawson's son, so you deserve it, Lark. Go get it. You're twenty-one now."

He'd left her bedside that night reluctantly, and that was the last time he'd seen her. She'd died early the next morning.

Larkin took her death very hard, for she'd been such a devoted, loving mother. He was to learn that all of the money he'd given to her had been saved. From that money he had purchased Raven. That was why the fine black stallion was so very special to him.

For several months he tried to shrug aside the idea of going to Gonzales County, but her voice kept haunting him until finally he went to Fred Compton and told him what was on his mind. "It's just something I've got to do before I can rest," he said to the rancher.

"Then take out, Larkin. Your job will be waiting for you when you come back," Compton had assured him.

A week later he'd left the Compton Ranch and headed for Gonzales County. He'd first stopped to see about work at the Big D Ranch and when that did not work out, he'd ridden to the Rancho Río. Tony Moreno had hired him immediately.

As most people living in the neighboring counties, the names of Moreno, Kane, and Lawson were well known. Old Mark Kane was a living legend in Texas.

It was after he was at the Rancho Río that he learned from the other men in the bunkhouse that Jeff Kane was Mark's son and Amanda's brother. Jeff had acquired the Big D Ranch after he'd married Mona Lawson and her father, David, had died. That would make Mona Lawson Kane his aunt, for she was Derek's sister.

It suddenly dawned on Larkin that she was also

Bianca's aunt, but that still did not make them blood kin, he reassured himself.

Larkin had not pursued all the plans he'd made in Guadalupe, nor had he checked out the vast spread of acres of the Big D Ranch as he would have surely done had Bianca Moreno not begun to occupy more and more of his thoughts.

Now that he'd held her in his arms and kissed her honey-sweet lips, finding that fortune didn't seem so important.

Bianca found herself very curious about what her father had talked to Rick Larkin about, but she could not ask either of her parents. When she didn't spot him around the corral or near the barn when she'd gone there to get Rojo to go for a ride, she was really perplexed.

Her inquisitive nature could not stand it any longer after the second day had gone by and she'd seen no sight of him so she approached one of the other hands. "Larkin drift on, Buck?" she asked in a very casual way.

"Oh, no, ma'am. He's gone over on the far side of the ranch to try to spot some cattle that roamed away a few days ago. He's camping out there for a few nights, I heard."

"I see. Hopefully, he'd find them," she replied and went on to Rojo's stall. She had to privately admit that Buck's news had eased her apprehension that he had left the Rancho Río.

She had ridden over to her grandfather's that afternoon without saying anything to her mother or father, for she did not want to be refused their permission.

Old Mark was delighted to see her. The two of them took a short stroll around his courtyard and they had not done this in a long, long time. "You've got to go to more fiestas, Grandfather," she teased him. "They're obviously a good tonic for you."

He gave out a chuckle. "That's a part of it, but the best tonic in the world for me is having you back here in Gonzales County instead of way back East where I didn't see you but once or twice a year."

She laughed softly. "Well, I'll pester you so much that you'll be wishing you hadn't said that."

"Never, little one. I never say anything I don't mean."

After she had spent an hour with her grandfather, Bianca knew that she needed to start riding back to the ranch before she did get in trouble with her parents. When she was preparing to go to Rojo, Kane called out to her, "How's Larkin?"

"Fine, I guess, Grandfather. I haven't seen him. He's out hunting for some strays," she answered him.

"Tell that young man to drop by to see me when he has some time."

She gave him a smile and nod of her head. "I'll do that, grandfather." Quickly she disappeared through the iron gate.

Long after she'd left, he sat there with a pleased smile on his face reminiscing about the nice hour they'd spent together.

Old Mark Kane thought to himself that his son Jeff and his wife had themselves a fine ranch, the Big D, and his daughter Amanda and her husband had a grand spread over at the Rancho Río.

Maybe the Circle K Ranch was meant to be Bianca's someday!

Nine

Larkin and the two other fellows rode into the Rancho Río and herded the six strays inside the gate. Larkin was ready for a good hot bath and to shave the two days' growth of beard. The next thing he wanted was one of the cook's hearty meals and then to fling himself into the bunk. The darn ground was awfully hard after the comfortable bunk he'd been sleeping on. He swore that he'd never complain about this bunkhouse again.

He bid the two men goodbye, went to talk to Moreno's foreman, José, then turned to go toward the bunkhouse. Suddenly from back toward the barn came a soft female voice. "Hey, Larkin! See you got back."

Before he could answer her, Bianca rushed across the barnyard toward him. He wasn't eager to encounter her looking as he did, not to mention he was bone-tired, but when she stood in front of him with that sweet, warm smile on her face, looking up at him with those big black eyes he found he forgot all about being tired.

Her dark eyes twinkled as they surveyed his unshaven face and tousled hair. "You're a sight for sore eyes, Larkin! Grandfather told me to tell you to come by and see him when you got the chance." She turned to rush hastily to the gate, but she could not resist looking back just once and waving her hand, for he was still standing there watching her.

A grin creased his face as he watched her. Everything about Bianca Moreno was exciting—the beauty of her face and the tantalizing movement of her curvy body.

By the time he'd had a warm bath and shaved away the growth of beard, he was feeling much better. Surprisingly, he wasn't ready to hit the bunk as soon as he'd finished devouring the food on his plate. But neither was he in the mood to join some fellows pulling up their chairs at the table to play cards. He politely refused their invitation and went outside.

He found himself rambling around toward the courtyard wall and he hesitated by the iron gate for a moment before moving on into the darkness. Soon, however, something urged him to get back to the bunkhouse.

The minute he walked into the bunkhouse he was informed by one of the men who'd been out with him rounding up the strays that the foreman had just come by. "He said we can have the next two days off," he informed Larkin. "He was pleased with the good job we did."

"Sounds good to me." He smiled as he ambled toward his bunk. Sitting down on the bunk, he took off his boots, then stretched out on the bunk. He drifted off to sleep swiftly, the talking of the men still playing cards proving no distraction.

Larkin slept late and awakened to a deserted bunkhouse. The other two fellows had family living nearby, so he figured that they were taking advantage of the two free days to visit with them.

Larkin found himself digging in his valise to pull out the old map his mother had given him with the specific directions Derek Lawson had drawn out. He suddenly felt possessed to seek out the truth about this man. Had he lied to his mother all those years ago and was there really a cache hidden in an old tumbledown shack at the north end of the Big D?

Had he just told the little saloon girl who he'd gotten pregnant this to soothe his own guilt and ease her fears so she would not appear on the Lawsons's doorsteps one day? It suddenly seemed important for him to know for too many things were weighing heavily on his mind.

According to the map Larkin had studied he needed no tools. He had only to find the old shack and in the floor was a trapdoor which led down to a dirt cellar. Down there on a wooden shelf in a tin chest was the cache.

He folded the map and quickly got dressed. A strange excitement was churning within him as he pulled on his black leather boots. But his practical side cautioned him to think about how many years ago that map had been drawn. The old shack might not even be standing now and those old wooden stairs down to the dirt cellar could be rotted. Before he left the bunkhouse he gathered up an extra strand of rope which might come in handy. A few minutes later he and Raven were riding out of Rancho Río. Bianca had chanced to be glancing out the window of the kitchen where she'd gone to help herself to one of the cinnamon rolls the cook had baked for their breakfast. She watched him gallop away on Raven and wondered if he was going to her grandfather's ranch. She had told him that Mark wished to see him when he had some time off and she'd heard her father telling her mother last night at dinner that Larkin and two of his other men had found all six of the straying cattle so Tony had given them some time off.

Her mother and father were gone to visit one of their neighbors who was ailing and Estaban had left the house early to spend three days with a friend of his over in Brazos County.

It did not help her mood that the sky was overcast and gloomy. She could go for a ride on Rojo, but she had learned the hard way that she could not control the fiery stallion when they were caught out in a storm. Once he had reared up in a panic and she'd found herself tossed to the ground.

It was beginning to look threatening outside.

By the time Larkin reached the end of the boundary of the Big D Ranch, the skies were hanging heavy with clouds rolling in from the southwest. This part of the Big D seemed to be deserted of ranch hands or cattle.

Suddenly right ahead of him was the old deserted shack that he was seeking. His heart started pounding with excitement.

He led Raven right up to the door and leaped off his back. He found it hard to open the wood door to the cabin, which had warped and settled with age, but he managed to get it ajar enough to enter. It was strange to see things left as they probably were when this man who was his father had last visited here, for it seemed to him that there had been no intruders. Blankets were

73

still piled on a cot and an old colorful Indian rug lay in the center of the small room. Scavengers would have taken these things if they'd have come this way, Larkin figured.

A kerosene lamp still sat on an old square rough-hewn table and there were a couple of old oak chairs around the table. Crude shelves lined a wall, and some jars and tins were placed on the shelves.

A strange feeling engulfed Larkin as he stood there carefully taking in everything. He wondered why a wealthy rancher's son like Derek Lawson would seek out a place like this unless he had done some despicable deed he wished to hide from his family. Larkin told himself that the money he'd spoken about to his mother had to be tainted or there would have been no need for him to hide it here.

He had only to pick up the Indian woven rug to find the trapdoor leading to the cellar below. But Larkin saw the deteriorated wood steps and knew that he didn't want to test them out.

He decided to lead Raven through the door of the shack and then he tied a secure knot around the stirrup. As the stallion was commanded to do, he stayed in the spot as Larkin lowered himself into the dark abyss below. There was no problem in finding the tin chest, for it was the only thing on the old wooden shelf down there.

Larkin lingered no longer than it took him to secure the chest underneath his arm. Below him he heard a sound that he didn't like worth a damn. The damned cellar was home to rattlesnakes! The minute he heard the rattle Larkin began to move up the rope swiftly.

By the time he was back to the plank floor of the

shack he heard the light patter of raindrops against the roof. He was glad to be out of that dark hole. He brushed away the cobwebs from his clothing and sat down on the cot to examine the contents of the old tin chest.

He took the time to light up a cigarette before taking out his knife to pry up the lid. Inside was the fortune his mother had spoken about! As he counted out the bounty, he wondered why Derek Lawson had felt the need to hide this cache of six thousand dollars. The one person who might have the answer was Mona Lawson Kane, but Larkin knew that he could not go to her.

Neither could he help himself to the money even though his mother had told him that it was rightfully his. If anyone had deserved that money it was his mother, but it was too late for that now. So he closed the lid on the tin chest and he felt that he was closing the door to a past that no longer mattered to him.

He was not about to go back down into the viper-filled pit so he left the tin on the rough-hewn table for the taking of anyone who might come to the cabin.

He pushed his hat onto his head and braved the shower of rain now falling heavier to mount up on Raven. He did not need to be spotted on Big D land if he had any intentions of lingering in Gonzales County for any length of time.

He followed the north boundary line of the Big D Ranch as he traveled back toward Circle K property.

He spotted some lightning in the direction he was riding toward and sensed the effect of the rumbling as he sat astraddle Raven. The huge black beast shook his head as though he was protesting. Larkin gave his silky black mane an assuring pat to try to soothe him, then veered from the open country to hit the thick woods a short distance away knowing that it would relax the stallion to get to the cover of the tall, thick-branched trees.

The minute they galloped into the dense thickness, he felt Raven's tenseness ease. He guided him through the woods and they crossed a small creek that cut through the wooded area.

He had heard no more rumbles nor did he see any more streaks of lightning, so he figured it to be merely a summer storm that passed quickly.

Everything was so peaceful, he would have suspected that he and Raven were the only ones in the woods when a wild shriek invaded the quietness.

He pulled up the reins and strained to listen. He heard a very familiar feminine voice angrily cussing. "Damn you, Rojo! You did it to me again!"

With a crooked grin on his face, Larkin reined Raven in that direction.

Ten

He followed the creekbed for almost a hundred feet before he came on the sight of the huge Rojo standing in the creek with his irate mistress sitting upon him! She had not heard Larkin coming and she was struggling to push her hat back atop her head. Larkin chuckled, for her dainty hands were grimy and so was her beautiful face and her hat.

Finally, he could not resist taunting her as she had teased him yesterday about his growth of beard. Urging Raven a little closer, he called out to her, "Bianca Moreno, you're a sight for sore eyes!"

She turned with a quick jerk to see Larkin within a few feet of her, a devious grin on his tanned face. Her black eyes were blazing like coals. "Damn you, Larkin. It—it isn't funny! I'll sell Rojo if he throws me one more time, I swear it!"

Larkin laughed as he leaped off Raven to help her out of the creek. "No you won't, *chiquita!* Right now you're just mad because you're all wet and muddy."

She took his hand as he lifted her up from the creek. She felt water dripping down her legs from her divided skirt and she saw the amused look on Larkin's face as his green eyes slowly surveyed her face.

77

"What is so damned funny, Larkin?" she asked indignantly.

He bent forward to kiss the tip of her nose and told her, "You're even beautiful with a dirty face."

A slow smile came to her face, for she found it impossible to be angry with him. She did not know how to explain the force this man had over her, but she knew that she'd never felt such overwhelming power before.

"Oh, Larkin—I know I look a mess! I should never have started out on Rojo with it looking so stormy. I have only myself to blame," she confessed as they got back to the grassy bank.

"Then why did you, *chiquita?*"

"I was bored," she told him as she began to squeeze the bottom of her skirt.

"I think poor Rojo knows you're out of favor with him," Larkin teased as she sat down on the ground to take off her boots.

"Well, good! I feel like I've got a gallon of water in each boot." She sat for a moment holding her boots upside down and she wondered how he happened to be on Circle K property. She did not hesitate to ask him about it.

"Just roaming around the country while I had some time off from work. I might ask you the same question."

She smiled. "I was just roaming, too, I guess."

"Well, I think the two of us have done enough roaming for one day. Besides, you need to get home and get those wet clothes off before you get yourself a cold," Larkin told her, fighting desperately the urge to take her in his arms and kiss her as he had the night in the gardens of her aunt's home.

"Guess you're right, Larkin," she drawled reluctantly, for she wasn't ready to return to the house.

Larkin sensed this and he found it intriguing that he knew exactly what was going on in that pretty head of hers without her saying a word.

He had no desire to part company with her, for the afternoon was early, but he knew nothing else to do or knew no place to take her where they could share private moments.

"Come on, honey. We better get you home now that it has stopped raining."

She said nothing as he lifted her up to straddle Rojo.

Together they rode toward Rancho Río. The rains had ceased, but the sky was still shrouded with heavy, threatening clouds.

There was no life around the sprawling hacienda when they galloped up the drive. Bianca knew when her parents went to visit their friends, Carlos and Marita Lopez, and it was always late in the afternoon when they returned to the ranch. There were no men moving about in the corral or the barn when they urged the horses into the barn.

Bianca lingered in the barn with Larkin while he unsaddled Rojo and Raven and put them in their stalls. As he went about the task, she asked him questions about himself.

"I worked on a ranch in Guadalupe County before I drifted this way, doing exactly what I'm doing now, Bianca," he told her.

She sauntered up to the stall. Her dark eyes carefully scrutinized him as she said, "Oh, but you are no drifter, Larkin! I find myself very curious about you. I've grown up around this ranch around hired hands."

A grin came to his face. The little minx was as smart as she was beautiful.

He came out of the stall to stand before her. "So you are curious, eh? I rather figured you just might be."

Boldly, she came closer to him. "Who are you really, Larkin?"

His strong hands clasped her waist, so tiny that they could almost surround it. His green eyes gleamed as bright as the emerald earrings she'd worn to the fiesta as he murmured huskily, "I'm a man being driven crazy to make love to you. You can't know what you're doing to me, Bianca. Damned if you can!"

"Kiss me, Larkin! Kiss me like you did in the gardens!" she purred softly.

"God, Bianca—do you know what you are doing?" His hands pulled her closer to him and his eyes searched her face for the answer she would give him.

"Perhaps I don't, but I know I want you to kiss me," she declared. He could not deny her, for he ached to do as she was asking him to do.

His lips captured hers in a long, lingering kiss and their bodies pressed most urgently against each other. The flames of passion soared to a mounting height as Bianca gave herself up to the wild, tantalizing sensations he was stirring in her.

Outside the barn a new burst of thunder exploded and the sharp flashing streaks of lightning lit up the barn, but Bianca and Larkin knew nothing about that, for they were too engulfed in the explosion within themselves.

Larkin swept her up to carry her to the unoccupied

stall at the back of the barn. He laid her down on the soft bed of hay. Reason had left him now, for he was a man ruled only by the reckless desire flooding him.

Her soft lips clung to his, wanting more and more of his kisses, but kisses were not enough to satisfy Larkin.

"Chiquita, I'm going to make love to you if you don't leave me right now," he declared as he started to unfasten the bodice of her tunic. She felt the gentle caress of his fingertips touching her breast and then his lips were playing the same kind of magic to the tips of her breast as they had to her lips. Her body undulated with fired desire to know more of this ecstasy he had ignited.

He heard her soft little moans of delight as his lips teased and taunted her. He knew now that she was certainly a woman of passion and fire, as he'd suspected.

His hands moved eagerly to remove her clothing and then, as anxiously, he ridded himself of his restraining pants and shirt.

Just as anxiously he was back at her side. The heat of his virile male body was eagerly accepted by her. He didn't know whether she was a virgin or not until he made his mighty thrust. Then, when he heard her gasp of a moment's pain, he knew and eased it with a touch of tenderness. His reward was the soft moan of pleasure. Together, their bodies swayed to heights of rapture.

When they returned to the world, Larkin suddenly realized what he had done to the daughter of Señor Tony Moreno. Stark reality hit him square between the eyes. But he had no regrets, for he'd never known such ecstasy. No other woman had made him feel this way nor had he tried to pleasure any woman as he had this woman on this rainy day in the barn.

81

When she finally looked up at him with a lazy expression on her face and her dark eyes framed with thick black lashes, he wondered if he would get a smile or a frown. All she had to say was, "Oh, Larkin! Dear God—I never expected it would be like this!" She snuggled closer to him and he was elated, for he knew that she was not disappointed or had any regrets.

"I probably signed my own death certificate, *chiquita,* if your father should find out."

"Why would you say that, Larkin? You didn't violate me! I gave myself to you willingly." She sat up, feeling no shame that she was completely nude.

"I don't think that would matter to Señor Moreno, Bianca." He let his eyes savor the loveliness of her satiny flesh, for this moment might never come again for him and he knew it.

Suddenly, Larkin's ears heard a sound that brought him alive. "Get dressed, *chiquita,*" he told Bianca. "I think your parents must be returning home." He hastily pulled on his pants and shirt. By the time the barn doors were being opened, Larkin was pulling on his boots.

"I'm going to take charge of their buggy," he whispered in Bianca's ear, "and when they go into the house you will have the chance to leave the barn. Get dressed!"

Quickly, Larkin left the stall and sauntered casually down the long row of stalls to where the buggy had pulled in through the double doors of the barn.

"Good day, señora and señor. I'll tend to the buggy for you. That rain is beginning to come down hard again, isn't it?" Larkin greeted the two of them.

Tony thanked him as he helped his wife down from

the buggy. It had not been the most pleasant of days. They had run in and out of rain showers going to and from the Lopez ranch.

Bianca had marveled at Larkin's cool, calm demeanor when he greeted her parents.

By the time Tony and Amanda left the barn, she was dressed and emerging from the stall. She ran her fingers through her tousled hair, then walked up to Larkin to say goodbye. He reached out to take her hand and have one last parting kiss. "I'll never forget this afternoon. I hope you won't, either."

"I won't forget it, Larkin," she told him as he released her from his arms.

More than ever he was glad he'd left that money back at the tumbledown shack!

Eleven

The light raindrops falling against her face felt pleasantly cool and refreshing to Bianca, as she was still feeling flushed from Larkin's lovemaking. She just hoped that she would not encounter her parents in the house.

She hoped both of them had gone immediately upstairs, since it was so late in the afternoon. Her mother usually refreshed herself before she came downstairs for dinner.

She certainly prayed that she didn't come face to face with her father. He'd see the glow on her face. There was no man any smarter than her father, she swore, and she always found it hard to try to fool him about anything!

When she got to the base of the stairs, she darted up them, not slowing her steps until she was ready to open her bedroom door. Only then did she give out a deep sigh of relief and collapse across her bed. But then she leaped up abruptly because she remembered her damp riding skirt. She got out of it and removed her tunic and damp undergarments also. She stood in front of the full-length mirror to gaze upon her naked body. For a moment she thought about how particular places on her body had been awakened to Larkin's gentle caresses. Dear God, she'd never imagined it would be like that!

She recalled how in that last moment she could have sworn she was soaring completely out of this world and up to the heavens.

Later, when she was luxuriating in the warmth of her tub and the perfume-scented water was covering her body, she thought about how Larkin's body had pressed and covered hers.

She had sent the little Mexican servant girl on out of the room, telling her that she could attend to herself this evening, for she wanted to be alone.

Stepping out of the tub she draped the huge towel around her and reached for her wrapper. From the armoire she picked out a simple little cotton gown with short puffed sleeves trimmed with an edge of lace. When she had the gown on and slipped her feet into the soft leather slippers, she went over to the dressing table to brush her hair. There was still some dampness at the back, so she tied a pale-blue ribbon neatly around the long tresses.

The hands of the clock told her that it was the time she usually met her parents in the parlor for the evening meal.

She splashed her favorite toilet water at her throat and behind her ears before going out the door.

Tony did not wish to make his presence known after he'd observed Bianca coming back from the barn. He had to conclude that she had arrived at the barn almost as soon as he and Amanda had left their buggy; he didn't want to think that she could have been there when they arrived. But he could not dismis the fact that Larkin was one damned handsome man. He was everything a young girl like Bianca would find exciting.

Tony saw that certain rugged quality about Larkin that he knew Bianca would be attracted to. After all, she was so very much like her mother, Amanda.

So he stood in his study with the door ajar, observing his daughter as she went down the hallway to the stairs.

She seemed in her usual high spirits from the radiant glow on her face. It had obviously not mattered to her that a rain shower had fallen off and on for the last few hours.

Tony thought he might just ride over to the Circle K Ranch to see old Mark tomorrow.

As the three of them dined, Bianca washed away any apprehensions Tony was harboring about seeing her come from the barn. Amanda had asked her what she'd done while they were at the Lopez ranch.

"I went for a ride, which I should not have done when I knew a storm was brewing," she candidly admitted.

"And you got caught in it?" Tony asked with an amused expression on his face.

"That darn Rojo heard the thunder and he reared on me and I landed in the middle of the creek sopping wet!"

Having seen her come into the house and knowing she was certainly not injured, her father exploded with laughter.

"Tony—she could have been hurt!" his wife admonished him.

"Look at her, *querida!* She is a tough little nut." He

grinned, his dark eyes darting across the table at his daughter with warm affection reflecting in them.

A smile broke on her face as she told him, "I know, Father, that you are going to tell me if I don't want to get thrown again to not ride Rojo out when it looks like a storm is going to break."

Now Amanda was also smiling as she watched the special warmth shared by father and daughter. She was glad that such a closeness was there. She had been lucky to have had that same kind of camaraderie with her own father, but she knew it did not always happen.

When she was Bianca's age, she had shared a closeness with her father, Mark Kane, that Jeff didn't. She had always been grateful that fences were mended as they'd both gotten older. But she often wondered just how much longer Jeff could go on managing two vast ranches. One of the ranches would suffer, and she feared that it would be the Circle K since the Big D Ranch was Jeff's home and had been since he'd married Mona Lawson.

Mona was her best friend, as David Lawson had been her father's dearest friend. For as long as she could remember, Mona had adored her brother, Jeff, but it had taken Jeff a long time to come to his senses and see what a jewel Mona was.

The Moreno family spent a pleasant evening. Bianca's escapade of falling in the creek seemed to set up a lighthearted atmosphere they continued to enjoy until the end of the evening.

After Larkin had eaten his evening meal, he sprawled

out on his bunk, his hands resting at the back of his head, thinking about the rainy afternoon he'd spent in the bower of hay making sweet love to Bianca Moreno.

He had had a very interesting day. The man who had sired him had not lied to his mother, but now he found himself curious to know more about Derek Lawson. He knew there were only a few people who could enlighten him, and they were all here within a few miles of Gonzales County.

He had one more day before he had to go back to work and he planned to pay a call on old Mark Kane tomorrow. He could prove to be a source of information for Larkin to learn about this stranger who was his father.

Larkin was up the next morning at the crack of dawn. When the rest of the hired hands were leaving the bunkhouse to go about their daily routine, Larkin was up along with them even though he didn't have to go to work. The fellows were laughing about old Bill and Willie not getting back to the ranch last night because they'd ridden into town yesterday. "They probably got themselves ground-crawling drunk. They better get themselves back here tonight or Señor Moreno will have their hides," one of the older hired hands remarked as they left the bunkhouse.

One of the other fellows turned to Larkin. "I'd have thought you would have been right there with old Willie and Bill, Larkin," he remarked.

"Sorry to disappoint you, Roy. I had other business to attend to," he declared with a grin on his face.

Roy commented to Pedro that Larkin was a very likable guy but that he couldn't figure him out. "He ain't like the rest of us, if you know what I mean, Pedro."

"Sí, I know what you mean, but he pulls his weight and this is what Señor Moreno looks for in his men. I've worked at the Rancho Río for over ten years and I wouldn't want to work any other ranch in Gonzales County," the Mexican told Roy.

Roy had to agree with him about that. Señor Moreno was a good boss man.

The sky was bright blue this morning, the gloom shrouding the countryside yesterday gone and the air fresh and clean. Larkin and Raven rode over the countryside, noticing the wildflowers and Indian paintbrush that were in full bloom in the meadows and pasturelands.

Larkin thought that Tony Moreno must feel like a king as he ruled his beautiful, vast dynasty of land and thousands of head of fine cattle, along with the impressive Thoroughbreds.

The same could be said of Mark Kane. The two impressive men must have found some kind of magic contentment in this Texas countryside.

He rapped on the front door to be warmly greeted by Estella. "Señor Kane will be delighted that you have come to see him," the Mexican woman declared as she invited him into the house. "He is having his breakfast out on the patio this morning. He was not happy to have to stay indoors all day yesterday and was eager to have his breakfast on the patio this morning," Estella told him.

"Guess I'd feel the same way if I had to be in for a whole day myself," Larkin remarked as he followed her out to the patio.

Mark Kane's face brightened at the sight of Larkin. He insisted that the young man sit down and have some breakfast with him. "In fact, Estella, when you bring Larkin's breakfast I could use two more of those biscuits," he told her.

When the housekeeper left them, Kane declared to the young man that Estella made the best biscuits in the state.

A short time later when Larkin was eating them, he had to agree that they *were* the best and he made a point of telling Estella this.

As they drank their second cup of coffee, Kane figured it was a good time to approach the young man. So in his straightforward way, "I've got something to talk to you about, Larkin."

"Then let's talk, Señor Kane," Larkin suggested.

Twelve

Ironically, Kane was to offer him the position of his foreman of the Circle K, which was exactly what Tony Moreno had spoken to him about.

"You don't have to give me an answer this minute. I'd want you to think about it," Kane said, then chuckled, confessing that he might be forced to soothe his son-in-law's ruffled feathers. "He might not take too kindly to me taking a good man away from him. There would be nothing else for me to consider but Tony's feeling, for my son Jeff is only running the ranch for me. But I've never given up being the boss here at the Circle K."

"I was going to ask if your son would accept me taking over the job. I've heard that Jeff has run the ranch since your accident."

"Well, young man, like I told you, I'm the boss. Ain't convinced I'll not ride again someday. I'm a stubborn man, as you'll find out if you come to work for me." He sheepishly grinned.

"I kinda figured you might be, sir," Larkin declared.

Kane liked Larkin's straightforward way of talking. It had been a pleasant time for him to just sit and talk with Larkin.

Larkin finally got up to take his leave after another hour had passed. Before Larkin left, Kane inquired of his granddaughter.

"Ah, she's just fine, sir. At least, she was the last time I saw her," Larkin told him. Privately, he was thinking about the last time he saw her — in the stall where they'd made love.

As Larkin was setting the black felt hat atop his head, he told Mark Kane he would give him his answer in a couple of days.

"Sounds good to me, Larkin," Kane replied as he watched Larkin's tall figure walking across the grounds to where Raven was tied to the hitching post.

Kane was pleased. He figured that he had himself a new foreman for the Circle K Ranch. Larkin would agree to it. He just felt it in his bones. As he often did since Jenny's death, he talked to her as if she was sitting on the patio with him.

"Ah Jenny love, maybe with Larkin's brawn and my old brain, the Circle K will be like it was some seven or eight years ago."

There was a small cottage a short distance from the main house. For years it had been occupied by Consuelo, Jenny's beloved housekeeper, and her husband, Juan. After both of them had died a few winters ago, the cottage had been emptied. All the furnishings were still there, for Jenny had provided the furniture for Consuelo and added to it during the long years she was in service at the house.

When Estella had come to work for Kane, she had her own quarters in the main house. Estella was already a widow when she'd come to the Circle K.

Later that day Kane gave Estella instructions to clean

up the little cottage so it could be ready for Larkin to live in if his answer was yes.

The next morning she and one of the servant girls went to the cottage, giving it a thorough cleaning. The floors were mopped and polished and curtains were taken down to be washed. The windows and doors were opened to give the cottage some fresh air as they worked.

By the time Estella and her servant left in the afternoon there was even a fresh set of sheets on the bed. The quilts and coverlet were hung to air on the clothesline.

As she went back to the main house, Estella was thinking how nice and cozy the little cottage was and how much the former servants must have enjoyed living there. In the small front room there was a small fireplace made of native stone. The one bedroom was about the size of the front room and the kitchen was the largest room in the cottage.

She hoped for Señor Kane's sake that everything worked out as he was expecting it to.

When Rick Larkin rode up the long drive toward the corral gate, he spotted Señor Moreno going toward the house and he called out to him.

Tony turned around and waited for Rick to ride up to him. Larkin dismounted from his horse. "I thought you should know, Señor Moreno," he said, "that your father-in-law offered me the job as his foreman. I couldn't believe my ears since you and I had just talked the other day about this same thing."

A smile came to Tony's face. "That old rascal already

had the idea himself. I'll be damned! Well, he always told me he could spot a good man the minute he met him, so I guess he got you pegged, Larkin. What did you tell him?"

"That I'd let him know in a day or two."

"Did he say anything about Jeff?" Tony wanted to know. There had been times over the years when Jeff had been indignant when he'd tried to offer him some advice about ranching which Tony had felt could be helpful.

A slow grin came to Larkin's face. "Well, he was very quick to tell me that he was the boss of the Circle K Ranch and always had been. He told me Jeff had just run the operation since he himself couldn't ride anymore."

Moreno laughed. "If anything galls that old man it's that he can't get in that saddle and ride over his land like he loved to do."

"Well, señor, I can tell you he hasn't given up on that. Told me today that he might just do it again."

Tony nodded. "I wouldn't count anything out where Mark Kane is concerned."

Before they parted company, Moreno told Larkin he was free to go to the Circle K Ranch at any time if he wanted to take the position.

"I'll give him my answer and go over there the same day, if that's all right with you, Señor Moreno."

"That would be fine, Larkin. The Circle K is in need of you, I think," Moreno told him.

Tony Moreno left him to go to the house. He took great delight in telling Amanda about the whole episode.

Amanda found it very humorous and broke into a

gale of laughter. "Oh, Tony, what a wonderful idea, and to think that Father had no inkling about what you were planning."

"I thought so." He was happy that she seemed to approve of the idea.

"It could be the best tonic in the world for Father, for he could still feel like he was at the helm."

Tony confessed to her that a few months ago he had spotted fences that had needed mending and in the last few weeks he had ridden that north boundary line of the property again and saw had not been mended. "As you know, hired hands have to have someone riding herd on them. Jeff can't be over at the Circle K every day and run the Big D, but if I was to make a guess I'd say the hired hands over at the Circle K lead too easy a life and spend too much time in that bunkhouse."

"Why haven't you said something to Jeff, Tony?"

"I tried that about a year ago when I first started seeing things going down. I didn't want to get your father upset, so I said nothing to him. When I finally mentioned it to Jeff, he did not take it too favorably, and I want no trouble in our families."

"Nor do I, but the Circle K will always be very special to me, and I know how much it means to Father."

"I know, too, *querida*. I had this in mind even when I hired Larkin. He impressed me as the hombre who could fill that position and I must confess to you when I hired him on here I didn't need him. I had a full crew of men around the Rancho Río but I didn't want to lose him if he proved to be the right man."

"Well, Tony Moreno! You are a sly fox!" she told him as she reached over to kiss him.

No one had to tell Amanda Moreno that her brother Jeff was not a powerful, forceful man like her father or her husband. He had become a very wealthy rancher and the Big D Ranch was one of the largest ranches in Gonzales County. But Jeff had it handed to him when he married Mona Lawson. Like her own father, Mona's father, David Lawson, had made the Big D Ranch what it was.

About six that evening, Estaban came riding into the Rancho Río accompanied by his friend, Ramon Martinez. Neither Bianca nor her mother was aware of their guest. Tony was the only one of the family who was still downstairs. Both of the ladies were upstairs preparing to dress for the dinner.

It had been three years since Tony had seen young Martinez and he was vastly changed. He was a very handsome young man now and Tony noticed how impeccably he was dressed.

"Ramon is going to visit with us for a couple of days before he goes on to San Antonio," Estaban told his father.

"Well, Ramon, it is a pleasure to have you here at the Rancho Río," Tony told him. "I'll leave you two young men to get settled in before we all meet in the parlor for dinner this evening."

When Tony went upstairs to the bedroom he knew that Amanda had just enjoyed a bath, for the room was scented with her bath oil. The fragrance of gardenia wafted throughout the room.

"Estaban is home, *querida,* and he has brought a guest, Ramon Martinez."

Amanda turned from her dressing table. "Estaban told me before he left that Ramon might come back with him. I've not seen him for a few years now. I suppose like our two, he has changed over the years?"

"Very much so! He is a very self-assured and quite a glib talker! He should be a very successful lawyer, I'd think." Tony smiled.

As Amanda turned back to the mirror to put the finishing touches to her hair, Tony went on into the dressing room to change his attire to a pair of fine-tailored pants and a white linen shirt. He made a most dashing figure who still could prove a delightful distraction to Amanda.

Tony told her how gorgeous she looked in her blue silk gown. After all these years, she still loved to hear him praise her. She hoped that Bianca would be as lucky as she herself had been to find such a man as Tony Moreno to fall in love with.

They had been husband and wife for more than twenty years but even more wonderful to Amanda was the fact that they were still lovers as they had been almost from the first moment they'd met each other.

"*Mi vida,* shall we go down to the parlor?" he asked as he held out his hand to her.

As they prepared to leave their bedroom, Amanda suddenly realized that she had never gone to Bianca's room to tell her about their guest.

It would be interesting to see her reaction when she met this handsome young man, Ramon Martinez.

Part Two
Summer's Magic

Thirteen

Señor Moreno and his wife were the first to arrive in their elegant parlor that evening. Tony had poured the two of them a glass of wine, for he was in very high spirits tonight. He felt that the problems at the Circle K might be solved now that Larkin was going to be taking charge.

As Tony and Amanda sipped their wine, Estaban and Ramon came into the parlor, which was brilliantly lit by the glowing candlelight. The Morenos greeted the young man in their usual warm hospitable way.

Estaban knew why he always felt such a pride when he brought friends to Rancho Río. His father was the perfect image of the dignified gentleman and his mother sitting in the brocade-covered chair was a rare beauty.

Bianca was the last one to enter the parlor. She had brushed her hair until it looked silky and glossy and had allowed it to flow softly and free over her shoulders and down her back. When she finally had slipped into a gown, it was not either the yellow or lavender ones she had considered. It was a vivid turquoise gown she did not wear often with hues of greens and blues. On her ears she had put on the long silver earrings with the turquoise stones that her grandfather Kane had given her. He'd told her that her grandmother's mestizo housekeeper, Consuelo, had given them to Jenny.

There were times when Bianca wondered why the evening meal had to be such a formal gathering when it was only her and her parents. Perhaps such traditional ways were important to them, but they weren't to her.

She came into the parlor and spied Estaban standing by the hearth talking to her mother but had not yet seen Ramon Martinez. She could not resist her usual sisterly taunting. "Damn, Estaban I didn't know you were back here!"

Amanda knew that Bianca had her father to fault for her daughter's vocabulary of cuss words. She looked over at Tony, but he had an amused grin on his face.

He knew some women created a certain excitement when they entered a room as his daughter had just done. And he had only to glance over in Ramon's direction to see how his dark eyes were flashing brightly at the sight of Bianca.

It was not until she had moved into the parlor that she saw the handsome Ramon Martinez sitting on the settee with her father, looking up at her as if mesmerized.

Estaban took charge and introduced his friend to his younger sister.

Ramon rose up from the settee and gallantly greeted the beguiling beauty standing before him in her colorful turquoise gown. "Señorita, it is nice to see you again."

Bianca gave a soft little laugh. "Ah, the last time we met was when I was considered Estaban's brat sister, sí?"

Ramon smiled, for what she said was true. Looking

102

at her now he could not imagine that any man would have considered her a brat sister.

"Ah, señorita, you could never be a brat. It is a pleasure to see you again. Memory fails me, I must confess, for I cannot remember the last time we met. It had to be at least four or five years ago."

Bianca did not remember Ramon Martinez being so handsome some few years ago. It was obvious that dark eyes were constantly on her the rest of the time they were there in the parlor, and as they dined later, it seemed every time she glanced up from her plate he was darting a glance across the table at her, a warm smile on his face.

Tony also noticed that Ramon couldn't keep his eyes off his daughter. He thought that it was just as well that his visit was going to be a brief one.

After dinner the three young people went for a stroll in the garden and Tony and his wife retired to the parlor. Amanda slyly smiled and told her husband, "Ramon finds our daughter very fascinating even though she's free with her cuss words. How long is he to be here? Did Estaban mention any time to you?"

"Just a few days was all he told me."

The garden was so pleasant with a gentle breeze blowing through the tall trees that Estaban, Ramon, and Bianca lingered there instead of going back into the house. By the time they did return to the parlor they discovered that the older Morenos had gone upstairs to retire for the night.

Bianca excused herself but not before she had accepted Estaban's invitation to go riding with him and Ramon in the morning.

After she had left the room and Estaban was pouring

a glass of wine for him and Ramon, his friend told him very candidly, "Estaban, your sister is the most beautiful lady I've ever met. It must keep you and Señor Moreno busy warding off would-be suitors swarming around her."

Estaban handed him the glass of wine and smiled. "Well, she's only been home a few weeks now from the East."

Like his parents, Estaban had to conclude that Ramon was smitten by his sister. As they sipped their wine, she was the main topic of Ramon's conversation.

Outside the courtyard garden, Larkin roamed around and puffed on his cigarette. He heard Bianca's lilting laughter within the walls and he could hear other voices, but even when he went by the iron gate he could not see who was out in the gardens with Bianca. He had been in the bunkhouse in the late afternoon packing up his belongings to go over to the Circle K Ranch, so he had not spied the strange horse in the stall next to the one where Estaban quartered his fine Thoroughbred. He did not even know that Estaban had returned home late this afternoon.

The next morning he got his first glimpse of Ramon Martinez as he spotted him jauntily walking by Bianca's side. She was looking up at the tall Mexican dressed in expensive riding garb and laughing about something he'd just said to her. He did not see Estaban with them, for he'd forgotten his hat and had dashed back into the house. Larkin concluded Bianca and this dashing-looking gentleman were going for a ride together all alone. He gave the corral fence an angry kick and went into the barn and got Raven. Swiftly, they galloped out of the barn and into the pastureland.

Bianca was startled by his mad dash out of the barn and she wondered where he was going off to in such haste. He had not even looked her way as he had ridden right past them.

Larkin was incensed with jealousy at the sight of her by the side of another man. As wild as the wind, he and Raven galloped over the countryside for a while. Finally, he slowed the horse's pace, for his temper had begun to cool.

It was the first time in his whole life that he'd ever felt jealousy over a woman, so now he knew for sure how involved his emotions had become for Bianca. She wasn't a woman he could make love to and turn to walk away as he had with other women.

The ride back to Rancho Río was at a slowed pace, but he had cleared his head. He thought it might just be in his best interest if he sought out Señor Moreno this afternoon to ask if he could just take on out this afternoon instead of tomorrow.

When he galloped into the long drive of the property, he saw Moreno going toward the barn.

"Señor," he called out to him, "could I have a word with you?"

Tony halted his steps as Larkin leaped off his horse. "I just thought if it's all right with you and since I've got all my gear packed up, I could ride on over to the Circle K this afternoon and get an early-morning start on things over there. Bert's off the sick list and back on the range this morning."

"Guess you might as well. I get the impression you're kinda anxious to get going on your new job." Moreno smiled, giving his shoulder a comradely pat.

"Guess you could say I am, señor."

"Well, why don't you come on up to the house with me now and let me settle up what's owed you," Tony suggested.

"Well, all right," Larkin replied, tying Raven's reins to the corral railing.

He'd never been inside the fine old stone house and he was impressed as soon as they entered the tiled entrance and wide hallway, where huge urns held giant palm plants towering almost six feet high. A young Mexican servant was scurrying on her way with a dust cloth in one hand and a mop in the other going about her morning chores. Moreno guided him down the hallway, but Larkin had a glimpse of the magnificent opulence of the parlor through the arched doorway. This room was furnished with the fine, elegant taste of Señora Moreno. When they came to Tony's study and he opened the carved dark wood door to usher him into the room, Larkin saw a completely different effect here.

Heavy furnishings of dark leather and highly polished wood dominated the room. Rich, earthy hues of rust, deep greens, and browns were here in the rugs and drapes at the window. A huge massive stone fireplace took up almost one side of the room, and on either side of the fireplace were shelves filled with numerous books.

Larkin thought this room as the señor's private domain. It was a completely masculine room.

Moreno went over to his desk and invited Larkin to have a seat in the chair by the desk. Before he opened the desk drawer to count out the wages he owed Larkin from the cashbox he kept there, he looked at Larkin.

"It's been a pleasant association with you, and should it not work out with Mark, then come back here. Your job will be waiting for you. You're a good worker, Larkin. But for Mark's sake and yours, I hope it does work."

A man could never question Moreno's sincerity, Larkin thought as he noted the señor's piercing black eyes that seemed to be able to look right into the core of a person. It was clearly from her father that Bianca had inherited those eyes of hers.

Tony handed him a very generous payment for his services of the last two weeks. Larkin knew that he'd been overpaid as he picked it up and thanked the señor and couldn't restrain himself from commenting. "Señor, I think you counted out too much."

"No, I count my money very carefully," Tony grinned. "I still owe you for something money can't pay you adequately for—saving my daughter from being ravaged by Ortega."

"You owe me nothing for that, Señor Moreno," Larkin told him.

Each rose up from their chairs at the same instant and reached out to shake hands before they said their goodbyes.

"Good luck, Larkin. Come back to Rancho Río to see us," Tony told him as Rick reached over to get his hat.

"Thank you, señor," he said, as he turned to leave the room.

Fourteen

As Larkin walked out the door of the study, a fragrant aroma came to his nose and he knew when he looked behind him he was going to face Bianca. She was the only one he'd ever known to wear that particular fragrance.

It was not Bianca but her lovely mother moving quickly toward him. "Good day, Larkin," she greeted him with a friendly smile on her face.

"Good day to you, señora," he replied with great relief that it was not her daughter.

"Is my husband in his study?"

"Yes, ma'am, he is. I'm—I'm getting ready to leave to go to the Circle K, so he was just paying me my wages. I'll be telling you goodbye, too, while I've got the chance."

She held out her dainty hand to him to give a parting handshake. "I'm very happy that you'll be taking over the Circle K for my father, Larkin, and I wish you the best."

"Glad you feel that way, señora. I'll try to make him a good foreman," Larkin told her.

She went into Tony's study to seek out her husband. She had decided while the nights were still so delightfully mild to have José prepare one of his delectable barbecues for their evening meal. "Lucia is cooking a huge pot of her beans with the chiles and onions that will be so good with José's barbecued pork and beef," she told Tony. "We shall have ourselves a little fiesta out on the patio and courtyard, *querido!* I thought it might be fun for Estaban and his friend. And Bianca has always loved dining out in the courtyard in the evening. What do you think about my idea?"

He smiled as he walked around to the front of his desk to take her in his arms. "I think it is splendid."

There was little wonder that he still found his fair-haired wife the most exciting woman he'd ever known. None of her zest for life had faded over the years. Amanda was the same vivacious woman she'd been when he'd first met her.

When he'd bent down to plant a kiss on her lips, she only allowed herself to give way to the amorous moment for a brief second before she urged him to release her. Giving out a soft, girlish giggle, she heaved a deep sigh. "I've a million things to do, Tony Moreno." As she quickly turned to leave the room a smile came to Tony's face, for he knew she *would* be busy all afternoon putting her own special touches to the patio while Lucia worked in the kitchen and José attended to the cooking of the meat outside.

Amanda remembered old Juan from her childhood. All her life, Juan and his wife Consuelo had been at the Circle K Ranch working for her parents. Consuelo had full charge of the Kanes's kitchen all those years and they were both like a part of the family. Amanda wanted to instill in her own family special traditions that she held so dearly. A Texas barbecue was always a special occasion.

109

She was just as devout in carrying out the traditions established by the first lovely lady who ran the spacious hacienda. Bianca Alvarada had been a most impressive woman who possessed a dignity Amanda had always admired. There was a very stately air about her that demanded one's respect. Yet, Amanda learned that she possessed a very earthy quality as well.

The same had been true with Tony's grandfather, old Estaban. She found him a most intriguing gentleman whose very aristocratic, dignified demeanor could mellow. She soon learned that there was a devious side of his character that endeared him to her. It was her deep love of this old gentleman that urged her to name their firstborn for him.

By late afternoon, the tables out on the patio were draped in bright red tablecloths and lanterns were hung to light up the patio area. The numerous pots of geraniums with their brilliant scarlet blossoms blended in perfectly with the setting she'd arranged.

When Bianca had returned from her ride with Ramon and Estaban, Amanda had told her about her plans for the evening and Bianca had thought it a grand idea.

She went on up to her room after speaking with her mother. She decided a simple gown was called for as she perused the contents of her armoire.

She quickly made the decision that the little cotton frock with its low, scooped neckline and short puffed sleeves would be perfect. The material was a mass of vivid colors of yellows, reds, greens, and blues.

As she laid out the sandals along with the gown on the bed, she noticed the hands of the clock and saw that it was still early in the afternoon. Something had been gnawing at her all the time she was out riding with her brother and Ramon. For a while she had dismissed it from her mind after they'd returned home and eaten a late lunch. Larkin was the source of that gnawing. Why had he ridden right by her without giving any sign of recognizing her?

She'd not seen him since the afternoon when she'd surrendered to his fierce lovemaking in the barn. She had to ask herself if he was trying to avoid her.

Well, he could hardly avoid her here on the Rancho Río and, he had to know that! After all, she was the daughter of Tony Moreno and no one trifled with Tony's daughter!

Her impatient nature urged her to go to the barn to see if he was there. There was plenty of time before she had to start getting ready for dinner.

She went outside through the kitchen. The aroma was enough to whet her appetite for the meal they would be enjoying later this evening.

She only prayed that she didn't run into her father. She knew that Estaban and Ramon were going to play chess after they'd finished lunch, so she did not have them to worry about.

No one moved around the corral, and when she entered the barn and walked along the stalls, it was just as quiet. There was no sight of Larkin. When she was getting ready to leave she spotted the little Mexican boy, Paco, sitting over in the corner with his straw hat pulled down over his face as he napped.

"Paco, where is everyone? Are you the only one around?" Bianca asked him.

"*Sí, señorita,*" he replied, quickly sitting up and alert.

"You mean Larkin and the rest have gone this early?"

111

"No, *señorita*. The rest of the fellows are still out on the range, but Larkin isn't."

"What are you talking about? Where is Larkin?"

"Señor Larkin left for the Circle K. Sure hated to see him leave. He was good to me," young Paco said, shaking his head.

"You mean Larkin went to the Circle K to *stay?*" Bianca was stunned that he had not even sought to tell her farewell before he departed for her grandfather's ranch. She'd heard her parents' discussion that he might be hired on as the foreman over there but she had not expected that it would happen so suddenly.

"Sí, señorita."

Bianca mumbled something to young Paco and turned quickly to leave the barn. She'd never known a hurt like this before and she fought back the tears. No man had ever caused her to feel such a pain. *She* had always been the one breaking the young swains' hearts.

If this was how it felt, Bianca wanted no part of love, she told herself as she marched angrily into the house. The tears that had almost begun to flow were replaced by a devious glint. She'd show that conceited Larkin that he had meant nothing to her!

He would also live to see the day that he'd regret taking his pleasure with her as though she was some servant girl.

Once she was in her room and had enjoyed a leisurely bath, she dressed with special care for the evening. She fashioned her hair as she had on the night of the fiesta and sent Cola down to the garden to cut a red blossom for her to pin in it.

She stood in front of the full-length mirror to appraise herself, and she was pleased with her reflection there.

When she got to the base of the stairs, she heard voices coming from outside and knew that her family was already gathered.

From the minute she made her entrance out on the lantern-lit patio, she made a point of being even more charming to Ramon than she had been before.

At first, Amanda and Tony did not think anything about her behavior and figured she was just in a light-hearted mood because they were dining out on the patio rather than the more formal dining room.

Ramon could not have been more pleased by all the attention being focused on him. He complimented her on how beautiful she looked.

She'd smiled sweetly and thanked him. "And you look very handsome, Ramon." Quickly, she turned to her father and Estaban to tell them how handsome they also looked. With her eyes twinkling brightly, she told her mother that her idea was perfect.

Ramon sat with a smile on his face just listening to her talk. A candle enclosed by a glass globe was lit as a centerpiece on the table and he thought she was so gorgeous with the candlelight reflecting on her face.

He could not imagine how he'd ever manage to get her completely alone, but he was going to try to manage it before this evening ended.

Tomorrow, he would be leaving and it could be a long time before he would be coming back this way again. Nothing would delight him more than taking the memory of one precious kiss from her nectar-sweet lips to San Antonio with him.

Long before Tony Moreno realized that his pretty

daughter was flirting with the handsome young man, Amanda sensed it, and she also noticed the displeased look on Estaban's face. She knew he was thinking his sister was acting too bold.

Ramon could not remember indulging himself with such a feast and he praised Señora Moreno for the special efforts she'd gone to for him. "I'll be wanting to come this way again, señora," he declared, giving her a warm smile.

"We'll hope so, Ramon."

As Ramon had expected, he'd had no time alone with Bianca, but there had been one brief moment when he'd been able to ask her if he might write to her after he got settled in San Antonio.

"Why, of course you can, and I will answer your letter, Ramon." She smiled sweetly.

His dark eyes had danced slowly over her face. "I'd like to get to know you better, Bianca."

"Perhaps we shall, Ramon," she told him with a provocative look in her eyes, which encouraged Ramon.

Suddenly, the evening was ending and everyone was going their separate ways. Ramon did not think he would see her in the morning as early as he would be leaving. But he had the memory of tonight to carry with him tomorrow.

Fifteen

Mark Kane could not have been happier to see Larkin and learn he was ready to tackle the job of being foreman of the Circle K.

"Got my belongings with me right now if you still want me, sir?"

"Damned right I do. Trust Tony took it all right?"

"Sent his best to you and wished the best for me. He's one fine man," Larkin said.

"You won't get any argument from me there," Kane declared, then confessed that he'd had quarters prepared in hopes that Larkin would use them. He summoned Estella to show Larkin to the small cottage, then turned his attention back to Larkin to tell him when he got settled in to come back to share supper with him. "Got something to talk over with you."

Larkin led Raven as he walked to the cottage, which was only about two hundred feet away from the main house. Estella ushered him in the front door. "I serve the señor's dinner at six-thirty and if there is anything you need you just let me know, Señor Larkin," she told him.

"Well, thank you, Estella. I remember that good breakfast I shared with Señor Kane." He grinned.

Estella smiled and thanked him, then turned to leave him in his new quarters.

When she got back to the house and her kitchen she added a few more potatoes to the pot.

It was pleasant for Mark Kane to have someone share the evening meal with him. He enjoyed conversing with Larkin. Estella heard the young man telling Señor Kane about his plans.

"I intend to ride this land over from one boundary to the other to see everything for myself, and whatever I find, I will report to you."

"Sounds good to me, Larkin. That is exactly what I used to do when I could ride. A rancher has to ride over his land to know what's going on there," Kane had told him.

After Larkin had said good night and Estella was helping Mark Kane to his bedroom, she remarked to him that Larkin seemed like a man who was not going to let any grass grow under his feet.

"It appears that way, doesn't it Estella."

Estella knew better than anyone how much it vexed Mark Kane that he could not oversee his beloved land as he yearned to do. But she knew he was happy about his new foreman!

Going to the Circle K Ranch when he had and throwing all his energy into riding over the Kane land was the best tonic Larkin could have had.

After the long days he put in, he fell on the bed and quickly went to sleep. Only the first night over at the

Circle K had Bianca haunted his sleep.

Already he was planning improvements around the ranch. He'd discovered various places along the borders between the Circle K land and the Big D Ranch where fences were down, so he'd sent one of the hired hands into town with an order for new fencing.

He saw that the hands worked from sunup to sunset just as he was. There were no more afternoon card games in the bunkhouse. Only two fellows had objected. They had enjoyed not working a full day for a full day's pay so they were none too pleased about Larkin coming and messing all this up.

Larkin had quickly spotted the two troublemakers and he let them know quickly that he was the boss. If they weren't going to take his orders and earn their pay they could move on.

He went by the main house daily to report to Kane what he'd done or checked out the countryside. It had not set well with Kane when Larkin told him about the fencing being down.

"Damn — now I wonder just how long it's been that way and how many head of Kane cattle roamed over into the Big D. Get that fence back up and buy new fencing. You just tell Jake you're my foreman and he'll let you have anything you want."

"I've already done that, sir, and most of it is back up. I'm working the fellows the same as I'm working myself, but I've got two lazy hands I may have to re-place."

Kane gave him an approving nod of his head. For a moment he'd sat with an intense, thoughtful look on his face. "Take a count of my cattle, Larkin. I'll be curious to know what you come up with."

117

Larkin had left the main house that night knowing that sooner or later he was going to be meeting Jeff Kane, and he already had it figured that it would not be pleasant.

By the time he had been at the Circle K Ranch for a week, Larkin was very settled in. The cottage was comfortable and cozy. Some evenings he shared dinner over at the main house, but he didn't wish that to be a nightly routine so usually he fixed his supper in the cottage. But Estella was always bringing him a piece of one of her fresh-baked pies or cakes, so Larkin was never lacking for good food.

Like Kane, he was anxious to see what the head count was going to be on his cattle. Larkin knew that he'd have no inkling if the count was short, but that old fox, Kane, would certainly know.

Larkin was feelng quite pleased with himself for all he'd been able to accomplish in that first week. He figured that in another two days all the length of fencing would be mended and, had he been losing cattle, it would cease now. And he was seeing that the men hired to work for Kane were now earning their wages.

But one of the things Larkin found the most gratifying was Kane himself. Yesterday, he'd approached Larkin with an idea: One of his oldest hired hands and one of the best workers was an hombre by the name of Turkey. "Think you and Turkey could lift me up on a damned horse, Larkin?" Kane had asked with a very serious look on his face.

"Don't see why not," Larkin had told him.

"Well, I know one thing—if I can sit in that damned

118

rocking chair, I can sure as hell sit in a saddle. As long as you were by my side, what would prevent me from a short ride around my property?"

"I think you could do it, sir."

"Larkin, you're my kind of man! It's settled! We're going to try it," Kane declared with a pleased smile on his wrinkled face.

Larkin's strength and daring was what Kane needed. This was one of the things Mark Kane liked so much about this young man from the beginning.

Usually when autumn approached the Texas countryside, Kane found himself getting very depressed, for it was in the golden autumn of the year that his beloved Jenny had died. But this late summer Kane was feeling in higher spirits, and even Estella had been aware of this. Larkin could take credit, the Mexican housekeeper felt. He had been able to do what Señor Kane's own family had not been able to do.

It was an ideal day to go to the Circle K Ranch, Amanda Moreno decided. She knew how her father always found this time of the year hard to cope with. She went to seek out Bianca to see if she would like to accompany her.

She found Bianca in the garden. "You're always such a joy to him! Come with me. Your father and Estaban are going hunting," she told Bianca.

Bianca could hardly refuse her, but she knew that conceited Larkin would think she was there to see him. "Of course I'll go with you, Mother."

"Oh, thank you, dear. I know that Father will be pleased."

119

That Sunday afternoon, the two Moreno ladies boarded their buggy to go to the Circle K Ranch. It was a glorious day, signaling that autumn was coming to the Texas countryside. The air was a little cooler and the sun not so bright and hot. Night fell sooner than it had a few weeks ago.

When they arrived at the Circle K and went through the courtyard, Amanda did not see her father. Her first thought was that he was not well enough to come out.

It was such a beautiful afternoon she could not believe that he'd wish to remain inside. With apprehension, she knocked on the door. Estella greeted her with a cheerful expression, so that eased Amanda's concerns.

"Ah, good afternoon, señora and señorita," Estella said, motioning them to enter.

"Good day to you, Estella. How is my father?" Amanda asked her.

"He is just fine, señorita." She led them into the parlor. "In fact, I haven't seen him so well in a long time."

Estella asked if she might bring them something to drink, but both of them politely refused the offer. When Amanda inquired where her father was since he wasn't in the garden or in the parlor, Estella grinned. "Would you believe that he has gone for a short ride, señorita?"

"Oh, one of the men has taken him for a ride in the buggy?"

"Oh, no, señora—he is riding his own horse, and I've never seen him so thrilled."

"Dear God, Estella! He has no business trying to do that," Amanda declared with a shocked look.

"Oh, señora—he will be fine. Señor Larkin is with him. He and another man got your father in the saddle. They have done this twice before, making very brief rides to just see how long he could last. Each time he's been able to go a little longer. He is so proud of this, señora. Señor Larkin has been the best medicine your father could have had. He's already done wonders around this ranch."

Bianca listened to Estella singing the praises of Larkin with a very solemn look on her face. She wished that she had refused to come along. Rick Larkin had obviously ingratiated himself to her grandfather and Estella after only one week and he had her willingly surrendering to him after she'd only just met him. She asked herself just who this green-eyed devil really was.

"Isn't that wonderful, Bianca?" Amanda exclaimed.

"Oh, it certainly is, Mother," Bianca said with a forced smile on her face. Next, it would be her mother falling prey to his charms!

"Señor Larkin will not keep him away too long, señora. So if you will excuse me, I'll get back to the kitchen to see to the pies I'm baking."

Amanda told her that they'd just make themselves at home.

Bianca paced around the parlor and glanced out the window to see if she could see the two men returning. She whirled around to face her mother. "Guess we weren't needed over here to cheer up Grandfather after all, Mother," she remarked. "I gather Larkin is doing a good job with that!"

"If this is so, then I'm very grateful to Rick Larkin, Bianca," she declared to her daughter. There was a sardonic tone in Bianca's remark which puzzled Amanda Moreno, for she had thought Bianca liked Rick Larkin after he'd rescued her from Ortega. She'd rarely been wrong about her daughter's feelings about someone for

Bianca's face was like an open book, unlike Estaban, who had always been able to shut her out if he wished to do so.

Neither of them had a chance to say anything else, for there came the sound of boisterous male laughter. Bianca felt herself grow tense; she knew she was soon to see Larkin and her grandfather.

She was curious what she'd see on his face when he looked at her.

Sixteen

With the help of Larkin's power, Mark Kane had been able to go a steady pace. As the two of them entered the parlor and Amanda saw the broad, happy smile on her father's face, she was convinced a small miracle had taken place.

"Well, hello, you old gadabout. Estella has told me about you two," Amanda teased him.

"Oh, she has, has she? That Estella has a busy mouth at times." He grinned, but he was ready to sink into a comfortable chair after the workout Rick had put him through the last hour. Yet, he'd loved every precious moment of riding down the lane along with Larkin.

It was only after he had Kane settled into the chair that Larkin allowed his eyes to cast in the direction of Bianca and her mother. He greeted them politely. Señora Moreno gave him a warm smile. "It appears that you two are getting along just fine," she told him. "Father hasn't looked so well in years. I must thank you for that, Larkin."

"No, señora — I can't take the credit. It was Señor Kane himself with that indomitable will of his. Me and Turkey just supply the strength to get him in the saddle. It is his courage to do it," Larkin told her.

Bianca's black eyes were staring directly at him. She thought he knew just the right words to use. It was obvious that a special camaraderie already existed between her grandfather and Larkin.

Larkin was just about ready to excuse himself from this family gathering when Kane called out to Bianca, "Come over here and give your grandfather a kiss, young lady."

Bianca forced herself to give out a soft little giggle as she got out of the chair to go to her grandfather's side to kiss him. Standing there beside Kane's chair, Larkin smelled the sweet essence of her and felt the same magic she always casted on him. A week away from Rancho Río and the sight of her had dulled none of the wild desire consuming his body. Right now he ached to kiss her sweet, tempting lips.

Old Kane patted her shoulder and declared, "Well, that's more like it!" He told her she looked as pretty as a peach in her coral-colored gown.

"Well, I have to look pretty for my grandfather, don't I?" she jested.

Larkin decided that this was a good time for him to get out of there and quit being tormented by the sight of her. As her grandfather had said, she was as pretty as a peach and when she'd bent down, his green eyes had ogled the soft flesh of her throat and the scooped neckline had revealed a part of that satiny skin he'd caressed. Recalling that rainy day in the stall, he had a fever in his blood that was raging.

"I'm — I'm going to my cottage, señor. I'll be there if you need me. Nice seeing you again, señora — and you, too, Bianca," he mumbled awkwardly as he started to

124

back away.

"See you at dinnertime, Larkin," Kane called back to him.

Amanda asked her father if Larkin dined with him every evening.

"No, Amanda—just occasionally. He works late some nights well past my evening mealtime."

"The cottage he spoke about—is that Consuelo and Juan's old cottage at the back of the house?" Amanda asked her father.

"Yes, and it seems good to have it occupied again. It puts Larkin close by if I need him. He's a good man, Amanda, and I'm more than pleased," Mark told his daughter.

She reached out to pat his hand. "Well, I'm pleased, too. You keep up with that horse and Bianca and I will come over some day to ride with you, won't we, Bianca?"

Bianca's eyes had followed Rick Larkin out the door and she was still glancing that way when her mother posed the question to her. "Oh—oh, sure we will," she stammered.

"Tony has given me the impression that you rarely ride anymore and usually go in that little buggy of yours." Mark grinned.

"Well, I've gotten lazy, Father. That Tony is like Estella. He talks too much sometimes."

Amanda's soft laughter ceased when she inquired of her father if Jeff knew about Larkin becoming his foreman.

"Couldn't very well tell him when he's not been over here, could I?" Kane told his daughter. But this week had awakened him to something he'd not been aware.

One day usually faded into another for Kane, but this last week because Larkin had been here, he'd realized Jeff had not even been over to check on things for him the last seven days.

"Well, if I had to be more exact I'd have to say it's been more like ten days, Amanda. That's why I need my own foreman to ride herd every day over here. Jeff's got more than he can handle between two big ranches—mine and David Lawson's."

It was interesting to Amanda that her father still referred to the Big D as ranch. To him, it wasn't Jeff's ranch even though he'd lived there and run it for years.

It had been a pleasant afternoon for Amanda, and she would be delighted to tell Tony that things were working out well at the Circle K. Tony had been absolutely right about Jeff, and he'd obviously spoken the truth about how things were not being properly cared for on the ranch.

The sun would be setting in an hour, so she told her father that she and Bianca had to get started for home. They said their farewells and Amanda and Bianca boarded their buggy.

Larkin watched the buggy roll down the drive until it faded from sight. He tossed aside his cigarette and sauntered back to the cottage he now called home.

How simple it would have been if she'd never come into his life, Larkin thought. But he had no sweeter memory to cherish than the moments he'd spent holding her in his arms and loving her.

As they traveled homeward, Bianca sensed that her mother was very happy about the condition of her father. And Bianca had to confess that she'd not seen him seeming so content since her grandmother Jenny had died.

"I hope your father and Estaban had a grand afternoon like we have," Amanda had told her daughter as she guided the buggy down the trail that led from Circle K Ranch to Rancho Río. "I hope they found themselves some of the wild turkeys back in the woods."

But Bianca could not agree that it was such a grand afternoon, though she did not admit that to her mother. "He usually does. Father's Sunday hunting trips have always provided us with our holiday feasts."

Bianca wished she had been the one riding with him this afternoon instead of being at her grandfather's.

"Next time, I shall ask Father to take me along. I should like to try my hand at shooting a turkey," she declared to her mother.

Amanda laughed and looked over at her daughter to see that she was very serious. "Well, I imagine that this could be arranged," she assured her.

A glorious sunset blanketed the western horizon as their buggy turned into the long drive at Rancho Río. The sky was a maze of golds, purples, and mauves. There was a rush of a sudden gust of wind that had changed its direction and Amanda noticed a shower of leaves falling off the tall sycamores. She knew that autumn was soon to arrive in Gonzales County.

To her, the golden autumn season was the most beautiful season of the year. She agreed with her mother, Jenny, about this.

Old Mark sat in his parlor after his daughter and granddaughter had left. It was very satisfying to Kane to know his only daughter had such a happy life. He'd never had to doubt throughout the years that Tony Moreno loved his wife. It was Bianca he sat thinking about after they'd left. She hadn't been her usual vivacious self. He knew her too well to be taken in by those forced giggles and brief minutes of lighthearted chatter.

Was she mooning over some young man? he wondered. She was about the age for something like that. From what he'd observed the night of the fiesta, she didn't give him the impression that any of the young hombres made her heart flutter, though.

Later, when Larkin came to the main house for dinner, he told Kane that he'd like his permission to hire a couple of new men and lay off a couple of the men he felt weren't pulling their weight around the ranch.

"You're the foreman, Larkin. Fire them if this is how you feel and go into town tomorrow and pass the word around at the mercantile store or livery that the Circle K is hiring."

"Well, I wanted to talk it over with you before I did take out to go to town," Larkin said, then turned his attention back on Estella's delicious food.

Seeing Larkin again had put Bianca in a depressed mood, so the next morning when she found out that Estaban was going into town to do some errands for his father, and pick up some items for his mother she eagerly asked him if she could go along.

That idea did not exactly please Estaban. It was always a challenge to protect her from some drifter roam-

128

ing the street or some cowhand who'd had too much to drink in the saloon. When they had a day off from any of the neighboring ranches, the first place they'd head for was the Sundown Saloon.

But he could hardly refuse her, so he told her to go get herself ready.

She did not have that much to do. She did not change from the sprigged muslin gown she wore, but she did smooth down her hair and fetch a white shawl to keep her warm as they traveled to town. Her black-and-white figured cotton frock would not have been warm enough with the slightly cool chill in the air. She picked up her black faille reticule and was ready to go back downstairs to join her brother.

As she prepared to go out the door her mother called out to her to enjoy herself.

"I will, Mother. I'll do your shopping while Estaban takes care of the business for Father," she answered her.

She was at the front entrance when Estaban came with the buggy. She had already leaped up to take a seat beside him before Estaban could get down to help her. He grinned, looking at her. "Guess I got to say that you don't keep a man waiting like most young ladies."

Her face glowed with a sweet sisterly smile as she told him, "Estaban, you can be very nice sometimes."

"Well, thank you, Bianca." He gave out an uncharacteristic gust of laughter. "You know Father and Mother would probably never believe that we can behave so civilly to each other."

Bianca laughed. "You're right, Estaban. I had not thought about that."

The two of them were enjoying each other's company as they did from time to time when they weren't having one of their brother-sister battles.

But Estaban was like all the other men who touched Bianca's life, for he found himself helpless to stay vexed at her too long.

Seventeen

When they arrived in town, Estaban stopped in front of Curtin's Mercantile to let Bianca out of the carriage. He could not resist admonishing his sister before he left her to be sure to remain inside the store.

"Don't you go traipsing down the street, Bianca. I mean it!"

"Oh, I won't, Estaban! I promise I'll be right here where you left me unless you piddle around too long and then I'm going to be hunting you up." She smiled slyly, for she was always telling him that he moved as slow as a snail.

When Bianca entered his store, Roy Curtin was waiting on another customer, but he paused a moment to greet her. "Señorita Moreno, good to see you."

"Good to see you again too," Bianca called out to him as she strolled to the center of the store. She remembered when her father would bring her here to Señor Curtin's store when she was only three or four years old. It was always a thrill to her when he'd lift her up on his huge horse and the two of them would gallop into town.

Before they'd leave the store she'd have a sack of lemon drops and taffy from the candy jars. Señor Curtin would always insist that she pick something from the numerous shelves that caught her eye.

While Curtin figured the items up for the customer he was waiting on, he thought how far back he'd furnished goods to the Moreno family, as well as to the Kanes. It was the pretty golden-haired Amanda Kane with her bright blue eyes who'd first come to his store with her parents, Mark and Jenny Kane. One generation had followed another as Tony Moreno had brought his little girl, Bianca, here.

Curtin knew Mark's dislike for Mexicans in those earlier days of this wild struggling state. Kane had done battles with rustlers, Indians, and Mexican bandits pouring over the border from Mexico.

But here in Gonzales County there were the respected families of Mexican descent like the Alvarado family and the Moreno family. It was as if fate had deemed the union of Tony Moreno and the daughter of an Anglo-American. Time had proved it to be right, for Curtin knew no man who drew more respect than Moreno.

By the time Curtin had finished with his customer, Bianca had gathered up the five articles on her mother's list and was browsing around the store. When Curtin offered to help her, she politely told him that she was just looking around.

"You just look all you like, señorita. I've got some beans to sack up. Let me know if I can help you."

The store had many counters laden with goods, and all the walls had a variety of things hung there to display them. Shelves were lined to utilize every inch of space.

Bianca was at the far end of the store when she heard a deep, husky voice speaking to Curtin. There was a familiar sound to that voice that immediately caught her attention and she slowly moved back toward the front of the store.

As she was almost in the middle of the store she spotted the tall figure of Rick Larkin standing talking to Señor Curtin.

He was a fine figure of a man in his simple working clothes, his black felt hat sitting on his head at a cocky angle. She did not seek to make her presence known but heard him telling Señor Curtin that the Circle K was looking for two men to hire on.

"I'm the new foreman at the Circle K, and Mr. Kane suggested that I leave word here with you." He extended his hand to Curtin and told him, "The name's Rick Larkin, and I'd appreciate any help you could give me."

Curtin shook his hand and told him he'd certainly pass the word to anyone coming in his store. "Known Mark Kane for over thirty years, so I'll sure do what I can." Curtin paused for a moment to measure the tall, husky man. "So you're Kane's new foreman, are you? Well, you look like you can handle that."

Slowly Bianca began to move around the counters which would lead her toward the front door of the store. Her curious nature demanded to know why he'd left Rancho Río without saying goodbye to her and telling her why he was leaving.

When he came ambling toward the front door, she addressed him. "Well, Larkin—fancy seeing you here."

He stopped short seeing her there. "Bianca . . . what—what are you doing here?" he drawled slowly.

"Shopping for my mother. I came with Estaban." She took a step closer to him before she posed her question. One hand went to her hip as she pointedly asked him,

"Did I not deserve at least a polite farewell from you?"

He answered her with his deep voice lowered so Curtin couldn't hear him. "I had intentions of doing just that, but when I was going to come to you, you were very occupied with one of your many suitors." His green eyes sparked with the fires of jealousy as he recalled seeing her with Ramon Martinez.

"You speak of Ramon?"

"How the hell would I know who he was? All I know is what I saw, so I made no attempt to intrude."

A slow, satisfied smile creased her face and she gave him a very provocative look. "Larkin," she purred, "you were jealous!"

He had to fight the temptation to take her into his arms and plant a kiss on her lips.

But he didn't do that. Instead, he told her in a very low, calm voice, "Yes, *chiquita*—I guess you could say I was jealous! But I won't play that kind of fool again."

He turned his back to her and walked out the door to leave her to think about what he'd said. But the look she'd seen in his green eyes was to haunt her the rest of the afternoon after Estaban picked her up at the store and they'd ridden back to Rancho Río.

Only one thing made her happy about her encounter with Rick Larkin today was his confession that he was jealous seeing her with Ramon Martinez.

Her romantic heart told her that if he cared that day, he surely still cared. What he could not know was that Ramon Martinez, as handsome as he was, did not thrill her like Larkin did. She was already thinking up a scheme to work on Larkin now that she knew he was jealous. She could not deny that she yearned to have his strong arms holding her again.

Larkin had said that he would not play that kind of fool again. Well, *she* might be playing the fool but she was going to chance it. She had to, for her restless, reckless heart would not allow her to do otherwise.

If she thought she was the only one affected by their encounter in the mercantile she was wrong. Larkin knew that his cool aloof air was hardly that as he stepped out the door to go on his way to the livery.

Bianca made him want to promise her everything. She made him want to love and protect her forever.

Once before in his life he'd thought himself in love, but the feeling hadn't been as intense as this consuming madness for Bianca Moreno.

He finally got Bianca off his mind when he talked to a man at the livery who told him he might know someone who would be interested in working at Mark Kane's ranch. "He'll probably be coming by here this afternoon," the man said. "Want me to have him ride out there to talk to you?"

"Sure appreciate you doing that. I'd like to hire two hands if I can find them."

He was back at the Circle K by midday. Estaban and Bianca were also back at the Rancho Río in time to join their parents for lunch. She'd made no mention to her brother about encountering Rick Larkin in the mercantile.

Estaban had mentioned to her his plans to pay a visit to their great-grandfather, Estaban Moreno. "He is really getting old, you know."

"Let me think about it, Estaban. When will you be leaving?" she asked.

"In a few days. But you've got time to decide if you'd like to go and if Mother will approve."

As they had arrived back at the ranch and were later sitting at the table having lunch, Bianca asked her mother about accompanying Estaban. She eagerly gave her approval. "I think it would be a splendid idea, don't you, Tony?"

"I certainly do." Tony turned to his son to tell him how nice it was of him to ask his sister to accompany him.

Bianca gave out a soft little laugh. "Oh, Estaban can be very sweet when he wants to be, I'm finding out."

Feeling still in his own lighthearted mood, Estaban taunted her. "Well, I'll pray I'm not kicking myself later."

"I'll be happy to oblige you." She laughed.

Tony and Amanda sat there laughing and shaking their heads as they listened to the two of them jest with each other.

Later, Bianca found herself pulled two ways about going with Estaban. She wanted very much to see her great-grandfather, for she adored him. But a part of her did not want to leave right now since she wanted to carry out her plans against Rick Larkin. In fact, she did not intend to waste any time in carrying out those plans. Tomorrow she was riding over to the Circle K Ranch.

As much as she adored her grandfather, her visit to the Circle K tomorrow had nothing to do with visiting him.

It was Larkin she was going to see!

Eighteen

After Bianca had dressed in her deep-green divided riding skirt, she turned back to reach in the armoire for the matching jacket. She might need it for her ride over to the Circle K. But she did not wear her flat-crowned felt hat. Her golden hair glowed from the brushing she'd given it and fell loose and free with its own natural curl draping around her shoulders.

Her parents and Estaban had already had their breakfast when she rushed into the kitchen to get herself a cup of coffee and some of the sugar-coated rolls in a pan.

The Mexican cook chided her for eating so fast, but Bianca only grinned as she kept munching heartily on the roll. Still chewing the last of the roll, she muttered, "Tell Mother I've ridden over to Grandfather Kane's this morning, will you?"

Before the cook could reply, Bianca had already disappeared through the back door on her way to the barn.

She put Rojo through a brisk, fast gallop as she rode from Rancho Río to Circle K. She loved to soar across the countryside with the wind whipping her long hair back away from her face as she sat astraddle Rojo's strong back.

She found the door ajar when she arrived at the ranch. She called out to Estella, but she did not come rushing through the kitchen door as was her custom. There was no one in the parlor or dining room, so Bianca marched into the kitchen to find poor Estella sitting there in one of the straight-back oak chairs with her foot propped up on another chair.

"Estella, are you all right?" she asked.

"I fell, señorita. I am so mad at myself."

"Well, you didn't exactly do it on purpose, Estella." Bianca had lifted Estella's cotton skirt to see the swelling. She told the woman to take off her stocking so she could get a cool cloth over the ankle. Estella thanked her and asked if she could check the kettle of stew she had simmering on the cookstove. Bianca did as she requested, then inquired about her grandfather.

"He went with Señor Larkin to speak to a man they are thinking about hiring. I had just served his breakfast and he'd left with Señor Larkin to go to the barn, I think." She explained to Bianca that she'd put on the huge kettle of beef stew to simmer slowly because it was the one day a week that she left the main house to go clean the cottage where Señor Larkin was living.

"I change his bed and sweep the floors."

"Well, you're not doing that today, Estella. You're going to have to stay off that foot as much as possible. Larkin can help Grandfather upstairs. What about the young girl who helps you here in the house?"

Estella said she would be coming shortly. Bianca declared in a very authoritative air that reminded Estella of Señor Kane, "Well, she is just going to have to work until your foot is better, Estella."

Bianca added water to the pot of stew and poured Estella a cup of coffee as well as one for herself. Her frivolous plans for Larkin had suddenly been swept aside, for she was more concerned about Estella who was so devoted to her grandfather.

The teenage daughter of one of Kane's hired hands served Estella at the main house and when she came into the kitchen, Estella introduced her to Bianca.

Juanita gave Bianca a nervous smile and mumbled a greeting. Immediately Bianca took charge. "Juanita, you will be taking responsibility over here in the kitchen and the main house until Estella's foot is healed. You go home to inform your mother and get some extra things for the next few days. I will stay here until you return," Bianca told her.

In less than a half hour the girl came back to the house. With the support of Juanita and Bianca, Estella was taken to her quarters. Bianca insisted that she lie on her bed to rest with her foot propped up on a pillow.

As Bianca and the young Mexican girl walked down the hallway, Bianca instructed her to check in on Estella and watch the stew simmering on the stove.

"Tell my grandfather if he should return to the house before I get back that I'm over at Larkin's cottage," she added. "I'll see that his bed is changed and his floors swept."

Bianca was to discover that Larkin was a very neat, meticulous man. She strolled through the cottage to find his clothing was hung properly and there were no dirty dishes on the counter. She only swept the floors and stripped down his bed.

The sheets were replaced and she was spreading the

coverlet back over the bed when a husky voice invaded the quiet of the cottage. Larkin stood in the doorway for a moment curious as to what Bianca was doing there taking over Estella's chores. It was a very titillating sight for him to behold her sensuous derriere as she bent over the bed.

For a few minutes he allowed himself the luxury of just enjoying and savoring the sight. At the same time he was thinking to himself that she was no helpless, pampered female. She could make a bed!

He could not resist alerting her to his presence for long. "Well, Bianca — I never expected to find you making my bed! I got to say you've done a damned fine job."

She turned with a jerk to stare up at his grinning face. "I'm not doing it for you, Larkin!" she responded. "I'm doing it for Estella. She fell and injured her foot."

He was the one suddenly feeling very foolish. For a moment he could not think of anything to say. She went about the chore and said nothing else to him. When he finally found his voice he asked how seriously Estella was injured.

When she moved past him out of the bedroom and through the doorway, she told him, "Your cottage has been swept and your bed is changed. Hopefully, Estella will be better in a week. If not, you can make your own bed and sweep your own floor!"

As she was moving through the front door, Larkin took long, striding steps to catch up with her. His hand snaked out to take her arm so he could stop her before she got to the front door.

"You didn't allow me to thank you for your kindness, *chiquita*," he declared in a deep, low voice as the two of them stood close to each other. Before she could protest, his head had bent down and his heated lips were kissing her. And before she could stop herself from responding, she was leaning against him and her lips were parting to welcome his kiss.

Larkin could feel the sweet release of the barrier she was attempting to put up against him. So he let his lips linger longer. He was convinced that her fire and passion were flaming just as intensely as his.

He finally released her lips, but his eyes continued to make love to her as he gazed into the jet-black pools. "No—no, Larkin," she stammered. "I can't. I must go." Her hands pushed against his chest and she moved away from him.

Larkin said nothing as she rushed out the door of the cottage, but he watched her hastily walk across the grounds toward the main house. He picked up the bed linens on the floor that she'd forgotten to take with her in her haste to leave.

A slow smile came to his face as he laid them in the chair. She could fight him if she wished, but the beautiful Bianca would be his. She was just fighting what her heart desired, but he had only to look in her eyes to know the truth.

All the way back to the main house Bianca could feel the flush of heat on her lips. She cussed Larkin for making her feel this way. He had to be the most conceited man she'd ever met to think all he had to do was take her in his arms and he'd have his way with her. By the time she'd reached the house, a little voice said to her: "But Bianca, that is all he does have to do, you know!"

She tossed her head in an arrogant air as if to sweep

the haunting voice away from her shoulder as she mounted the front steps.

The minute she walked through the front door her grandfather was calling out to her, "Bianca, is that you?"

"Yes, Grandfather," she answered him as she went into the parlor to join him.

"Well, young lady — you certainly took charge, I've been given to understand by Estella. I appreciate that, honey, and poor Estella thinks it was awfully kind of you to help around here and take care of her."

"Well, it was necessary. She has to stay off her foot."

"Juanita will be able to manage the kitchen and house for a few days with me and Estella bossing her." He grinned.

"Well, Larkin can help you since he's close by," Bianca pointed out.

"I understand you were over there doing Estella's weekly chore for him," Kane remarked.

"Yes, but Larkin can sweep his own floor for a while and make his own bed. If he doesn't know how, then it's time he learned," she declared.

Kane roared with laughter. "Oh, Bianca — I can see that you're going to make a very demanding mistress in your own home someday." But he was secretly admiring her attitude and how she'd taken charge of things.

Bianca glanced up at the clock on the mantel. "Oh, God, Grandfather — I've got to get started for home before they have a searching party out for me. I've been gone a long time. I had no idea of the time."

"Think maybe you better be hightailing it home then," he told her as she bent down to plant a kiss on his cheek.

142

He watched her go, her golden curls bobbing up and down, and he swore she could have been his Amanda at that age.

Amanda had been pacing the parlor floor for over an hour, looking out the window in hopes of some sight of Bianca.

Usually her visits to Mark's ranch were never this long and she'd even told herself that her father had possibly urged Bianca to remain and have lunch with him before she rode back home. But even so, she should have been home by now, for it was almost three.

When she was about to turn from the window and ask her son to go in search of his sister, she spotted Bianca and Rojo coming up the drive. She smiled and sunk down in the chair, finally able to relax.

Being the mother of such a beautiful girl was not easy sometimes!

Nineteen

When Bianca explained to her mother why she'd been detained at the Circle K, Amanda not only understood but she felt very proud of her. "I'm sure that your grandfather was very grateful to you, dear. I'll go over there tomorrow." She went to the kitchen to have her cook bake some extra bread and a couple of pies so she could take them with her in the morning.

Estaban had laid his book aside when his sister had arrived. After their mother had left the room, he asked Bianca if she had made up her mind if she was going to go with him to San Antonio to visit Grandfather Estaban.

"Right now, the only thing I've made my mind up about is that I'm starved. It just dawned on me that I had no lunch."

Amanda was still in the kitchen when Bianca breezed through the door. "I've gotta have something to eat. I'll faint if I have to wait until dinner."

The cook smiled. "Let me slice that child a piece of ham and some bread," she told Amanda. "We don't want Señorita Bianca fainting."

The cook and her mother finished their conversation and Bianca sat there devouring the ham and bread along with a glass of milk.

By the time she left the kitchen the pangs of hunger had left her and she was ready to go up to her room for a bath and to change into a fresh gown.

Later, as she was sitting in the tub enjoying the soothing warmth of the water and the aroma of the bath oil, she thought about Larkin. She realized the dangerous game she was playing. He was not a man she could tease with her coquettish ways, as she had Julio, Emilo, or Armando.

Larkin was different from the likes of them, and she was not in control when she was around him as she was with the young men she'd known most of her life in Gonzales County.

The same could be said of Ramon Martinez, for she did not feel nervous or unsure of herself with him — not like she did around Larkin. It perplexed her that this tall, handsome stranger had such a power over her.

But there was consolation in knowing that she was not the only one beguiled by his charm, for obviously her grandfather had been very impressed to have offered him such authority at the Circle K Ranch. Her own father had also been impressed by his performance when he'd worked at the ranch.

By the time she had slipped into her challis gown of gold-and-brown figured material and sat down at the dressing table to brush her hair, she was thinking that it would be best for her to go with Estaban to San Antonio. She put the gold-hammered hoop earrings her great-grandfather had given to her on her last visit to his house on her ears, pulled back her thick golden hair, and tied a brown velvet ribbon around the long mane.

By the time she went downstairs to join the family

she had firmly decided that she was going to tell her brother that she was going with him.

As she walked into the parlor she was greeted warmly by her father. "Well, I hear that there was a new boss lady over at the Circle K for a few hours today, Bianca," he playfully teased her as he took her hand and led her over to sit on the settee with him.

"Did my best." She smiled up at him.

Tony Moreno was happy to hear Bianca say that she was going to accompany Estaban to San Antonio, for his grandfather's days were growing shorter all the time. He, like Mark Kane, adored his beautiful great-granddaughter, Bianca.

He poured Bianca a glass of sherry. "When will the two of you leave?" her father asked her.

"He told me at the end of the week, Father."

Estaban came into the parlor and Bianca was quick to inform him that she'd decided to go to San Antonio with him.

Estaban looked over at his father and grinned. "Am I asking for trouble, Father?"

"You'll just have to be man enough to handle it, son," Tony told Estaban.

The next morning Bianca still slept when her mother left in her buggy with her loaves of fresh-baked bread and pies to go to the Circle K.

When she finally got out of bed and got dressed she went downstairs for her usual cup of black coffee and a couple of breakfast rolls. She returned to her room quickly to see what clothing she wanted to pack for her trip.

She included two of her fancy gowns in case the occasion arose that she and Estaban were invited to some social affair. And she could not dismiss the thought that she would be seeing Ramon Martinez during her visit with her great-grandfather.

There had been a time before age caught up with him that Estaban Moreno had been quite the gentleman about the city of San Antonio and grand parties had been given there in his mansion often.

By the time she had chosen her clothing, she knew exactly what her brother would say. He was going to swear that she was taking her entire wardrobe.

However, she was patting herself on the back that her choices of gowns would not make it necessary for her to take but two pair of slippers.

She left the packing up to one of the young servant girls, for she intended to have an afternoon ride on Rojo before she left. While she was gone he would not be taken out except when her father sought to ride him. So for the next two afternoons she planned to give him a nice run.

For an hour she rode over the countryside before reining Rojo to head for home. As she was approaching the trail leading up to Rancho Río she spied her mother's buggy, and rode up to join her. The rest of the way home she slowed Rojo's pace to ride along beside the buggy so she might inquire about Estella. The two of them chatted as they traveled up the winding drive toward the barn and corral.

"You put in a long day, Mother."

"I know, but I sat by Estella's bed to visit with her, for she's very vexed that she can't be puttering in her kitchen. I think she feels that Juanita will have every-

147

thing out of order." Amanda laughed. She told Bianca that her father had said everything was going along without any problems at his ranch.

"I'm glad to hear that." She could not resist asking about Larkin.

"As a matter of fact, he just stays there at the main house when he walks over for the evening meal. That way, if Father needs anything at night, Larkin is there to see to it."

"Guess that would be the best arrangement," Bianca mumbled.

She quickly sought to change the subject by excitedly telling her mother that she had chosen her wardrobe to-day before she went out to ride.

"Well, I'll wager that Estaban hasn't got that done yet for himself!" Amanda laughed.

Tony saw his wife and daughter coming up to the door and he was glad that neither had been at the house this afternoon when his angry brother-in-law had come here.

When he and Amanda were alone after Bianca excused herself to go upstairs, he told her about Jeff's visit. "He figured that I'd manipulated the whole deal because Larkin was working for me. I admitted that I did have it on my mind to talk to his father about Larkin, but before I'd had the chance Mark approached Larkin himself," Tony told her.

"Well, he could hardly hold you at fault then. Besides, Jeff has to realize that it's father's body that's ailing and not his brain. Why, that old fox is as sharp and shrewd as he ever was!"

"Well, after he cools down a little and thinks about it, he'll see that it was the best thing that could have happened for him and your father."

"Well, we'll hope so. Jeff certainly doesn't make it a habit to check on Father or the ranch. That's enough to tell me that he doesn't need to be trying to handle both ranches."

She bent over to plant a kiss on her husband's cheek and tell him that she felt the need of a bath and a fresh frock before dinner. Her bright-blue eyes gleamed warmly as she looked at him and said, "Jeff has never been the man you and my father are, and he never will be. I've known this all along. But for dear Mona and her devoted love I don't know that Jeff would even have become as much man as he is."

Tony knew that everything she'd said was true.

He well remembered those days over twenty years ago when Jeff and Mona Lawson's brother, Derek, were two hell-raising hombres.

In the end his own wickedness had destroyed him before Derek Lawson celebrated his thirtieth birthday. But his evil doings had corrupted Jeff, his best friend, and destroyed his father, David Lawson. Never had Tony Moreno forgotten that a bullet from Derek's pistol could have killed him.

It was obvious that his beautiful Amanda had never forgotten, either!

Twenty

All evening Mona had noticed her husband's quiet, brooding mood. She had known throughout all the years they'd been married that Jeff was a man given to childish pouts. Often, she'd found him more difficult to deal with than their children.

At least after three children and some fifteen years of marriage she had finally become wise enough to not accept the guilt which had always seemed to lie at her feet. Once she was able to do that, she was able to deal with the times when he sunk into one of his sulking periods.

In a dignified way, she left the parlor to go to her bedroom without saying good night. This room reflected the soft pastel colors Mona loved, and it was here she found peace instead of the sitting room downstairs. It was here she could calm her frayed nerves.

She immediately undressed and slipped into her silk nightgown and wrapper of light blue which matched the coverlet on her bed. She went to sit at her dressing table to comb out the coil of her hair. Once it had been as black as a raven's wing, but now it was slightly streaked with gray.

Her black eyes studied the reflection in the mirror

and finally she had seen what Amanda Kane Moreno had told her back when they were both sixteen. She was a most beautiful woman! But she was so reserved, and often she had wondered how she and Amanda could have been such good friends. Amanda was her complete opposite with her vivacious, adventuresome ways.

Because she had been so shy, it had not mattered to her that Jeff was not a man who possessed the hot-blooded passions of Amanda's Tony. So she was already seasoned when he decided to have his own bedroom some years ago. This became her own private haven.

Their last baby had been stillborn some ten years ago and the doctor had told them that she should not ever try to have another one or it could mean her life. That was when Jeff had started to sleep in one of the guest bedrooms. However, he had never sought to return to her bedroom, and Mona had said nothing even though it had hurt her.

Mona had found great joy in the daughter born some thirteen years ago whom she'd named for her very dear friend and sister-in-law, Amanda Kane Moreno.

Her two older sons had been gone from the Big D for a few years and had their own families. One lived in El Paso and the other in Austin. She had been well aware of how devastated Jeff was about their desire to leave the Big D to pursue their own lives away from the ranch.

But Jeff had never formed a close bond with either of them and she could not help thinking that the same had been true between him and his father, Mark

151

Kane. God knows, there was never any bond formed between her father and her brother, Derek!

Mona decided she was going to pay his father a visit and she told Jeff of her plans the next morning when they were having breakfast.

"What for?" he angrily snapped at her. The expression on his face was so strained and tense.

"What for, Jeff? I want to visit with him. I haven't seen him since the fiesta. There's surely nothing wrong with that, is there?" Mona asked with a skeptical frown on her face.

"No, nothing is wrong with that," he mumbled.

Mona turned her attention back to the food on her plate. After she'd taken a few more bites, she asked him, "By the way, when was the last time you saw your father, Jeff?"

"For Christ's sake, Mona—I can't tell you. I don't know," he said as he rose from his chair and scooted it back. "I got to go, Mona. I'll see you this evening."

Mona watched him go, feeling as perplexed as she had last night as to what was plaguing him. After she finished her coffee, she, too, left the dining room, which was glowing from the bright sunshine streaming through the windows. This was why Mona had put so much greenery in this room, for it had seemed to flourish here. But this morning it was shrouded with gloom.

With a basket filled with a tin of fresh-baked cookies, a jar of pear preserves, and gooseberry jelly, she was ready to board her buggy and in a short time was guiding it through the impressive high archway over the roadway that announced the Circle K Ranch. Mona was thinking how often she and Amanda had traveled between the two ranches to see each other. She recalled how she'd envied Amanda having her dear, devoted mother, Jenny, around to comfort. Mona's own mother had died when she was very young.

Guiding her buggy up to the house she thought that this particular area of the ranch had not changed at all.

But the vast acres of pastureland had been neglected and numerous heads of cattle had been allowed to roam from the property of Kane over into Big D land. Jeff had not considered a few head here and there mattered knowing the thousands there on the Circle K. He had justified the fences down and the cattle coming over to the Big D of no consequences since it would all be his and Amanda's someday when Mark Kane died. It never entered his mind to think that it would be any other way.

Mona received a warm reception from her father-in-law. She'd known that Mark Kane had always liked her ever since she'd first met him and her parents visited the Kanes or the Kanes came over to their ranch.

"Damn, Mona—I think you just keep getting prettier as the years go by," Mark declared as she came into the parlor to greet him. She'd given the basket of treats to Juanita as she'd entered the house.

She gave him an affectionate pat on the shoulders. "You look so good, Mr. Kane," she declared. "You really do! I thought so the night of the fiesta but I *know* so today."

"Well, I do feel better and I'm riding a little, Mona. That's the best medicine I could have. I've my new foreman to thank for that. He's been helping me to get back to what I used to be."

153

She was taken by surprise by his announcement. "I—I didn't know there was a new foreman here at the Circle K. Jeff hadn't told me," she spoke in a hesitating voice.

"He doesn't know 'cause he's not come over for me to tell him, Mona. I hired Rick Larkin on my own."

"Well, Jeff does not always tell me about what goes on around either of the ranches."

"I understand, Mona." There were times Kane had found himself feeling sorry for Jeff's pretty little wife. He knew his son wasn't the easiest person in the world to live with.

"Well, you can tell him for me that I've a damned good foreman and that all my fences are now mended. You can also tell my son that my men are taking a head count of my cattle. I figure a hell of a number of my cattle roamed over to the Big D all that time the fences were down."

"I will tell him, Mr. Kane. I—I am happy you've found yourself a good man. You are obviously pleased with him." In an effort to change the subject, she inquired about Amanda and Tony and how she wished they got to spend more time together. "But I can understand how wonderful it has been for Amanda to have her daughter back at Rancho Río after being away for the last three years," Mona told him, as she went on to rave about how gorgeous Bianca was the night of the fiesta.

A chuckle came from Mark Kane. "She is as sweet as she's pretty. I know that there are those who think she's spoiled, but even though that's true, she's not so self-absorbed that she can't be very generous with people." He told Mona what she'd done the morning

154

she'd ridden over to discover Estella injured.

Kane was enjoying his visit with his daughter-in-law so much that he'd forgotten about the ride he was supposed to take with Larkin until he saw him come sauntering through the parlor door.

"Well, Larkin—I've a lovely lady for you to meet. This is my daughter-in-law, Mona—Jeff's wife. Mona, my new foreman, Rick Larkin."

Rick Larkin had to agree that she was a very lovely lady. She had the warmest black eyes he'd ever seen as she looked up to him and extended her hand to greet him.

"My father-in-law has been singing your praises and I'm so happy he has found himself a good foreman." Mona was carefully surveying this young man standing in front of her.

"Well, ma'am—that's nice to hear," Larkin told her. He was also scrutinizing Mona, who, if Derek Lawson was truly his father, was his aunt.

It was apparent to Larkin that Kane was very fond of his daughter-in-law. "Larkin, I might just have to forget about that ride with you since I've such a pretty lady here with me to keep me company. I'm thinking you could understand that?"

"Sure can, sir!" Larkin agreed, a crooked grin on his face.

Neither of them noticed the very sober, startled look on Mona's face at that moment. For her it was like looking back in time when she stared mesmerized at that particular expression on Rick Larkin's handsome face. She carefully studied the fine-chiseled features of his face, the very defined arch of his brow, and the shape of his sensuous mouth. His hair had an unruly wave that seemed to want to fall over a part of his forehead.

Oh, the eyes were not the same but everything about this young man reminded her of her brother, Derek!

She sat there looking at him and she was shaken to the core of her being.

She gathered all the strength she could muster as she tried to control her voice from cracking. "Oh, you two go on your ride, for I have to get back home anyway. I was just about to leave when you came in, Mr. Larkin. I really was. But I'm glad I've had the opportunity to meet you."

She was already getting up from the chair, soothing Mark Kane's protest. She wanted to leave desperately, for her head was whirling with all kinds of crazy thoughts. She felt the need of fresh air on her face as she traveled in her buggy alone to sort out the tormenting thoughts parading through her mind. It had been a long, long time since thoughts of her brother Derek had haunted her.

But today they did when she had gazed upon Rick Larkin, and it was enough to disturb her very much.

By the time she had said her farewells to Mark Kane and Rick Larkin, Mona had to tell herself that she was a very good actress, for neither man would have suspected the tumultuous torment she was experiencing.

All the way back to the Big D Ranch Mona kept telling herself that Rick Larkin was young enough to be her own son so he could certainly have been Derek's son. Was it possible that Derek had sired a son that no one ever knew about?

156

Her brother was a handsome devil who had many women fawning over him. Knowing him as she had, she also knew that none of those women ever meant anything to him.

Only one woman had conquered his reckless, restless heart. That woman was Amanda Kane but her heart belonged to Tony Moreno.

Twenty-one

After her visit to the Circle K today Mona was convinced that Jeff knew there was a new foreman. Gossip traveled between ranches; she was sure he'd heard the news and that was what he was sulking about.

She had every intention of letting him know that she knew about the new foreman. But there was more than just Larkin troubling Mona. She had listened to Mark Kane tell her about the unmended fences separating Big D land from the Circle K. Jeff had to have known about that, and she found herself dwelling on the time when Jeff and her brother, Derek, had rustled both their fathers' cattle to pay for gambling debts they'd incurred playing cards in the back room of a saloon in town.

Dear God, she was thinking of things that had been forgotten years ago; now suddenly here they were all popping up again this afternoon because she chanced to see a young man who looked so much like her brother Derek that she could not dismiss it from her thoughts.

She wondered if Amanda had felt that way when she'd seen him. She knew that she was going to be going over to Rancho Río very soon to see Amanda and seek out an answer to this thing that had stirred such a fury in her.

All Mona Lawson Kane knew by the time she arrived back at her home was she had to have some answers to questions that were gnawing at her soul.

Mark Kane took his ride with Larkin as planned after Mona departed his ranch. As curious as Mona had been about him, Larkin found himself curious about her and her family. He knew if anyone could tell him about the Lawsons it would be Mark Kane. So as he rode with Kane he made a point of asking questions about Mona and he found Kane very eager to converse about his dear friend, David Lawson.

"Your daughter-in-law sure is a nice lady, sir."

"Isn't she. But her brother was no one to be admired, I can tell you. He was a damnation to his family, and David deserved a better son than that."

Larkin prodded Kane for more information about this man who was supposed to be his father.

"What kind of man was he, sir?" he asked Kane.

"I'll tell you. He lived by the sword and died by the sword. He stole from his own father to pay a gambling debt. He was a young man who had a powerful influence over my own son, which made Jeff forget the principles his mother and I had taught him all his life. He even tried to kill Tony Moreno because my daughter Amanda was in love with Tony and not him. He was a despicable man! It was good riddance when he was killed!"

Larkin listened to this sad report Kane was giving him and he had to respect it as the truth. He knew that he could never let the Kane or Moreno families know that he was the son of Derek Lawson.

He was cussing the day that he'd made the decision to come to Gonzales County. How much simpler his life would have been to remain in Guadalupe County and work on the ranch where there were no complications.

His mother had not lied to him for there had been a bounty of money in the shack. But he wanted no part of the tainted, soiled money.

After a while Larkin suggested that they start back, and Kane agreed that he was ready to head for home.

Larkin realized he could never reveal to Bianca who he really was, for it was his father who'd tried to kill her father. Forever, it would be a barrier between them.

By the time they got back to the main house and Larkin had helped Kane inside, he knew that the elderly gentleman had had a full day. He told him that he would not be over for dinner but he would spend the night there. He went directly to his cottage as soon as he left Kane back at the main house. He had not had a drink of whiskey for several days, but this late afternoon he felt the need for one, so he went directly to the cupboard to get the bottle he kept there and a glass.

As he sat there in the chair and sipped his whiskey he thought about the past and his honest, hard-working mother. His father had obviously not been an admirable character from what he'd learned from Mark Kane. He was glad that he'd listened to his gut instinct that day when he'd discovered the tin of money in that old shack on Big D land. He wanted no part of it now.

He went into the bedroom and opened the drawer where he'd placed the old map that had guided him to the shack. He tore the paper into numerous pieces, wanting to be rid of it and wash it completely from his thoughts.

His name was really Larkin Miller, but for the rest of his life he would go by the name of Rick Larkin. No Lawson blood flowed in his veins as far as he was concerned.

This was a secret he intended to carry to his grave.

Jeff and Mona Kane shared a strange dinner that evening. She would have expected that her husband inquire about his father since he knew that she had gone to the Circle K. She was at the point of bringing up the subject when Jeff finally asked about his father.

Mona told him about the contented gentleman she'd spent over an hour chatting with. "I've not seen him look so well in a long, long time. I also met his new young foreman and I was very impressed. By the way, he told me to tell you about him if you'd not heard about it."

"I'd heard. I would have expected him to speak to me about hiring the guy before he did it. Obviously, he didn't feel the need to do it," Jeff muttered.

Mona saw from the expression on his face that he resented what his father had done.

"Well, Jeff—how could he? You've not been over there for several days."

"Damn it, Mona—I can't run myself ragged between these two big ranches," he snapped at her.

"That's why your father made a wise decision to hire himself a foreman for the Circle K."

"It depends on just how good a job this hombre does," Jeff replied.

"Well, from what I was told today he's doing the job well. All the fences that had been down for months have been put back up," his wife informed him.

A strange expression came to Jeff's face. As if to defend himself, he was quick to point out to her that a fence down could have allowed Big D cattle to roam over to the Circle K just as easily as Kane's cattle to cross over to Big D land.

"Well, they're taking a head count over at the Circle K. Maybe you should tell your men to do the same, Jeff," she suggested.

Never could he recall that his very docile wife had suggested anything that he should do in the way he was running the ranch. A fury ignited within him as he glared across the table at her.

Mona felt a share of her own resentment. She met his stare, her own black eyes piercing him. "The Big D is my ranch, Jeff. You share it only because you married me. If I choose to take a part in running it or make a decision that is my legal right. I think that you'd best never forget that!"

Her stinging remark left him numbed for a minute. When he finally got over the shock of her blunt remarks, she had gotten up from her chair and marched out of the dining room.

Flinging his napkin down on the table, he, too, marched away from the table. Once he was in the study behind the closed door, he went directly to the liquor chest to pour himself a generous drink of whiskey.

Something was happening lately to make everything go wrong. Things had run smoothly for so long. When had all the trouble started, he was questioning.

Mona was proving to be the biggest puzzlement of all!

He sat in the dimly lit study sipping the whiskey and thinking about what she'd said to him. It was the truth that the Big D was his only because he'd married Mona.

He also confessed to himself that Mark Kane was just as sharp as he'd ever been. No one outsmarted him. Jeff had to admit he had been at fault in not repairing the fences but he'd just put it off to do whatever else demanded his attention around the ranch.

He would go over to the Circle K the first thing in the morning and see his father, he decided. Besides, he was anxious to get a second look at this Rick Larkin who seemed to be enchanting everyone.

He stayed in his study that evening until he had drunk enough to dull the pain gnawing at his gut. But this pain had nothing to do with Mona. This was something he'd lived with from the time he was just a young lad. He knew that he could never be the man to step into the shoes of Mark Kane. It had not eased this torment when his sister had married Tony Moreno, for he had the force and powerful personality of his father.

Now another obviously strong, imposing man had made an appearance. Rick Larkin had to have some very impressive qualities to urge his father to hire him as his foreman. He knew how Mark Kane measured a man.

Jeff realized that his father must be thinking he'd failed to run the ranch properly. For Larkin to have accomplished all these repairs within the first two weeks made him look bad in his father's eyes, he was sure.

When Mona told him about them taking a head

163

count Jeff knew that Mark Kane was determined to find out just how many of his cattle were missing. But tomorrow he intended to point out to him that the same could be true for Big D cattle. There was one sure way to find out the truth and that was the branding.

This was a point he was going to make to his father.

Twenty-two

There was an instant feeling of mutual dislike between Jeff Kane and Rick Larkin when they met each other the next day at the Circle K. When Jeff arrived at the ranch, Larkin and Kane were just returning to the barn from their daily ride together. Jeff didn't know that his father had been riding his horse again and that Larkin had been riding along beside him.

He was appalled to see his father sitting astride his favorite roan mare, Maude.

Mark knew what his son was thinking so he quickly made a point of telling Jeff that it was his idea. "I'm glad I did, Jeff. I'm getting better all the time. I ride a little farther every time we go out."

Larkin figured that his wife's visit yesterday to the Circle K must have whetted his curiosity about the new foreman his father had hired.

Larkin leaped down from his horse and went around to the side of the mare. "Want to help me get your father down from the horse?"

"Sure, I'll help," Jeff quickly replied to this man who seemed to be so cocky and self-assured.

There was no question that Larkin was in charge as

they lifted Mark Kane off the mare. Once his feet were on the ground, it was Larkin who took full charge of Kane as he began to move toward the house.

Trailing along with his father and Larkin, Jeff had the chance to scrutinize the young man very carefully. He was the type of rugged individual who would impress his father. There was an air of authority about him that could not be easily dismissed.

As they made their way to the house, Larkin could almost feel the touch of Jeff's cold eyes staring in his direction. Larkin sensed that there was nothing friendly in Jeff Kane's feelings toward him.

When Larkin had Kane comfortably settled in the parlor, he excused himself. "See you later, Mr. Kane. It was nice to see you, Jeff," Larkin said as he left the parlor.

"Yeah, nice to see you too, Larkin," Jeff told him.

Mark Kane had also sensed the tenseness in his son, but he knew the reason. So he merely gave Larkin a wave of his hand and a smile.

Larkin wondered what it would have been like to be reared in a family like the Kanes or the Morenos, where there was a father and a mother. What would it have been like to have lived in a big house instead of one room.

He'd never known any other life until he went to the ranch outside town. The cozy little cottage was the most luxurious place he'd ever lived in his whole life.

He was finding that life at the Circle K Ranch was proving to be good. It was gratifying to Larkin to see Mark Kane improving daily. He was also proud of the things he'd been able to accomplish around the ranch.

With the fences all mended and two new men hired, Larkin was ready to tackle a new project to make more improvements.

He had no doubt that he was the topic of conversation between Kane and his son Jeff back in the main house.

About a half hour later he glanced out the window to see Jeff mounting up on his horse. He didn't seem to have a very pleased look on his face. Larkin thought that Kane's son and daughter were certainly nothing alike.

But his private musings were interrupted by the rapping on his door and when he opened it, Juanita stood there with his laundry. "Your clothes, señor. Estella told me to tell you that she was mending one of your shirts, so I will bring it by later."

Larkin took the bundle she handed him. "No reason for you to do that, Juanita. I'll pick it up this evening or tomorrow."

"I'll tell Estella, señor," she said, and turned to quickly move away from the door to scurry across the grounds back to the house. As young as she was, Juanita had done a remarkable job of running the house for Estella the last several days. He'd wager that she was more than eager for Estella to take charge again so she could return to her parents' cottage and have to come here only a part of the day.

While it was true that she was very weary of the number of chores she had to see to daily here at the main house, Juanita had found herself enjoying spending the nights over here instead of the small cramped cottage where she shared her bedroom with a noisy six-year-old brother. Her fourteen-year-old brother and her four-year-old brother had to share a cubicle which had been a small back porch that her father had boxed in for their sleeping quarters. It had been a delight to her to have the nice little bedroom all to herself when she had finished in the kitchen. It was also wonderful to have so much good food to eat, for the meat and potatoes were not rationed out among two adults and four children as they had to be at her house.

Although she knew that the handsome Rick Larkin did not know or care that she existed, she thought he was the most handsome hombre she'd ever seen. She could not stop herself from daydreaming about him when she was alone in her room at night. She could not control the trembling her young body experienced when she was close to him.

But she had been carefully instructed by her mother about how she should conduct herself when she was working at Señor Kane's house and she always obeyed her parents.

It came as a surprise to her when she saw that Estella was sitting in the kitchen there with a smile on her face.

"Estella? You should be resting," Juanita told her as she went over to the stove to stir the food she was preparing in the cast-iron kettle.

"No, Juanita—resting time is over for me. I intend to start testing this foot out. I'll let you prepare the dinner tonight and breakfast in the morning. If I do as well as I think I can, then I'm going to let you return home midday tomorrow."

"Are you sure, Estella?"

"No, niña—I'm not sure at all, but I'll never know

168

unless I try. If I can't, then I'll send Señor Larkin over to get you back—*sí?*"

Juanita nodded and went about her other chores.

Estella insisted that she would set up the dining-room table before she returned to her room to rest and praised the Mexican girl for the fine job she'd done in keeping her kitchen spic and span.

Everything was going smoothly for the brother and sister on their trip. They had arrived at the Arnaldo ranch just as the sun was setting that evening. Bianca had captured the admiration of the entire Arnaldo family by the time dinner was over.

By the time they were ready to depart the next morning to head on for San Antonio, they had an eager invitation to stop back as they returned home to Gonzales County. Estaban had assured them that they would.

Renaldo Arnaldo, the oldest brother, made no effort to disguise his feeling to his friend Estaban as they stood alone while Bianca was bidding the rest of the family farewell. *"Madre de Dios,* Estaban—she is the most gorgeous lady I've ever seen. I dread to hear your answer, but I must know if she is already spoken for?"

Estaban smiled. "No, Renaldo—she is not spoken for. Bianca is only seventeen and my father is very strict. She's just returned to Rancho Río from school back East."

Renaldo heaved a deep breath. "Ah, *amigo*—this makes me a very happy man!"

Estaban stood watching Renaldo say his farewell to

his sister before they mounted their buggy. Never had he seen him display such charm.

He was wondering as the buggy rolled out of the Arnaldos' drive how many more hearts would Bianca win or break before they returned to Gonzales County.

Twenty-three

Old Estaban Moreno was past his mideighties, but his eyes had not dulled to the sight of a beautiful woman. Tonight he sat at his table seeing a most beautiful young lady who just happened to be his great-granddaughter.

It was a wonderful surprise this late afternoon when Ignacio announced to him that his great-grandson and granddaughter were in the parlor.

Eagerly he'd left his room to go downstairs with Ignacio. His manservant was not much younger than old Estaban himself and a younger Mexican now served both of the elderly gentlemen. Ignacio stayed on as Estaban's devoted companion.

The last time Bianca had been to San Antonio was the spring of her fourteenth birthday. She had blossomed in the last three years and Estaban was hardly prepared for the sight of his great-granddaughter. Young Estaban had not made such startling changes as she had.

He was elated that they were going to visit with him for a few days. He'd immediately asked Ignacio to go to the kitchen to tell Elvira that there would be guests for dinner and to get some of his fine Madeira wines from the cellar.

Old Ignacio had moved to the kitchen in a slow, lagging pace to do as Señor Estaban had requested. He'd encountered José, the young Mexican now serving as the elderly Moreno's manservant.

"Señor will be needing you to assist him upstairs, José," he told him. "I am going to my own room to rest." Ignacio found himself very weary after the last hour's activity.

José had a lot of spare time for the wages he was paid by Señor Moreno. He found the elderly señor a kind man who had made José aware from the beginning that he was to serve the old devoted servant Ignacio as loyally as he did Señor Moreno himself.

José napped in the chair as Señor Moreno and his great-grandchildren visited for almost an hour. When they were shown up to their rooms, he assisted the señor back to his bedroom. José informed him that Ignacio had gone to his room to rest.

Estaban told him that he intended to do the same thing until the dinner hour and dismissed the young servant.

It had been a long time since the dining room had been so alive. Laughter resounded as the three of them dined together this first evening of their arrival.

Old Estaban knew what immortality felt like tonight as he gazed across the table at this fine-looking young man who'd been named for him. He saw how a part of him would go on forever with both young people sitting with him.

He now had the answer to why he'd saved some particular gems which had belonged to his beloved wife. So much of the vast collection he'd given to Tony's wife, Amanda, because he'd adored her from the first time

172

he'd met her. He had been reluctant to part with the emeralds which his wife had always cherished. Now, he knew the reason, for they were meant to be given to his great-granddaughter, Bianca.

What a magnificent time this would be to present them to her while she was here visiting him!

Bianca felt happy about her decision to come along with her brother to see her great-grandfather.

She had always adored her grandfather Kane and she now wished she'd been able to spend as much time with this very intriguing, dignified man who represented the other side of her heritage. It made her realize what a rich, wonderful legacy was hers.

Suddenly, she was no longer envious of her mother's beautiful blue eyes, which she always felt would have been a perfect match for her fair hair. She was glad she had the black eyes of the Moreno family whose ancestors had come from Spain to this country. Her father had told her that the first Morenos had left Spain to settle in the Canary Islands before they migrated to this new country to settle in San Antonio.

A part of the Moreno ancestors had traveled on into Mexico to settle, and this was the faction of the family who were Tony Moreno's great-uncles and -aunts.

His aunt had married a very wealthy Mexican rancher named Alvarado. Rancho Río had always been their home. Tony never knew his aunt Bianca's husband because she was a widow when he came to Gonzales County. He was soon to realize that the middle-aged lady ran the vast ranch with an iron fist as forceful as any man's.

He came to admire her tremendously over the next few months and she felt the same way about him. She saw that Tony had a great passion for the ranch, as she did. Her son, Mario, felt no love for the land at all, and her only daughter, Delores, was unable to fill her shoes, for she was married to a doctor and occupied with raising her family. When she realized her health was failing, she summoned a lawyer friend of many years to draw up a new will.

Mario and Delores shared a very generous inheritance, but the land, Rancho Río, was left to her nephew, Tony Moreno. He was overwhelmed when he found himself the proud owner of the ranch he'd already grown to love. That was why for the last twenty-two years he'd devoted his energies to keeping it the fine ranch it had been when Bianca Alvarado had owned it. He would have hated to think that he had failed that grand old lady who'd had so much faith in him.

Amanda had suggested that they name their daughter for her, and this was more than agreeable with him.

Bianca and Estaban felt their great-grandfather must be getting tired.

"I'm feeling the need for rest, Great-grandfather," Bianca finally said. "Coming from San Marcus and having such a hearty dinner has made me lazy. Besides, we will have several days more to enjoy," she told him. "Shall I summon José or shall Estaban and I assist you to your room?"

"Summon José, *niña*," he told her. The proud old gentleman did not wish to mention to her that José had to help him get out of his clothes and into his bed. It was very depressing to him to be so helpless.

Her great-grandfather saw a lot of Amanda Kane's fire in Bianca. As José helped him up the stairs and assisted him out of his clothing and into his nightshirt, he thought how he wished he wasn't do damned old. He'd had the great joy of seeing his grandson, Tony, marry the lady he loved and raise his fine family. But he was greedy, for he now wanted to see his great-granddaughter live her life. He wanted to see the young man who'd be lucky enough to capture her heart.

When Bianca got to her room, she was not tired and unpacked her clothing and hung her gowns in the huge mahogany armoire. All the furnishings in the room were so massive, as they were in all the other rooms of this old mansion. There was an air of grandeur and opulence here that was not present in the sprawling red-tiled hacienda at Rancho Río.

Once she'd got all her gowns hung and her slippers neatly placed, she got out of her silk gown and put on her nightgown and wrapper. The hands of the clock were at ten as she sat down at the dressing table.

When Bianca had brushed her hair until it glowed, she walked out on the small balcony enclosed with an iron railing. A glorious autumn moon was gleaming down on her. That same moon was shining down on Gonzales County tonight, she thought. Rancho Río must be very quiet with her and Estaban gone. Over at the Circle K, her grandfather was probably comfortable in his bedroom, as her great-grandfather was. Larkin was back at his own little cottage after having dined with her grandfather Kane.

Now why would she even think about Larkin when she was in this very exciting city of San Antonio?

She had a feeling that Ramon Martinez could help

her sweep away any thoughts of Larkin. Estaban had remarked this afternoon that he was going to pay a visit to Ramon's office tomorrow. She wondered if this was one of the reasons her brother had decided to make this trip to San Antonio. Perhaps he was thinking about coming here to live, for the ranching life had never seemed to appeal to him. He had no great love of horses as she had, and the breeding of good cattle did not whet his interest, either.

Maybe seeing Great-grandfather Moreno was only a small part of Estaban's reason for coming to San Antonio, Bianca mused as she left the balcony to go back inside.

She found the warmth of the coverlet soothing as she crawled into the bed. Amazingly, she fell asleep quickly even though the hour was not that late.

Twenty-four

Rick Larkin finally had a tally of the number of head of cattle on the Circle K Ranch, but it told him nothing since he had no inkling of the numbers grazing in the back pastureland. Since the fences had been mended he now saw Big D cattle roaming on the pastureland on the other side of the fence. When he'd first come to the Circle K he'd seen no cattle in the back pasture so he had to assume that they roamed on the other side of the ranch.

But his hired hands had rounded up some twenty head of cattle with the Big D brand on them. He was going to tell Mark Kane this tonight.

"Take them back," Kane told him at dinner. "I don't want anything that doesn't belong to me, Larkin but I also want back what is mine. If you've found that many Big D cattle over here, then I've got double that over there. You tell my son that I expect him to take a count and check the brands on his cattle. You tell him I want a figure in a week's time," Kane told him.

"Yes, sir. I'll do it the first thing in the morning,"

Larkin told him. It was not going to be a pleasant scene when he relayed Mark Kane's message to his son. Larkin figured that he was going to receive the brunt of his scorn.

Larkin bid the elderly man goodnight and walked out of the house to be greeted by the same golden autumn moon Bianca had seen from the balcony of her great-grandfather's mansion. He thought about her and how the gold of the moon shining in the sky reminded him of her beautiful golden hair.

Even after he returned to the cottage, her beautiful image still haunted him. He knew he had to be a fool to dare to dream that there could be any kind of future for him and Bianca. What could he offer her? Such a pampered girl could only marry a young man from a family like her own. But Larkin could cherish the thought that he was the first man who'd ever made love to Bianca. This he knew!

Once Estaban sought out his friend Ramon and let him know that they were visiting their great-grandfather in San Antonio, he came to call on Bianca and invited her to lunch with him. She did not hesitate in accepting his invitation. It did not surprise her that Estaban was not included, but she did not know that Ramon had first asked Estaban's permission to take her out.

Ramon was going to take her to a quaint, romantic little sidewalk cafe down by the river that weaved through the city of San Antonio.

Ramon planned to pick her up in his carriage and take her a beautiful bouquet. They would enjoy a leisurely lunch, then walk by the river that ran by the cafe.

Later, he would take her on a tour of all the interesting places seeped with so much history of this state. And finally, they would go to a very beautiful park, where there were many secluded spots that provided a romantic atmosphere. If he was very lucky, he would find the right moment to have a kiss or two from her sweet, luscious lips.

Bianca was very pleased that Estaban was agreeable to her accepting Ramon's invitation and didn't seem out of sorts that he was not asked to accompany them. She was rather excited about the next day and she chose her gown and the slippers to match it with special care. She picked the pale-yellow frock trimmed with brown velvet piping and she took her new brown velvet bonnet out of the box with the matching brown velvet reticule. She had never worn the pretty bonnet before, for there'd been no occasion to wear it at the ranch.

She thought it was very sweet of her brother to suggest to Great-Grandfather Estaban that they might take a little jaunt around the city if he felt up to it. Without any hesitation, the elderly Estaban accepted the offer.

The next morning Bianca woke up to a glorious day, and at midmorning she started getting dressed. There would be no need for the brown velvet short jacket today, for it was mild, she discovered when she walked out on the small balcony just outside her bedroom door.

An hour later, she and Ramon were saying goodbye to Estaban as they went to Ramon's carriage.

Bianca could not resist plucking one of the beautiful yellow rosebuds from the bouquet that Ramon had brought her, and she gave them to one of the servant girls to put in a vase to take to her room.

Bianca gave Ramon a warm smile. "That was awfully nice of you. Roses are so beautiful "

"Not half as beautiful as you are, Bianca," he said, as he assisted her up to the seat.

It was just a few minutes past noon when they arrived at the Casa Rosa, but the many little white iron tables were already filled.

Bianca was convinced that this would be one of her favorite spots in the city as they ate a very delicious lunch and she watched a pair of graceful swans swimming on the river.

All along the walkway tall majestic palm trees seemed to climb up to the heavenly blue skies. A constant flow of people strolled by, enjoying themselves this late summer day.

A sudden strange sound invaded the serene setting and Bianca glanced over to see a very colorful parrot perched in a huge gilded cage.

She laughed. "I hadn't noticed that fellow when we came in."

"Oh, he puts on quite a show sometimes," Ramon grinned.

"You must come here often, Ramon," she remarked.

"I try to come once or twice a week. You like it, Bianca?" His dark eyes danced over her lovely face.

"Oh, I certainly do. This is the first time I've ever dined outside."

"A lot of the countries Estaban and I traveled

through in Europe have restaurants in the open air," he told her.

"It hardly seems fair that girls aren't allowed to take jaunts to Europe like young men are," she declared to Ramon.

"Ah, but Bianca, it would not be wise for a pretty girl like you to travel without a protector. Another young lady would hardly be the wise companion, either," he pointed out to her.

"Well, I suppose so, but look what I'm missing!"

"How long will you be in San Antonio?"

"About a week, I think."

"Well, we will pretend this is France or Spain and I will show you old missions and parks and I will take you to very elegant restaurants and quaint little shops as nice as any Estaban and I went to in Europe."

"Oh, Ramon—it does sound like such fun!"

"Well, shall we start right now?" He reached over to take her hand. His black eyes warmly gazed across the table at her.

But he was not the only gentleman darting admiring glances in Bianca's direction. Ever since they'd been seated at the table Ramon had been aware of the various men turning around to admire her. Several young ladies were green with jealousy that their swains were ogling another lady.

As Ramon guided her by the tables he felt a certain pride, knowing he was envied by the men sitting there. Bianca had insisted that they go by the parrot's cage.

"You're a pretty one," she told the parrot.

Just as she and Ramon were starting to move on,

the parrot began to chatter, "Pretty lady! Pretty lady!" Bianca gave out a soft gale of laughter.

"You're right, Pépe—" Ramon declared, "she is a most beautiful lady!"

Twenty-five

Bianca had not had so much fun since the night of her tío Jeff's fiesta. She found Ramon Martinez entertaining and charming, not to mention very good-looking and debonair.

He'd taken her by the old structure which was once the Alamo, forever a shrine to all Texans. A more serious air came upon him as he told her, "I'm glad we weren't standing where we are now thirty-four years ago, Bianca."

Ramon was soon ready to leave and recapture the happy feeling they'd both had before they came to this very sacred place.

He saw by the large cathedral clock that one hour remained before he'd promised Estaban he'd get Bianca back to the mansion.

"Now I will show you a beautiful park," he declared, and she noticed that he was holding her hand again as they went back to the carriage.

Ramon guided the carriage off the main road. Thick groves of trees lined both sides of the winding roadside. Riders came down the trail prancing their fine Thoroughbreds and buggies were parked at various spots.

Bianca spotted some peacocks strutting around through the grove of trees and Ramon told her that they roamed everywhere around the vast park area. They came across people enjoying a late-afternoon picnic by the side of a little pond in the park.

"Oh, Ramon—this is a beautiful place. San Antonio is a beautiful city. I can see why you wanted to come here."

"You'll love it even more before you go back to Rancho Río, Bianca," he declared as he guided the carriage to a secluded place where giant tropical plants grew profusely and a small pond was surrounded by them. Huge goldfish swam around in the pond and clustered water lilies floated atop the water.

Ramon helped her out of the carriage so they could sit down on the small iron bench by the pool.

After Bianca had watched them swimming around in the water and coming up to the surface, she turned to Ramon to tell him what an absolutely wonderful afternoon she'd had.

He gave her a warm smile and was encouraged enough to be even bolder. His hands turned her shoulders so that she was facing him. "You must know that I'm very attracted to you, Bianca. I want the chance to know you better and I want you to get to know me."

"I'd like that, too, Ramon," she told him. She sincerely meant it, for there was something about him she found very appealing.

"That is all I need to hear you say, Bianca."

Bianca felt the warmth of his hands on her shoulders and his touch was tender and gentle. When she saw his head moving closer to her she knew he was

184

going to kiss her, but she did not protest.

Gently Ramon urged her closer and his arms held her tighter as his lips came down to capture hers. Bianca responded to his caress, for Ramon had a very sensual way to him. She was aware of things now that she'd had no knowledge about before Larkin's lovemaking.

She allowed him to kiss her and hold her until she sensed his passion beginning to mount; then her hands began to push at his chest. "Ramon — Ramon!"

"Oh, Bianca, don't be offended, but you are so beautiful that you take my breath away and perhaps my good sense," he muttered, slowly moving back away from her.

"I'm not offended, Ramon, but if we want to spend more time together in the future, I think I better be getting home." She gave him a slow, easy smile.

"You're right. I don't want to get in disfavor with my best friend."

As they rode toward her great-grandfather's house, he asked her if she would like to go to the Plaza Room for dinner with him tomorrow night. He added that he would have to include Estaban. "He would not allow you to go without him in the evening, and I can't say that I would blame him. If you were my sister, I'd feel the same way."

Her black eyes twinkled with mischief as she told him, "Well, I guess then we must ask Estaban to go with us."

"I guess we must! But that is not to say that I can't have another afternoon or two with you before you leave, does it?"

Ramon knew their afternoon was growing to a

close. Once they left the carriage for him to escort her inside the house he wouldn't have a chance to say anything else to her. Right now, he was feeling like an eagle soaring in the heavens. He'd felt her respond to his kisses! For the rest of the week he knew his work would pile up, for he was determined to grab every precious moment he could to spend time with her.

When he had said his goodbyes to Bianca and Estaban and got back in his carriage, he decided to go to his office instead of home.

He gathered up a pile of papers on his desk, and headed for the little house he called home.

His little Mexican housekeeper seemed to understand that a bachelor lawyer did not keep regular hours. But he always could depend on Theresa to have his dinner ready when he came home and his house was always put in order.

As he traveled toward his house this late afternoon and dusk began to gather over the city, Ramon was not feeling the need of dinner.

His hunger was for more of Bianca Moreno's kisses!

Old Estaban dreaded to see the two young people leave his house to return to Gonzales County. He'd enjoyed the ride and the conversation with young Estaban this afternoon, and it had been another delightful evening for him sharing dinner with his two great-grandchildren. The days were passing by so fast. Estaban had told him he was thinking of casting his lot in San Antonio, and that pleased him exceedingly. Old Estaban had told him about an entire wing in the mansion where he could live. There was even a private entrance and stairway leading up to the second landing and long balcony.

His great-grandfather's offer had whetted Estaban's interest. He was very eager to discuss some things with his friend Ramon tomorrow night when he and Bianca dined with him at one of San Antonio's most elegant hotels. He understood why Bianca was so excited, as she'd told him about everything she and Ramon had seen.

Estaban knew that he would be coming back to San Antonio soon. Here was where he wanted to be and not back at Rancho Río. Perhaps when he was older he might enjoy the quieter life there on the Rancho Río.

The next day, he and Bianca stayed around the mansion all day to be with their great-grandfather until it was time for them to get dressed for the engagement with Ramon Martinez.

"Would you help me into the study before you go up to your room, dear?" he asked Bianca, for Estaban had already gone out the door.

"Of course, Great-grandfather." She took his arm and led him down the hallway very slowly to the study. "This is such a magnificent old house, Great-grandfather. I'd forgotten just how grand it was. I'm so glad Estaban asked me to come with him."

"If he hadn't brought you, I'd have taken my cane to him," he chuckled as he sunk down in the leather chair at his massive desk. "Sit down, dear, for just a minute. I know you have to get yourself all pretty for your evening engagement."

Bianca did as he'd requested, wondering what it was that he was searching for in his desk drawer.

"This is something I was going to give to you before you left, so I thought I'd just go ahead and give them to you tonight since you're going to be wearing a fancy gown," he declared. "These belonged to your great-grandmother." He handed her the case.

She opened the top to see the stunning emeralds inside. "Dear God, Great-grandfather, they're—they're exquisite!" She gasped. Her hand trembled as she picked up the glorious ring with diamonds surrounding the pear-shaped emerald. The matching necklace and bracelet were just as impressive.

"They are exquisite just like you, Bianca, and I know your great-grandmother would wish you to have them. I gave most of her lovely jewelry to your dear mother, but somehow I could never part with these, and I know now why I didn't. I must have known that I was going to have a great-granddaughter someday and she was to have the emeralds."

"Oh, I thank you from the bottom of my heart, Great-grandfather. I'll treasure them forever. I shall surely wear them tonight proudly!" She kissed his wrinkled cheek.

"I rather thought you might just do that. Now, be off with you, but let me see you before you leave, eh?"

"Oh, I will. I'll come down to see you as soon as I get dressed," she told him as she excitedly turned to dash out of the door.

As she rushed up the steps with the emeralds in the velvet case clutched in her hand, she had changed her mind about her gown for the evening. She would

188

wear the cream-colored satin, not the pale-blue one.

How magnificent the emeralds would look with that gown!

Twenty-six

Bianca had styled her thick golden hair as she had the night of the fiesta so that the beauty of the emeralds on her dainty ears would be displayed. She had been extremely pleased to find that the ring fit her finger perfectly and looked so marvelous with the bracelet on her tiny wrist.

Never had she felt more elegant than when she walked down the steps to show herself off to her great-grandfather and Estaban.

Old Estaban had already told his great-grandson about the emeralds so her brother knew how exciting this night was going to be for Bianca. She was a bewitching vision as she walked into the parlor. He could well imagine the effect she was going to have on his friend Ramon this evening.

Old Estaban was visibly shaken with emotion; he had never seen a young woman more beautiful than the one who stood before him now.

"You enhance the emeralds, *niña!*" He cautioned her brother that he should keep a watchful eye on her tonight, for all the young men would be beguiled by her charms.

As they got into the carriage, Estaban excused himself to go back into the house. He realized she might be needing her shawl by the time they returned home, so he went to her room to get the cream-colored wool shawl.

Ramon was glad for the private moment. He reached over to give her a kiss. "God, I couldn't resist that," he murmured. "You look so divine! You'll be the most beautiful woman in that dining room tonight. It is a good thing there are two of us to watch over you!"

"Oh, Ramon!" she laughed.

Estaban rushed back to the carriage and it began to roll down the drive and into the street.

When they arrived at the hotel, Bianca was sure that she'd picked exactly the right gown to wear for dinner, as she saw all the ladies dressed in fancy gowns of silk or satin.

Bianca was reminded of the brilliant starlit nights back at the ranch when she saw the massive candelabras twinkling so brightly from the ceiling.

Huge gilt mirrors lined the walls and the chairs were covered in a rich deep-red velvet with the table draped in the same deep red cloth. Frosty white napkins lay by the plates with fine-cut crystal goblets sitting next to them. Each table had its own miniature cut-crystal vase holding white rosebuds and baby's breath sprigs.

"This is quite a grand place, my friend," Estaban remarked.

"Nothing but the best for my friends, the Morenos," Ramon smiled.

"I'm impressed. Your law practice must be getting off to a fine start," Estaban said.

Ramon was quick to let him know that there were

unlimited possibilities in San Antonio.

"I've been impressed by all the things I've seen since I've arrived," Bianca was quick to say.

Ramon knew he was going to find it difficult to concentrate on conversation with Estaban tonight when he wanted to gaze in Bianca's direction constantly. But he could not be that unfair to his old friend, so he tried desperately to direct part of his attention to him.

The three of them sipped their wine and enjoyed the very special thick, creamy soup of chicken and fresh vegetables always served here. Bianca found it delicious, but didn't know what she wanted to have for dinner. There were a number of intriguing meat dishes she was trying to decide between.

"What would you suggest, Ramon?" she finally asked him.

"I'm going to have roast duck with an orange sauce. I've never eaten anything as good."

"Then that is what I shall have, too," Bianca smiled at Ramon. "What about you, Estaban?"

"Well, you and Ramon can enjoy your duck. I had it once when we were in Europe and that was enough for me. That lamb chop sounds good to me," he told the two of them.

Unlike her brother, Bianca enjoyed the succulent meat of the duck and the herbed rice served with it. Her lovely cream satin gown was feeling overly tight after the meal and she could not bring herself to touch the fancy little pastry they were served later.

As they were dining she heard the enchanting melody resounding through the room and saw a man playing a violin across the room.

Bianca was thinking what an exciting evening it was

and she was going to go home with so many wonderful memories and so many things to tell her mother and father.

While Ramon had had a wonderful evening dining with Estaban and Bianca, the most exciting thing had been the one little kiss he'd managed to get before they left the Moreno house. He had an engagement with Estaban the next day, for he had asked if they could have a talk. Ramon was certainly not going to refuse him. However, he would have preferred Bianca's company.

But Ramon drove away from the old Moreno mansion that night convinced he was going to try to win the lovely Bianca, for she was the woman he wanted for his wife. She made all the other ladies look pale in comparison.

Ramon found himself staying up late after he got home so he could go over some papers he needed to read before he went to his office in the morning. When he finally dimmed his lamp and put all the papers in his leather case, he was thinking that some way he had to manage to have one more afternoon with Bianca before she left.

By the time he sunk down on his bed he was weary and sleep came quickly.

Sunrise came all too soon for Ramon. The extra hours he'd spent trying to make up the time away from his office were taking its toll on him. Until Estaban and Bianca had come to San Antonio he had not had many social engagements. Getting himself settled and established had been his all-consuming passion.

Social affairs could come along later, he'd reasoned. But he knew Bianca would be leaving soon, and there were only two or three days left for him to try to win her heart.

By the time he was ready to leave the house to go to his office, the clock in his parlor was chiming seventhirty. He promised himself that tonight he was coming home when he left the office and staying there all evening.

He knew what Estaban wanted to talk to him about and he wasn't sure of what he was going to tell him. Though they were good friends, he and Estaban had different approaches to things and Ramon liked working independently. He was just getting his office into the shape he wanted it, so he had no desire to uproot himself to move into larger offices that would accommodate a partner.

But he knew he could be facing a ticklish situation, for Estaban could be oversensitive. On various occasions when they'd traveled together in Europe he'd found out how easily offended he could get.

Bianca had slept almost as late as her great-grandfather the next morning. Estaban had left the house before either of them had ventured out of their bedrooms.

She had spent the most of the day with her greatgrandfather, for she knew that their visit was more than half over. Two more days after and they would be leaving to return to Gonzales County.

Old Estaban did not know exactly the day they were to leave, but he knew it was going to be too soon to please him.

It was late in the afternoon when Estaban arrived back at the house, so Bianca figured that he and Ramon had spent several hours together. He told Bianca that Ramon wished to take her for another jaunt around the city since it would be his last chance.

"He'll pick you up about the same time he did the other day. He has another place he wants to take you for lunch," Estaban told her, seeming very reserved and solemn.

"Well, you and Ramon had a full day's visit apparently. I fear, Estaban, we are proving to be a distraction to poor Ramon. He will get behind in his work."

"Well, one more day and we'll be out of his hair. The truth was, I wasn't with him that long today. He had too much to attend to, so I was with him only about an hour."

"Oh, I see," she said but she couldn't dismiss the sharp, curt tone to his voice. "I thought it was day after tomorrow that we were leaving."

"No, Bianca, you must have misunderstood me. Tomorrow is our last day here," he told her before he turned to leave the room. She left feeling a little perplexed as to what had made him change his mind. She knew she had not misunderstood him as he was now trying to say that she had.

Whatever it was, she had to conclude it had to do with something that had happened between him and Ramon Martinez today.

Perhaps when she was with Ramon tomorrow, he would give her some clue as to what had suddenly made her brother have such a sour look on his face.

Estaban was glad that she didn't try to challenge him

as she usually did. But he didn't fool himself because he now appreciated the clever mind of his sister.

She knew he had changed his plans.

Twenty-seven

Three hours later, Bianca was to have her curiosity eased. Estaban made the announcement as the three of them dined that evening that he was returning to San Antonio after he got his sister back home and packed up his belongings.

"Great-grandfather, I'm going to accept your generous offer to allow me to have that wing of the house because I'm going to be opening my law office in San Antonio."

Bianca would never forget the thrilled look on her great-grandfather's face.

"Oh, Estaban, how happy you've made me tonight! I can help you contact many people who will be delighted to have a Moreno as their lawyer. You will be very prosperous and I shall sit back boasting that this is my great-grandson," he chuckled.

Bianca smiled, seeing how absolutely happy he was and relieved that nothing had gone wrong between Estaban and Ramon.

The night became more pleasant for her after Estaban had made his announcement. After dinner, she left the two men in the parlor alone, for it seemed that they had much to discuss. Knowing this was going to be her last tour of the city with Ramon, she

197

wanted to choose the gown she would be wearing for the occasion and also the outfit she would be traveling in the next morning when they left. She had some packing to get done, so she could spend more time with her great-grandfather tomorrow night.

She glanced over all her garments hanging in the armoire and held out the one riding ensemble she'd brought. She would wear this for the trip home.

She debated between the deep purple frock with its matching cape and the berry-colored gown trimmed in black braid with its matching short jacket. She finally picked the berry-colored gown and the black bonnet with the little plume feather in the band. All she had left to put out were her black leather slippers and black reticule.

By the time she was ready to dim the lamp by her bed she heard the light patter of raindrops pelting her window. She heaved a deep sigh, hoping that it would pass during the night and a bright sunshiny day would greet her in the morning.

But that light rain falling over the city during the night was still lingering as the sun rose.

"Oh, no," she moaned, knowing that she and Ramon would not be doing too much sightseeing on a day like this. All the time she was dressing she kept hoping the rain would cease, but it didn't.

The parlor was very quiet, and she smiled, thinking that Great-grandfather, as well as Estaban, were both sleeping late.

Ramon arrived promptly. He was disappointed in the weather too, and decided to take her to Torero's that day, a quaint little Mexican restaurant. He'd chanced to come upon the place when he was exploring the city and he'd found it very cozy. Its owner was a Mexican named Antonio Ramos, a bullfighter who'd been gored and injured so badly that he could not fight and so he and his wife had opened this little establishment.

The food was delicious. Ramon went there whenever he felt the urge for tostadas made to perfection or tortillas lavishly ladened with meat and chiles.

He was delighted that Bianca liked the place as much as he did. He sat with her in this small little restaurant enjoying himself as much as he had the night before in the elegant dining room when she was all dressed up in her fancy gown and exquisite jewels.

"Oh, Bianca, I have to tell you that I'm going to be very lonely when you leave. It's been a wonderful week for me."

"Well, Estaban might just have himself a guest from time to time. He told us last night that he is going to come back here to open an office."

"I know and I hope you will come often. So he has definitely decided to open his own office?" he quizzed her.

"You—you did not know?"

Ramon told her of Estaban's proposal and that he had to turn it down. "I don't think he was too happy when he left me, Bianca, but a man has to do what his conscience tells him to do. I like being independent."

"Then that is what you should do, Ramon. It would not be right otherwise," she told him candidly.

"Thank you, Bianca. It is important to me that you understand why I had to refuse Estaban even though I consider him my best friend."

"Oh, I do, Ramon, and I admire you for doing what you did."

Ramon no longer minded that it was a miserable, rainy day. He suggested that he take Bianca to one of the streets lined with various shops. For an hour they went in and out the shops and Bianca bought her grandfather Kane a magnificent pipe and a soft black wool shawl for Estella. When a hammered silver cheroot case caught her eyes, she knew that this would please her father, so she bought it for him.

When they went into the last shop on the street, Bianca looked at Ramon and sighed. "I have to get my mother something and I've seen nothing yet that I think is right for her."

He smiled. "Look around. We are in no hurry, Bianca. I've the rest of the afternoon."

As she moved around the little shop he also looked for something he could buy for her to serve as a memory of this rainy day. He finally found the perfect brooch and earrings and he summoned the clerk while she was occupied in her search for a gift for her mother.

By the time she came back to him with her black eyes flashing with excitement, he had purchased the black onyx brooch and earrings. They were securely tucked in his pocket of his coat.

"I found the perfect thing for her, Ramon—a peau de soie bonnet in a shade of blue to match her eyes and they have a matching reticule."

She was so enchanting when she was excited and

200

her black eyes gleamed so bright, Ramon thought. That was why the black onyx jewelry seemed so perfect for her.

The rains were still coming down when they left the shop. He carried all her purchases as they moved to board his carriage. He knew that he was not ready to say goodbye to her and he had yet to give her his gift.

"Before we call it a day would you like to see the Mission San Jose, Bianca? The rain can't interfere with that."

"Oh, I'd love to. I remember my father talking about it and how the Indians had built it years and years ago."

He took her arm as they went toward his carriage, then Ramon guided it toward the old mission.

The raindrops fell on the branches of the numerous palmettos lining the stone walkway. The mission grounds seemed to be deserted today and Ramon figured that the usual crowd had stayed away because of the weather.

As they entered the old stone structure a darkness engulfed them. Bianca tightened her hand in his. "Oh, Ramon, we're walking back through history — through decades!"

He found her so different from most girls her age. She had so many sides. She could be the frivolous, carefree young girl. She could also be the very sophisticated lady, as she'd been the other night in her fancy gown and exquisite jewels. This afternoon at the mission he saw that she had a very serious side.

She was a woman a man rarely encountered in a lifetime. Ramon had been very impressed when she had accepted without question her decision to not accept the proposal her brother had made to him.

She went over to sit down on the wooden bench and stared up at the high ceiling just above them. "It's amazing to me how the Indians ever managed to build such a high structure back so many years ago." She turned toward him. "Ramon, you have taken me to so many places and I've enjoyed seeing all the wonderful sights around the city," she told him. "I have you to thank for being so generous with your time. I know that you've had to neglect your work."

He took her hand in his and smiled. "Don't you worry your pretty head about that. Besides, it has been my pleasure to escort the prettiest girl in the state of Texas around the city."

"Oh, Ramon," she gave out a soft laugh.

"I mean it sincerely, Bianca. I think you're the most beautiful girl I've ever seen. I don't guess I have to tell you that I care very much for you."

"I—I like you, too, Ramon."

A very serious look came to his eyes. "I want you to come to love me someday. You see, I think I must surely be in love for the first time in my life."

"But we've only known each other for a short time, Ramon. I do like you very much, but love is such a serious thing."

"Sometimes love can happen quickly—in the blink of an eye, so I've been told," he grinned.

He had moved closer to her and she knew he was going to kiss her. She did not resist him as he bent down to take her lips in a long, lingering kiss.

"That kiss may have to last me for a long time.

Your lips are as sweet as that wine we drank the other night."

Bianca smiled up at him. Ramon would be easy to fall in love with, she thought to herself. He was a very suave, handsome gentleman. Any number of young ladies would be impressed by him.

"I just want you to take something back to Rancho Río to remind you of me." He took out the package he'd placed in his pocket.

Bianca opened it to see the dainty black onyx earrings and brooch. "They're lovely, Ramon!" she exclaimed. "Thank you so much."

"Your eyes are as black and beautiful as that onyx."

As much as she hated to bring the afternoon to an end, she knew she must, for she could tell that it was getting late.

"I've few hours left to spend with my great-grandfather, Ramon," she told him. "We'll be leaving early in the morning if I know Estaban."

They left the mission and all too soon he was telling her goodbye. He dared not take a farewell kiss as he would have yearned to do.

It had been a wonderful interlude for Ramon and he was hoping this was not the end of it!

Twenty-eight

As Bianca had expected, Estaban had gotten up at an ungodly hour to leave the next morning. Dear elderly Estaban had insisted on rising to see them off when he normally would have slept for another few hours.

Estaban and Ignacio stood out on the front entrance waving to them as they rolled out the drive. From the time they left San Antonio and traveled down the road, Bianca chatted on about all the wonderful sights she'd seen during their brief stay. "And Ramon told me there was so much more to see, so I'm anxious to make another visit to San Antonio."

"I sort of figured you'd be wanting to come visit me once I'm settled in," he grinned.

Bianca kept the few stolen kisses shared with Ramon her little secret. But she did wonder what Estaban would have said if he'd known.

By the time they stopped in a hamlet for some lunch and she'd climbed back in the buggy, its rolling motion made her sleep. Estaban enjoyed the quiet after she'd chatterboxed all morning. He'd kept the bay at a fast pace, for with any luck they could make it home by early evening.

As she'd slept, a handsome face haunted her, and his eyes were green, not black like Ramon's. For a few days, Ramon had intrigued her, but now she found herself thinking about Larkin. She was anxious to see him. She found herself comparing Ramon's kisses to the ones Larkin had so forcefully taken.

Both men were handsome and very intriguing with their particular brand of charm. Ramon Martinez was the type of man her parents would expect her to marry instead of the rugged Rick Larkin.

Ramon would live his life in a city like San Antonio, whereas the rugged Rick Larkin would be miserable living where he could not ride his horse over the Texas countryside. Larkin was a free spirit the city would restrict!

Even though she'd promised Ramon that she would not forget him, his face was already fading now that they were drawing nearer and nearer to Rancho Río and the Circle K Ranch.

Estaban smiled as he saw her sit up straight in the seat. "Going to be home in a few minutes now, little sister."

"Yes, I know, Estaban. We'll be there for dinner."

Estaban could imagine all the stories she was going to be telling their parents about her experiences in San Antonio. Her excitement about the city might just make his announcement easier for them to accept.

It had been a very quiet eight days around Rancho Río. Both Tony and Amanda missed their daughter and son sharing their dinner table with them.

Amanda had made a point of going over to her father's ranch on a couple of occasions, and each time she'd returned to the Rancho Río singing the praises of Larkin to her husband. Tony was naturally pleased. At the end of the week Amanda decided to pay a long overdue visit to her brother and his wife, Mona.

She was only there a short while before she knew there was tension in the household. As close as she and Mona had always been, she insisted on knowing what the trouble was.

Mona had been reluctant at first to confess to her good friend what was making her husband difficult to be around. "Amanda, it's Larkin," she finally sighed. "He's a thorn festering in Jeff's side."

"Why, Mona? Dear God, I'd think he'd be happy that the man's taking a load off Jeff's shoulders."

"That's not the way Jeff's taking it. He's resentful because he feels his father thought he wasn't capable of handling the job. All the things Larkin has done like mending the fences and bringing back cattle that had strayed only point out to Jeff that he wasn't handling things like he should have."

"Two ranches the size of those two would be an overwhelming task for any one man," Amanda pointed out.

Mona told her how she'd tried to tell Jeff that many times and that Larkin could prove to be a blessing to both his father and him. "But Jeff doesn't see it that way."

"Then my brother is being very childish, Mona," Amanda declared.

"I'm glad we agree on that, Amanda. You've always helped me when I've had a problem with Jeff. I don't know what I would have done sometimes if I had not had you to talk to."

"We've *always* talked. Oh, Lord, Mona, we've shared a whole lifetime together. Can you believe that we're forty years old? Where did the years go?"

Mona smiled. "I ask myself that all the time, Amanda."

As they laughed and reminisced about the past, Mona immediately thought about something she could not dismiss. Only with Amanda could she have approached this subject. Today seemed like the perfect time.

"Tell me, Amanda—tell me when you look at Rick Larkin if he reminds you of anyone?"

Amanda sat thoughtfully for a few moments before she replied, "No, Mona—I can't think of a soul."

"The next time you're at the Circle K, notice Larkin's walk and the way he tilts his head and his crooked grin."

Amanda shook her head and sighed. "I don't know who you're talking about."

"Amanda, I'm surprised that you haven't noticed that Rick Larkin looks so much like my brother," Mona told her.

"Larkin looks like Derek? No, I can't say I'd noticed that, Mona."

"Then take a long hard look at him the next time you visit your father's ranch. The very first time I laid eyes on him I saw Derek on his face. Oh, the color of the eyes are different, but replace Larkin's green ones with Derek's blue eyes and look for the other things I've mentioned."

"Well, I shall, but what are you trying to tell me, Mona?"

Mona shook her head and admitted that she didn't exactly know. "It was an eerie thing to gaze at someone who looked so very much like my dead brother, Amanda. Oh, I'd dare not discuss this with anyone but you. Jeff would scoff and call me crazy so I've not said a word to him."

When Amanda guided her buggy home about an hour later, she could not dismiss what Mona had told her, for she'd known Mona Lawson Kane long enough to know that she was a very level-headed person not given to foolish fancy.

By the time she arrived at Rancho Río she had decided that she was going to the Circle K to study this young man for herself. Amanda reminded herself that she'd tried to forget that Derek Lawson had ever existed. To think of him only opened wounds of the past. As much as she loved Mona, she hated Derek Lawson for the evil he did to anyone whose life touched his.

Once she stepped through the front door of her home, Amanda forgot all about this unhappy time of her life, for her handsome husband was there to greet her with a warm kiss and her son was sitting in the parlor. It was obvious he and Tony had been having a talk.

Giving both of them a smile, she told them she felt the need to refresh herself before the dinner hour. "I'm going to enjoy a nice bath if you two gentlemen will excuse me."

Once she was in her bedroom alone she found her thoughts drifting again to Mona's words about Larkin looking like Derek. She also had to ask herself how that could possibly be. Derek had never taken himself a wife who could have borne him a son, for he was killed before that could ever have happened.

Rojo had greeted his mistress eagerly. He seemed to know that she was ready for the two of them to take their regular ride over the countryside.

His nostrils flared and his silky black tail swished to and fro as she led him out of his stall. He had missed those daily jaunts and Bianca sensed this. Her hand patted his black mane as she cooed to him, "I missed you, too, fellow. I truly did!"

She wasted no time leaping up on him with a small canvas bag clutched in her hand filled with the gifts she'd purchased in San Antonio for her grandfather, Estella, and Larkin.

Try as she might she could not deny her eagerness to see Rick Larkin again. Now she had been kissed by another sensuous, handsome man, but Ramon's kisses did not make her want to surrender willingly to him.

Only Larkin could ignite a wild recklessness in her that she seemed unable to control!

Twenty-nine

Larkin was just coming out of the barn when he saw the big red stallion galloping up the winding drive with Bianca atop him. Her glorious crown of golden hair flowed back away from her face and swung to and fro around her shoulders. She made a very striking sight in her black twill divided skirt and vest, her black leather boots on her small feet. A brilliant blue blouse was opened at the neck and the soft material seemed to cling to her full breasts. Larkin knew his hands could span her tiny waist.

He lingered in the barn for a moment as she leaped off Rojo and tied the reins to the hitching post by the gate. He stood watching her walk to the front steps.

Larkin lit up a cigarette and a thoughtful look was on his face as he sauntered out of the barn. Damn it, he'd missed seeing her beautiful face! Señor Kane had told him about her and Estaban going to spend some time in San Antonio with her great-grandfather, and he had to figure that she had also seen her brother's Mexican friend while she was in the city. A wave of jealousy engulfed him with a fierce force.

All week as he'd gone about his work on the

ranch, those little demons of jealousy had stabbed at him. At least, she was back here in Gonzales County.

As he walked around the barnyard, young Juanita was coming to the main house to help out Estella as she'd been doing for the last week even though Estella was back in full charge of her kitchen. She kept hoping that Larkin would notice her or stop her to engage in conversation. She always gave him an inviting smile and a flirting gleam in her dark eyes. So far Larkin had not sought to take the bait she had tossed his way. But Juanita was not discouraged because she knew she was pretty; many young hombres had told her that and so did her mirror.

One day this handsome gringo was going to become aware of it, she kept telling herself.

Larkin had been aware of the young girl flirting with him as he was working around the corral or barnyard. Her father was one of the best hired hands on the ranch and he was not about to get himself involved with Juan's seventeen-year-old daughter who was a very pretty little señorita and an obvious flirt.

She was only going to get a polite greeting from him. Besides, Juanita was not the señorita he was interested in. It was Bianca Moreno he could not take his thoughts away from, though he knew any future for them was probably impossible.

As stubborn and determined as he was to have his own way, Bianca Moreno was just as obstinate. Her grandfather and Estella were very pleased with their gifts she'd brought them from San Antonio. There was only one gift left in the canvas bag she brought with her, and that was the emerald-green silk neck scarf she'd chose for Larkin. So far, he'd not appeared over at the house. She'd tried to be very discreet as she'd quizzed her grandfather about how things had been going around the ranch with Larkin running it.

"Good man, Bianca. He really is. Worked his damned tail off since the day he got here," Mark Kane told her.

"Well, then I'm glad I brought him a little gift, too," she casually remarked.

"Larkin will be thrilled that you thought of him! Bianca, you're a very sweet young lady," her grandfather declared.

"Well, I'm just glad that he's doing such a good job for you, Grandfather," she said.

She lingered only a few more minutes with her grandfather. "Guess I'll stop by the barn to give Larkin his gift before I head for Rancho Río," she told him as she breezed out the door.

Kane watched her go rushing out the door. She was as sweet as the fragrances permeating the gardens his beloved wife loved so very much.

It meant a lot to him that when she was in San Antonio having herself a good time that she'd thought of him and Estella.

Mark Kane made a sudden decision.

The Circle K Ranch was going to be willed to Bianca! He didn't care what the rest of the family thought, for it was his land and he could damned well do with it what he wished. Besides, they would not know about it until he was dead and gone.

There would be only one person to know what he was doing and that would be Clint Carpenter. And

Clint would be sworn to secrecy.

Clint had been a good friend as well as his lawyer for well over thirty years now, so the two of them had shared many confidences throughout the years.

Estella was feeling as kindly toward the señorita as her grandfather. She was touched that Bianca had thought of her and purchased her the soft wool shawl when she was in San Antonio. Not only was Señorita Bianca beautiful of face, but she was also beautiful of heart and soul.

Bianca left the house and went to the barn in search of Larkin. She did not see him anywhere, so she called out, "Larkin! Larkin—where are you?"

"Up here, Bianca," he called down to her from the hayloft. He'd been inspecting some rotted wood in the loft one of his booted heels had discovered was ready to crumble. "I'll be right down."

As he was almost at the bottom of the ladder he turned to give her a smile, then walked toward her. "Welcome home, *chiquita!* I trust you had a nice visit with your great-grandfather."

"I did," she told him. Already he was having his effect on her and she turned her eyes away from him to fumble in the canvas bag. Finally she lifted the soft silk green scarf from the bag. "I brought this back for you, Larkin." She felt very awkward standing there with the scarf in her hand. But Larkin did not feel uncomfortable at all accepting it. In fact, he was feeling more than pleased. That she'd thought of him while she was away was more than he'd dared hope for.

"Oh, Bianca—it's a handsome scarf and I thank you! I'll think of you every time I wear it. Tie it around my neck, Bianca," he urged her in that deep but gentle voice of his.

She did as he'd requested, and as her hands were raised, his head began to bend slowly so he could capture those honeyed lips of hers that were tempting him so.

She felt his arms snaking around her waist. She felt the force of those strong-muscled arms enclosing her until she was pressed against the front of him. Instinctively, she leaned against him to feel the heat of his body.

He was so hungry for the touch of her lips that he never wanted to let her go. When he finally did, Bianca was gasping breathlessly.

A slow, amused grin came to his face as he watched her taking a deep breath. "I missed you, *chiquita*. Missed you damned bad!"

Trying desperately not to allow him to know the overwhelming impact he had on her, she heaved another deep sigh. "A girl could faint away, you know!" She moved slightly back from him.

A grin was still on his face. "Not you, Bianca. You'd never faint." He scrutinized her flushed face and those eyes gleaming with black fire.

Bianca was certain she best make a hasty exit before she found herself back in that stall again with this handsome devil who rendered her so helpless. Her grandfather had known she was coming to the barn and he would be questioning why she'd remained there. All he had to do was look out the window to see that Rojo was still there by the hitching post.

"I — I've got to go, Larkin." She began to move back a few more steps.

He made no effort to stop her but stood there with his hand playing with the scarf.

She gave him a smile and nod of her head as she swiftly turned to run out the barn door. The scarf was enough to tell him what he'd felt was true about Bianca Moreno. She did care for him, but she just didn't want to admit it. She was afraid of this wildfire of passion both of them felt when they were together. But she could not deny it even when she tried to, and this was enough to satisfy Larkin.

Back at the main house, old Mark Kane had been sitting in his favorite chair glancing out the window. He was beginning to wonder what was taking Bianca so long to present her gift to Larkin.

When she finally came running out of the barn to mount up on Rojo, he directed his attention back to a journal he'd been reading when she'd arrived. But he lowered the journal down to his lap a few seconds later, a thoughtful look on his face as he got to thinking about the length of time she'd spent in the barn with Larkin.

Was it possible his feisty little granddaughter had an eye for his foreman? There was no denying that Rick Larkin was one fine figure of a young man. Handsome enough to turn any girl's head, Kane figured.

Well she could certainly make a worse choice than Larkin, Kane concluded. He knew it was going to take a very powerful, strong-willed man to tame that little minx and Rick Larkin just might be that man.

He knew one thing he was going to be observing the two young people more closely in the future.

Part Three

Autumn's Anguish

Thirty

A wagon was pulled into the barn to accommodate all the cartons of personal belongings Estaban had been busily packing for the last three days to take to San Antonio.

Amanda had left her father and Estaban to attend to the task and left to pay a visit to the Circle K.

She was not going to rest until she satisfied her curiosity about Larkin, she knew.

Over at the Big D Ranch, Mona didn't know what was ailing her husband after he returned from town. This morning when he'd told her he was going into town to pick up some supplies, he'd been very nice and asked her if there was anything she needed. She'd given him a list of three or four articles he could get for her at the mercantile.

But she noticed the difference in his mood as soon as he'd returned and slammed the things on the dining-room table. As abruptly, he marched out of the room and the house.

She could not know the torment plaguing Jeff as he'd gone to the barn where he could be alone and think. He was beginning to wonder if he was ever going to be free of the past.

No one had to remind him of how wild he'd been when he and Mona's brother, Derek roamed the countryside raising hell. But he had always been glad that he'd finally seen the light about Derek and not allowed him to drag him down any further. Derek had been the one in charge back when they were young. To this day, he was still riddled with guilt that the two of them had rustled cattle from their fathers' ranches to pay for their gambling debts at a local saloon in town.

Derek had a wild side to him, and he was so greedy that he didn't care who he hurt to get what he wanted. Yet he could be very likeable.

Jeff had fought to keep all these bad memories in the back of his mind. He'd worked to make Big D a prosperous ranch since he and Mona had married. No man could have asked for a better, more devoted wife than Mona. They had a fine family and he could have been a happy man but for the torments of the past.

He could not put his finger on it but the torment had seemed to begin again when Rick Larkin appeared and ended up taking charge of the Circle K for his father.

And now, today, he chanced to meet a man he'd not seen for almost thirty years, and dear Lord, Russell Harlin was a part of the past he wanted to forget.

When he was coming out of the mercantile with the articles he'd purchased for Mona, he'd almost bumped into Harlin. Jeff was ready to walk on by him when Harlin spoke up. "Damn, Jeff—you going to walk right by me?"

"What did you say?"

"You don't remember me? Harlin—Russell Harlin is the name. Now does that jog your memory?"

Jeff looked at his face and saw a typical drifter. For a moment he just stood there, for he did not recognize the man.

"The back room at the saloon some thirty years ago, Jeff. You recall those nights when you and old Derek sat there at the poker table with me and the other dudes all night long?"

"Well, thirty years is a long time," Jeff gave out a nervous laugh. "I'll take your word for that, Harlin—isn't that what you said your name was?"

"That's right, Kane." Harlin's beady eyes surveyed the rancher's face and he saw some apprehension reflected there. Down on his luck and having been fired from a ranch he'd been working at in Bandera County, he'd decided to come to Gonzales County when he'd heard about Jeff Kane running the vast Big D Ranch.

Harlin remembered that Derek's father had been the owner of the Big D at the time he'd sat in that back room playing poker with the two young bucks.

Since he'd drifted into Gonzales County he'd learned that Jeff Kane had married Derek's sister, Mona, but Harlin rather doubted that Jeff Kane's little wife knew what he knew about her husband. So he figured to feather his nest.

Luck was with him when he'd happened to meet up with him in town, for he had intended to ride out to the ranch later that afternoon.

He wasted no time letting Jeff know that he needed a job and it would be to Jeff's best interest to hire him on. Being no fool, Jeff had caught the innuendo he was baiting him with, and told Harlin he would hire him on for the rest of the season.

"I'm going to be laying off hands in a few weeks, Harlin, so it's going to be a short spell. Winter will be coming soon," Jeff had told him.

"Well, that will do for now and give me enough to be on my way somewhere else," Harlin had told him with a cocky grin.

Jeff had taken his leave from this unsavory character and gone to his wagon, but he knew that he was going to be facing more challenges from Harlin before he was through with him. This was the agony he was going through when he had returned to the Big D and faced Mona. But how could he burden Mona with what was troubling him? She still did not know all the dastardly deeds he and her brother had done. He prayed that she would never know.

What his beautiful Mona also did not know was that he had never felt worthy of her complete, devoted love.

Mona was a rare, exquisite young lady who demanded a young man's absolute respect. Often he had questioned how she and his sister Amanda had been such good friends, for they were such opposites. Amanda had defied her father and the conventions of their Anglo-American family once she'd met Tony Moreno. Everyone in Gonzales County knew of Mark Kane's hatred of Mexicans, but Amanda had to follow the dictates of her heart.

Jeff knew of no couple who'd been happier. He also knew that his father held Tony Moreno in the highest esteem. It was men like Tony and his father and

David Lawson who'd made this great state of Texas what it now was. They'd fought the Indians to save the lands that they'd loved so dearly and they'd also faced the Mexican bandits and outlaws who were out to steal and rustle their cattle. When all this was coupled with weather that could be fierce, the rancher was one hell of a gambler. Those who survived were men to be admired. The Alvarado family and the Morenos were held in the same respect as those Anglo-Americans. Long before Tony Moreno had taken over the helm of Rancho Río, the Alvarados had fought the battle of the bandits, outlaws, and Indians to preserve the lands they loved with as much passion as the Kanes and Lawsons.

Mark Kane and his daughter enjoyed a nice visit for over an hour before Larkin appeared to take the elderly Kane for a jaunt around his land. Her father had boasted to her that he was riding longer and farther over his land.

"That is wonderful, Father. Larkin seems to be a godsend to the ranch and you," Amanda told him.

"Larkin is a most unusual man, I've come to realize," Kane told his daughter.

When Larkin came into the parlor this early afternoon, Amanda scrutinized him, recalling the particular things Mona had mentioned to her. There was no question about it; he did look a lot like Derek now that Mona had made her aware of certain features. A sudden chill crept through her as Amanda sat listening to her father speaking with his young foreman. When he was about to leave the room after he and her father had finished their conversation, he said goodbye to her and gave a tip to his hat. There was that crooked grin on his face just like Derek's!

Amanda didn't linger too much longer at the Circle K. As she traveled back to Rancho Río she thought of how she'd never wanted the memories of Derek Lawson revived—but now they were.

It was rare that she and Tony had secrets, but she wasn't going to say anything about this to him, at least for a while.

When Amanda stepped inside her front door and felt the comforting warmth of her home, she found that the memories of Derek quickly began to fade once more.

All she needed were Tony's strong arms encircling her to make her completely healed from the pain of the old wound.

Later, the laughter of her daughter and son as the four of them sat in the dining room having their dinner made her completely forget the unpleasant afternoon.

Estaban told his family that he was packed and would possibly leave midday tomorrow. Amanda was not prepared for this quick departure. "So soon, Estaban?"

"I'm eager to get started, Mother. I'm sure you can understand that?" He smiled across the table at her.

Nodding her head, she returned his smile. "Of course, Estaban. I understand, but we'll miss you and I expect it won't be too long before you pay us a visit to tell all the glowing news of your new venture."

"Oh, I will. It will be a pleasant reprieve to come from the city to the quiet countryside on weekends."

"You see what he is saying, Amanda *mia* — that this ranch is too quiet for him," Tony laughed. "I remember what it was like to be your age, Estaban. I just happened to be attracted by a pretty girl over at the Circle K and that was enough to entice me to stay here."

"Well, I've not found such a beautiful girl here, so maybe I'll find her in San Antonio," Estaban laughed.

Thirty-one

Jeff had hoped that Russell Harlin wouldn't arrive the next morning, but he had been on his way to the barn in early morning when Harlin came riding up the drive.

Jeff knew that he might have made a bad mistake by hiring him on, but if he'd refused to, he knew that he could have faced worse trouble.

Jeff took him to the bunkhouse and showed him where he could put his things. He told him his foreman would be here soon and that he would be the one giving him his chores. "Dixon is the boss here, Harlin, after me. I'll expect to get a full day's work for a full day's pay. I'll leave you on your own to get settled in," Jeff told him as he turned on his booted heels to leave the bunkhouse.

Harlin watched him go, a smirk on his face. Jeff Kane was as naive as he had been years ago. It was always Derek who was the sly fox. Jeff just tagged along with him. If he thought he was going to break his back on this ranch he was crazy. There was only one reason he'd hired on out here and that was so he could be free to search the ranch for that cache he knew old Derek had hidden. But he had no map or instructions; he had only the recollections of a drunken, bragging young dude. Harlin had recognized Derek at the tavern, so he'd gone over to keep him company. For the next hour he'd encouraged him to talk about how he'd hoodwinked his buddy, Jeff, out of his share of a bounty.

Harlin had pumped him to the limit. "Buried it for safekeeping out in that thick woods around your pa's ranch, I bet."

"Damned if I did!" Derek had blurted out. "In a place better than that and easier to get to than having to dig it up. I got it close by right there on the Big D so I can grab it anytime I want it."

By the time he helped the very drunk Lawson up to his room he was mumbling about an old shack and the old dirt cellar where the tin chest of money was stashed.

It was only a few weeks later that he'd heard about Derek Lawson being killed. Harlin decided to make a fast departure from Gonzales County, so he headed for the Big Bend country and stayed around that area for the next fifteen years.

He had somehow slowly moved back northward staying a few months in one place and then another until a month ago he found himself in Bandera County. That was when he'd thought about both Derek Lawson and Jeff Kane.

It was then the idea was born to seek out Jeff Kane, who he had heard had become a prosperous rancher.

So now he was back where it had began over twenty years ago. Since old Derek wasn't around to enjoy his spoils, Harlin figured that he might as well take advantage of it. And then he would be more than eager to leave the Big D Ranch.

Jeff's foreman, Dixon, and Harlin felt a mutual dislike. They weren't hurting for more hands right now, and he certainly wasn't impressed by this dude.

He made a point of working Harlin's butt off to just test him. Harlin's assignment for the day was shoveling manure out of the barn stalls.

But Dixon was not the only one questioning Jeff's hiring of this new man. Mona didn't like the looks of him either, or the way he'd stared at her when she'd gone by the barn to get into her buggy to take some food to an ailing neighbor.

That evening at the dinner table she'd asked her husband about him.

"What's his name? And I thought you'd just said that you had a full crew?"

"Dear God, don't tell me you're going to start bossing me about how many men I hire around here," Jeff said in annoyance.

She, too, could run out of patience. "It is hardly bossing you, Jeff, if I ask you a simple question about something here on our ranch. That is my privilege. I am your wife and this ranch belonged to my father long before you married me."

"Oh, you remind me often enough about that, my dear wife," he barked at her, slamming his napkin down on the table and pushing back in his chair.

"Only when you force me to do so, Jeff. Amanda and Tony can discuss the business of their ranch, so I see nothing wrong with us doing the same thing. Tony asks your sister's opinion on many things. I—I'm not a stupid woman, Jeff."

228

She had hit a sore spot with him when she mentioned Tony, for he had listened to the praises of him throughout the years. If it wasn't his sister raving about her wonderful husband, it had been his own father spouting his admiration for Moreno.

"You'll excuse me, Mona. This talk is going to get us nowhere," he told her curtly as he moved to leave the table.

Mona's dark eyes watched him leave the dining room and she gave out a deep, depressed sigh and shook her head. She had to accept that the husband she loved so dearly would never be the man her father or Amanda's father was. Nor would he ever be the man Tony Moreno was. It was easier for Jeff to turn his back and walk away rather than face something unpleasant.

Well, *she* wasn't going to turn her back. Whether Jeff liked it or not she was going to take more interest in this ranch, for it had been her father's life and blood that had furnished them with it.

A few days later, she met up with Dixon Barnes and made a point of inquiring how everything was going on the ranch.

"Oh, yes, ma'am, guess the ranch is going along just fine, Mrs. Kane. I do have something I've got to speak to Mr. Kane about, though. This new fellow ain't worth his salt. I'm ready to let him go as far as I'm concerned."

"Lazy, eh?"

"More than lazy, ma'am. He just ain't no ranch hand. It's a waste of good money to keep him on."

"Why don't you come to the house and talk to him. If this is the case, then I'd say we should let him go at the end of the week, Dixon," Mona said in her soft voice. Jeff should just let Dixon hire the men, she considered.

"I'll talk to him before I leave for home this evening. I'm ready to be rid of him." Dixon watched her return to the house and thought that she would be easier to work for than her husband. He'd lived in Gonzales County long enough to know all the Lawson family and never had he heard a harsh word spoken against Mona Lawson Kane. She was a very lovely lady with a kind, gentle heart.

He stayed around the barn for a while in hopes that Jeff would be getting back from town soon. Best he get this behind him as soon as possible.

An hour later, Dixon went home a much happier man, for he had had his talk with Jeff. Mona had overheard enough of it to know Jeff had finally told Dixon to let Harlin go at the end of this week. She was pleased to hear this before she went upstairs to refresh herself before dinner. Her daughter, Amanda, should be arriving shortly after her visit with the Mortons and Mona was looking forward to having her back home.

Her pretty little blue-eyed daughter was the joy of her life. She was fairer skinned than Mona and her bright blue eyes were exactly like her father's. But she had inherited Mona's black hair with its natural curls.

Jeff had been more doting and liberal with his affections with his daughter than he had been with his two sons. She hoped seeing Amanda would put him in a better mood.

Promptly at five, Mona saw the Morton buggy coming up their drive. The few days her Amanda had been gone had seemed like months. It would be very lonely for her if Amanda wasn't here.

Bianca did not like admitting it but she had missed her brother after he left Rancho Río. She had no one to parry with at the dinner table. But she had been very pleased to have received a letter from Ramon Martinez telling her how lonely he was since she had left San Antonio. He wrote how much it had meant to him to have spent those special times together while she was visiting her great-grandfather. He had ended the letter by telling her how much he cared for her and that he hoped she'd not forget that while they were separated by so many miles.

Bianca folded the letter and put it in the drawer of her desk thinking that she had just received her first love letter. Tonight after dinner she would write back to him.

That afternoon as she took her usual ride on Rojo, she instinctively reined him in the direction of the Circle K.

She had to wonder if her frequent visits were all too obvious, for her grandfather had teased her as they sat in the parlor chatting. "I find it very wonderful, Bianca, that you want to spend time with an old man like me."

"You know I've always found you an interesting fellow," she smiled.

"You sure it's me or that good-looking foreman I hired?"

"Larkin isn't the man you are, Grandfather."

"Larkin is a lot of man and you and I know that, eh, Bianca?"

He saw a rosy blush come to her cheeks and he knew he was right. "Well, I don't care if that is the reason for your coming, Bianca, because it allows me to see you. That is more than I get from my grandson. Estaban did not even stop by here to see me as he was leaving to go back to San Antonio."

"Oh, Grandfather, he was so anxious to get back. I'm sure that he didn't mean to slight you." She was trying to soothe his feelings.

He patted her hand as he told her, "I'm sure that was it, honey." Mark Kane had never felt the closeness with his grandson as he had with his granddaughter. Kane had always known that it was not in Estaban to ever be a rancher as he was, so that might have explained it.

Bianca left the Circle K without a glance of Larkin, for he was nowhere around the corral or the main house. He had been riding the back range of the Circle K land and was pleased with the way things looked until he rode down the length of land bordering the Big D Ranch and spied a rider pulling up to the old deserted shack. He was curious about any hired hand on Jeff's ranch coming to this shack, so he paused to see what the rider was up to. He watched him dismount from his horse and walk up to the door. Instinct told Larkin that the man was up to no good.

He stood there by the door for a moment before busting through it. Larkin detected sounds of things being shuffled all around.

Russell Harlin knew that he had to get to the old shack this afternoon after Dixon had given him his walking papers. Only yesterday he had spied the shack when he and some other of Kane's men were herding up stray cattle.

After he'd searched the shack and found old Derek's bounty, he would be more than happy to leave here and be on his way. In shuffling things around the old rug had moved and Harlin discovered the trapdoor in the floor leading to the cellar below.

But there was no steps and Harlin pondered how he could lower himself down into the black abyss below. So he frantically searched the three small rooms for something he could use to get below. He found a long thick pole of wood about ten feet long and when he propped it against the trapdoor and lowered it downward, it worked with over a foot of the pole to spare.

The treasure he sought was right on the table where Larkin had left it weeks ago after he had discovered it in that snake-infested cellar. His hand could have reached out and touched it from where he was standing in the kitchen.

But the trip down in the black hole yielded up nothing for Harlin and, like Larkin, he was to become suddenly aware of the rattling and hissing of the snakes coiled up in the dark corners. He scampered quickly back up the pole.

When it had become quiet inside the cabin Larkin decided to enter. He found the rug tossed aside and the trapdoor opened. Larkin knew whomever this man was that he, too, was privy to the tale his own mother had told him.

He sunk down on the old cot against the wall of

the front room and posed his pistol ready to use if he had to. He heard the deep gasp of the fellow below as he rushed up the pole, and a smile came to Larkin's face, for he recalled the vipers below.

By the time Harlin had reached the top of the pole, he was out of breath. "Who the hell are you, fellow?" he asked in a faltering voice.

"Just getting ready to ask you the same question," Larkin shot back at him. Larkin never trusted a man who had shifty eyes like this dude, so he kept his pistol targeted directly on Harlin.

"I work here on the Big D, so I know you don't. Guess that gives me the right to inquire about you," Harlin said, swinging his leg up.

"I hardly think ransacking this shack is what Jeff Kane hired you to do. By the way, what did you say your name was?"

"Not that it's any of your business, but it's Harlin. Now suppose you tell me your name and why you're aiming that damned gun in my direction?" Harlin insisted.

"The name's Larkin and I always draw my pistol when I face danger."

Harlin gave out a nervous laugh and declared that he posed no danger to Larkin. "Hell, I don't even know you. Never saw you before in my life, young man." But the longer Harlin stood there looking at this powerfully built young hombre lounging on the cot, there was something about him that reminded him of the young Derek Lawson. He was seized by an idea which he knew had to be insane, for Derek was so young when he was killed. But that was not to say that he could not have fathered a son. The age would have been just about right, Harlin thought.

"Well, am I free to go on my way or are you going to shoot me, fellow?" Harlin bluntly asked.

"You are free to go as soon as you tell me what you were looking for, Harlin," Larkin told him.

"Well, what the hell, if you must know, I was hunting for some money that was supposed to have been hidden here years ago. Figured it was mine as much as anyone's. My buddy who'd hidden it here has been dead a long time." Harlin lit up a cigarette and shrugged his shoulders as he muttered, "Hell, he was a liar back then, so I should have known that there would be nothing here and there wasn't."

"Before you go, would you mind telling me who your buddy was, Harlin?" Larkin asked him.

"Can't see why not. His name was Derek Lawson, and the truth is you look a hell of a lot like him. Since I answered your question, perhaps you'll answer one for me. How come you happened to be here?"

"I'm the foreman over at the Circle K and this is the back range," Larkin told him.

"Well, we won't be running into each other again 'cause I've been given my walking papers by the Big D."

Larkin lingered on the cot watching Harlin saunter out the door of the shack.

This time when Larkin left the shack he took the money with him. He planned to put it to good use. Old Juan Escobar who worked so hard on the Circle K could use a helping hand with his many children.

He was going to see that Derek Lawson's tainted money would end up doing good. With the money

235

placed in the inside pocket of his vest, he left the shack and climbed back over the fence to mount up on his horse.

He could have a good feeling about the money in his pocket but there was no good feeling about the man who'd fathered him.

Derek Lawson was a no good sonofabitch!

Thirty-two

Mark Kane owed Larkin so much for getting him back on his horse and patiently putting him through the paces almost daily. Kane could feel the growing of strength in his aging body.

His lawyer, Clint, had even commented about the vast change in him. They'd had a pleasant visit and also taken care of drawing up Mark's new will.

He sensed that Clint was taken by surprise that he wanted to leave the Circle K Ranch to Bianca. He had protested to Mark that she was so young, but Mark had quickly pointed out to his old friend that Bianca loved the land with a passion he didn't see in her older brother, Estaban. "Someday she will marry a young man who will feel the same way if I know my granddaughter as well as I think I do," he added.

Kane spoke with such a convinced, assured way that Clint saw there was no point in arguing with him. "But what about Amanda and Jeff, Mark?" he asked.

"What about them? Amanda and Tony have the Rancho Río and Jeff has the Big D. Young Estaban will most likely inherit the vast holdings of his great-grandfather. You see, Clint, I've got faith in that pretty little granddaughter of mine 'cause she thinks like I do. She's a person who won't be ruled by stupid conventions any more than I ever was. But the thing about Bianca I admire most is her kind, generous heart." He told Clint how she had taken charge the day she'd come to the Circle K to find Estella injured. "It amazed me, Clint how that young lady of only seventeen put the house in running order. She's the person I want to take over this ranch I've loved so dearly all my life."

His lawyer now understood why Kane wanted Bianca to be the one to inherit his property. Always, he had admired and respected the wisdom of Mark Kane. There was no man in Gonzales County he held in higher esteem than this old rancher who'd done battle with the rustlers, Comanches, and renegades to keep this Texas land he loved so much.

"I'll be pleased to draw up your new will, Mark. I've got to see this granddaughter of yours—it's been almost four years now," Clint told him.

Kane chuckled. "Well, Clint, be prepared for a surprise, for Bianca is not the little girl you last saw."

Kane said goodbye to Clint and was feeling in high spirits by the time Larkin came to the main house to share the dinner hour with him.

Larkin was feeling in high spirits himself this evening, for he looked forward about what he was going to do with the money he'd taken from the cabin. He could think of so many good people here at the Circle K he could help. Tonight, Larkin was reminded of Fred Compton and what a difference he'd made in his life when he'd hired on at his ranch as a young lad of eighteen.

Fred had been like the father he had never known.

238

Larkin planned someday to go back to pay a visit to the Compton Ranch. Now that he was on the Circle K he found himself looking up to Mark Kane as he would have if he was his own grandfather. It was pleasant for Larkin to come to the main house a few nights a week and sit in the dining room to share the camaraderie he did with Kane. He felt that the things he'd been denied as a youngster were coming his way now.

As Larkin and Kane played a game of dominoes after dinner, they also talked. Mark decided to ask Larkin some questions about himself.

Larkin told him about Compton and working on his ranch. He also told him about his mother, and he did not try to hide the fact that he was a bastard. "My father never wed my mother, señor. I never met him, but can't say I wanted to."

"I'd say he was the loser—missed knowing a fine son, in my opinion," Kane told him.

"Well, he missed a lot of things. He missed a lot of years of life 'cause he got himself killed at a pretty young age."

"So did my brother, Larkin. Damned Comanches raided the Circle K and almost killed him. A year later, Mexican bandits *did* kill him. There was a time when I hated every Mexican I came across. Life has to be crazy 'cause my daughter ends up marrying one and the granddaughter I adore is part Mexican," he chuckled.

"My mother always said that life travels a full circle and I'm just beginning to see what she meant by that."

Kane felt as if he knew this young man better after they'd talked so long that evening. Kane was more than ever certain that Larkin had justified his faith in him.

Larkin was ready for bed by the time he got back to his cottage for he was used to getting to bed about an hour earlier than this for him to get up at the crack of dawn and start a new day.

The next morning, Larkin was reluctant to crawl out of the cozy bed and get into his work clothes. One of the new men he had just recently hired was already in the corral when he sauntered in that direction. Harry Tully was proving to be a good man and all the old hands found him a very likable fellow.

Larkin had found that he could tell Harry what he wanted done and Harry saw that it was carried out. The wiry young man saw Larkin coming through the gate and called out a good-morning to him.

"Morning to you, Tully. How about you taking over for me this morning so I can get Señor Kane a ride. He didn't get to go out yesterday."

Larkin found Mark in the kitchen having his breakfast. He brightened as Larkin told him he was free to take him out for a ride.

"I'm ready, Larkin. You tell him, Estella, that I don't sleep half the morning away like I used to," Kane declared.

"It's true, Señor Larkin. He gets up much earlier than he used to," Estella confirmed.

It was the perfect autumn morning for a brisk ride over the countryside, and Kane could go at a faster pace now that Larkin had been taking him out for regular rides. Kane felt that the day would soon come when he would no longer have to depend on Larkin.

By the time the two of them arrived back at the

house and Larkin helped Kane down from his horse, not needing additional help from old Turkey, it was almost time for Kane to have his light lunch.

Mark suddenly spotted the rider approaching the drive. "Wonder what's bringing Clint out here again today?" he muttered.

"Clint, sir?"

"My lawyer, Larkin. Did some business with him yesterday. Sure didn't expect to be seeing him again today."

Mark greeted him and asked Clint what brought him to the ranch.

"Nothing to do with you, Mark," Clint smiled. His attention was turned to Rick Larkin. "I'm assuming you have to be Rick Larkin, who this man has been talking so much about."

"Yes, sir—I'm Rick Larkin."

"Well, it is you I've come to see to discuss a matter that had come into my office."

Larkin's green eyes flashed with puzzlement. He could not figure out what Kane's lawyer could be talking about.

Kane had no inkling, either, but he knew from his cheerful demeanor that it was not bad news Clint was bringing.

When they reached the parlor and Larkin had Kane comfortably seated in the chair, Clint asked Larkin if he wanted him to discuss the matter in front of Mark or privately.

"I do not mind Señor Kane being present," Larkin told him, and the lawyer did not hesitate to sit down then.

"I'd advise you to have a seat, too, Mr. Larkin before I tell you why I've come," Clint told him. Larkin did as

241

he'd suggested.

Clint told him he had received a letter from one of his lawyer friends in Guadalope County this morning. "He was asking my help in tracking you down, since he had information you'd come to Gonzales County."

"Why was he wanting you to do that, may I ask?"

"Well, young man, I'll tell you why. It seems that you have just inherited a rather large ranch back in Guadalope County. A Mr. Fred Compton left you his entire spread of land over there and my friend is handling his estate. He left you the ranch and his only sister all his other holdings when he died."

Kane and his lawyer exchanged glances when Larkin gave out a moan of protest. His face was etched with anguish. "Mr. Compton dead! God Almighty!"

"It happened about a month ago, and I'm very sorry to be the bearer of news that saddens you so, but I'm sure it also has to make you feel happy to know that this man thought so much of you that he left his ranch to you," the lawyer tried to console him.

"Oh, it does," Larkin mumbled.

The rest of that day was a foggy maze to Rick Larkin and Kane sympathized with him, for he knew what it was like to lose someone you cared for.

Thirty-three

Mark Kane spent the rest of the day in thoughtful solitude, and it was a bittersweet time for him. He was happy for Larkin and his good fortune. But now he would be a wealthy rancher and he'd have no reason to work as a foreman at the Circle K Ranch.

Kane knew he'd just have to accept what had happened. Long ago, he had learned when things were rolling smoothly, it was inevitable that something would disrupt it. So it came as no surprise to him when Larkin came to the house for dinner and said he was going to have to go to Guadalupe County. "I trust you will understand that I must do this, but I know I'm leaving you in good hands. I've talked to Tully this afternoon and told him what I expect him to do for you."

"I do understand, Larkin, and I thank you. I know you have to go."

Both men searched the faces of the other and Kane saw that Larkin was a man torn in two directions. That made him admire him even more.

"I'll be back, Señor Kane, I promise! I'd not let you down."

Kane gave him a nod of his head. After all, he and

his ranch were in much better shape than both had been several weeks ago. His fences were mended and he had a fine crew of men working for him now. The shiftless ones had been let go. The slow winter months were approaching now, so activity around the ranches would slow down until springtime.

"You won't let me down, Larkin. I know that, son," Kane told him.

Larkin realized just how fond he'd become of the old man. They gave each other a warm, comradely embrace and Larkin admonished him to take care. "Don't want all our good work to get undone. I'll try to get back to the Circle K in ten days."

Kane's wrinkled hand patted his shoulder. "I'm going to hold you to that, Larkin," Kane told him. "God go with you. The Circle K will miss you and we'll eagerly wait for your return."

Larkin had left the ranch early that morning and Mark knew that he would not be going out for a ride, so he'd contented himself with a stroll in the gardens after breakfast. Several weeks ago, that would have been a major undertaking, but this day he was not tired.

Bianca breezing into his parlor was exactly what he needed. "Well, *niña* — what a breath of fresh air you are!" he greeted her, seeing that she looked as lovely as the golden leaves falling out in his gardens. She wore her riding skirt and russet-colored tunic. Atop her gold tresses a perky wide-brimmed, flat-crowned hat sat at an angle, a cluster of colorful feathers tucked into its band.

She and her grandfather had sat in the parlor chatting as they enjoyed the coffee Estella had brought to them along with some delicious rolls glazed with sugar icing and cinnamon.

Mark Kane thought she seemed to grow more beautiful each time he saw her. "Let's you and me go for a ride over this countryside we both love so much, Bianca," he asked her impulsively. "Would you go with your old grandfather?"

"Of course I would! You know that! I'll just have Larkin get you up on that horse and then we'll go for that ride."

"We have to get someone else, honey. Larkin is going to be away from the Circle K for a while."

Had he slapped her across the face it would not have stunned her more than his revelation. "Wha—what do you mean, Grandfather?"

"Larkin left this morning to go to Guadalupe County. He found out yesterday that he has inherited a ranch, Bianca. I fear that I've lost a very good foreman. After all, he'll have no need to work here now." Kane noticed the strange look on his granddaughter's face.

She sat there saying nothing for a few minutes. It was as if she had forgotten that he was even in the parlor with her.

"Bianca, is there something you need to tell your old grandfather?" His eyes searched her face for an answer for her strange behavior.

"Yes, Grandfather—and you are the only one I've told this to, but I think I'm in love with Rick Larkin." Her eyes met his.

"I see," he mumbled. He knew that a man such as Larkin could whet her interest.

"Oh, Grandfather! He will come back, won't he?"

Kane patted her hand. "He promised me he would, Bianca, and I believe him."

But what he could not promise her was how long he'd remain once he did come back. He saw her lovely face suddenly change from the sad, stunned look to one of anger. "Oh, damn him! I wish I hadn't fallen in love with him, Grandfather. Really, I mean it!"

"Our hearts just don't listen to our heads all the time, Bianca. I'm a man who knows that very well. Guess you could have lost your heart sooner."

"No other man ever held my interest like Larkin did from the minute I met him."

A warm look came to Kane's wrinkled face and he nodded his head in understanding. "Does Larkin feel the same way about you?"

"I can't say, Grandfather. If you're asking me if he's asked me to marry him, then no, he hasn't," Bianca confessed.

Kane thought that if Larkin felt the same way about her, then that might be an incentive for him to return to Circle K Ranch if the Compton ranch had a good foreman.

"Well, honey, any man alive would certainly be taken with you. If Larkin is half the man I think he is, he won't take a chance on losing you by staying away too long."

"Oh, I don't know, Grandfather. I never knew finding yourself in love could hurt so."

Kane reached over to take her soft hand in his wrinkled one. "Oh, Bianca—loving can hurt something fierce sometimes and don't you ever forget it, but it can also give you more happiness than anything else in your life."

"Well, I'll take your word for that, Grandfather. I've never caught you in a lie yet." She gave him a weak smile and suggested that they go for that ride together.

With the help of a couple of the hired hands, Kane was lifted atop his horse and the two of them cantered down the drive. It was the first time Kane had gone out on a jaunt with anyone except Larkin, but he felt perfectly at ease with his granddaughter riding by his side.

An hour later, they returned to the house and she bid him goodbye as she prepared to ride back to Rancho Río. But she was quick to tell him before she left that she was going to have a few things to say to Larkin when he returned to Gonzales County.

"I've no doubt of that, Bianca!" Kanev chuckled.

Estella had overheard the two of them talking and she, too, knew Señorita Bianca was in a temper and suspected it was about Larkin she was talking.

Señor Kane confirmed this and the two of them laughed, knowing that Larkin was in for a good tonguelashing from her.

Estella had suspected for quite a while that Señor Larkin was very attracted to Señor Kane's granddaughter from the way he looked at her. Now that he had inherited that fine ranch over in Guadalupe County he would be free to court her. Just being a foreman for her grandfather had probably made him reluctant to do so. Estella was thinking how wonderful it would be if those two nice young people did get together.

She inquired of Mark Kane if there was anything she could do for him before she went to her room to rest now that Juanita was going to be taking over the chores for the rest of the afternoon.

He assured her he was fine, so she went back to the kitchen to give Juanita a few more orders before she enjoyed a long siesta.

Juanita's dark eyes had searched all around the grounds for the sight of Rick Larken. Estella had told her that the dinner she was to start preparing would be only for Señor Kane.

So when Estella came back into the kitchen to tell her to mop the kitchen this afternoon, Juanita tried to sound casual when she inquired, "I trust Señor Larkin is not ill, since Señor Kane will be dining alone tonight."

"Oh, no, he is away for a few days, Juanita," Estella told her as she turned to leave to go to her room. It was going to be nice to stretch out on her bed, for her foot still bothered her after she'd been working for a few hours.

"I see," Juanita mumbled as she turned her attention to her chores.

By the time she had completed everything and had the pot of beef stew simmering on the back of the cookstove, Juanita was tired. She was sitting at the small square wood table enjoying the cup of coffee she'd just brewed in hopes that it would revive her for the half-mile walk to her home.

The other Mexican servant, Nola, came into the kitchen, for she'd just finished her chores for the day. She had worked all day on the upstairs rooms. Like Juanita, she was more than ready to call it a day, but before she left, she asked Juanita if Estella had told her why Larkin had left.

"She just said that he would be gone for a few days," Juanita said.

"Well, I'm not so sure of that. You see, I happened to overhear the conversation this man had yesterday with Señor Larkin when he and Señor Kane returned from their ride. It seems our foreman has suddenly inherited a big ranch of his own."

"Señor Larkin will have his own ranch?" Juanita stared up at Nola. She didn't know whether to take the young girl seriously, for she was known for not always telling the truth.

But two hours later after she'd arrived home, she overheard her father telling her mother the same tale. News around a ranch traveled like wildfire.

This time Nola had not been lying!

Thirty-four

Bianca announced the news about Larkin to her parents that evening. His daughter's announcement filled Tony Moreno with mixed feelings, for everything had been running so smoothly over at the Circle K Ranch since Larkin had taken charge. Now all of this would surely change for if Larkin was now the owner of a big spread in Guadalupe County, he would hardly want to remain as foreman for Mark Kane.

"Grandfather said he promised to return, Father," Bianca quickly informed him.

"Oh, I'm sure he will, but that doesn't mean he will stay."

None of the Morenos realized the very quiet moods they'd sunk into as they left the dining room that evening. Bianca excused herself very early to go to her room to leave her parents in the parlor.

Amanda thought about the last time she was at her father's ranch and her reason for going there.

As yet, she had still not mentioned anything to Tony nor did she intend to tonight, but she did ask him if it was Guadalupe County Larkin had come from when he hired him.

"That's right," Tony confirmed. "He'd worked for about two years on the Compton ranch, he'd told me. Now, he's the owner of it! Isn't that ironic?"

"He obviously has an overwhelming impact on people, but I have to ask myself why he left the Compton Ranch if he had such a good job."

"I can't answer, *querida*. Only Rick Larkin can give you the answers to that," Tony smiled at her.

"I find him a most mysterious young man, Tony."

Tony, too, had felt there was a mystery surrounding Larkin. As Larkin had proved himself to be such a good hand, he'd tried to dismiss the one thing that had always prodded at him.

Madre de Dios, he would never have voiced his innermost feelings to his beloved wife about the first time he'd met the young man out there in the corral yard. Rushing images of the past came vividly to him, for he saw a young man who reminded him of Derek Lawson. Like any man who'd almost been killed, Tony remembered every feature of Derek Lawson's face. The day he'd hired Larkin it had set off a flurry of memories of the past, but other things had taken over to occupy his time and thoughts, like Bianca returning to Rancho Río.

Unbeknownst to him, Amanda had been affected by the resemblance of Rick Larkin to Derek Lawson, too, and it was one of those very rare times they'd kept a secret from each other.

The family received their first letter from Estaban.

251

He was all settled in at his great-grandfather's house. A boyish excitement was reflected in his letter as he wrote about his office that was now completely furnished and ready for him to occupy.

Old Estaban was already rallying his many wealthy friends and acquaintances, enlightening them that his great-grandson was going to be practicing law in San Antonio and having them over for dinner to meet young Estaban.

Tony had laughed. "Sounds like Grandfather is as enthusiastic about our son's venture as he himself is."

"I am happy for Estaban, Tony. The ranch was not for him," Amanda told her husband.

"I know, *querida,*" he agreed with her. But she saw a hint of sadness, for he had wanted his son to carry on with Rancho Río.

When Tony and Amanda had left the house Bianca sat in the parlor to read Estaban's letter over. As she was refolding the letter she glanced out the window to see Sheriff Warner riding up.

She watched as he went over to the corrals to speak to her father. They talked for the longest time and she instinctively knew that the conversation concerned something of a serious nature from the tense look on her father's face.

The minute the sheriff rode away, her father came into the parlor. In his strong, authoritative voice, he told her, "Bianca, I want you taking no rides on Rojo today, you understand?"

"May I ask why, Father?"

"You may, and I shall tell you. Ortega escaped early this morning from the jail in Austin where they'd taken him. The sheriff told me that they're al-

252

most certain he's going to be heading this way. He's got a score to settle with the Moreno family." His black eyes sparked with fury. "I should have killed him the day he did what he did to you and then we would not be facing this now. If I even see his ugly face again, I won't hesitate a minute."

Suddenly, he was gone from the room and she knew it was to seek out her mother.

As her father had ordered her to do, she stayed inside the house, but it was a miserably long day. But she did go to the barn to visit with Rojo and console him as well as herself.

During dinner, she was to find out just how serious her father was taking the news, for he'd posted night guards around the grounds of the spacious hacienda.

When one day went by and then another, Bianca felt like she was smothering. Her free spirit was rebelling at being kept a prisoner within the walls of the house courtyard. By the fourth day, she was ready to scream.

Like a caged animal, she roamed the courtyard each evening, but it was not the same as taking her daily rides on Rojo.

She'd sat in the moonlit gardens the last three nights and thought about Larkin. How she wished he was back here. She told herself that he would take care of Ortega swiftly as she remembered the day he had rescued her from that ugly Mexican.

Sitting on the little iron bench by the spraying fountain with the moonlight playing across her face and golden hair, she gave way to the desolation she was feeling. "Come back, Larkin! Come back to me, for I need you so much," she murmured to the darkness of the gardens and the gentle winds resounding through the branches of the tall pine trees. She heard the sound of a night bird calling out to its mate as she was crying out to Larkin. Suddenly the night bird's call could not be heard, so perhaps its mate had come. She could only hope that the man she loved would come to her.

Nostalgia flooded him as he rode up the drive to the house where Fred Compton had lived. Larkin only wished that he would have seen him once more before he died. He was coming with misgivings; if his one and only sister did not approve of his will, he decided he would ride away. He'd not fight her for her brother's land.

He was still in a state of utter shock at Compton's actions. It was going to take some time to get used to the idea that he was the owner of this ranch.

But once he had entered the house and met Compton's sister, Frances, a lady in her seventies with eyes as bright and blue as the Texas skies, he was feeling less apprehensive. She'd wasted no time telling him she was delighted that he'd arrived. "I'm ready to leave here and get back to Austin. Fred knew I could never have taken over this ranch. I like city living. I hate it out here. It's too lonely for me. I gladly turn this all over to you, young man, and you look like you'll be able to handle it very nicely. Fred's lawyer will be available when you need him."

Larkin took an instant liking to this lady and he was relieved that she did not resent her brother leaving the ranch to him.

"Truth is, Fred didn't need to leave me all that money," she said candidly. "I've got more than I can possibly spend, and I can spend a lot! I had a very wealthy husband who had the audacity to die on me before he should have, so now I have two fortunes to try to spend before I die."

Larkin could not resist laughing. He found himself enchanted by Frances Beaumont.

They shared a pleasant evening meal together that the cook, Ola, had prepared and served to them. "Fred had a very perceptive sense about the people he hired, Rick. You'll find this out after you've been here a while. He left Ola a nice sum of money for her years of devoted service to him and I hope that you'll find the need to keep her here. I'm sure she is quite concerned about her future," Frances Beaumont told him.

"Oh, Mrs. Beaumont, I'll certainly have a need for her services in this big house. I'll ease that worry for her for sure."

"Good. I'm happy to hear you say that. I'll be leaving in the morning, for I've two very lonely cats back in Austin and a house I'm anxious to get back to even though I, too, have a very dependable housekeeper keeping things in order for me," she smiled. She went on to tell him that he would find a list she'd made for him back on Fred's desk. She told him Fred's lawyer, Joel Bowman, was a fine gentleman and she was sure he'd find the association with him as pleasant as she had.

"I really appreciate this, Mrs. Beaumont. I have to admit all this is earthshaking to me. I need all the advice you can give me," Larkin confessed to her.

"Well, I'm more than happy to do what I can. Now, I guess I don't have to tell you what a good man Miles Golden is, for he was here when you used to work for my brother and he had nothing but nice things to say about you. You'll find him as eager to do a good day's work for you as he did for Fred. It's like I said, Rick, Fred had a lot of good people around him."

They spoke of many things before the evening ended and Larkin went to the quarters which had been Fred Compton's bedroom and office. It seemed strange to him to be taking this finely furnished room. Frances Beaumont had obviously removed all Fred's personal belongings. The alcove which served as Fred's office had been untouched, for Frances felt that the papers in the desk pertaining to the ranch should be in Larkin's possession. Pictures and personal mementoes had been removed and all of Fred's rifles and pistols had been given to his faithful foreman, Miles Golden.

Larkin sat on the side of the bed thinking that this would be a fine enough home to bring Bianca to as his bride. One of the things that had nagged at him when he'd found himself falling more and more in love with the beautiful Señorita Moreno was what he could offer her. He had no fine ranch to take her to like the grand hacienda she had lived in all her life. He was not a wealthy man like her father and grandfather. Now, it seemed that fate had taken care of all those worries. He would be a wealthy man.

By the time he was in bed, he was thinking that there was nothing to stop him now from asking Bianca Moreno to be his wife. He gave way to the fantasy of how he and the beautiful Bianca would live here and raise a family. Together they would ride over the rolling hills and valleys on their fine Thoroughbreds.

He could not imagine a happier life!

Thirty-five

By midday Frances Beaumont's carriage was rolling out of the drive into the road taking her back to Austin. She could not have been happier, for she knew now why Fred had left his ranch to the nice young man she'd met only yesterday. Fred might have been her younger brother, but she had always admired him tremendously for the wisdom he possessed.

When Rick Larkin commented about Fred's never marrying, she had told him that he could have had any girl he wanted. "Fred was not only a very good-looking man, but he was also a man whose emotions ran very deep and intense," she explained. He had loved only one young woman and she had died. He never found another quite like Rosemary, so he remained a bachelor the rest of his life. That was just Fred; he'd never settled for second best."

Larkin had told her that he could understand a man feeling that way. What he didn't say was he was beginning to think he was that sort of man himself.

Bianca Moreno was the lady he loved and had wanted no other since the day he'd rescued her from Ortega. The temptation of little Juanita had not inspired him to accept her obvious invitation back at the Circle K Ranch. Other men would have been ready to

258

take the dark-eyed little señorita to the hayloft, but Larkin had ignored her.

After he had said his farewells to Frances Beaumont, he took a tour of this fine house that was his now. All the time he'd worked for Mr. Compton he had only been in the parlor and the kitchen.

He surveyed each of the rooms. His head was still whirling to think that this was all his. When he entered the bright, sunny kitchen with its many windows, Ola was there putting things in order. Larkin felt very awkward and ill-at-ease about his new status, but he wanted to assure the middle-aged housekeeper that she still had a job.

Ola wiped her damp hands on her apron and brushed back a stray hair from her forehead. "I want to tell you I'm sure going to need you desperately to run this big house for me and I'm hoping you don't have any plans to leave me now that Mr. Compton is gone," Larkin told her.

He could tell by the way her voice cracked and her speech stammered that she was thrilled by his declaration. "Oh, Mr. Larkin—this has been the only home I've known for several years. I'm just happy you want me here."

"Well, I sure do, Ola. I know I'm not Fred Compton, but I hope to be as fine a man as he was someday."

"You are a fine man as far as I'm concerned and Mr. Fred surely had to feel that way, too. That's good enough for me."

By the time Larkin was ready to leave the kitchen, Ola was so eager to please him that she was asking him what his favorite foods were and what time he would like to have his evening meal.

"What time were you used to serving dinner to Mr. Compton?"

"Six every evening," she told him.

"Then that sounds about right for me, Ola," he smiled as he turned to walk out of the room for his meeting with Miles Golden, the foreman.

Miles, like Ola, did not know what to expect from this young man who'd be his new boss. He'd found Rick Larkin a likable dude when he'd worked on the ranch and he was one of his best hands. But Miles also knew that sudden wealth could give a fellow a big head, so he did not know what to expect.

Larkin was at the fence before Miles got there, so he climbed over the top railing and swung himself over to the ground. Extending his hand, he told Miles it was good to see him again. "I—I just wish it had been under different circumstances," he added. "Never figured that last spring when I left this would happen."

"Good to see you too, Larkin, and I know what you mean. Mr. Compton was a man who kept his problems to himself, but I'd seen him have a couple of those attacks over the last year and a half."

"Mrs. Beaumont told me that it was his heart," Larkin told him.

"Yeah. He'd finally got to the doctor about three months ago, but I don't know what he was told," Miles said.

Larkin's intense green eyes looked directly at Miles as he told him in a sober tone, "Miles, I can't fail that man. God knows I can't, but I'm going to need your support. I'm damned well going to try to fill his shoes! Can I count on you to help me?"

Golden was older than Larkin by some fifteen years and he knew sincerity when he saw it, and he saw it now on this young man's face. He also had known Fred Compton long enough to know that he had made his decision to leave the ranch to him for a very good reason.

"You can count on me, Larkin, and old Fred wherever he is, is going to be smiling about how well this ranch is going to run. We'll take good care of it for him," Miles assured him.

A heavy load was lifted off Larkin's shoulders, for he felt he had the support of Miles and the housekeeper, Ola. Next, he had to do the same thing with the men who worked the Compton Ranch.

"I want to ride out with you tomorrow, Miles, but this afternoon I've got to go into Bandera to see Joel Bowman."

The two of them went their separate ways. An hour later, Larkin left the ranch to go into Bandera. Joel Bowman had been just as cordial as Ola and Miles to him. After he had spent an hour in the lawyer's office, Bowman told him that he knew Fred Compton for over thirty years and held him in the highest esteem. He added that he did not question his judgment when he told him he wanted to draw up a new will, that he knew he had a very good reason for doing what he did.

"Well, Mr. Bowman, Fred Compton was the closest thing to a father I ever had and I well remember when I went out to work for him that I tried to imitate everything he did. I worshipped the man. Got myself a hat just like him with my first wages."

Bowman laughed. "Well, you could not have found a

better man to imitate, Larkin. Fred told me once that you were the son he would have liked to have had."

"I wish I had been his son. But at least I learned a lot from him about what a man should be. I credit him with that," Larkin said.

"I'm sure that is why he made that last will, Larkin. He knew that Frances had more than she would ever need the rest of her life. He also knew that she didn't need the bother of the ranch so he left the ranch to you. But he also knew what you would need to run the ranch, so you were left a sizable account in the bank, too. You have your work cut out for you, Larkin, but I'm here to help you whenever you need my advice."

Larkin reached out to shake his hand. "I'll probably be talking to you quite often, sir. If Mr. Compton trusted you, then that's good enough for me."

"You can trust me, Larkin, and I feel the same way about you." He handed him the huge portfolio of documents he'd been holding.

"You're a very wealthy young man, Rick Larkin, and you're a man who will know the true worth of such an inheritance. Often I feel very sad that I have to turn over the helm to unworthy heirs who are usually a bunch of wastrels."

"Thank you, sir. Thank you very much." Larkin gave him a final handshake before he went out the door.

Joel Bowman sat there at his desk and removed his spectacles to dwell quietly. Fred Compton had been a friend of his. He had been a man Joel admired tremendously.

But he was going to leave his law office feeling very good. He was very impressed by Rick Larkin, for he was cut from the same strip of cloth as Fred Compton

262

himself. Bowman knew it instinctively the minute he walked into the office. There was that same authoritative though not overbearing arrogance about him that Fred Compton had possessed.

But what was even more impressive to Bowman was the look on his face when he spoke about Fred, a look of honesty and sincerity.

Fred had made the right decision to leave the ranch to Larkin!

For the next few days Larkin got acquainted with the men at the ranch. They all seemed like good, hardworking fellows and none of them showed any signs of resenting him.

He figured it was time that he educate himself about the details of running the ranch. So after he had had his dinner, he went to his bedroom and office. The massive desk seemed to be left just as it was when Compton had died, and the drawers were filled with various documents and records.

It was time-consuming for Larkin to read over all the material in the drawers, but each night he did just that until he got sleepy and couldn't concentrate on what he was reading.

For three nights now he had sat at the desk and he realized why Compton had been such a successful rancher. He was a planner and a good businessman as well as knowing about cattle and ranching.

The last drawer he was to go through was the narrow one in the center of the desk. It was there that he realized Frances Beaumont had made a thorough survey of the drawers because he found a small box. When he'd opened the lid he found a note she'd written. It stated that she had first thought about taking the article in the small velvet case when she'd left, but after meeting him she'd decided to leave it in the desk. "I wanted you to have this, Larkin. Perhaps you'd like it for the lady you marry, since Fred never got the opportunity to do so. It is a most exquisite ring as I'm sure you will agree, and Fred would be happy to know that it was enjoyed," the noted had stated.

Larkin opened the small case to find a wide gold band with a large, magnificent stone centered on the band. For the longest moment he just stared at its rare beauty. He knew that there was only one woman who would ever wear that ring, for her rare beauty rivaled this magnificent gem.

He closed the lid and put it back in the drawer — when he went back to Gonzales County he would take it with him.

There was nothing to prevent him from asking Bianca Moreno to be his wife. He had a fine home to offer her and he was going to have a future to share with her.

Now, he had a beautiful ring to slip on her finger when he asked her to be his wife!

Thirty-six

The forceful, energetic air of Rick Larkin was infectious around the ranch.

Larkin sensed the happy atmosphere around the grounds and the house, so he could not have been a happier man himself.

At the end of two weeks, Miles Golden and he were having one of their many talks when Miles turned very serious. "Rick, the men like their new boss and I just felt the need to tell you this. I also have something to say to you and I'll hope you'll take it the way I mean it. This has been the Compton Ranch for many a year, but Fred Compton is no longer alive. You now own this land and you need to establish your identity as the new owner. It needs a new name."

For a few minutes he was silent. "I'll have to give that some thought, Miles," he finally said.

He did give it just that, and the next day when he and Miles were riding over the range together, he told him with a grin on his face, "I thought of a name, Miles, but I wanted your opinion about it. If you like it, then we'll get busy putting up a new sign over the archway out by the main road."

"Let's have it, Larkin."

"Happy Valley Ranch. What do you think?"

"Damn, I like it! Yeah, I like it a lot!" Miles gave him a big, broad smile.

"Well then, I'll leave the rest up to you to see that the sign is changed," Larkin told him.

"Get Monty busy tomorrow. He's got the talent for the job. I always tell him that he should have been an artist and not a cowhand, but he swears he'd starve. And he likes to eat too much."

Larkin laughed. "It doesn't mean he couldn't work on it in the evenings."

Miles told the men what the ranch would be called in the future. All of them liked the sound of it.

The next day Larkin had to make a trip into Bandera and when he returned in the late afternoon, he was pleasantly surprised to find the new sign was up over the archway of the drive. For a moment he pulled up on the reins of his horse to just sit in the saddle and stare up at it.

Happy Valley Ranch was going to be a happy home and haven. He had never dreamed he would ever own a ranch as grand as this one.

Now that he felt that everything was in working order around here his thoughts were consumed with another ranch and the elderly old man he'd promised he'd come back to. But it wasn't only Mark Kane haunting his thoughts. It was his granddaughter, Bianca, who Larkin was aching to see.

Miles was here to run the ranch and Ola was certainly capable of tending to the house. Everyone had been paid their wages for a month, so Larkin felt that it was time he returned to Gonzales County. The only thing troubling him was what he was going to tell Mark Kane. He could hardly do a proper job of being his foreman and handle Happy Valley Ranch at the same time.

The next day he told Miles that he was going to be going back to Gonzales County for a few days.

"You go do what you've got to do, Rick. Happy Valley will be here to welcome you back."

As dawn was breaking the next morning, Rick Larkin rode out of his ranch to head for Gonzales County. In the pocket of his leather vest was the ring that Fred Compton had purchased years ago for the lady he loved.

It had seemed strange to Bianca to pay her visits to Grandfather Kane and see nothing of Larkin around the corrals. She knew how much he missed Larkin and their regular rides.

She also noticed that Estella did not seem so cheerful on her last two visits. There was no question that the atmosphere over at the Circle K was gloomy with Larkin's absence.

Bianca had to accept the possibility that now that Larkin had inherited a ranch he might never return to Gonzales County, no matter what he had promised her grandfather.

It was a pleasant surprise to Bianca when her mother announced to her that they had received a letter from Estaban saying that Great-grandfather Estaban was going to have a grand gala to introduce him formally to San Antonio society and he wished them to come for the weekend.

"Oh, it sounds like such fun, Mother. We're going to go, aren't we?" Bianca had excitedly asked her.

"Of course, we will, so pick out the gown you want to wear, for we won't have time to have new ones made, dear."

Bianca immediately left the parlor to start going through the armoire. The thought of going to San Antonio and attending a festive affair was a tonic she needed right now. There in San Antonio was the handsome Ramon Martinez. He could help her forget Larkin, she told herself.

But she wished that she could think of something that could fill the void left in her grandfather's life when Larkin had left the Circle K. She thought to herself that she wasn't going to assume anything where Larkin was concerned, for she might just find herself with a void in her life as Grandfather Kane was feeling right now.

She finally made a decision on the gown she would wear to the gala. The rich green taffeta with its low, scooped neckline and long, fitted sleeves would display her great-grandfather's magnificent gift. She also picked out a black-and-white striped gown, so she might wear the black onyx jewelry Ramon had given to her. She felt sure that he would be asking her to go to lunch with him while they were in the city. When she had decided on the ensemble she would wear to travel to San Antonio, she finally was ready to go to bed. Tonight she wasn't going to allow herself to think about Larkin. She was going to think about going to San Antonio and having herself a wonderful time for the weekend she was there.

She even had herself convinced that Ramon was just as handsome as Larkin. When he kissed her the next time she would not allow the cloud of Larkin's face to haunt her. No, she would surrender to Ramon's kisses with as much fervor as she had to Larkin's, she vowed.

The next morning she awakened in the highest of spirits and she greeted the new day with a cheerful air. She'd been foolish to mope around over Larkin, she decided.

Amanda was glad to see her daughter so happy, for she had noticed lately that she wasn't her usual vivacious self and she'd wondered why or what had caused it. She'd even suspected that it could be Larkin's departure from her father's ranch. This was enough to make her ask just how involved Bianca had become with the handsome young foreman.

Never had she regretted her decision to marry Tony!

The morning the Moreno family left Gonzales County to travel westward to San Antonio Rick Larkin was leaving Guadalupe County to ride eastward to return to Gonzales County. But their paths would not be passing, for they were traveling on different roads.

Larkin put his huge black horse into a fast pace, so he was to arrive back at the Circle K Ranch much sooner than the Moreno family arrived at their destination in late afternoon.

He received a most enthusiastic welcome from Estella. "Oh, Señor Larkin, it is so good to see you back!" He saw the happy look on her face.

"Good to be back, Estella," he told her as he walked on into the entranceway. She had begun to wonder if he would ever return to the ranch. She knew she was going to have to make some changes to the dinner she had planned.

When she led him into the parlor where Mark Kane was reading a journal, he exuberantly greeted his young foreman with a warm handshake and pat on Larkin's shoulder. "You're a damned good sight to see, Son!"

"You are, too, Señor Kane, and I've got to say, you're looking fit as a fiddle," Larkin told him, taking hold of his arm to lead him back to his chair.

Mark told Estella to bring them some hot coffee. "Me and Larkin have a lot of catching up to do. Been quiet around here with you gone, hasn't it, Estella?"

"Sí, señor—it has," she replied.

Mark motioned for him to sit down in the chair beside him and tell him everything that had happened to him since he'd left the Circle K.

"Well, sir, that's going to take a long time," Larkin smiled.

"Well, I've got all the time in the world and it's quite a while before dinner," Kane told him. He was also thinking this was the day that Bianca was leaving with her parents to go to San Antonio for the weekend. Kane was naturally wondering if this was to be a brief visit from Larkin and he would be returning to the ranch he'd inherited.

So he urged Larkin to start telling him about his

two weeks in Guadalupe County. Just his presence in Kane's parlor was enough to enliven it for him. The two weeks Larkin had been gone were enough to tell him how he'd come to rely on the young man and his company.

Rick Larkin had given a new meaning to his life and Kane would never forget that!

Thirty-seven

Larkin told him all about the ranch with its rolling countryside and fine pasturelands and the nice stone ranch house.

Kane listened intently as he spoke about Fred's sister, Frances, and how she was eager to get back to her home in Austin.

"Guess she is the only family Mr. Compton has and she had no objections to her brother's will."

"Well, I'm glad that there was no trouble for you on that score," Kane told him.

"Oh, no, sir. Everyone is very nice. Compton had himself a fine foreman and he's going to stay on. His housekeeper was very happy to hear I wanted her to stay on, too. Had a good talk with the lawyer and it seems Mr. Compton was a very thorough man and all things were in order."

They had been talking for over an hour and Larkin had finished two cups of coffee when he suddenly realized he'd left Raven at the hitching post instead of taking him to the barn after his long, hard ride. It made Larkin realize just how eager he had been to see Kane.

"Maybe I better get Raven comfortable in his stall and me settled in my cottage. I do have an invitation to Estella's good dinner, don't I?" he jested with Kane.

"Sure you do, for we've got more talking to do. Go take care of your horse and get yourself unpacked and I'll see you at dinnertime," Kane urged him.

"See you then," Larkin said as he moved swiftly toward the front door.

Once he had Raven in his stall he told the young Mexican boy working in the barn to give Raven a good feeding and watering. He made for the little cottage carrying the leather bag holding the belongings he'd taken when he left the Circle K.

Obviously, Estella or Juanita had cleaned his cottage while he was away, for everything was dusted and polished, and the bed was made up. It was when he was placing his clothing back in the drawers of the chest in the bedroom that he remembered the money he'd brought with him the day he'd encountered Harlin in the shack.

He'd had second thoughts about that money. It was not his to distribute as he wished. That money should rightfully go to Mona Lawson Kane, Derek's sister. After all, it was money he'd stolen from their father.

He had forgotten all about the money when Kane's lawyer had come to the ranch to bring the news about Fred Compton.

He pondered how he could possibly manage to see that Mona Kane got the money. That was going to take some thought. But right now it would have to wait.

He felt the need to wash his face and get a clean shirt on before he went back over to the main house to share dinner with Kane.

A stiff wind was blowing out of the north and there

was a chill to the air. Autumn would go and come as quickly as the summer was now just a memory, Larkin thought as he ambled across the ground toward Kane's courtyard. He went through the iron gate and up the flagstone pathway toward the front door. Estella had the house blazing with lamplight, and he could already smell the grand aroma of the food they would soon be eating.

Mark Kane was already in the parlor having himself a glass of his favorite whiskey and branch water. He offered Larkin some of the same. "A little celebrating for your return."

"Sounds good to me," he replied.

As they sipped on the whiskey and branch water, Larkin inquired about Harry Tully.

"Got no complaints about Tully. He's a damned hard worker," Kane told him. "But I've been missing those rides of ours. Bianca took me out once and that was good for me. Bianca is always a good tonic for me." Being a sly old fox, Kane watched Larkin's face as he mentioned Bianca's name.

But he got no inkling of anything, for Larkin's expression gave away nothing. What he did tell him was that they'd go for a ride tomorrow if he'd like.

"Damned right I would. Winter will be right around the bend and that plays hell with this old leg of mine. I get stiff as a poker!"

Neither of them had to be urged to come to the dining room when Estella announced dinner. Both of them ate like two hungry wolves, and a pleased smile was on Estella's face, for it told her how tasty her food was.

By the time they were ready to leave the table, Larkin had told him the name of his new ranch. Kane told him that he was glad to hear that he'd changed the name.

Later when they were in the parlor, Kane figured that there was no reason to put off asking Larkin just where this all left him. He dreaded hearing the answer, but he might as well face it.

Once they were settled in the cozy, overstuffed chairs in the parlor, he looked at Larkin and he asked him straight out.

"I can't answer you tonight, but I've been thinking about something that would work out for both of us. Now that I've been to Guadalupe County and have things squared away there, I just want to sort a few things in my own mind before I talk to you."

"Sounds fair to me, Larkin," the elderly man told him.

Later, Larkin lay in bed wondering if his idea could possibly work out. He just could not desert the old man. He meant too much to him. Besides, there was Bianca to think about.

As soon as he'd taken Kane out for a ride, he would go to Rancho Río to see Bianca. He had no intentions of delaying the trip over there one more day.

For the longest time, Larkin lay in the dark room staring up at the ceiling and thinking. The miles separating the Circle K Ranch from his ranch, Happy Valley, were not that many. For the next few months the demands on a foreman or a hired ranch hand would decrease. He had a good foreman and Harry Tully could end up being a good one, too. Larkin could foresee no problem if he spent some days each month with

Kane at Circle K Ranch to oversee things. He knew what it would mean to the old man if he could manage such a routine!

Tomorrow he would approach Kane about it and see how he felt about his idea.

Kane felt good being astraddle a horse again and Larkin there riding by his side. Kane had missed their camaraderie.

As they rode over the countryside and through the groves of trees, Larkin told him about what he had in mind.

"What would you think of me allowing Tully and his wife to take over the cottage so he could be close to the main house? I've bedrooms to spare when you come here for a few days, Larkin," Kane suggested.

"Well, let us try our little plan for a while and see how it works."

The elderly rancher was so touched by this young man's devotion to him. His granddaughter should not allow him to get away from her. He hoped she would be as determined to pursue the man she loved with as much fervor as her mother had when Tony Moreno had conquered her restless heart.

By the time they returned to the house, Kane was ready for lunch and then a good long rest during the afternoon.

Larkin took Kane's horse back to the barn where he told Tully of the plans he and Kane had just discussed. Tully was more than pleased to think about him and his wife living in the nice cottage and him taking charge as the foreman.

Tully realized that Larkin didn't have to do this and he sure admired him. Now he could understand why Kane held him in such high esteem. Larkin was giving him a golden opportunity and he was going to work his butt off to prove he was worthy of Larkin's faith in him.

Now that he'd had his talk with Tully and taken Kane on his ride, Larkin was going to do what he was most eager to do: go see Bianca Moreno.

He felt no need for lunch after the hearty breakfast he'd eaten. His hunger was for the sight of the beautiful señorita with her flashing black eyes.

So he rode as wild as the wind toward Rancho Río. Larkin had no way of knowing that Bianca and her family were gone. Kane had never got around to mentioning it to him.

A boyish eagerness churned in him when he guided Raven up the long drive toward the sprawling hacienda. But all that was completely shattered when he was met at the front door only to have the Mexican servant girl tell him that Señorita Bianca and her family had gone to San Antonio and would not be returning home until Sunday evening.

Larkin said nothing as he turned around to leave, but his high spirits were dampened. Disappointment washed over him as he mounted up on Raven to ride back to the Circle K Ranch.

At least she would not be gone for a whole week as she had when she went to San Antonio before. Sunday wasn't too far away, he told himself. At least he tried to comfort his impatient nature by thinking this.

Thirty-eight

The Saturday evening Larkin and Kane shared was a quiet one compared to the one being enjoyed by the Moreno family in the old gray stone mansion where candelabras and candlelights sparkled brilliantly throughout the house. The rooms were vivid with color as the ladies in their fancy gowns strolled around the parlor where cut-crystal vases held beautiful clusters of flowers and greenery.

The guests sipped the sparkling champagne old Estaban's servants served. He had not given a dinner party for a long time, but he still knew what it took to make it an evening everyone would remember.

Many a grand affair had taken place in this parlor and vast dining room over the years he'd lived here. He had personally seen to the foods to be served and the champagnes to be brought up from his cellar.

Invitations had been sent out to his friends and their wives over a week ago. Since his great-grandson had not had a chance to acquire friends in the city, old Estaban had suggested he invite his one friend, Ramon Martinez. Old Estaban was delighted that Tony, Amanda, and Bianca were coming in from Gonzales County. Bianca would surely add spice and spirit to the affair.

Old Estaban, looking debonair in his fine attire, had

Ignacio help him downstairs so he could survey the house to see that everything was exactly as he wanted it.

When he was satisfied that it was, he went into his parlor and had Ignacio pour him a glass of his favorite wine to sip on as he waited for Tony and Amanda to join him.

It was Bianca who came breezily swaying through the parlor door to greet him gaily, and the sight of her made the old man gasp. She was wearing the exquisite emeralds he'd given her, and her emerald-green gown was so gorgeous. She would be the center of attraction this night.

"Good evening, Great-grandfather! Now aren't you the dapper gentleman!" she told him as she rushed up to plant a kiss on his cheek.

"*Ah, bella!* It is a damnation for a lady to be as beautiful as you, *nieta!*" he declared with an admiring smile on his face.

Bianca laughed liltingly. "Oh, Great-grandfather! May I join you with a glass of wine?"

"Of course, *nieta.*"

She came to sit next to him by the hearth. "Everything looks so festive and grand, Great-grandfather. It is going to be a wonderful evening!"

"What makes it so perfect is that you are here. Seeing you tonight in that gown I know more than ever why I gave you those emeralds. *Madre de Dios,* if only your Great-grandmother could have lived to see you!"

Before she could make a comment, Tony and Amanda came into the parlor. Tony led his beautiful wife up to old Estaban and Bianca. He had already told Amanda how beautiful she looked in her gown the

279

color of the blue wildflowers that grew in their pasture-land. She'd piled her thick golden hair into an upswept hairdo that made her look very elegant, he thought, and she was wearing her sapphire earrings and neck-lace. He viewed his daughter in her rich emerald-green gown and the emeralds dangling from her ears and he thought what a lucky hombre he was, for he had a wife that was as beautiful as the day he'd first met her and she'd given him the most beautiful daughter a man could have.

Amanda greeted old Estaban with a warm, affection-ate kiss. "Look at him tonight, Tony!" She sought to tease him. "You look awfully spiffy tonight, Grandfather Estaban."

Tony stood there smiling at the two of them. He had always known the deep affection they shared. Old Esta-ban had been as stubborn in his own way as Mark Kane, for he had expected Tony to marry a nice girl of Mexican descent. But he'd defied tradition by marrying a gringo's daughter.

Amanda Kane had changed his thinking. Tony could see tonight that Estaban was still beguiled by her. No other young lady would have won his praise as Amanda had.

The younger Estaban made his entrance into the par-lor only a few minutes before the first guests started to arrive. Tony observed him for the next half hour as he was introduced and greeted his great-grandfather's friends and finally decided that his son had made the right choice to come to San Antonio. Ranch life would never have satisfied him as it had him.

Estaban would probably pick for his wife some nice young lady who would pose no challenge to him and be very agreeable to anything he wanted to do, Tony thought. But Tony knew he was going to miss the thrill of what it was like to love a real firebrand, like his mother.

Estaban liked this type of atmosphere and circulating through the elite gathering of wealthy older people, Tony observed. So he should do very well in his newly established law office here in San Antonio. He thought back to the years when he'd gone to Gonzales County for U.S. Marshal Brett Flannigan to help him break up a ring of rustlers. He'd first met Amanda and her father, Mark Kane, then, and he had given him the name of Tony Branigan. It was this mission for the marshal that had entwined his life with the Kanes.

But this sort of adventure would never have intrigued his son.

As Tony was enjoying his observations, so was Amanda. She saw how Bianca's eyes began to spark when young Ramon Martinez arrived. As soon as he had graciously greeted Estaban and his great-grandfather, he immediately rushed to go to Bianca who was talking to some of the guests.

Amanda watched the two before she finally turned her attentions back to her husband and the gentleman he was talking to. There was no question that Ramon was a very dashing, handsome young man with a very suave air about him. As Bianca's mother, she could not object to him being a suitor if Bianca wished him to be. She'd seen the beautiful onyx jewelry he'd given to her.

But as handsome and charming as Ramon Martinez was, Amanda still did not see him as the man to tame her beautiful Bianca's restless heart. Yet, she had only

281

to observe young Martinez to know that he adored Bianca.

Each time she glanced over in their direction, she saw that he was staying close by Bianca's side. He had been the one to escort her into the elegant dining room as the guests gathered to enjoy the grand feast.

It was a shattering blow to Ramon to find out that tonight was going to be the only time he would share with the beautiful Bianca, for they were to leave the next day. "Walk with me in the garden, Bianca," he was prompted to whisper in her ear after dinner.

She gave him a smile as the two of them slipped out the terrace doors into the darkness. He removed his coat, draping it around her shoulders. "I was hoping to have more time with you, Bianca! I've missed you." His dark eyes were devouring her as his hands were holding her wasplike waist. Bianca could not deny that Ramon with his hot-blooded Latin nature did not affect her.

She decided that she would allow herself to be freed of the spell Larkin had put on her. So she turned slightly to face Ramon to tell him that she also wished that they would be staying longer. But she never got to declare this to him, for Ramon could not restrain himself from pulling her into his arms and kissing her passionately. When he finally released her lips, he whispered huskily in her ear, "I'm madly in love with you, Bianca!"

There was no denying that his kiss had left her breathless and she gave out a gasp. "Oh, Ramon!"

"I am not taking this lightly, Bianca, and if you don't feel the same way, then tell me right now. I know I love you, but I also know that you are very young. Do I have a chance with you?"

Bianca didn't know what to say to him. "I am very young as you said, Ramon. I don't know about love. I like being with you as we are tonight."

Ramon looked on her lovely face and he saw the face of a sweet innocent virgin. It endeared her all the more to him, for he knew how protective her family had always been with her. Never would he have guessed that this beautiful girl with her angel face had known the ecstasy of wild passion and the desires of a man making love to her.

"That's enough for me to hope I have a chance to win your love, Bianca. I can't imagine any other woman ever being my wife now that I've known you. I want to marry you, Bianca." His black eyes danced over her face and his arms were still encircling her possessively.

"Oh, Ramon, you are so sweet. You—you are just going to have to be patient with me. I don't know whether I'm ready for marriage."

"I understand, Bianca. But I am a very patient man. All I know is I want to marry you and I just want you to know how sincere I am about it," he declared.

He turned her around so they could start back down the pathway to go back toward the terrace, for he certainly did not want to get in disfavor with her parents. He was well aware of the strict traditions of a family like the Morenos. He had been brought up with those same restricted traditions, but Bianca had been allowed more liberties than his five sisters, Ramon knew.

He figured that this had to come from the more liberal attitudes of her Anglo-American mother, Amanda Kane Moreno, and was probably why the very strict Mexican families in Gonzales County considered her to be rather wild and reckless.

This didn't matter to Ramon, for all he knew was she was the most exciting young lady he'd ever known, as well as the most beautiful. He certainly didn't mind being patient with her if that was what it would take to win her love and affections.

With his handsome dark looks and Latin charm, Ramon had found it easy to make his conquests with pretty señoritas, but to win Bianca's love was a challenge.

Before they moved out of the concealing shadows of the tall tropic plants, he rewarded himself with one more kiss from Bianca's luscious lips and she gave him no protest.

At least she had not told him no when he'd mentioned marriage to her, so he was feeling very encouraged.

By the time they had entered the parlor as discreetly as they'd left, he had no more moments with her alone. A short time later he bade her and all her family farewell as he prepared to depart from the old mansion.

Later, Bianca was to think about Ramon's proposal. She had not told him no, but neither had she told him yes. She could not have brought herself to do that. Though his kisses had made her feel a certain titillating sensation, it was not a fierceness such as Rick Larkin stirred within her, and this was what she could not sweep away later that night when she lay there in the darkness of the bedroom.

She could not imagine abandoning herself to the wild, reckless passion she'd shared with Larkin!

Thirty-nine

Bianca spent the longest time thinking about the evening. Most of the guests were older than her own parents. There had been no lively music and dancing as there had been at her tío Jeff's gay fiesta. Everyone seemed so very sedate and proper and all the ladies were so very demure and prim.

Ramon Martinez was the only exciting person she was with and his amorous kisses were the only thrilling thing that had happened. But it was a party for her brother, after all, and he seemed to enjoy himself very much and was confident that the affair was going to bring some of these people to his office for his legal counsel and services.

She lay staring at the crescent moon gleaming through her window because she was not all that sleepy. Now that the night was over, she wondered why she'd gotten so elated about coming to San Antonio for the weekend. She found herself ready to leave and go home.

She smiled as she thought about the reaction of her family if she told them that she had received her first proposal of marriage from her brother's friend, Ramon. Well, she was not going to announce it to them.

"You don't love Ramon Martinez," a pestering little voice taunted her.

She boldly argued with the voice that it was possible that she might just love Ramon and didn't realize it yet. But the voice stubbornly argued with her. It told her she couldn't love Ramon, for her heart already belonged to another. It admonished her for trying to fool herself. Rick Larkin was the man she loved.

She flung herself over on her side. "Oh, shut up!" she muttered as she tried to will herself to go to sleep.

But as strong-willed as she was, she saw those green eyes that seemed to devour her when they gazed down on her face. The distance did not seem to reduce the intense spell Larkin cast on her.

Because it was so late when she finally went to sleep, she did not wake up until long after the rest of her family had already had breakfast.

When the elderly Estaban asked about her absence at the table, Amanda laughed. "I fear she is like her mother. She isn't an early riser, Grandfather."

It became necessary for Amanda to go up to the room to rouse her, for Tony wanted to leave San Antonio so they could get started back to Rancho Río.

Bianca reluctantly crawled out of the bed and began to get dressed in the comfortable riding ensemble she'd worn for traveling to the city Friday morning. She did not bother styling her hair but just brushed it loose and free before she placed the felt flat-crowned hat atop her head.

When all her things were packed, she instructed the servant girl to see that her valises were brought downstairs. She then rushed out of the room and down the steps to join the rest of her family sitting in the parlor.

The minute she entered the parlor, her brother sought to tease her about being a sleepyhead.

"Oh, Lord, Estaban, at least I don't have to put up with this now that you are in San Antonio," she retorted.

The elderly Estaban and her parents roared with laughter. Tony explained to his grandfather that this was their usual way when the two of them were around each other.

"It's true, Great-grandfather! Keep him here around you, for he won't do that to you. It's me he likes to pester because I'm his younger sister," she laughed as she went over to her brother to plant a kiss on his cheek. "Truth is, I miss you, Estaban," she told her brother.

"Well, Bianca—that's sweet of you. I'll try to be nicer to you in the future I promise." Estaban told her.

Tony announced that they must leave. As soon as fond farewells were said, Tony, Amanda, and Bianca were in their carriage and ready to return to Gonzales County.

Long before sunset, they were on the familiar road leading them toward the ranch. "The days are growing shorter, *querida*," Tony observed. "Winter will be here before too long now. And it is so wonderful that we shall have our daughter with us this winter." He gave Bianca a wink of his eye.

She blushed. What a rogue he must have been when he was young, she thought as she gazed at his still-handsome face. As she sat there in the carriage it dawned on her what it was about Larkin that had attracted her from the first minute she'd seen him. It was that indomitable manner of his. He was the same kind of man as her father!

As she could see the red-tiled roof of the sprawling hacienda in the distance, Bianca was glad to be getting home. She thought that she would have liked to have known the grand lady she was named for — Bianca Alvarado — who had once lived in this house. She had to have been a fantastic lady.

She also had to admit that it was fun to go to a city like San Antonio for a brief stay but this was where her roots were. This was where she wanted to live. She loved this country with its beautiful wildflowers in the pastureland and the fine cattle roaming and grazing. She thrilled to see the new colts bred by the Thoroughbreds in her father's stables.

If she wanted to kick her heels up and dance, it would be at one of the fiestas the ranchers would give and not a sedate dinner party like the one she'd just experienced at her great-grandfather's mansion. She had always adored her great-grandfather, but it was her grandfather Kane she had worshipped since she was a tot.

Bianca unpacked her valises and hung her gowns in the armoire. She indulged herself in a leisurely bath before the dinner hour and felt most refreshed by the time she dressed for dinner.

Already, she was anticipating a ride on Rojo in the morning. To live in a city would cramp her life if she could not ride her horse as she loved to do.

She wore a simple gown of sprigged muslin and her hair was brushed to a glossy sheen when she joined her family for dinner that night. Obviously, her mother was feeling in the same casual mood, for she had dressed quite simply with her hair in a coil.

The three of them enjoyed a very relaxed dinner and evening. Each of them felt good to be back here at Rancho Río.

Later when Amanda and Tony were in their bedroom, she pointed this out to her husband. "Bianca would not be happy to live in San Antonio like Estaban seems to be."

"I've always known that it would be Bianca who had a love and passion for the land, Amanda. I can't deny that I would have liked our son to have that passion, but he doesn't and I don't fault him for that. Estaban has to follow his heart."

Tony had always been a most amorous lover and the years had not dimmed that. He took his wife in his arms to declare to her, "You see what you created years ago when you caught the eye of a Tony Branigan who came to Gonzales County to catch some thieves and rustlers for U.S. Marshal Flannigan and ended up losing his heart to a blue-eyed lady by the name of Amanda Kane."

"I could not help myself, Tony Branigan or Tony Moreno. The minute we met I knew that no man was ever going to do what you did to me."

"*Mi vida*, I've never had any regrets about anything in our lives. There can be no man happier than I am. You are my life—my everything!"

They mounted the stairs and, in the privacy of their bedroom, they recaptured the magic that had always been theirs.

After all these years, they were still lovers!

The next morning as soon as Bianca got up and dressed, she was ready to take a ride on Rojo, which she'd not done now for four days. She knew he was going to be more than ready to exercise his long, powerful legs.

She had hardly entered the kitchen for a quick cup of coffee, before she was leaving to dash out the back door to go to the barn.

Rojo gave his mistress an ardent greeting by bobbing his head up and down and swishing his black, silky tail to and fro.

"Ah, Rojo, you're glad to see me, aren't you, and I'm glad to see you. Ready to go for a ride? Well, that's exactly what we're going to do," she told him as they galloped down the road. By the time she slowed their pace, she was reining Rojo to go up the long drive at the Circle K Ranch.

She was sure her grandfather would be as happy to see her as Rojo had been. Grandfather Kane was her confidant, and she would reveal to him that she had had her first proposal of marriage while she was in San Antonio. She wondered what he would say about that!

When she had secured Rojo at the hitching post she went to the front door, not bothering to knock since she was sure Estella would be busy in the kitchen. In her hasty move through the door she found herself blocked by the firm, hard-muscled physique of Larkin.

She gasped surprise as she looked up to see his familiar face grinning down at her. "Well, good morning, *chiquita!*"

"Larkin! Wha—what are you doing here?" she stammered.

"I told your grandfather I'd be back. I always try to keep my promises, Bianca."

His eyes stared down at her and she thought that he was doing the same thing to her he always did when they stood this close together with his eyes devouring her. Damn, he could fluster her so!

"Are you back to stay or just a visit now that you have your own ranch?" she candidly asked him.

"I'm going to be here part of the time and at my own ranch the rest of the time. At least, we're going to try that and see how it works out."

"I see," she remarked.

"I rode over to Rancho Río to see you and found out you and your family had gone to San Antonio for the weekend," Larkin told her. Larkin found himself feeling a pang of jealousy, knowing that the young man he'd seen her with was in San Antonio. "I trust you had a nice time?"

"I had a very nice time, Larkin," she casually commented.

There was a serious air about him as they stood there together. "I would like to come over to see you before I have to leave to go back to Guadalupe County, Bianca," he told her.

"You can come over anytime you'd like, Larkin."

"Well, I've got to go now to do some things for your grandfather. You'll find him in the study." He took a couple of steps to leave her and then turned back around to look at her. "By the way, Bianca," he said, "I've missed you."

She smiled as she saw the taunting green fire in his eyes. "I've missed you too, Larkin," she responded softly.

Forty

"Well, you're back!" Mark greeted Bianca.

"Yes, I'm back and glad to be. Rojo misses me too much when I'm away too long, Grandfather. Besides, city life isn't for me," she declared as she sank down in the leather chair in front of his desk.

"Wouldn't be for me, either, honey. I'd feel smothered in a city."

"I saw Larkin just now. Guess you were glad he came back."

"Sure was. Can't tell you how long he'll stay, though. But at least he's here for now. He's a good man and an honest one, Bianca. He doesn't need to help me out for wages. He has his own ranch and it is a fine one, I'd say. But he's offered to come back to help me oversee the Circle K and we're going to let Tully be the foreman. He's done a good job since Larkin left."

She thought this a very generous offer on Larkin's part and was more than pleased to hear that he would be spending time at the ranch. It wasn't as if he was leaving the Circle K for good.

She told her grandfather all about the dinner party her great-grandfather had given to introduce Estaban to his friends in the city. A smile came to his face as he remarked, "I'm sure Estaban was feeling very happy about the affair."

"Oh, he was but it was very dull, Grandfather. I like our fiestas here on the ranch where there is music and dancing."

Kane laughed. "And so do I, honey. Those fancy parlor gatherings never did a thing to excite me. But then Jenny always told me I was a ring-tailed tooter when she was alive."

Bianca exploded with laughter. "I can believe you, Grandfather. And who knew you better than Grandma Jenny. I miss that sweet lady and was glad I got to know her for a few years before she died."

"So am I, Bianca, and I miss her more and more all the time. Most people thought my little Jenny was a quiet little lady and allowed me to rule the roost. Well, I'm here to tell you that wasn't the case. She could be a real hellcat when she got her feathers ruffled. She put as much into the ranch as I did and I took her advice a lot of times about things here on the ranch 'cause she was one smart lady."

"Ah, Grandfather—I hope one day I can say the same things about the man I marry. But I've got to have a particular man to look up to, for I've always had such paragons like you and my father. Both of you are strong and forceful and take no quarter from anyone. Yet I know both of you have a very gentle, tender side when you love someone. That is the kind of man I must have, Grandfather."

Kane nodded his head for he understood what she was trying to tell him. "Well, there is such a man out there. You've told me how you felt about Larkin. Do you not think he meets all these requirements?"

"Larkin perplexes me sometimes, Grandfather. I think I love him, but then I start having doubts." What she could not bring herself to tell him was that even though she'd surrendered to him and he'd told her how he adored her, he'd never asked her to marry him as Ramon Martinez had.

"There's also the possibility that you could perplex Larkin, Bianca. After all, until just recently he had nothing to offer a young lady like you."

By the time she left the Circle K, she found herself understanding things about Larkin and his reluctance to make her any promises.

Bianca was in a thoughtful mood as she rode back to Rancho Río. She recalled that Larkin had asked if he could come to the ranch to talk to her. Was he now ready to ask her to marry him? Did she dare hope that this was the reason?

She was so absorbed in these pleasant thoughts that she did not hear the rider coming out of the grove of pines. Before she could have spurred Rojo into a faster pace she faced a bearded man who was grabbing the reins from her.

She found herself being taken at a swift pace as they weaved through the thick grove of trees. They traveled at this swift pace for several minutes. Bianca was not sure if they were still on Circle K land or if they were now entering the Big D Ranch. All she did know was that they were traveling away from Rancho Río.

By now, she had recognized the grizzly face of her captor. He was the same Mexican who'd tried to abduct her back in the late spring. But this time Larkin was not there to rescue her.

There was no question in her mind that he intended

to seek his revenge against her for what her father had done to him. It was a revenge that had been smoldering for a long time, but Larkin had aborted his first attempt.

When they came out of the wooded area into a clearing, Bianca's eyes scanned all around her in hopes of seeing something that would tell her where she was. But the pastureland they were now riding over could have been either Circle K or Big D land.

Ortega had chanced upon the old deserted shack on the far end of the Big D Ranch after he'd escaped from jail and headed back to Gonzales County. He didn't see any of the cowhands from the ranch riding near the shack, so he'd felt safe to camp out there for the last three weeks.

He was driven by his obsession to have his revenge on Tony Moreno and it didn't matter to him how long it took to get the job done.

He had no doubt that the sheriff had warned Moreno about his escape, but somehow he seemed to keep missing the pretty little daughter of Tony Moreno. He had worked on the ranch long enough to know that it was her habit to go out riding almost daily.

Each day he'd failed to spy her riding around the countryside, his anger seethed more intensely. The only time he'd seen her was when she was accompanied by her parents and Ortega didn't choose to encounter Tony Moreno.

Ortega was no fool. He didn't want to be a dead man and he knew Moreno would not hesitate to kill him to protect the two beautiful ladies with him that day. Ortega had heard tales about Moreno being a pretty rough hombre when he was a young man. He never doubted for a minute that there was still some of that rugged character within him, recalling that day back in late spring.

It was the daughter he'd singled out to be his victim. Nothing would pain Moreno more. That old deserted shack was the perfect place to take her. No one could hear her screams.

All the time they had been riding she had not spoken a word to the ugly, bearded Mexican, but now she yelled out in as loud a voice as she could muster. "Hey, Ortega—you are going to be a dead man this time. My father will not waste time taking you to a sheriff. He will take care you himself!"

"Shut your mouth, bitch!" he growled. For such a tiny señorita she had a loud voice on her.

"I'll not shut my mouth, you *bastardo!* I'll scream my head off!" She was wondering why she had not yelled and screamed at him earlier to hopefully draw some attention.

Her sudden outburst had rattled Ortega and he'd slowed his pace. He turned around to look at her, a wicked gleam in his black beady eyes. He shook a warning finger at her as he snarled, "That mouth of yours is just going to give me more pleasure punishing you, señorita."

"And I will delight in watching your own punishment," she declared to him with her head held high and defiant as her black eyes challenged him.

The Mexican had to admire her boldness. She showed not one ounce of fear of him!

He suddenly pulled up on the reins of his horse and leaped down from his horse. Marching back to Rojo, he ordered her to get down, but she refused. Like a bolt of lightning she felt herself yanked down from the horse and she saw the dirty kerchief in his hand. She figured he was either going to gag her or cover her eyes so she took advantage of his huge hands releasing the reins of her horse. With her one free hand, she swatted Rojo's rump and ordered him to go home.

As if he understood exactly what she was telling him, Rojo broke away into a mad gallop like the demons of hell were after him.

For that little act, Bianca received a cruel slap across her face that caused her to stagger and fall on the ground. "You sonofabitch!" she angrily hissed.

"Get up!"

Not sure of what he might do next, she began to rise up slowly. As she suspected he would do, he rammed the filthy kerchief in her mouth. "Now I will be free of listening to that mouth of yours," he growled as he jerked her along beside him. She did everything she could think of to slow down their departure, walking with hesitating steps and mounting the horse with reluctance. She figured every moment she could delay Ortega would be to her advantage. He had no inkling of the foxy little game she was playing on him. Bianca knew the minute Rojo galloped up to the corrals without her on his back, her father would know that something was drastically wrong.

She did not need him to tell her that they were arriving at their destination when she spotted the run-down shack by the edge of the woods. Giving her a sharp blow on her back to urge her to move on ahead of him, she did so but as slowly as she possibly could.

The minute she walked through the door, she was overwhelmed by the musty odor. The first thing he did when they entered was to pull two narrow strips of leather from the back pocket of his pants. In the next few minutes she found herself rendered helpless as he bound her wrists and ankles. The only way she had to protest was to glare at his ugly face with her eyes.

Bianca shuddered when she looked out the windows and saw that the sun was setting and darkness would soon cover the countryside.

As Bianca had known he would do when Rojo came to the corral fence without her atop him, Moreno immediately mounted his horse and galloped as swiftly as he could toward the Circle K.

All the time he rode to the ranch, he was cussing himself for not demanding that she remain at the ranch and not take those daily rides of hers.

Rojo had not thrown her, Tony knew. The only time that would happen was on a stormy day if Bianca was foolhardy to take him out for a ride. No, this was something else! This was what scared the hell out of Tony Moreno!

He knew one thing, and that was if any harm had come to her he'd never forgive himself!

Forty-one

Tony knew he'd caused his father-in-law grave concern when he had inquired about Bianca and the hour at which she'd left the Circle K, but he was terribly worried about her.

"Damn, that was over an hour and a half ago, Tony!" Kane's voice cracked with the deep emotions he was flooded by at the thought of any harm coming to Bianca.

"I found no sign of her between the two ranches as I rode over here, and Rojo returned without her. Now that I know she left here that long ago, I'll be on my way. I've a searching party to organize at once." Mark Kane gave him a nod of his head, for no words would come. He saw the overwhelming desperation that was reflected in Tony's black eyes. It was the first time he'd seen Tony scared.

Neither Kane nor Tony Moreno was aware of Larkin entering the house. What he'd heard was enough to chill him. He immediately left the house and mounted up on Raven to ride out of the ranch.

There was less than an hour of daylight left to search the countryside and he was going to make full use of it. By now he knew the countryside quite well between the two ranches. It was not the open country he was concerned about, for Bianca rode Rojo at a fast pace over the clearings. He reined Raven toward the wooded area for some signs of . . . something.

The sun was setting fast and he was finding nothing to lead him to her. He felt a desperate panic akin to Tony Moreno's. Suddenly he spotted a brilliant object lying on the grass. Upon careful inspection, he found it to be a ribbon which was the same color Bianca had tied on her hair when he had had his brief encounter with her this afternoon.

Larkin didn't know which way to veer through the vast growth of trees, but he allowed instinct to guide him. Soon he came across the dainty black leather glove she'd dropped to lead someone to her.

Once again he reined Raven very slowly through the trees, for the sun was going lower and lower. Larkin knew that he was soon going to be leaving Circle K land and entering Big D property.

A carpet of golden leaves was beginning to layer the grounds of the woods, and Larkin knew that he was going in the right direction when he came across Bianca's other black leather glove.

Suddenly it was as if he needed no more clues to guide him to the woman he loved more than life itself. A primitive instinct pulled at him urging him to guide Raven in the direction which would lead him to that old secluded shack on the far side of the Big D.

Moreno had returned home and told his wife what had happened to cause him to ride out of Rancho Río so quickly. He wished that he could have said something to ease her pain and concern. "I'm going to get a searching party organized, Amanda, so don't hold dinner for me."

"Who could eat, *querida?*" But you get going and I will be here waiting and hoping," she told him.

Amanda's instincts told her that the culprit had to be the hired hand who'd tried to do harm to her once before. It wasn't as if they had not been warned by the sheriff he was on the loose. For a week Bianca had remained close to the house. Amanda could only excuse herself from not cautioning Bianca after they'd returned from San Antonio because the fear had faded. When the whim hit her, she obviously had left the ranch to ride Rojo over to see her grandfather.

She found nothing could content her to pass the time after Tony left. So she roamed the house like a caged animal and constantly moved back into the parlor where she could look out the wide windows in hopes of seeing Tony and his searching party returning. The sun was down now and the countryside was enveloped in darkness.

Larkin's pace had slowed, since the woods had become completely dark. All the time he guided Raven, he kept praying that he was going in the right direction.

Like Señor Moreno, he had a feeling that it was that damned Mexican, Ortega, who'd grabbed her as she was en route to Rancho Río.

Larkin's heart pounded harder and harder as he rode along. If he had harmed one hair on her beautiful head, Larkin swore under his breath that he'd take great pleasure in killing him.

Larkin was not familiar with this woods and he found himself suddenly coming out of it into a small clearing. He had some light from the hazy moon now, so his eyes immediately saw the familiar shack right ahead of him. It had always been the trail just to the south of the woods that he'd taken to go to the shack.

He tensed immediately when he saw the glow of dim light shining through one of the small windows. There was a brown horse tethered to an old gate post. The gate laid there on the ground.

He dismounted from Raven right then and moved stealthily across the ground toward the shack. He heard no sounds or screams and he was grateful for that.

But Bianca could not have screamed as frightened as she was, for the gag was still stuffed in her mouth as it had been for well over an hour. Her ankles were still bound as were her wrists. For almost an hour she had endured the debasing ogling of the Mexican as he sat in the old oak chair gulping whiskey and giving out lecherous sniggers as his beady eyes stared in her direction. The only defense she had was to close her eyes so she could not see the look of lust on his ugly face.

But to have to lie on that old cot with nothing clothing her but her divided riding skirt, since he'd taken a long-bladed knife to rip her jacket and tunic top, was horrible. His hand had fondled the nipples of her bared breasts for a few moments and he'd given out a roar of laughter. He'd turned to get a jug of whiskey and started to gulp it down and just stare at her.

In a husky, accented voice, he'd told her, "Before the night is over, señorita, I'm going to play with every little part of you! *Sí,* you can believe that it is going to be a long, long night, so I am in no hurry. I'll just sit here and enjoy a little whiskey before I start my pleasure with you."

He might have expected to see fear in those lovely black eyes of hers. Not that she wasn't petrified, but her eyes reflected the hate she felt for the animal sitting a few feet away from her.

She knew that it would be too much to hope for that he would drink so much whiskey that he would pass out and not be able to carry out his intentions. Her other prayer was that her father would come and find her.

Larkin did not try to step up on the plank front porch, for he remembered how the old rotten planks squeaked, so he moved around to the side of the shack to peer into the small window. What he saw was enough to chill his blood. Bianca's bare back told him all he needed to be told, but he could not miss the lustful eyes viewing her soft, satiny flesh. A madness consumed Larkin and, like a flash of lightning, he exploded into action. Swinging up on the porch with his pistols drawn and ready to fire, he slammed through the rickety old door like an angry, raging bull. As he pulled the trigger of both the pistols he cussed Ortega.

Ortega had only one split second to blink his eyes before the jug he was holding fell to the floor and a rivulet of whiskey streamed along the floor. Larkin didn't have to assure himself that the Mexican was dead for both pistols were aimed at Ortega's head.

He rushed to Bianca and removed the gag from her mouth, but she could not say anything for a moment. All she could do was look up at him with her black eyes beginning to mist with tears. His arms cradled her protectively and he whispered her name over and over

303

again. She answered him in a sobbing whisper, "Oh, Larkin! Larkin, I was so scared."

He felt the violent trembling of her body next to his and he released her only long enough to free her from the leather straps binding her ankles and wrists. But then, he took her in his arms again to just hold her. Neither of them said anything. It was only when her trembling eased that he released her long enough to remove his jacket and put it on her.

She was still sobbing when she moaned, "Oh, Larkin—he was terrible. He was an animal!"

He held her close to him and his hand brushed away the hair from her face as his lips kissed her cheek. "I know, honey. I know. But he'll never bother you again. I'm going to get you out of here, *chiquita*. I know your parents and grandfather will be very happy to know you are all right," he told her.

He buttoned the jacket for her, because her hands were still trembling, then scooped her up in his strong arms to carry her to the spot where he'd left Raven. When he had her hoisted on Raven's back, he leaped up behind her.

As they rode through the darkness, she suddenly murmured to him, "I think I love you, Larkin. I think I truly love you."

He leaned closer so that his cheek could gently caress her, for he'd seen the ugly redness on her face back at the shack. "Tell me that, *chiquita*, when you're not in a stunned state as you are now. I want nothing more than to hear you say those words, for I know I love you, Bianca Moreno."

She turned to look into his green eyes so warm with adoration. But she said nothing. Her small hands reached out to cover his holding the reins and guiding Raven toward Rancho Río.

When they emerged out of the woods, Bianca knew the men coming toward them were her father's search party. "You take me the rest of the way home, Larkin. I want you to take me—please!"

His deep voice soothed her. I'm taking you all the way home, *chiquita*." He felt her immediately relax and lean against his chest. Before they were joined by Moreno and his men, he whispered once more in her ear, "I love you, Bianca. I guess I have since the first moment I saw you."

There was no time to say more for a most anxious father was riding up to them with a very pleased look on his face when he saw his daughter atop Raven.

Just to have her there in the safe circle of his arms was enough to make Rick Larkin a happy man!

Part Four

Love's Legacy

Forty-two

Larkin's black stallion coming toward them with Bianca in the saddle in front of him was the most glorious sight Tony Moreno could have seen. He spurred his horse to go faster to meet them. When he joined them, he reached over to kiss her. "Oh, Bianca! Bianca, I thank God you are all right!" But as soon as he'd said it he had spied the ugly redness on her beautiful cheek. His eyes darted to Larkin, who was holding her so protectively in the circle of his arms.

In a faltering voice, Bianca told her father, "I—I just want Larkin to get me home, Father."

"I understand, dear. We're going right now." Once again he and Larkin exchanged glances and Tony didn't need for her to say anything else to him. He turned his horse around.

When they arrived back at Rancho Río, Tony quickly dismissed his men with a word of thanks for their efforts so he could join his daughter and Larkin. Larkin had dismounted and was helping Bianca off the horse. Once again, he took her up in his arms and was going toward the front entrance when Tony joined them.

The anxious Señora Moreno came out of the parlor

with tears streaming down her face to give her daughter an affectionate hug.

I think I should get Bianca right to her room, Señora," Larkin suggested, "and then I'll take out to get back to Circle K to tell your father she is home safe. He's a worried old fellow."

"Oh, of course, Larkin! Follow me," she stammered. Amanda led the entourage up the steps. Behind Larkin, Tony followed them up the steps.

Larkin followed the señora into the bedroom, and as she lit the lamp, Larkin gently placed Bianca on the bed. "I'll leave you now, *chiquita,* because your grandfather will be eager to hear from me. I'll see you tomorrow," he promised her.

"Thank you from the bottom of my heart, Larkin," Señora Moreno told him as she turned her attention back to her daughter.

As Larkin left the room, Tony Moreno followed him out of the room. He had to talk with Larkin to know just what kind of circumstances he had found his daughter in.

"God knows you've earned a hearty shot of brandy before you make that ride to Circle K."

They went downstairs to Tony's study, where Larkin told him how he had luckily found the ribbon Bianca had untied from her hair and dropped to the ground as Ortega was leading her into the thick woods. "I'd seen her about an hour earlier so I knew it was the ribbon. Then I came upon the gloves she'd dropped as a clue."

"It was Ortega, wasn't it?" Moreno asked, an incensed look on his face.

"Yes, Señor—it was Ortega, and I killed him. He was sitting there drinking his whiskey and enjoying humiliating Bianca. I guess you want me to tell you the whole truth, which is what I'm doing, but I don't intend to tell Señor Kane all this. I want to spare him. Ortega had apparently slapped her around from the look on one side of her face. I—I can't tell you if he had raped her, but I don't think so. I think I luckily got there in time."

"I am damned glad of that, Larkin. Now you get back to the Circle K and ease my father-in-law's mind and I'll take charge here. There is no way I can thank you for what you've done."

Larkin's green eyes met his boldly. "I did what I did because, you see, I love Bianca very much." He did not wait for Moreno to comment, for he had already set down the empty glass and was starting for the Circle K.

Moreno was left in the room to think about what Larkin had declared to him. He was to recall another young man who'd dared to be so bold to Mark Kane. It was himself he was reminded of. The truth was, he liked a man looking him straight in the eyes to make an honest declaration. And God knows, Larkin had proved his love for her!

Tony went upstairs to see his daughter and wife. Amanda told him that Bianca was having a bath. "She said she wants to wash all of Ortega's filth off her. Oh, Tony!"

"I know, *querida*." He soothed her and put his arm around her shoulder. "But I don't think she was raped if that is what you are afraid of. Larkin told me everything. Bianca will be just fine once she gets over the shock of what happened to her. And we've no cause to worry about Ortega anymore, Amanda. Larkin killed him. I'll be sending one of my men in shortly to inform the sheriff. I'm glad Larkin killed him, but I can't help wishing I had done it myself!" he declared to her.

"It's been an exhausting night for us, too," Amanda said. "We need to eat something and relax, Tony."

Tony was ready to relax, and as soon as they'd finished their light evening meal, he dozed off to sleep in his favorite overstuffed chair. So Amanda slipped out of the room and went upstairs to check on Bianca.

The warm bath and Celia's dinner tray had made her sleep, and Bianca wasn't aware that her mother had even entered the room.

Just as she had descended the stairs, John appeared at the front door to tell Amanda the sheriff had been informed of Ortega's death. "He said to tell Señor Moreno that it was good riddance and there'd be no charges against him or anyone who got the lucky shot in."

After John left, Amanda welcomed the sweet comfort of her own chair. She sat looking out the window, feeling so content that her daughter was safe at home. It had turned into a wonderful autumn night with a crescent moon glowing up in the dark sky.

The ordeal had taken its toll on her and she, too, drifted off to sleep.

At Rancho Río, Estella had not even announced dinner, for she knew Señor Kane was agonizing too much over the fate of her granddaughter to think of food.

It was Estella Larkin encountered first when he rushed through the door. "She's fine, Estella! Where's Mr. Kane?"

"In his study, señor, and God bless you! God bless you for finding her!" Estella stammered, feeling such joy she knew that she was surely going to burst into tears.

Larkin went into the study to announce Bianca's safe return to Kane.

Kane's ashen face began to flush with elation. "Oh, dear God, Larkin! Come here and tell me everything. Figured that you'd left to go hunt for her, too."

"Yes, sir, I was in the hall getting ready to come into the parlor when I heard what Señor Moreno was telling you so I just took out right then."

He told Mark Kane the general facts about Bianca's abduction, but as he'd promised Señor Moreno, he omitted telling him the degrading state he'd found his granddaughter in when he rescued her.

"She wasn't harmed, you said?" Tom Kane asked when Larkin had finished speaking.

"Oh, he'd slapped her and she might have a bruise on her face in the morning but certainly nothing that won't heal in a short time," Larkin told him.

"Well, Larkin, why don't you and me have us some supper. Hell, I'm hungry now! How about you telling Estella she's got two hungry men to feed?"

Larkin left the parlor to go to the kitchen, but as he'd suspected, Estella was already dipping the vegetables out of the pot and the roast was already resting on the huge platter. Larkin told her that Señor Kane was now ready to have dinner.

"I was sure he would be after you told him your good news, Señor Larkin. You and him come to the dining room and I will have it all on the table."

"Sounds good to me, Estella!" Larkin gave her a smile as he turned to go out of the kitchen.

Estella's tasty dinner cast a pleasant languor over both men. Larkin told Kane he was ready for the comfort of his bed and a good night's sleep.

Kane made the same confession to him, so Larkin assisted him to his bedroom, then went to his own quarters. As soon as he got undressed and sprawled out on his bed, he drifted off to sleep.

Forty-three

Moreno greeted Sheriff Duncan when he arrived at the ranch the next morning, and he told him all Ortega's debasing acts against Bianca. He felt it was in Larkin's best interest that he do so, for Larkin had saved Bianca from a fate worse than death.

"The shack where you'll find Ortega's body is on Big D property, Duncan. I'll ride with you over to my brother-in-law's if you'd like. I haven't had a chance to tell them about any of this."

When they arrived at the Big D Ranch they found Jeff and Mona still lingering at the breakfast table.

Tony told them of Bianca's ordeal, and he had only to look at Mona's eyes to see how upset she was. "Is Bianca all right, Tony?" she asked.

"She is just fine, Mona," he assured her in that slow drawl of his that convinced her to believe him. Tony had a way of calming and assuring a person. Her father had been the same way. When she was a little girl he was always there to soothe her fears away. She thought about him often.

"I'll ride with you, Sheriff," Jeff told them. "Damn if I hadn't forgotten about that old shack. I don't guess I've gone by there in ages. It's at the far end of the ranch and there's been no reason."

315

"It was probably the spot Ortega made for when he first broke out of jail since it's so isolated back there," Tony pointed out to him.

Sheriff Duncan made a point of reminding them both that Ortega knew the countryside. "He had worked at various ranches in the area, though he never lasted long at any of them."

Tony suggested that Jeff have one of his men bring along a flat-bedded wagon to carry the body out of the shack. "I'd figure you want to be rid of it as soon as possible, Jeff," Tony told him, noticing that his brother-in-law seemed to resent his suggestion.

Moreno had always known that Jeff felt a certain amount of resentment toward him; he could never decide if it was because he was a Mexican or because of a jealousy he felt due to the high esteem Mark Kane held him in.

An hour later the distasteful task of removing Ortega's body from the shack was done and Jeff's driver was following the sheriff back to town.

Tony bid his brother-in-law farewell as he prepared to return to Rancho Río and Jeff turned around to go into the house. Neither Tony nor the sheriff knew what it had been like for Jeff to see that old shack again. Years had gone by since he'd last been there and yet the memories were so vivid to him of he and Derek meeting there to conjure their madcap schemes.

He had finally accepted the truth about himself and what caused him to allow Derek to influence him back then, but damned if it didn't haunt him still! He wasn't a strong-willed man. His sister had inherited that from their father and that was why she and Tony Moreno

316

had been so perfectly matched. Neither he nor his sweet little Mona were of the calibre.

Jeff didn't want to go into the house to face Mona with all the questions she would be asking him, so he went toward the barn. He needed to be alone for a while.

Mona had to question what was happening to their peaceful countryside. She could not dismiss the feeling that everything had begun to change when her niece Bianca had returned home and at the same time Tony had hired on Rick Larkin a few weeks earlier. She was not faulting these two young people for anything, but it was most assuredly a strange coincidence!

Yesterday, Mona had received a very mysterious letter with a considerable amount of money in it. The note had been printed and not signed and was another thing linking to the past and her brother, Derek. The note had stated that the enclosed money was stolen by Derek Lawson and rightfully belonged to David Lawson but that since he was dead, it should now be hers. Who was this person who seemed to know all about their past?

She'd said nothing about this to Jeff yesterday, but this morning she had intended to do just that when the sheriff and Tony had arrived at the house.

It had made her more depressed to hear the horrible news about what had happened to Bianca. She could imagine how Amanda was feeling this morning! She sought the answer for all this madness that seemed to be sweeping over the three ranches whose borders joined.

And the uncanny resemblance of Rick Larkin to her dead brother, Derek.

She was going to insist to Jeff that the old shack be torn down immediately. Tonight, she and Jeff were going to have a talk whether he wanted to or not.

With that decision made, she got busy attending to her greenery and giving the cook instructions about what she wished prepared for their dinner. She also went in search of her daughter, who was very puzzled by her reserved mood earlier, Mona knew.

For the rest of the day she tried not to think about the ghosts of the past. But even the people she loved so dearly like Tony and Amanda were reminders of that past that had been haunting her so much lately.

It was good news to Larkin when he rode over to Rancho Río to see Bianca that Moreno had had a visit from the sheriff and no charges would be pressed against him for killing Ortega.

Moreno suggested they go inside the house to see Bianca. They were met in the hallway by Señora Moreno, who greeted them with a warm smile. Tony gave her an affectionate kiss on her cheek. "A good night's sleep did wonders for you, *querida.*"

"Thank you, Tony. I feel just fine." She turned her attention to Larkin. "I trust you got back to the ranch and got a well-deserved meal and rest, Señor Larkin?"

"I did, and so did your father, señora. His appetite returned immediately after I told him the good news about Bianca."

The three of them were laughing as Bianca came down the steps, her hand lifting the long flowing robe of dark-green velvet. The robe was heavier than the one she usually wore, but she had awakened feeling chilled. She thought about that long miserable hour she'd lain on the cot in the shack with her chest bare. She just could not seem to rid herself of that eerie chill.

All of them turned at the same moment to see her floating down the steps with her silky golden hair flowing around her shoulders. She looked very refreshed after her ordeal except for the bruise on the side of her face.

As she greeted them breezily, Larkin just stood watching her intensely, and anger flooded him to see the ugly bruise on her gorgeous face.

Bianca had never feared anything or anyone before in her life. Now she knew what fear was and what it could do to a person. She wondered if she could ever take off from the ranch astride Rojo to ride alone to her grandfather's ranch or over to the Big D to see her tío Jeff.

The thought of such a weakness in her repulsed the usual spirited Bianca Moreno! She had to fight it, she'd told herself this morning.

But she'd stood for a long moment looking out her window at the boundary of the walled courtyard garden and thought to herself that within this house the walls of the courtyard were the only places she would feel safe.

It didn't matter that Ortega was dead. Dear God, she'd seen Larkin kill him last night! The fear was more than that, and she could not fight it, for she didn't know what it was. Until she knew, she would be wearing a mask to hide the turmoil churning within her.

319

She still had some pride and dignity left after last night and she was determined to hold on to that dearly! But the humiliation and degradation she'd suffered by Ortega had left a scar that would last far longer than the ugly bruise on her lovely face.

Forty-four

Amanda and Tony made an excuse to leave the parlor to allow the young people to be alone.

Celia had brought a carafe of coffee to them. As soon as the servant girl had left, Larkin asked Bianca if she was all right.

"Thanks to you, Larkin! I can't bring myself to think about what would have happened if you hadn't come when you did. In fact, I've tried to blot out last night."

He wanted to tell her that the memory was always going to be there. He wanted to tell her to face it and go on, but he didn't. But he had to know if she was going to be repulsed by his touch. So he reached out to her to take her hand in his in a most gentle motion and his deep voice declared to her that it would fade in time.

She did not flinch, and that encouraged Larkin, but her black eyes had a haunted look in them as they met with his. She looked childlike and helpless and he loved her deeply. But she was not the carefree young lady she had been, Larkin sensed. The night before had had a tremendous impact on her!

"I'm not going to stay too much longer, Bianca, but I did want to ride over to see how you were. I'm going to try to get some things squared away for your grandfather before I leave to go back to Happy Valley Ranch."

"I like the new name, Larkin!" A smile came to her lovely face. "Tell me about it before you leave, Larkin— please."

He gave her a very visual description of it. He told her about the little fishing pond a short distance from the house and the verdant pastureland. "Raven seems to like it," Larkin laughed.

He went on to tell her of the fine house Fred Compton had built and the middle-aged housekeeper and cook, Ola. "Got myself a good foreman, too, Bianca, and that is why I've told your grandfather I would come back every few weeks to check over things for him, too. You see, I love that old fellow. Couldn't leave him at a drop of a hat."

Her dark eyes glowed. "Oh, Larkin, that's wonderful! Grandfather would have been devastated to know that you wouldn't be coming back to Circle K."

"Would you be devastated, too, Bianca?" he dared to ask her.

"Oh, Larkin, you devil! Of course I would!"

He was glad to hear that hint of the little firebrand he adored in her. "Good, then I will have to come back, won't I?"

"You certainly will!" There was a spark in her eyes that reassured Larkin that she was going to be just fine.

Reluctantly, he told her he had to be leaving now and bent down to give her a kiss on the cheek. Nothing could have pleased him more that she wanted him to kiss her.

In a deep husky voice filled with the depth of emotion he whispered to her, "Dear God, Bianca! I—I love you so very much!"

He wanted to place the magnificent ring that he was carrying in his vest pocket on her finger, but somehow he knew that it was not the right time.

The right time would soon come, he told himself.

The report Larkin gave Mark Kane on how he had found his granddaughter pleased him. He brought him up to date on things that he and Tully had discussed concerning the running of the ranch for the next three months. "Winter is on its way and you won't need so many hands. I told Tully to give three of them two weeks notice today."

"And am I to take it that you're preparing to leave in a few days, Larkin?" Kane asked him.

"Yes, sir, I'll be leaving day after tomorrow. I need to be getting back to Happy Valley. I love that ranch already. That's where I'll live and raise my family someday, sir."

"You do just that, Larkin, and you'll be a very happy man," Kane declared to him.

"Oh, I'm going to be a happy man, sir. You see, when you're born a bastard, it makes you want to prove something to yourself and show the world that you can do what the man who sired you didn't do. I'm not that kind of man, señor."

"I know that, Larkin. I've always known that," Kane told him. "Can I ask you if you know who your father was?"

"Yes, sir—I know. Someday, I shall tell you his name, for you knew him." Larkin could already see the

323

wheels turning in old Kane's head. An amused smile came to Larkin's face.

He told Kane he would be taking all his remaining belongings with him when he left this time so that Tully and his wife could move into the cottage.

It seemed that there was nothing Larkin had left undone to prepare the Circle K Ranch for the next few months. He'd even mentioned to Kane that he'd assigned one of the hands to cut wood to stack it for Estella's cookstove and all the fireplaces in the house.

Kane hoped that come the New Year he would be hearing that Bianca was going to be the mistress of Larkin's Happy Valley Ranch. There was no man who would be a more perfect match for his granddaughter, Kane was convinced.

He wondered if Larkin had any idea that Bianca thought herself in love with him. Now that he'd come to her rescue, surely she was more convinced about it.

The next day he and Kane had shared a late leisurely breakfast together. After that, he went out to the barn to have a last talk with Tully. He'd told him the cottage would be ready for him and his wife.

By early afternoon, he was ready to be on his way to Rancho Río. On the chance that the right moment would present itself, he slipped the ring into his vest pocket.

It was almost two in the afternoon when he galloped up the long drive of Rancho Río. When the Mexican servant girl ushered him through the front door, Bianca was just coming down the stairs.

"Larkin you did come back!" she greeted him with a

warm smile, as she spritely bounced down the steps.

"You never doubted that I would show up, now, did you?" he laughed.

"Well, I guess not." She came to the base of the stairs.

"You're looking much perkier!" he observed.

"I feel better after being lazy all day yesterday." She guided him into the parlor and he noticed that she was dressed in her black twill riding skirt.

"Were you planning to go for a ride?" His green eyes danced over her face as he questioned her.

"Only if you would go with me," she confessed to him. Last night she'd thought about this fear within her and had decided if Larkin did come over today she was going to ask him to go for a ride with her.

"Of course I'll take you for a ride if you feel up to it."

"Let me run upstairs to get my jacket and tell Mother where I'm going and I'll join you in just a minute," she declared as she hastily dashed out of the room. A smile creased his face. He should have known Bianca would come out of the ordeal she'd been through with flying colors.

A short time later, she was riding beside Larkin. He had no idea the apprehension she was fighting as they left the drive to enter the road running by the ranch.

He allowed her to take the lead as to where they would ride. It did surprise him that she went in the opposite direction from the one that led toward the Circle K and Big D.

"Thought we'd take in a different countryside today, Larkin. I didn't want to go over the same old trail."

Larkin put no importance to why she'd not wished to

go in the other direction.

For a while they put Rojo and Raven into a fast pace, and Larkin was glad to see her enjoying herself so much.

Suddenly, she slowed up on Rojo and laughed. "Ah, that felt good! It's exhilarating to ride like that."

Larkin had always appreciated what a fine figure she made astride her horse and he had known since the first time he'd seen her back at Rancho Río while he was working for her father that she was a skilled horsewoman. He'd figured that Tony Moreno had put her up on a horse when she was only a tot.

They were riding slowly now side by side. "You look beautiful today, Bianca, and I'm glad you suggested that we go for this ride. I'm leaving the first thing in the morning and I can't imagine a more perfect way to spend this last afternoon with you."

"Oh, Larkin, I shall miss you terribly!" she sighed.

"I want you to miss me terribly, Bianca Moreno, for that would tell me you feel about me as I feel about you," he told her, moving Raven a little closer to Rojo.

"Oh, Larkin—you know how I feel about you. You've known that for a long time."

He felt the moment had arrived. "Hold out your hand to me, Bianca." She did as he asked. The horses had both come to a halt as Larkin reached into his pocket to take out the ring and slip it on her finger. "Say you'll marry me, Bianca. Tell me you love me enough to become my wife."

She stared down at the magnificent ring. Her grandfather had told her that Larkin was a very wealthy young man now and she could certainly believe it as she looked at the ring. It had to have cost a huge amount of money.

She was bedazzled both by it and Larkin's proposal of marriage. "I—I don't know what to say, Larkin."

His green eyes looked at her with intensity. "Do you love me, *chiquita,* or is there some other man clouding your mind about that?"

"There is no other man, Larkin. I've never cared for any man as I do for you."

"And if I have my way that's the way it will always be. I want no other man to have you and love you as I have."

She bent forward so that his arms could encircle her as they sat there on their horses. His lips took hers in a kiss, but it proved to be awkward to hold her as he yearned to do.

But her eager response told him all he needed to know. "You do love me, Bianca, so don't try to deny it," he huskily whispered in her ear.

"Yes, Rick Larkin—I love you!"

"You will marry me?"

"Yes, I'll marry you!" she grinned.

"And we'll start the New Year as husband and wife. I'm not a patient man. We'll just have to make your parents understand that there will be no long engagement as they might want. I want my bride with me at Happy Valley by New Year's Day. Will you agree to that?"

She gave out a soft gale of laughter. "Oh, what a demanding man you're going to be, Larkin!"

The two of them rode back to Rancho Río at a slower pace. So many things had changed for Bianca. Larkin's proposal of marriage and the exquisite ring on her finger had made everything else pale.

327

All she could think about was how her parents would take the news about her accepting Larkin's proposal! Somehow, she felt that they would approve.

She knew her grandfather Kane would certainly approve!

Forty-five

They made a striking couple riding up the drive. The sandy-haired Larkin sat on his black stallion and by his side rode the beautiful Bianca in the saddle of her reddish-brown Thoroughbred. The look on their faces would have been enough to convince anyone that they were in love.

When they arrived at the house, Bianca recognized her tío Jeff's buggy at the entrance. "I hope Tía Mona came with Jeff," she said to Larkin. We can tell them of our plans to be married."

Larkin sensed that Jeff Kane wasn't too fond of him, but he gave Bianca no inkling that he wasn't looking forward to meeting up with him again.

After they had dismounted from their horses, Bianca reached for Larkin's hand as they went up the front steps. She turned her face toward him to tell him, "Oh, Larkin—I'm so happy! And I do love you!"

He bent over to give her a featherlike kiss on the cheek. "Not half as happy as I am, *chiquita.*"

Together they entered the parlor where her parents were sitting with Jeff Kane, his wife, Mona, and their young daughter.

Amanda Moreno had only to gaze upon her daughter's glowing face and see how possessively she was holding Larkin's hand to know that the young people were in love. She was thinking how they reminded her of herself and Tony at that age.

Bianca's impulsive nature would not allow her to wait any longer to announce her news and she rushed over to the settee where her mother and father were sitting to display the ring to them and announce, "Larkin has asked me to marry him and I've accepted."

There was a brief moment of silence, for neither Tony nor his wife were prepared. Tony made the first gesture toward Larkin as he walked over to clasp his hand. "I am very happy for the two of you," he said. "You don't have to be told by me or Bianca's mother how we feel about you. You've proven that to us already, Larkin."

Amanda moved toward Larkin, and declared in a soft voice, "I wish you and Bianca the same happiness Tony and I have known. May your new ranch, Happy Valley, be the happy home our Rancho Río has been for us."

"I thank you, Señor and Señora Moreno. Your blessing means very much to me," Larkin declared to them as Bianca came back to join him after displaying her ring to her tío Jeff and tía Mona.

"Heard about your inheriting the Compton Ranch," Jeff Kane remarked. "Guess one could consider you a lucky man, Larkin. A ranch and the prettiest girl in Gonzales County to be your bride all in a month's time."

Larkin detected the innuendo of sarcasm immediately, but he just smiled at Jeff and answered him in a cool, calm voice. "I'd say I was the luckiest man alive."

As quickly, he turned his eyes toward Bianca in an effort to ignore Jeff Kane. But Jeff was not ready to let it go at that, so he inquired about what his father was going to do without a foreman.

"He isn't. He will have Harry Tully tending to the ranch, and he is a good man. Worked it real well while I was up in Guadalupe County getting my own ranch in order. I happened to be lucky again, Mr. Kane, and I have a good foreman at Happy Valley. So I don't have to be there every day. I'm going to come back to Circle K from time to time to check on things for your father."

Jeff didn't like the arrogance of Larkin at all. It was obvious to him that Larkin didn't hold him in very high esteem. And so the feeling was mutual.

"Well, two ranches the size of Circle K plus the one you inherited is a hell of a lot of land to oversee. I know, because I did it for a few years," Jeff retorted defensively.

"I'll agree to that, but it's a matter of hiring good people. One man can't carry the load. I've got good people at Happy Valley and the Circle K has some good hands now." Larkin considered Jeff had invited these blunt remarks.

Indignation rose up in Jeff Kane. "Are you saying that the Circle K wasn't run right until you came on the scene, Larkin?"

"I'm saying, Mr. Kane, that there were some men not worth their salt and drawing wages they didn't earn."

Tony found himself admiring this young man who had the courage to speak the truth to his brother-in-law. Larkin's reasonings about the Circle K had been his for the last two or three years when he'd seen it going down and things not properly taken care of.

But he also considered that it was time he stepped into the conversation because he knew Jeff's temperament and he was obviously getting frenzied.

"Larkin, I think it would be grand for you to stay and have dinner with us. After all, we have something to celebrate, don't we?"

The atmosphere was not conducive for Larkin to want to remain, so he graciously refused the invitation by telling Tony, "I'm leaving very early in the morning, señor. I've got to get back to the Circle K. I've got my things to pack tonight so Tully can move into the cottage to be close to Señor Kane."

Larkin wasted no more time saying farewells to the Kanes and Morenos. Bianca went with him to the door. She was very perplexed by her uncle's attitude; she did not feel that he'd been very cordial to Larkin at all. This disturbed her.

Larkin did not deny himself a farewell kiss when they reached the front door. "Start making wedding plans, *chiquita*," his green eyes teased her, "because I'm anxious for our wedding to take place." He folded her into his strong arms and kissed her farewell.

She assured him that she was going to do just that. "It's going to be a long few weeks for me. That kiss will have to do until I get back, I guess," he grinned down at her.

"Well, just be sure you get back here that soon, Rick Larkin, or I'll come to Guadalupe County hunting you up," she teased him.

His hand went up to caress her cheek tenderly and he told her, "Take care of yourself, *chiquita*. I want nothing happening to the lady I love."

He reluctantly turned to leave and she remained at

the door until she finally saw him riding away on Raven. So much had happened in the last few hours that her head was whirling crazily. She would never have expected to be wearing Larkin's magnificent ring or had his proposal of marriage. She felt she needed to pinch herself to make sure this wasn't a madcap dream.

She was now engaged to be married soon to the man she loved. She found herself ready to explode with happiness. She wanted to get to her room to be in quiet solitude until she absorbed all this.

Right now she was not in the mood for chitchat with Tío Jeff and Tía Mona. Right now she couldn't say her tío Jeff was in her favor. And she didn't exactly find her aunt friendly and warm as she usually was. She was a little upset by their manner.

She wasn't thrilled that they were going to remain for dinner.

"Well, I'm going to have to ask you all to excuse me. I need to change clothes after taking the ride this afternoon with Larkin. I'll see you all at dinner," Bianca told all of them.

In her room she found the privacy she sought just to stare at the beautiful ring and think about Larkin. She was wishing that she could have a tray sent up to her room, but she knew that she couldn't so she immediately prepared to take a bath and get dressed.

At the appointed hour, she joined the rest of the family downstairs. Her tía Mona was asking questions about her terrible experience. There was no way for her to hide the ugly bruise on her face, but it made the evening miserable for Bianca. Amanda sensed her discomfort; it was a rare thing for her to get annoyed at her sister-in-law. However, by the time dinner was over, she found herself glad that Jeff suggested they get back to the Big D before the hour got any later.

Tony and his wife exchanged glances with each other as they began to amble slowly into the parlor. It was understandable to both of them why Bianca went directly upstairs.

Tony had always to look at the blue fire in Amanda's eyes to know when her temper was riled. Tonight it was most assuredly riled!

She sunk down in the chair. "Would you pour me a glass of wine, *querido?*" When he had handed the glass to her and went back over to the liquor chest to have a brandy for himself, she asked him, "What under God's green earth was the matter with the two of them, Tony?"

"Trying to figure that one out myself, Amanda. Mona wasn't her usual self today. At first I thought they had come here out of concern for Bianca, but they did not even ask about her or where she was when they arrived."

"And Jeff was hardly civil to Larkin. I felt sorry for him and Bianca after they'd announced their news to all of us. It's not hard to figure out Jeff and why Larkin is a thorn in his side. He's jealous of Larkin and his association with Father. It was Mona who really puzzled me. I think I may have that figured out but that still doesn't explain why she was so thoughtless and unfeeling, constantly prodding Bianca with her questions during dinner," Amanda declared.

There was something very exciting about Amanda when she was angry. Tony Moreno had found her intriguing back when she was a young hellcat about Bianca's age and she was just as enchanting now.

"I've got to remind myself to get you angry more often, Amanda *mia*. You are so exciting when you're furious," he grinned.

"Oh, Tony Moreno—you smooth-talking devil!" she softly laughed. "Age has not changed you."

"Sitting here with you tonight I feel as wonderfully young as I did in my twenties."

A part of the evening had not been too pleasant, but now both of the Morenos were feeling blissfully relaxed and happy once again.

Forty-six

Larkin was a happy man, for his ring was on Bianca's finger and she'd promised to marry him. Before the next year came in, she'd promised him that they would be married.

There was almost a boyish eagerness about him as he and Raven rode over the countryside and thought about all the things he wanted to do at the house before she arrived as his bride.

He had naturally been very happy that Mark Kane had seemed elated over the news. "Got to admit I thought the two of you made a good pair," he'd confessed to Larkin. "Always knew it would take a hell of a man to tame and brand that granddaughter of mine. I think you're the man, Larkin."

"Well, sir — I hope I'm the man! I've never loved a woman as I have Bianca. She's like no other woman I've ever met."

Larkin entered the archway of Happy Valley by midday. It was a good feeling for him to tell himself that this was his land and ranch. A couple of hands were milling around the corral and they greeted him as he rode up. He took off his saddlebags and turned over Raven to one of the hands as he went on into the house.

He gave Ola an enthusiastic greeting, which she returned. "Sure glad to see you back home, Mr. Larkin. Sure am!"

"Well, I'm glad to be back, Ola, and I've got some very good news. I'm going to be bringing a new bride here by the end of December. What do you think about that?"

"Well, sir—I think that that is real fine. Always wished that Mr. Compton had a nice lady. A man needs a good wife to make his life whole."

"You're absolutely right, Ola. I'm going to have myself the most beautiful wife in the whole state of Texas," he proudly boasted to her.

"Oh, I bet she is, Mr. Larkin and I can't wait to meet her." She hated to have to tell him anything that would dampen his high spirits, but it was necessary to do so now that he was back. She'd sought Miles Golden's advice and he'd suggested that she let Larkin handle the situation.

"Uhhh, Mr. Larkin, there's something I've got to talk to you about. We've got ourselves a guest."

"Oh, Mrs. Beaumont come to visit?" Larkin asked her.

"No sir—wish it was that nice lady. This lady arrived yesterday. Calls herself Cornelia Mason and says she's Fred Compton's daughter."

"Compton's daughter? Well, I don't give a damn whose daughter she is, she isn't staying here. Where

337

is this so-called lady?" As far as he knew, Compton had no daughter.

"Put her in the back guest bedroom, sir. Said she wasn't leaving until she had a chance to speak to you. Says she has proof that she was Mr. Compton's daughter and she's going to get her just dues."

Larkin told Ola to not worry about anything.

With his saddlebag flung over his shoulder, he marched down the hall to the guest room. Rapping firmly at the door, his deep voice called out to her. "Miss Mason, this is Rick Larkin and we've some talking to do."

Like a lazy cat, Cornelia moved to prop herself up on the pillows, giving a flippant fling to her black hair. She had no intentions of covering her voluptuous breasts that were displayed to advantage in the pale-pink gown she was wearing. "Come in, Mr. Larkin."

When the door opened and she saw the tall figure of Rick Larkin, his emerald-green eyes glaring down at her, Cornelia was hardly prepared to react as she did. He was a most handsome man.

Something told her that he was a most indomitable individual and that she would have to use all her wiles to get what she wanted. But she was prepared to do just that.

"I don't take very kindly to you invading my house and upsetting my housekeeper while I was away, Miss Mason. What is this claim that you were Fred's daughter? It's the first I've heard of it, and if you are, then you were illegitimate. So that gives you no claim to anything."

"I have a letter written by Mr. Compton himself,

but I can hardly get out of bed to get it with you standing there, can I?"

"Oh, come, Miss Mason—one would hardly figure you as being shy after you intruded into my house," Larkin smirked. "But I'll play your little game and turn around while you get out of bed." He turned around to face the wall.

With the sheer gown clinging to her voluptuous body, she got out of the bed and picked up her velvet reticule from a nearby chair. She crawled back into the bed and propped herself up against the pillows, draping her black hair over her shoulders. She knew she was a very sensuous-looking lady. Her good looks were an asset, she'd found.

"All right, Mr. Larkin, you can turn around now." In her hand she held the letter she was speaking about. She explained that it was written to her mother Agnes just a few months after she was born. "I think you will have to admit that Fred Compton knew my mother when you read this."

The signature looked like Compton's, but he hardly admitted to fatherhood. He had merely sent the woman a check and told her to do with it what she could because he would send no more.

He did not hand the letter back to Cornelia. Instead, he tucked it in his vest pocket, and when she began to protest, he quickly and firmly told her he had no intentions of returning it to her.

"Now, you let me tell you exactly what we're going to do, Miss Mason. In the morning I am riding to Austin to turn this over to my lawyer and I'm taking you to a hotel in Seguin until this is settled. You are not remaining here, is that understood?"

Cornelia did not answer him but sat there with a pretty pout on her rosy lips. She'd never met a man yet that she couldn't lure to her bed.

There was this afternoon and evening; that should give her plenty of time to change his thinking, she reasoned. He said nothing else as he turned to leave the room.

When Larkin had done his unpacking and prepared to go out to find Miles, he left the letter tucked in his vest pocket. When he left his bedroom, he went to seek out Ola and tell her what his plans were concerning their unexpected guest. "I'm going out now to see Miles, Ola, but I want you to keep an eye on her while I'm gone. She is not to be treated as a proper guest. Let her do for herself, and you can tell her I gave those orders."

It was going to give the housekeeper great pleasure not to have to trot after the demanding young lady as she'd done the last day.

An amused look was on Ola's face as she returned to her kitchen and Rick Larkin left the house. Once she was back in her kitchen she began to prepare the vegetables laid out on her worktable for the beef stew she was going to cook for dinner tonight.

Cornelia Mason soon came swaying into the kitchen. "Guess I'm ready for some of those eggs and ham like you fixed me yesterday morning, Ola. Lord, I sure need some of that black coffee," she drawled.

"Coffeepot's on the stove, miss, and I'm busy right now, so I'll have to leave you on your own to fix your breakfast," Ola casually informed her.

"Wha—what did you say?" Cornelia demanded to know.

340

"I think you heard me, Miss Mason. Coffeepot's on the stove."

Ola never looked up once from her peeling, but out of the corner of her eyes she saw the vexed Cornelia going slowly over to the cupboard.

With the cup of hot coffee in her hand, she started to leave the kitchen announcing to Ola, "Mr. Larkin is going to hear about this, Ola. I can assure you I'm going to tell him!"

"You do that, Miss Mason. He is the one who told me that I wasn't to wait on you. He doesn't consider you his guest," the housekeeper quickly retorted.

Cornelia Mason was to realize what kind of man she was dealing with and that it might not be all that easy to work her cunning wiles on him.

She took the cup of coffee and went in the parlor. This was certainly one grand house Fred Compton had built and furnished for himself. It was too bad her mother had not been a more clever lady and gotten him to marry her.

She went back to the kitchen to pour herself a second cup of coffee, but Ola had her vegetables chopped and her pot simmering, so she had left to attend to her household chores. Yesterday, she'd cleaned and dusted the parlor and dining room. Today was the day she did the same thing to Mr. Larkin's bedroom and the study.

But there was little to do in his bedroom since he had just returned this morning, so she immediately prepared to go on to the study. To her amazement when she entered the room with her feather duster and cloths, she spied Cornelia Mason there nosing around.

"Miss Mason, you looking for something, 'cause I don't think Mr. Larkin is going to take too kindly to you roaming in here. This is his private domain," Ola informed her.

"Mercy! This isn't a very hospitable place, I must say!" Cornelia gave a flippant shrug of her shoulder.

"Oh, I wouldn't say that, Miss Mason. Happy Valley is one of the nicest ranches I've ever worked at and Mr. Larkin is the same nice kind of gentleman as Mr. Compton. But there are private rooms in a house that a person isn't privy to wander around in."

"And I suppose you'll just have to tattletale to your Mr. Larkin?" Cornelia asked in a catty tone.

The housekeeper looked the haughty Cornelia straight in the eye and told her, "Never question for a moment that I'm completely loyal to Mr. Larkin." Now she understood why Mr. Larkin had told her to keep her eye on this Miss Mason. He probably suspected that she might try doing something like this.

"Well, I'll just get out of here so you can slave away at your household chores, Ola," Cornelia said with a smile on her face. "Don't work too hard, Ola."

Cornelia was not prepared for the housekeeper's arrogance in asking her, "And what do you do, Miss Mason, to earn your living?"

Whirling around, Cornelia left the room seething with anger, for nothing was going as she had planned it!

Rick Larkin was a cold-hearted bastard who seemed to be made of stone. Now that he had returned, his housekeeper had become very hateful toward her. Cornelia was feeling very shaky about her scheme so cleverly plotted when she'd heard about Compton's death a couple of weeks ago.

But she'd figured it was worth a try. It was not a man like Rick Larkin that she'd expected to encounter!

Forty-seven

Larkin sat in his dining room at Happy Valley Ranch with Cornelia Mason at the table with him. The dutiful Ola had told him everything that had happened during the afternoon while he'd been occupied with Miles Golden.

He'd had a good report from Miles. Knowing that Miles was aware of the arrival of Cornelia Mason he told him about his plans for the next day. "I'm personally seeing that she leaves this ranch in the morning with me. Not that she deserves it, but I'll get her lodging at the hotel at Seguin and then I'm going on to Austin to talk to Mrs. Frances Beaumont and the lawyer. I don't want the likes of her popping up at the ranch when I'm going to be bringing my new bride here."

"A gal like Cornelia can play all kinds of hell for a dude. Met a few like her I'm sorry to say. Glad to hear you're getting her out of here tomorrow," the foreman told him, then nodded his head and said it was good to have him back.

* * *

When the dinner hour was ending Larkin broke his silence to compliment Ola on her fine dinner. As he was pushing back in his chair and preparing to leave the table, he directed his remarks to Cornelia. "I'd advise you, Miss Mason, to get your packing done tonight and get a good night's sleep, for I will be leaving at the crack of dawn.

Ola had now left the dining room and they were alone together. "I am prepared to pay for your lodging in Seguin for two days and nights, Miss Mason, and then you are on your own unless my lawyer tells me different tomorrow."

"You are a hard man, Larkin! Very heartless!"

He was very aware of her effort to attract him with all her feminine charms this evening. The low, scooped neckline of her mauve-colored gown displayed the cleavage of her breasts. There was no denying that she was a damned attractive lady, but Larkin was not ignited with any desire to taste her lips or hold her curvaceous body, for he was still warmed by Bianca Moreno's kisses.

"Well, you are not Fred Compton's blood kin, Larkin!"

"Well, I don't know that you are either, Miss Mason!" he told her as he went to his study.

She flounced around to go to her bedroom. She found him the most perplexing man she'd ever met. Everything about him made her tingle, but he seemed so cold and aloof to all her obvious charms. This was enough to fluster Cornelia.

Why could she not charm him as she did other men?

Right now, she was feeling very unsure of herself

345

and she did not even have the letter written by Fred Compton in her possession. By the time she got to her room, she had convinced herself that she had to get the letter back from Larkin. She remembered that black leather vest he'd stuffed the letter into this afternoon.

It did not take her long to pack her belongings. She left out the outfit she would wear in the morning and she checked her reticule to see how much she still had in it after making the trip here. She still had a place to return to if this didn't work out in her favor. There was a gentleman who found her a lady he liked to do nice things for to make her happy and content.

But Cornelia was greedy and she was the first to admit it, especially after she'd seen this ranch and fine home that had belonged to Compton. She could envision what a life of ease she could enjoy if this was all hers instead of Larkin's.

She thought what high esteem Fred Compton must have felt for Rick Larkin to have willed this entire ranch to him! That was enough to tell her that he was a rare breed of a man!

She had her packing all done and she had undressed when she heard his heavy footsteps going down the hallway. She wondered if she could manage to slip into his bedroom once she knew he was sound asleep and search that vest of his to find the letter. What did she have to lose? She was no fool and she was a worldly young lady. She knew that once he consulted with his lawyer, he was going to be told that she proved to be no threat.

She decided to linger for a while in her bedroom and wait out the time it would take him to go to sleep. After all, he had ridden from Gonzales County and put in a busy day at the ranch after he'd returned, so he should be ready to go to sleep as soon as his head hit the pillow.

But Cornelia did not know Larkin. He did undress and crawl into his comfortable bed, but he did not drift immediately off to sleep, and the letter he'd kept was tucked under his pillow for safekeeping.

Larkin was well aware of the type of woman he was dealing with and he would put nothing past her. After a half hour had gone by, he was feeling himself drifting off to sleep and he didn't try to fight it. If she did come through the door, all she was going to find was him sleeping. She could search the drawers of the chest and the desk, she'd not find the letter. He knew he'd outfoxed her, but he had also seen the stunned look on her face when she realized he was keeping the letter, so it told him how much value she put on its importance.

When he was just about to go off to sleep, something made him become alert, but he didn't move a muscle and continued to lie very still. A bright autumn moon played through the windows. Lying on his side, he had a good view of the figure noiselessly moving like a cat across the room to where he'd flung his clothing on the chair. She knew exactly the article of clothing she was looking for. First, she'd picked up his pants and then his shirt. It was the vest she was searching for. He lay there amused as she examined the pockets before she angrily tossed it back in the chair.

His green eyes followed her shadowy figure as it moved over to his desk and surveyed the top of it. She picked up a paper laying there thinking that it might be her letter, but the moonlight shining through the window told her it wasn't when she walked over closer to the window to examine it.

By now Larkin was weary of the game and was ready to get some sleep, so he finally spoke up. "All right, Cornelia, get yourself out of my room so I can get some sleep. You're not going to find what you're hunting for, I can assure you of that. I expected that you might try something like this."

She said not a word as she left the room, for once again he had outsmarted her. Damn him, she thought as she went back to her room and slammed the door angrily! Never had she met someone like Larkin.

There was nothing for her to do but go to bed and get some sleep. So that was that she did.

It seemed like moments before a sharp rapping was sounding in her room. "Get up, Cornelia. I'm going to be leaving in an hour and so are you, ready or not!"

She grimaced as she flung away the covers. She didn't doubt for a minute that if she was standing in her undergarments, he'd come barging through that door and drag her out to the buggy.

She made a point of being dressed long before an hour was up and she and her valise were in the parlor. She went directly to the kitchen to get a cup of coffee for herself and said not a word to Ola. With the cup in her hand, she went into the parlor to wait for Larkin.

Ola had to smile to herself as she watched her. Larkin had already had a couple of cups of coffee, but he'd taken no time for one of her hearty breakfasts. He'd only helped himself to one of her biscuits and spread it with some of the berry jam. Then he'd left to go to the barn to get the buggy ready for their departure. Shortly, he was returning to the house and was surprised to find Cornelia sitting in the parlor sipping on her second cup of coffee. Her fancy bonnet matched the berry-colored gown she was wearing. Draped over the back of the chair she was sitting in was a matching cape trimmed in black braid. Larkin figured to have such fancy attire she had not been hurting for money.

There was an expressionless look on her face as she turned to glance in his direciton.

"I'm ready whenever you are, Larkin," she told him.

"I'll be ready as soon as I have a word with Ola, Cornelia," he told her, disappearing from the parlor but returning a few moments later.

"Let's go, Cornelia," he called out to her, but when she started to pick up her valise, he went over to take it out of her hand. "I'll get that."

"Well, Larkin—guess you aren't exactly heartless after all," she smirked.

"Not completely, Cornelia."

It took him less than an hour to get to Seguin and get her a room at the Cattleman's Hotel. He paid up three days' rent instead of two days as he'd planned to do.

He wasted no more time in Seguin, for he was anxious to get on his way to Austin. Had he allowed Cornelia to stay at the ranch while he traveled to Austin to talk with the lawyer and Francis Beaumont it would have been a swifter trip atop Raven, but he wanted that woman away from the ranch.

It was to Francis Beaumont's house he went first

when he arrived in Austin, and she was pleased to see him standing at her front door.

As soon as they were comfortably seated in her parlor, she had her housekeeper bring them a pot of tea and some spice cakes. Larkin didn't have the heart to tell her he detested tea, so he slowly sipped it as they talked.

"I needed to talk to you, Mrs. Beaumont. I've had a young woman show up at the ranch claiming to be Fred's daughter. Her name is Cornelia Mason and I have a letter I want you to read." He took out the letter from his pocket.

Francis took but a minute to read the letter before she began to laugh. "Dear God Almighty—is Agnes Mason never going to give up on poor Fred? Ignore it, Larkin, and kick the girl off the ranch. Her mother hounded Fred to marry her and he wouldn't. Now, it seems the daughter is determined to do the same to you."

"I've already gotten her off the ranch. I put her up at a hotel in Seguin for three days."

"Well, I'd say that you were most generous to do that. It's more than she deserved, for she isn't Fred's daughter, Larkin. Fred couldn't stand Agnes Mason, but she was one of those pushy ladies who could not take no for an answer. My brother was a gentleman who didn't like being nasty to people. He obviously sent her some money to help her out, but he certainly didn't father any child of hers, and her daughter could never prove that, I'm sure."

"Fred assumed no responsibility in his letter and I told Cornelia that. But it was important to me to know your feelings," Larkin told her as he took back the letter from her.

"Well, Larkin—my advice to you would have been to kick her off the ranch as you've already seen fit to do. The other thing I would say is save yourself the fee of consulting with your lawyer. You don't need his advice. You have nothing to concern yourself about."

"Well, thank you, Mrs. Beaumont. I think I'll do just that. I'll forget about the lawyer and get back home."

"Well, I'm glad you came to talk to me and I got to see you. Is everything going all right at the ranch other than this little fiasco?"

"Just fine, Mrs. Beaumont. I'm going to be a married man by the first of the year and that's why I wanted to get this thing straightened up before I brought Bianca to Happy Valley. I wanted nothing marring that."

"Well, congratulations, Larkin! That was the one thing Fred didn't do. I always wanted him to find himself a good wife, but it just didn't happen." She had a sad look on her face, but it did not remain there long. "You will end up being a happier man, Larkin, than Fred was. And I shall be most eager to meet this young lady."

"Happy Valley will always welcome a visit from you, Mrs. Beaumont, and I thank you for your advice," Larkin told her.

"I'm happy to be able to help you, Rick, and don't worry about anything where Agnes Mason or her daughter are concerned. Just be sure you warn your little bride so she will not be upset should this Cornelia decide to reappear," she warned him as he prepared to leave.

"I'll remember all you've said, Mrs. Beaumont," he told her as he bid her farewell.

Larkin started back toward Happy Valley Ranch early enough in the afternoon that he'd get there before sunset. Mrs. Beaumont had eased any concerns about Cornelia Mason.

Forty-eight

By the time the sun was setting, Larkin was riding into Happy Valley convinced that he could wash his hands of Cornelia Mason. He could tell when he entered the house and Ola greeted him in such a cheerful mood that she had been happy to be rid of the obnoxious young woman.

"Thought you might be ready for a big meal after all your traveling today, Señor Larkin. Baked a big fat hen for you with a lot of cornbread stuffing. How does that sound?"

"I'll swear I can't think of anything I'd rather have. I think I'd better marry *you*. I want to keep you around to cook all these good meals for me," he teased her.

A blush came to the housekeeper's face. "Oh, Señor Larkin—be off with you! You know I'm going to cook for you as long as you want me, and I just hope I'll please the young mistress of the house."

"You will, Ola. I have no doubt about that. But I'm going to hold you to what you just said," he told her as he went out of the room.

The topic of conversation around Rancho Río centered around her marriage to Larkin. Amanda had

353

made a point of having a talk with her daughter the day after she and Larkin had announced their intentions to be married.

"I apologize to you, Bianca, for my brother's behavior, as well as Mona's. You know I love them both dearly. We could not understand their attitude last night," she'd told Bianca.

"Nor could I, and I don't have to tell you how I feel about Tío Jeff and Tía Mona, but they don't seem to like Larkin. That does not matter to me, because I love him."

"Well, that is all that is important *niña*. I felt exactly the same way when I fell in love with your father, and I should remind you that your grandfather did not exactly like Mexicans. We shall plan you a beautiful wedding and we will go into San Antonio to shop for a beautiful wedding gown. Would you like the wedding to be right here at Rancho Río?"

"I would love it, and I think Larkin would, too. I would want only our family present, Mother."

Amanda assured her that it would be that way, but she reminded Bianca that surely her great-grandfather and her brother would be there for the gala occasion.

"Oh, that goes without saying!"

Amanda was finding herself becoming very excited about planning her first wedding in the family. She certainly wanted everything to be perfect.

"Then we go to San Antonio next week, Bianca. On our way back home we will stop by Larkin's ranch and tell him of our plans."

This was enough to give Bianca something to look forward to. She found that she could not bring herself to go for a ride on Rojo by herself, so she had lingered around the house. But she swore that she was going to force herself to ride Rojo tomorrow, for she could not make herself a prisoner, she'd told herself. Besides, she was anxious to tell her grandfather about her impending marriage to Larkin and show him the beautiful ring she was wearing on her finger.

She also wanted to go over to the Big D Ranch, for she needed to have a talk with her aunt and uncle. So she went to bed that night making a vow to herself that she was going to overcome her fear by going not only to the Circle K but to the Big D Ranch, which was farther away.

The next morning after she dressed in her riding ensemble, she rushed down the steps to the kitchen to have a quick cup of the steaming coffee before she went out to the barn to get Rojo ready.

A few minutes later she was dashing toward the barn. Rojo was anxious to take a jaunt across the countryside. This was enough to make Bianca forget the fears welling deep inside her.

They galloped on by the archway of the Circle K Ranch and Bianca was feeling no fear. Soon she found herself entering the Big D Ranch, and she told herself proudly that she had done it! She had ridden over the countryside alone as she used to, without the fear that had been gnawing at her since the incident with Ortega.

With high spirits she dismounted from Rojo and entered the house. The young servant girl ushered her into the room that her tía Mona called her sun room, because of all the windows in the room and the abundant flow of sunshine through them.

Mona was pleasantly surprised to see her niece and

greeted her, setting down the watering can that she'd been using to water all her greenery.

"Well, I thought I'd pay a visit to you and Grandfather today before I got too busy with my wedding plans."

"My goodness, dear—is it to be so soon? I assumed that you would not wed Larkin for a few more months since you just accepted his proposal," Mona said with a skeptical look on her face.

"We don't want a long engagement, Tía Mona. He wants us to start the New Year off as husband and wife." Bianca could see that she was not pleased by this news.

"Oh, that is only about two months away now, Bianca. How—how can you and your mother do all the things that will be necessary for you to be married so hastily?"

Bianca laughed. "We'll manage, Tía Mona. It won't be a large wedding, for I don't want that and I know that Larkin doesn't, either."

Mona wore a sad look on her face. "Oh, Bianca dear—I just wish that you weren't rushing so headlong into a marriage to a young man you've known such a short time."

Bianca minced no words by asking her aunt why she didn't like Larkin.

"I—I don't dislike him, Bianca. I truly don't know enough about him. I guess you could say that is the problem, that none of us know enough about him or his background. A person's background can be very important, Bianca," Mona pointed out to her.

"I'll admit that I've not known Larkin long, but it doesn't take long to fall in love, Tía Mona. But since

356

Larkin came here after working a few years for Fred Compton and Compton left him his whole ranch, one would have to assume that Señor Compton had a high opinion of him," she replied, a hint of haughtiness in her voice.

"I would have to say you are right about that, Bianca, but I also have to ask why, if Larkin had a good job on the Compton Ranch, he left it to come here. Did you know that he came to the Big D Ranch before he rode on to Rancho Río?"

"No, I did not know that," Bianca confessed.

"Well, he did, but your uncle told him that he needed no more hired hands so he went on over to the Rancho Río and your father hired him," Mona told her.

Bianca shook her head and smiled. "I don't see what you're getting at and why it would really matter, Tía Mona."

"Because, Bianca, the young man had to have some reason for coming to Gonzales County when he had such a good job and a fine rancher as Compton to work for. You think about that, dear."

"Well, I have no doubt that Larkin would not hesitate to tell me if I came right out and asked him, Tía Mona," she remarked flippantly. "Perhaps I shall do that when he comes back. Then I will be able to ease your mind about him, I'm sure."

Mona's dark eyes warmed as she looked at her pretty niece. "I only want the best for you, Bianca. You must know how dearly you're loved by your uncle and me."

"I know, Tía Mona, and I love both of you, too," Bianca told her as she prepared to leave to go next to pay a visit to her grandfather.

"I'll let you know when the wedding's to be, Tía Mona," she promised as she went out the door.

Once again she and Rojo were galloping across the countryside separating the Big D land from the Circle K Ranch.

Her grandfather greeted her news about the wedding more enthusiastically than her aunt had. He looked at the ring on her dainty finger. "Just about as beautiful as you are, little one, but not quite."

She told him about their plans to be married before the year had ended. Kane remarked that this would just about make her the same age her mother was when she'd married Tony Moreno. "Got to admit that I wondered if she was ready for marriage, for she was a reckless little madcap like you, Bianca."

"Now, Grandfather . . ."

"Don't you try to kid me, Bianca. I heard from your parents about all those broken-hearted Yankees back East and I got to admit I'm glad you've settled for a Texas man."

"I'm glad you approve of Larkin, Grandfather," she told him, hugging his neck. "I don't think Tío Jeff or Tía Mona do, but they'll change their mind. I'm going to see to that."

"And just how are you going to do that, niña?"

"Ah, I can't tell you that right now but I will!"

"I've no doubt that you will do just that. I can't figure out any reason why Mona and Jeff wouldn't like Rick Larkin in the first place," he drawled.

"Tía Mona doesn't think I know enough about his background and feels none of us do," Bianca commented.

"That doesn't sound like Mona!" he barked. "I judge

a man by his actions. Mona should be the first to know that. Her older brother, Derek, came from two of the finest people me and Jenny ever knew. David Lawson and his dear wife were our best friends, but they had a son that wasn't worth the powder it would take to blow him to hell!"

He patted her hand and assured her to not worry about what the two of them thought.

She rode away from the Circle K Ranch convinced that there was an awful lot of her Grandfather Kane bred in her.

She thought and felt about things as he did.

Forty-nine

Tony Moreno was feeling like an outcast a lot of the time the next week as his wife and daughter discussed things about her wedding that he seemed not to share a part of.

Amanda had been delighted to receive Estaban's letter telling them that he would be coming to Rancho Río at the end of the week for a couple of days. "This is wonderful, Tony," she'd told her husband, "for Bianca and I shall return to San Antonio with him and spend the week shopping for a wedding gown for Bianca and other things. You could come to bring us back home."

It was settled that Bianca and her mother would go to the city with Estaban. By the time Estaban arrived at the Rancho Río, his mother and sister had made the plans for the wedding to be held in their parlor to be followed by a reception for their guests in the spacious dining room. Bianca had insisted that since Larkin had no family, she wanted only her family in Gonzales County and her great-grandfather and brother to be present.

Amanda respected her wishes and did not insist on any of their rancher friends attending the ceremony.

Bianca had arranged with her mother that it would be a late-morning wedding, so the luncheon reception would be over in time for the newlyweds to reach Happy Valley, where they would spend their honeymoon.

The afternoon Rancho Río was expecting Estaban's arrival, the house permeated with the aroma of his favorite meal of roast beef and herbed vegetables. Celia had baked his favorite juicy cherry pie.

Amanda had gone to refresh herself earlier than usual so she would be ready to greet her son when he arrived home. She wondered why Tony had not come to the house yet, since he knew Estaban would be arriving any time.

As soon as she got downstairs she saw Tony being supported by two of the Mexican workers coming through the door.

"Dear Lord, Tony—what happened to you?" she asked, deep concern etching her face.

"Oh, I got a good sprain, I think, Amanda." He instructed the two men to get him on up the stairs and Amanda heard a muffled moan of discomfort coming from Tony. She hastily moved ahead of them and went down the hallway to guide them to the bedroom, opening the door for them.

Amanda graciously thanked the two men after Tony was situated on the bed. She removed his boot so she could take a look at his foot. It did appear to be a sprain to her and the swelling had already started.

She smiled down at him. "You're going to be having your dinner on a tray, so you might as well get that jacket off and I'm going to get your foot propped up on a pillow. How did it happen, Tony?"

361

"I don't want to talk about it, Amanda, for I'm too angry with myself. Here Estaban is due in any minute and I've had a stupid accident," he grumbled.

"Tony Moreno, you quit acting like a sulking little boy and tell me how it happened," Amanda demanded.

"I fell over a damned bucket and was looking back to talk to one of the men. Tried to get up and couldn't put any weight on it. So there you have it, *querida*."

"Oh, Tony—what a shame! Well, you just lie still while I get some things I need to get that foot doctored." Before he could make any objections, she was gone from the room.

She stopped only long enough by Bianca's room to tell her what had happened and ask her to go down to the parlor as soon as she was through dressing. "I cannot possibly leave him like this by Sunday, Bianca. I know you will understand," Amanda told her.

"Of course I do, Mother, but there is no reason why I couldn't go on to San Antonio with Estaban and then maybe you could join me there in a few days," Bianca told her.

"We'll talk about it, Bianca. Right now I've got to attend to your father."

As her mother had requested, she lingered no longer in her room but went on downstairs. She did not have long to wait before her brother arrived.

"Welcome home, Estaban," she called out to him as he entered the parlor. She quickly explained to him why their parents were not there.

Estaban asked how Tony's accident had happened,

and Bianca told him. "A bucket?" he inquired with a slight grin on his face. "I can't imagine that."

Now that she had told him the unpleasant news, Bianca thought, she would announce her happy news. With a bright twinkle in her dark eyes, she told him. "There's going to be a wedding, Estaban!" She was about to extend her hand out for him to see her ring, but his next words stopped her. In a hesitating voice he asked her, "How could you know that?" The only one guilty of passing the news on was his great-grandfather.

"How could I know it? Now, that's a dumb question, Estaban. I ought to know about my own wedding, shouldn't I? I'm the one getting married, my dear brother!"

"You, Bianca? But—but so am I, and that was the reason I came home this weekend to tell my family. I've found a most beautiful girl I'm madly in love with. Her name is Rosita Armendez and her family has known Great-grandfather for years. Needless to say, he is overjoyed. We're going to be married the first week of February."

"Well, congratulations, Estaban! But I'm going to beat you, because I'm going to be married the last week of December!"

Estaban laughed. "Should know you'd manage to do that, Bianca, and who is this lucky fellow you're going to marry?"

"Rick Larkin."

"Larkin? Larkin the hired hand who worked for Father before he went to work for Grandfather Kane?"

"That's right, Estaban! What's the matter? You

have a strange look on your face," she grinned over at him.

"I guess I find it hard to picture you as the wife of a ranch foreman, Bianca. You've led a different lifestyle from the ordinary rancher's daughter." He couldn't believe that his parents would give their approval to Bianca marrying Rick Larkin.

"Larkin doesn't have to work as anyone's foreman now, Estaban. He has inherited his own fine ranch over in Guadalupe County." She went on to explain to him what had happened in the last few weeks. "In fact, Mother and I were planning to return with you Sunday so we could shop for a wedding gown in the city. I don't know now what Mother's plans will be."

"Well, I'm going to have to get used to the idea that my younger sister is going to get married, but meanwhile I'm going to go to my room and deposit this luggage. Think I'll peep in on Father and see how he is doing."

A short time later, Estaban and Amanda joined Bianca in the parlor and it was only the three of them having dinner in the dining room tonight. Amanda ordered a tray sent up to her husband.

After she ate, she excused herself to go back upstairs to see her husband. It gave Bianca a chance to speak to Estaban about her going back to the city with him if Amanda could not accompany her.

"Of course you can, Bianca," Estaban declared. He had to admit that listening to all the things she had told them while they dined alone put a different slant on the prospect of Larkin being his sister's husband. The ring she was wearing was a far more impressive and expensive one than the one he had purchased for

Rosita.

Their conversation was interrupted when Amanda returned to the parlor to tell Estaban that his father wished to talk with him. He was most anxious to have a talk with his father, for he had not planned to announce his wedding plans to his sister before he told his parents. It had just happened that way.

Bianca had had to bite her tongue to keep from saying anything to her mother while the two of them were alone in the parlor. But she did tell her that Estaban had no objections to her going back with him if Amanda felt she could not leave Rancho Río Sunday.

"You will do fine without me. Besides, I've got to get your father walking before your wedding," Amanda told her.

Fearful that her tongue would surely slip and she would tell Estaban's news before he had a chance to do it himself, Bianca bade her mother good night with the excuse that she should get some packing done if she was to leave with him Sunday.

Amanda did not linger, for she figured Tony and Estaban might be having a lengthy conversation this evening since it was his first evening home in so long.

So she dimmed the lamps in the parlor and mounted the steps to go up to the small sitting room adjoining their bedroom. She snuggled up in the comfortable floral chintz-covered chair and read a book until she heard Estaban leave his father's bedside. She put her book aside then and went through the door to the adjoining room, which was their bedroom.

"You two had a nice chat, I figure. Estaban seems to be very happy, doesn't he?" she said as she ambled over to the bed to plant a kiss on her husband's forehead and check his foot.

"He has every reason to be in such high spirits, *querida*. He, too, is in love. In fact, we are to have two weddings in the Moreno family, it seems. Estaban is getting married only a few weeks after Bianca marries Larkin."

"Estaban is getting married?" she stammered, for she had figured it would be a long time before her son would ever marry.

Tony saw the stunned look on his wife's face. He knew that she had been taken utterly by surprise by the news. However, he always felt if Estaban met a very special young lady, then he would fall head over heels in love with her. It had obviously happened!

Estaban had given him a very vivid description of this exceptional young señorita, Rosita Armendez. Tony recalled the family when he was in San Antonio visiting with his grandfather. Like the Moreno family, the Armendez family were among the first settlers there in San Antonio.

Tony thought that Estaban had picked himself the perfect lady for his bride. He watched his wife slowly pacing around the bedroom before she finally took a seat at her dressing table and he could not miss seeing the thoughtful look on her lovely face as she began to let down the coils of her long hair.

"Tony, we could be a grandfather and grandmother a year from now. That is going to make me feel very old," she told him.

He could not restrain his laughter and he wished

he could leap out of that bed to go to her, assuring her that she would never grow old as far as he was concerned. But he couldn't, so he had to say what he felt as he lay on the bed. "Ah, Amanda *mia*—to me you will always be younger than springtime! You are still the most beautiful woman in the world and to me you'll always be."

"Then that is all that matters to me, Tony Moreno! It's all that has ever mattered to me," she declared as she left her dressing table to join him there in bed.

Fifty

Tony Moreno was an impatient man and it was vexing him that by Sunday, he was still unable to leave the bedroom. So he had to tell his son and daughter a fond farewell from his bed. Amanda accompanied them as they left the room to go downstairs to board Estaban's buggy.

She was still bedazzled that her son and daughter were both going to be married and leaving Rancho Río forever to have their own homes. It seemed only like yesterday that both of them were just tots running and playing on these grounds.

As happy as she was for Bianca and Estaban, she felt a pang of sadness and she wondered if Tony was sharing her feelings.

Amanda had two dinner trays sent up to the bedroom, where she shared dinner with her husband. This was a routine she followed for the next four evenings.

On the fifth day, Tony found that he could move around the bed very cautiously. So he was going to surprise his wife tonight by insisting that they dine downstairs.

By the dinner hour, he was ready with the aid of a cane to tackle descending the stairway. Amanda was delighted to see how well he was moving around their bedroom. She, too, was ready to enjoy his company downstairs, so she eagerly rushed to inform the cook that they would be having their meal in the dining room tonight.

She made herself look especially pretty and arranged to have Tony's favorite foods prepared.

The last four days had been busy ones for Bianca, but she had accomplished much of the shopping she had wanted to do. In wandering through the various shops of San Antonio, she had found the wedding gown she wanted, so she had immediately purchased it, for it fit her perfectly. In the same little shop she found the other accessories she needed like white satin slippers and lacy undergarments.

The very practical side of Bianca urged her to purchase a couple of new divided skirts and matching jackets. Since she was going to be the wife of a rancher she would be more in need of clothing like that instead of her fancy gowns and afternoon frocks. Besides, she had an armoire filled with gowns. Before she called it a day she visited a boot shop to purchase a fine pair of brown leather boots.

She knew her great-grandfather's driver was glad when she finally announced to him that she was ready to go home.

When they arrived back at the old gray stone mansion, Orlando helped her out of the carriage before he attempted to gather up all the packages to take into the house.

She thanked him graciously and told him she would need his services again the next day about eleven.

"Sí, señorita," he agreed.

Bianca was feeling quite proud of herself, for she had accomplished everything she'd sought to do. There were three days left, so she could use the rest of her time to just enjoy herself. It was perfect when Estaban told her at dinner that evening that he was taking her to lunch with him and Rosita the next day.

Being in the company of her brother and his bride-to-be made Bianca lonely for the sight of her handsome Rick Larkin. It seemed like months since they'd last said goodbye and he'd left Gonzales County.

It was obvious that the beautiful Rosita was very much in love with Estaban. Her eyes warmed with adoration every time she looked at him. Bianca was reminded of her tía Mona whose delicate dark beauty was like Rosita's fine features. She was a very petite young lady, so Estaban towered over her. But her brother was still not as tall as their father or Rick Larkin.

The three of them had enjoyed a delicious lunch and Bianca was delighted to have the opportunity to get acquainted with the young girl Estaban would soon marry.

Rosita found Bianca an easy person to warm to. Being more demure and quiet, she admired and envied Bianca's liveliness.

After they had finished lunch and before Estaban took Rosita back to her home, he took his sister to their great-grandfather's house. "I can't let you two pretty ladies keep me out of the office all afternoon," he'd teased the two of them.

As Bianca was preparing to leave the two of them to go into the house, Rosita told her that she hoped that

370

they would get to see one another again before she left to go back to Rancho Río.

As Estaban urged the carriage into motion to take Rosita to her home, he was feeling very happy about how well his sister and Rosita had seemed to enjoy each other's company. He had hoped they would like each other, for it was very important to him that his family would approve of her. Quite different from Bianca, Estaban was ruled by conventional ways. Rosita confirmed her feelings to him as the carriage moved out of the drive. "I like your sister, Estaban, and I think she likes me, too. She is so very beautiful!"

Estaban laughed. "Oh, Bianca liked you, I can assure you. If my sister didn't like you, you would know it. That's the way she is."

"Oh, it is going to be nice to have her as my sister-in-law," Rosita exclaimed, looking up at Estaban affectionately.

Bianca wandered through the downstairs of the old house to find it deserted, so she figured her great-grandfather was upstairs having his afternoon rest. There was no sign of old Ignacio, either. She wondered what one of them would do without the other, for they'd lived so many years together that one would not know what to do without the other.

She went upstairs to the guest room she had been occupying since her arrival here. She sought to make herself comfortable as soon as she was inside the room by removing her slippers and the bonnet atop her head.

She wondered if her mother would be coming to the city; if she did not arrive by this evening, Bianca was certain that she would be going back home alone.

Then her thoughts began to wander from Gonzales County over to Guadalupe County where the man she loved was. Her eyes suddenly sparked very brilliantly and she was consumed by a very impulsive idea. She saw no reason why she shouldn't do it, she told herself. After all, she had all her shopping done and she'd spend some pleasant time with her great-grandfather. Today she'd had lunch and met Estaban's bride-to-be. So what was to stop her from having Orlando drive her into Guadalupe County, which was only about a two-hour journey.

The more she thought about it, the more the idea appealed to her. What fun it would be to surprise Larkin by appearing at Happy Valley! She could tell him about all the plans she'd been making and about the beautiful wedding gown she'd bought.

But a short time later as she was enjoying a leisurely bath, a much better idea came to her. Instead of having Orlando drive her, she would ride that high-stepping little bay mare to Happy Valley herself. She'd just tell Orlando that she was going to take Poppy for a ride.

She could make much faster time if she rode Poppy there and back. She knew that she could not spend much time at Happy Valley but just to see him and have his arms hold her for a brief moment was worth the ride.

No one would ever know where she'd gone for the few brief hours. Great-grandfather Estaban would never be any the wiser and she would be home long before her brother came from his office.

All during the dinner she shared with her brother

and great-grandfather, her thoughts were consumed with going to Happy Valley tomorrow. She was not listening to their conversation. After dinner, Estban did not linger long in the parlor. "I've got to get to the office early in the morning, sir," he'd told old Estaban as he prepared to go to his own private wing of the house.

It gave Bianca the opportunity to also say good night and go up to her room. But she was too excited about her plans for tomorrow to try to go to sleep, so she got one of the new riding skirts she'd purchased and her new brown leather boots ready to wear in the morning.

Since her mother had not arrived by late afternoon she was sure she would not be coming during the day tomorrow since Bianca was due to leave for home the next morning.

The night was endless for Bianca and she got little sleep. The minute the sun was rising and shining through her window, she got out of the bed. Only the thought of seeing Larkin would have urged her out of that bed. She was dressed and ready to go downstairs to see if the cook had a pot of coffee brewed before she went to the stables to get the bay ready for her ride. She knew that she was going to give Orlando a terrible shock by appearing so early.

She was certainly right about that, for Orlando came slowly stumbling down the stairs from his quarters above the stable when she'd called out to him, his hair tousled and fumbling with the buttons of his shirt.

"Sí, Orlando. I wish to ride the bay. You don't have to take me anywhere today, but I wish to go for a ride. Can you saddle the bay for me?"

He soon had the feisty roan saddled and readied for the señorita. Bianca was eager to be on her way so she quickly mounted up and galloped out of the stable.

She could tell that she and Poppy were going to get along just fine. She wasn't a huge animal like Rojo, but she had a lot of fire and spirit and Bianca liked that in a horse.

Soon they had reached the outskirts of the city and were heading for the open countryside. Soon, she told herself, she was not only going to be seeing the man she loved with all her heart but she was going to be seeing the place she'd be calling her new home.

What a perfect name that seemed to be for the home she would share with Larkin. It would certainly be a happy valley!

Fifty-one

The rolling countryside was beautiful, with its fertile black land and groves of pine trees. There was a peace and serenity in that hour of the morning as Bianca rode along the dirt road. She passed by some ranches where she could see the movement of men around the grounds.

She was aware when she'd entered Guadalupe County and her excitement mounted until she found herself riding down the country road that was going to lead her to the old Compton Ranch. She knew she'd made the right decision to ride Poppy instead of having Orlando bring her here in the carriage.

Only now did she begin to slow down the bay's pace, but she suspected that Poppy had rather enjoyed kicking up her heels instead of pulling a carriage as she usually did.

When she finally came to the archway telling her it was Happy Valley Ranch, she pulled up the reins. For a moment she just sat on Poppy to survey the land and all the surroundings before she rode on through the archway that would lead her up to the house. It was not a house like the one she'd always lived in. There was no red-tiled roof and no courtyard gardens surrounding the house like there was at Rancho Río.

The house was a one-story structure of sand-colored stone. She could see the barn and other outbuildings to the back and side of it. She liked the clustered groves of trees along the drive leading up to the house. Her father would have said that it was a ranch that had been given tender care and devotion.

She was ready to urge Poppy to move through the archway and up the drive. When she reached the hitching post, she saw a buggy there and wondered if Larkin had visitors this early in the day, for it was not yet midday. She glanced over in the corral but saw no sight of Raven prancing around the grounds.

An impish smile etched her face as she bounced up the steps to the porch. She was already anticipating the look on Larkin's face when he saw her there.

But it wasn't Larkin who opened the door nor was it his housekeeper, Ola, for she was in the barn gathering up the eggs. In fact, Ola was not aware of the unannounced arrival of Cornelia Mason. Since Cornelia had seen Larkin riding away in the opposite direction from the one her buggy was traveling, she had not hesitated in entering the house without knocking.

She had barely taken off her bonnet and cape when she heard the galloping hooves of a horse coming up the drive. Looking out the window, she observed a gorgeous creature dismounting from her horse.

When she knocked on the door, Cornelia went to open it as though she was the mistress. "Welcome to Happy Valley," she flippantly greeted Bianca, who was not exactly expecting to be greeted by the sultry, dark-haired beauty with her low, scooped-necked gown.

Bianca could not see this woman as Larkin's house-keeper, and if she was, then she wouldn't be working here long after they were married.

"I've come to see Larkin. Is he here?" Bianca asked as she stepped inside.

"No, honey, he isn't," Cornelia told her.

Bianca decided she might as well satisfy her curiosity by asking her, "Are you the housekeeper?"

Cornelia broke into a gale of laughter. "Now, I don't exactly look like a housekeeper, do I honey? No, I'm Cornelia Mason, and who are you?"

"I am Bianca Moreno. You said Larkin wasn't here, so could you tell me when he will be back?" By now, Bianca was becoming very upset even though she was able to appear calm and composed. She had to know why Larkin had a woman like this in his home.

"Larkin doesn't tell me when he will be returning when he leaves the house, so I can't tell you when he'll come back. You're welcome to sit down and wait, though," Cornelia told her, for she saw the perplexed look on the pretty girl's face.

"So you stay here at Happy Valley?" Bianca asked, trying to keep her mounting temper in check.

"Well, I have, if that's what you mean, Miss Moreno." By now Cornelia was having herself a devilish good time. Larkin was going to have a devil of a time getting back into Miss Moreno's good graces, she figured. Oh, she appeared to be calm and collected, but Cornelia had seen the black fire in those eyes of hers.

"Well, I can't wait, so I will be leaving." Bianca hastily whirled around to go out the door. As she was almost through the door, Cornelia called out to her, "Shall I tell Larkin you dropped by?"

"No, it was not that important, Señorita Mason," Bianca muttered as she rushed out to the porch and down the steps. By now, she did not try to keep the tears from flowing as she went to the hitching post to mount up on Poppy. No one could see her tears now. Only she knew how brokenhearted she was!

Wild as the south winds blowing, she rode away from Happy Valley, for she wanted to leave Guadalupe County as fast as she could. Never would Happy Valley Ranch be her home!

Ola returned to the house with her basket filled with eggs and she had no inkling that Mr. Larkin's bride-to-be had been here and left. But she did wonder at the strange buggy at the front of the house.

As soon as she walked into the house she knew who their visitor was. That sickeningly sweet fragrance she smelled could only mean Cornelia Mason had come here again! Ola gave out a sigh of despair, for she had hoped that they were rid of her.

A grimace creased her face as she marched into the parlor to find Cornelia Mason sitting there making herself very much at home.

With a scowl on her face, Ola inquired what had brought her here. Mr. Larkin is not going to be too happy when he returns to find you here," she commented.

"Well, *Mr. Larkin* as you call him, may just have to be unhappy, Ola. Just go about your chores and I'll wait here for him," Cornelia told her. Ola was hardly able to toss her out of the house so she turned to leave the room. Mr. Larkin would have to do that when he returned home. In the meanwhile she put the eggs away. She had her kitchen to sweep, and when that was done she went to sweep off the porch. While she was making ready to sweep off the two front steps, a brown woolen glove caught her eye. Bending down to pick it up, she saw the embroidered initials on the folds. It certainly did not belong to Cornelia Mason she was sure. Yet, the initials B M could have belonged to someone in her family.

When she went back into the house, she observed Cornelia's fancy attire. Her keen eyes saw the bonnet and cape trimmed in black velvet laying on the chair. A pair of black gloves lay with the reticule.

"What are you staring at, Ola?" Cornelia asked the housekeeper.

"Just checking to see if you had two gloves there. I found a brown one out on the front step, but then yours are black and this one is brown, so it wouldn't be yours."

"No, it isn't mine. I never wear brown anyway!"

"Well, I guess Happy Valley has had another visitor this morning that I didn't know anything about. Someone lost their glove and it is surely a lady's glove," Ola remarked as she prepared to leave the room.

"Oh, there was some young lady who came, but she left as quickly when she found out that Larkin wasn't here. I think her name was Bianca Moreno. Yes, that was her name," Cornelia casually informed Ola.

That name matched the initials on the gloves and Ola instantly recognized that name as Mr. Larkin's bride-to-be.

Ola turned to leave the room, for she was very disturbed about what that poor man was going to be facing now that his bride-to-be had come to the ranch which was to be her home only to encounter a hussy like Cornelia Mason. Mercy, what that young lady must be thinking!

Ola put the glove in her apron pocket for safekeeping, then busied herself in the kitchen attending to her chores.

She made no effort to offer Cornelia any lunch when the midday hour arrived nor did she offer so much as a cup of coffee to the intruder in the parlor.

It was almost one when Larkin hit the back door to come into her kitchen and she immediately told him about Cornelia.

"Oh, God! That woman!" Larkin moaned. He flung his hat down on the kitchen chair and marched out of the room.

Larkin was wondering what that bitch was going to hurl at him now. Whatever it was, he was determined that she was not going to get one more cent from him.

There was no gentleness in his voice as he addressed her when he entered the parlor. "Make whatever you have to say to me fast, Cornelia, for I'm a busy man. Why are you here? We have nothing more to talk about, and my lawyer has assured me of that."

"I merely wanted to thank you, Larkin, because those three days' stay at the hotel in Seguin enabled me to meet a very nice wealthy bachelor, so I'm on my way to Austin and a most comfortable life. You see, Larkin, I was going to thank you for doing me a favor."

She rose up from the chair, swung the cape around her shoulders, and picked up her reticule and gloves as she sashayed out the door.

Larkin was happy to see her go, and he had to admit that he was pleasantly surprised that she wanted nothing more from him.

He ambled back toward the kitchen to tell Ola the good news and help himself to a cup of coffee. She would be glad to know that the house was free of Cornelia Mason once again.

She hesitated to show him the glove in her apron pocket, for she knew that it was going to cause him grave concern to know that his bride-to-be had come to see him only to encounter the likes of Cornelia Mason.

But she had to do it even though it pained her, so she pulled out the brown glove from her apron pocket and held it out to him. "We had another visitor today, Mr. Larkin, but I did not know it until I came back from the barn where I'd been gathering the eggs to find Cornelia sitting in the parlor. I did not know about her arrival or her departure until I found this on the steps of the front porch."

Larkin had only to look at the dainty glove with the initials B and M to know it was Bianca who'd come to the ranch.

He could well imagine what that devious bitch had said to plant seeds of suspicions in Bianca's mind. For her to have made such a hasty departure, Larkin knew what she must be thinking.

Ola watched as Larkin heaved a deep, heavy sigh. She saw the tension etching his handsome face.

"I'm so sorry to tell you this, Mr. Larkin. I—I just wish that I'd been at the house when this young lady arrived, for I figured that this had to be your bride-to-be."

"She probably won't be now, Ola."

"Oh, Mr. Larkin, she's got to believe that you had no part of that Cornelia Mason being here this morning. You'll just have to convince her of that and I can cer-

381

tainly back you up on that," Ola said.

"That's mighty nice of you, Ola, but Bianca Moreno is not a lady you convince of anything too easily."

Ola felt very sorry for him. He looked so desolate and gloomy and she knew what she had told him had caused it. She wished that she could ease the pain she'd caused him.

She wished she'd gotten to meet this lady Rick Larkin loved so much, for she had to be very special. She never had a doubt that he would lose her, for he loved her too much to allow that to happen.

It did not surprise her when he announced to her that he might be leaving the ranch tomorrow for a few days.

Fifty-two

It was only when she had led Poppy into the stable that Bianca realized how harshly she had ridden the bay back to San Antonio. She felt very guilty about it. She should not have punished the horse when it was Larkin she wanted to hurt as she had been hurt.

Somehow she managed to get through the evening meal and get back to her room without giving away the feelings she was flooded with. She could not bring herself to tell her great-grandfather or her brother that there would be no wedding. Her fierce Moreno pride would not allow that. Later they could be told. Right now, she just wanted to leave San Antonio and get back to Rancho Río to figure out what she must do now that she knew that Larkin was not the man she'd thought he was.

So she left the next morning with Orlando driving the carriage bearing her back to Gonzales County with her many purchases of lacy garments and the fancy wedding gown that she knew she'd not wear. When she left the old gray stone mansion, neither her brother nor her great-grandfather had an inkling that there would be no wedding at the end of December. She'd insisted that Estaban not accompany her back home and interrupt his work. She wished to travel back home alone.

Larkin's ring had already been removed from her finger and tossed into her reticule. Now she regretted that she had not accepted Ramon's pleas that she have lunch and talk with him while she was in San Antonio. Bianca knew that Ramon Martinez would eagerly marry her in a minute if she encouraged him. But she could not do that, for Bianca had faced something else while she was in San Antonio, and it had also told her how naive she had been. She was hardly the sophisticated young lady she'd credited herself with being. There was every reason for her to suspect that she might be pregnant!

Madre de Dios, she'd never thought of that possibility!

If she was forced to live up to her reputation as the reckless daughter of Tony Moreno, she could always marry Ramon to preserve the family honor and give her baby a name. Ramon would be most eager to be her husband, she knew She had a few weeks to think about this.

She would have to tell her mother and father that there would be no wedding. There was no way of getting out of it, for she could not allow her mother to carry on with her plans now that she'd decided not to marry Larkin.

More than anything she dreaded this, and then there would be Grandfather Kane to tell. She also dreaded having to disillusion her grandfather, knowing the high esteem he felt for Larkin.

This first night she would give them no inkling of what was on her mind. Tomorrow she would tell them, she promised herself.

It was just about noon that Orlando guided the carriage into the drive of Rancho Río. Her parents came out the door to greet her. Her father was finally walking, though with the aid of a cane. He did not attempt to come down the steps to help her down from the carriage but allowed Orlando to do that. Her mother rushed down the steps to give her an affectionate hug and kiss. "Ah, good to have you home, *niña!*"

Tony gave her a warm, fatherly hug and told Orlando to bring the packages and luggage into the house.

As soon as they'd all entered the house, Tony instructed Orlando to come with him and he took him to the kitchen, motioning him to have a seat at the little kitchen table. He asked the cook to fix the young man a plate of food. "You'll need some lunch before you start back, Orlando. Celia will take care of you."

"Gracias, señor," Orlando said with a broad smile. Tony Moreno was not exactly a stranger to him, for he'd seen him often when he'd visited his grandfather's house in San Antonio.

Bianca told her mother that she was not hungry after eating a huge breakfast before she'd left San Antonio and would unpack and have herself a bath before stretching out on the bed for a while.

An excited look came upon Amanda's face when she asked her daughter about her wedding gown. "I trust you found exactly what you wanted, Bianca."

"Oh, yes, Mother, I found a beautiful gown. I'll—I'll show it to you later when I get all this mess hung up," she said, trying to show the excitement a young bride-to-be would display when speaking about her wedding gown.

Two servants were summoned to get all the numerous packages up to Bianca's room, along with her luggage. Bianca was glad that she'd got through the homecoming without any problems. Now that she was alone she could relax until she joined them for the dinner hour, which was some five hours away.

She was grateful that her mother had not insisted on coming to the room with her to see the wedding gown. The sight of it as she took it out of the box was enough to make her cry, so she quickly put it in the armoire and out of her sight.

She sunk down on the bed for a minute to wipe the tears from her cheek. In a low soulful moan she muttered, "Damn you, Larkin! How could you have another woman in the house that was to be ours?"

Once her tears were wiped away, she made herself get up from the bed to finish taking the other articles from the boxes to place in the chest or the armoire.

It was when she was at the point of unpacking the last few articles left in her luggage that she realized that she had only one of the brown gloves she'd worn the day she'd ridden Poppy over to Guadalupe County and Happy Valley.

She hoped that it was Larkin who chanced to find the glove and not that black-haired hussy! Then he'd know that she'd been there. If he thought he was getting away with his little escapade with that Cornelia Mason, then he got a hell of a shock!

There was a part of her that wished she'd not found out and lived in her fool's paradise, but then, in the end, she would have been sorry. No, it was far better she found out before there was a wedding, the practical side of her said.

By the time all the things were neatly put away, Bianca was ready to have a bath. After she had indulged herself in the scented water, she put on her wrapper, laid across the bed, then took a long nap. It was almost dark outside her window when she roused.

She dressed in a paisley light wool frock in shades of pale blues, pinks, and lavenders. She pulled her long hair back to tie a blue velvet ribbon around it. On her ears she placed the topaz earrings that her great grandfather had given to her while she was in San Antonio. It never dawned on her to think that her mother or father would notice that she was not wearing Larkin's ring, which she'd angrily pulled off her finger.

When she was dressed, she went on down to the parlor to find that her parents were not down there yet, so she helped herself to a glass of her mother's favorite sherry. She sat looking out the window into the darkness and her mood became thoughtful, for she had expected this to be the most glorious holiday season she'd ever known. Around Rancho Río, it was always such a festive time with that magical blend of her mother's customs and those customs of her father's Mexican and Spanish background. Now, it was probably going to be the saddest time of her life, she thought as she sat there alone.

Tony and Amanda joined her in the parlor and they all shared a glass of wine before they retired to the dining room to enjoy the evening meal together. "I can't believe that Christmas is almost here. It doesn't seem possible. Where did autumn go this year?" she smiled at both of them.

In talking about the holidays of the past, Bianca found it distracted her parents from talking about her approaching wedding. Bianca was grateful for that.

But for all her lighthearted chatter, her mother was wondering why her daughter was not wearing her ex-

387

quisite ring. Her observant blue eyes had noticed it this afternoon after Bianca had arrived back home. And all evening until the time Bianca had bid them good night she'd mentioned not one word about anything pertaining to her wedding. Her mother found that a little puzzling, too. She wondered if Tony might have sensed this strangeness, so when the two of them were alone in their bedroom she brought up the subject.

He had not been as observant as his wife, but he tried to soothe her concerns by jesting with her. "Amanda *mia*—you are just the typical mother worrying over her children."

"I hope that you are right, Tony. Oh, I truly do. But I think I know Bianca, for I have only to remember myself at her age. She has certain ways so like mine. I shall hope this feeling will leave me by tomorrow, Tony, but I feel very intensely that something is wrong."

"Tomorrow will prove you wrong, *mi vida*," he told her in such a positive tone that she found herself convinced that he was surely right.

He always had the capacity to sweep her worries away. By the time they were going upstairs, she was sure that she had just been overly concerned.

There had to be a very simple reason for Bianca not wearing her ring!

Fifty-three

Bianca knew that the best tonic for her would be to take a ride on Rojo as soon as she awakened the next morning. Besides, she did not want to linger around the house because she knew that her mother would surely begin to talk about the wedding.

She was glad that she had told her mother that she wished only the family at the wedding. If it had been otherwise, invitations would have already been sent out to all their rancher friends. She was going to be spared that embarrassment!

She had given her mother a hasty good-morning greeting as she rushed out of the house to go to the barn and get Rojo saddled up for the ride over to the Circle K.

She was quickly up on the horse and spurring him into action. He was more than ready to break into a fast-paced run over the countryside. Riding at this wild pace Bianca could forget all her cares and concerns.

As Bianca galloped toward the Circle K Ranch, Larkin was riding at just as fast a pace out of the Happy Valley Ranch. He had tossed and turned all night long wondering what Bianca had to be thinking when she found Cornelia in the house that was to be their home. He knew exactly what she was thinking, but he'd convince her it wasn't true if he had to hogtie her down to make her listen to him.

He pushed Raven hard, for he could not get to Gonzales County fast enough to please him. In his saddlebag, he had put Bianca's glove.

Ola had felt very sorry for him as she'd watched him gulp down two cups of coffee this morning. She just hoped that he could convince the lady he loved that he was innocent of any wrongdoings with that Cornelia!

For the first hour Bianca and Mark Kane visited, Bianca said nothing about her plans to call off the wedding. But she knew before she left that she must say something to him. There was no way to do it but come forward with that particular candor of hers.

She told him in great detail the story of what had happened when she went to Happy Valley Ranch. She was taken aback by his cool and calm reaction. "Did you speak to Larkin and ask him what this lady was doing there?" he asked her.

"No, I left, Grandfather, just as quickly as I could."

"Then Bianca, I've got to tell you that you did not act wisely. You should have sat yourself down and waited to face Larkin to see what he would have told you. You played right into this Cornelia Mason's hands. When a woman loves a man she's willing to stand her ground and fight for him. You didn't do it!"

For the first time in her life her grandfather had admonished her harshly and she was a little befuddled by the sharp snapping tone of his voice. "I was too hurt to stay there," she told him.

"This I can understand, my dear, but Larkin deserves to be heard and Bianca, you've got to have faith in the man you love as he must have in you, the lady he loves. That is what it's all about. Ask your mother about the faith she had in Tony Moreno. Ask her about their tumultuous love affair. Anything worth having is worth fighting for, Bianca, and maybe life's been too easy for you."

She'd never had such a stern lecture from her beloved grandfather before and it was all very disconcerting to her by the time she told him goodbye.

Now, she found herself wondering how her parents would react when she told them that she was going to call off the wedding to Larkin.

If she found no more understanding from them than she had from her grandfather, she was going to feel very desolate.

When she arrived at the ranch and rushed into the house she had every intention of telling her mother that she was calling off her wedding. Amanda heard her daughter entering the entrance and called out to her. "Come join me, Bianca," her mother urged her as she announced that they'd received a letter from Estaban.

As Bianca went into the parlor, Amanda gave her a warm smile as she told her, "Ah, Estaban seems so very happy. I'm glad to see both of my children so happy, Bianca."

It would have been the perfect moment for Bianca to tell her that only one of her children was to be married. Instead, she simply told her mother that she was happy for Estaban, too. "I liked Rosita very much and I'm sure you and father will when you meet her," she added. "It was obvious to me she worships Esta-ban. She is a very beautiful girl. She reminds me of Tía Mona."

"Ah, then she is very beautiful. I am most anxious to meet her and I'll get to do that at your wedding, for Estaban says that he will bring her here with him for the event."

Once again, Bianca could not tell her mother that they would not be coming to her wedding. She simply couldn't! She knew now just how hard it was going to be for her.

Quite abruptly, she rose up from the chair using the excuse that she needed to refresh herself after her brisk ride on Rojo.

"Of course, dear, you go ahead. I've a couple of things to attend to anyway," Amanda told her as she laid Estaban's letter on the table and accompanied her out of the parlor to go toward the kitchen.

When she had had a brief chat with her cook, Amanda went on to the study, but Tony must have finished what he was doing in there and left to go to the barn. So she just sat down for a moment in one of the black leather chairs by her husband's desk. What was going on with that pretty daughter of hers? she wondered. Something wasn't right, and her mother's instinct cried that out loud and clear to her.

The ring was still not back on her finger today, for Amanda had made a point of looking to see if it was there. This was enough to arouse Amanda's suspicions. She decided that the next time they were together she was going to ask Bianca about her ring and why she wasn't wearing it.

It did not surprise Mark Kane when Rick Larkin arrived at the Circle K Ranch less than an hour after Bianca had left to return to Rancho Río. He was thinking what a damned shame it was that she had not stayed a little longer or he'd not arrived a little earlier.

Mark wasn't fooled for a minute by that happy-go-lucky air he was forcing himself to display. "Put me up for a couple of days, Mr. Kane," he grinned at Mark.

"Couple of weeks, if you'd like, Larkin. I'm glad for this unexpected visit. Things going all right with you, Larkin?"

"Ranch is doing just fine, sir."

"Good! Glad to hear that. Didn't expect to see you again so soon, Son. By the way, you just missed Bianca. She hasn't been gone more than an hour," Kane deliberately baited him.

"Hadn't planned on coming back so soon myself, sir. It's Bianca who brought me back here so soon, I've got to admit to you, sir." He did not hesitate in telling Mark Kane his version of what had happened and what a headache Cornelia Mason had caused him since the minute he'd arrived in Guadalupe County. "Bianca saw her there at the house and took it all wrong," he finished his explanation.

"Well, you'll just have to set her straight, Larkin."

"That's what I intend to do, but you know how stubborn she can be."

Kane laughed. "I'm the first to agree with you about that, so I guess you'll have to be a little more stubborn and determined, won't you, Larkin?"

"You can bet that I will be if that's what it takes."

"Then get your things up to the room and hightail it over there if that's what you want to do," Kane told him.

"I'll give Raven a little time to get some rest first. I pushed him pretty hard all the way from Guadalupe County."

Kane admired a man who considered his horse. It said something about his character. Never had any hand stayed on his ranch if he found them to be cruel to the horses or cattle. It was something he wouldn't tolerate for a minute.

Larkin took his gear up to the guest bedroom before he led Raven to the barn to rid him of the saddle and make him comfortable in the stall. When he came through the back door Estella was pleasantly startled to see him. "Señor Larkin, how nice to see you!"

"Good to see you! Ah, you made those delicious apple turnovers just for me, I bet!" he playfully teased her.

"*Sí, señor*—just for you. Here, have one of them while they are nice and warm," she offered.

Larkin eagerly accepted the delectable pastry and even took a second one before he left the kitchen to go back into the parlor to join Mark Kane. But Kane had gone up to his room to have himself a nap before dinner, so Larkin went to his room to take a bath and get shaved before he made the trip to Rancho Río.

He could not deny that he was feeling a little apprehensive about going to Rancho Río, for he wasn't sure what his reception would be from Bianca or her parents. After all, they might not be feeling too kindly toward him when Bianca told them of the woman she'd encountered at his house. It didn't appeal to him to have an audience of her family around when he was attempting to convince her that he was innocent of any wrongdoing. But family or not, he had to see her!

Fifty-four

Tony and Amanda had no inkling of the very volatile scene taking place in their parlor. Larkin had been ushered into the house by one of the Mexican servant girls and told that he'd find Señorita Bianca in the parlor.

"Bianca, we've some talking to do," he immediately declared with a serious look on his face and her brown glove in his hand. "Here—here is the glove you dropped the day you came to Happy Valley."

There was no warmth in her lovely black eyes as she glared up at him.

"I've nothing to talk to you about, Larkin. There is nothing for us to say to one another, for my eyes saw what they saw. Nothing you can say will change that," she snapped at him.

"Oh, yes, there are some things to say, and you're going to listen to them," he told her. His green eyes pierced hers with their intensity. "Cornelia Mason means nothing to me and I didn't even know she'd come to the house that day."

She paced across the room and turned her back on Larkin, but his strong hand reached out to grab her wrist and whirl her around to face him. "Look at me, you little hellcat! I'm going to have my say whether you like it or not!"

"I'm in my father's house, Larkin. Take your hands off of me!" she angrily demanded him.

"This woman has tried to lay claim to my ranch declaring that she was Compton's daughter. I consulted Compton's sister and a lawyer and proceeded to kick her off the ranch."

There was a smirk on her face when she asked him, "Are you going to tell me that she never spent a night under your roof?"

"Under my *roof*, but not in my *bed*. She had come to the house while I was away here in Gonzales County."

She wanted to believe him with all her heart and he spoke in such a convincing way she was finding it hard not to rush into his arms. Larkin could charm her so effortlessly but she was determined to stand her ground. She would not share the man she loved with any woman even if it was just a brief moment of fancy for him.

"So you kicked her off the ranch and she comes back. Is this what you're telling me, Larkin?"

"This is what I'm telling you, Bianca, and you can believe it or not." For one fleeting moment he thought he saw a mellowing of the icy glare in her eyes and he gave way to the impulse to yank her into his arms as his hungry lips captured hers in a kiss, long and lingering.

He held her until her hands began to press against his chest and she began to protest breathlessly, "No, Larkin—no! I must think! I must!"

His eyes danced over her face and his hands took hers in his. It was then he became aware that his ring was not on her finger. He held her hand up to inquire why she was not wearing it.

She saw the rage and indignant look on his handsome face. "I—I have it, Larkin! I took it off when I was very angry with you."

He abruptly released her hand and his deep voice was laced with emotion as he turned away from her to start for the door. "I would have expected you to put more worth on the love I thought we shared, Bianca Moreno. If need be, I would have expected you to be a woman to fight for me as I have done for you. You see, I wanted to save this wonderful love I felt we had. But I won't come here again."

Tony and Amanda overheard all this. Both of them stood frozen at the second landing as Larkin emerged through the parlor door. They watched as he stood there only long enough to tell her, "I'll be at your grandfather's two more days and if you love me, you come to me with my ring on your finger."

Then he vanished out the door!

Amanda and Tony exchanged glances and were feeling quite helpless as to whether they should go on down the steps or retreat back to their bedroom for a few moments. Now, Amanda knew that her instincts had been right and something had most assuredly gone wrong since Bianca had returned from San Antonio. Neither she nor Tony had heard enough of the couple's discussion to know the cause of their quarrel.

Tony urged her to go on down the stairs. He himself had no intentions of pampering his beautiful daughter after the remarks he'd overheard from a very hurt young man.

He was not a man who passed judgment on anyone until he knew the whole story, but he was convinced that Larkin loved his daughter.

Amanda was having her own private musings. She knew not if they were to find an angry young lady there or a tearful one. A flood of memories washed over her and her own tempestuous love affair with the dashing Tony Moreno. Deep passionate love can often be very painful, as well as giving ecstasies of pleasure, she knew.

When she and Tony walked into the parlor Bianca seemed deep in thought, so absorbed in the ultimatum Larkin had tossed at her that she was not even aware for a moment that they had entered the parlor.

When she suddenly looked up to see them standing there, she knew that she could not lie to them. They had surely seen Larkin vanishing out the door. "Did you see him and hear us?" she candidly inquired.

"We saw Larkin leave and we heard only his last words to you, Bianca," her father told her. He searched her lovely face and he knew that she was fighting back tears that wanted to flow. Oh, she was a prideful little lady and she had inherited this trait from him, Tony knew.

He suggested that all three of them have a glass of wine before dinner. They sipped at the wine but carried on little conversation during the time. It was the same when they sat at the table. None of them had their usual hearty appetite, not even Tony.

After dinner, Tony decided to make himself scarce so that his wife and Bianca could be alone. It was a time in Bianca's life that she might need a woman's sage advice and wisdom.

Amanda knew Tony Moreno well enough to know exactly why he'd made his exit, and she appreciated his sensitivity to the needs his daughter might be having to have a talk with her mother.

He was not gone from the room but a few minutes when Amanda told Bianca that she had noticed the absence of Larkin's ring on her finger. "I knew something was not right, Bianca. But I was waiting for you to come to me."

"I found it hard to do, Mother. I found it awfully hard."

Amanda's blue eyes mellowed with compassion as she looked at her daughter. "Oh, Bianca—when I was so desperately in love with that handsome father of yours I went through the hurt and pain of being disillusioned and having doubts."

"With Father?" Bianca's black eyes flashed with surprise at her words.

"With your father! We had violent arguments, I can assure you. He was stubborn and so was I. Both of us were unbending and unwilling to give in to the other."

"I can't imagine you and Father being that way with one another."

Amanda gave out a laugh. "Ah, Bianca—you have much to learn about a man and woman in love. We still have our arguments, but that is the way it is when you are truly in love. When the man you love so much takes you in his arms and kisses you, you forget what it was you were arguing about. It doesn't seem important, *niña*." She knew Bianca was absorbing everything she was saying to her from the intense look on her face. With the same look on her own face, Amanda Moreno asked her daughter, "Do you love Larkin so much that the thought of not having him in your life would leave you desolate, Bianca?"

"I love him as I've never loved another man, and yes,

400

I think I would be devastated if I lost him," she confessed to her mother.

"Then you better fight to keep him, for you will be a very unhappy lady if you let this man slip away from you. Larkin is a proud man too. You would not respect him if he wasn't, Bianca. I always knew that it would take a certain kind of man to win your heart. No ordinary man like Emilo or Julio would have held your interest. I think I sensed that Ramon Martinez, with all his sophisticated airs, did not intrigue you like Rick Larkin did."

Bianca had never more admired her than tonight. She knew that she could come to her to bare her soul if need be and not feel ashamed.

This was very comforting to Bianca. "I'm glad we've had this chance to talk. I'm a very lucky girl to have a mother like you."

"Then I suggest that we go to our rooms and get a good night's sleep. Tomorrow is a new day, Bianca."

Once Bianca was in the privacy of her bedroom, she immediately went to seek out the velvet reticule she'd dropped Larkin's ring inside when she had been so angry.

Sitting down on her bed, she dug into the reticule to get the ring, and she looked at it for a moment before slipping it back on her finger. Never would she forget the fury she'd seen in Larkin's eyes when he'd discovered the ring missing from her finger.

With the ring back on her finger she was now asking herself if she could humble herself to get on Rojo and ride over to the Circle K Ranch to see him as he'd told her she must do if she loved him.

If she was to heed her mother's words of wisdom and

the urging of her heart, then she would ride Rojo as swiftly as she could to the Circle K Ranch in the morning.

By the time she had crawled into her bed and pulled the coverlet up over her, she had made her decision.

As her mother had said all that mattered was tomorrow and the future!

Fifty-five

As soon as the sun's rays came streaming through the windows of her bedroom, Bianca awakened. It was the tomorrow that her mother had spoken about, so she did not intend to waste one precious moment of it.

With an eagerness she would not have normally felt at this early-morning hour, she got dressed in her riding skirt and pulled on the new leather boots she'd purchased in San Antonio. With the flat-crowned felt hat atop her head, she was ready to leave her room and start for the Circle K Ranch. Amanda Moreno, having just gotten out of bed and staring out the window and leisurely stretching herself, chanced to observe the petite figure of her daughter rushing out to the barn. A pleased smile brightened her face, for she knew where Bianca was going this morning.

Last night she had told Tony about their discussion and he had praised her for the advice she'd given to Bianca. He was already gone from the room this morning, but she was going to be most anxious to tell him about seeing Bianca leave the ranch if he was not aware of it.

As she went about getting herself dressed and her hair brushed neatly into a coil at the back of her head, she was thinking to herself that there was going to be a

403

wedding at Rancho Río after all. In fact, it wouldn't surprise her if the wedding date was not moved up after they got together this morning!

All the time she was riding Rojo toward her grandfather's ranch Bianca hoped that she would meet up with Larkin before she had to enter the house.

Larkin had gotten up even earlier than Bianca, and he'd told himself that he might as well have stayed up all night because he'd done nothing but toss and turn all night long. It was a hell of a harsh ultimatum he'd laid down for Bianca, and as soon as he'd left Rancho Río he'd been tempted to turn Raven around and ride back there.

He knew that he had not been very good company to Mark Kane during the evening. Larkin had confessed to Kane what the conditions he'd laid down to Bianca.

"Oh, Son—wish you hadn't done it that way. A little sweet persuasion would have worked a lot better with Bianca. Tell her she's got to do something and she really gets stubborn and bullheaded," Kane informed him.

"Well, sir—it's a little late to do anything about it now. That's what I told her and I can't take it back now, but I got so damned mad when I saw that ring off her finger I blew up," Larkin declared to him.

For the next twelve hours Larkin had not thought about anything but Bianca. From the time he and Kane had had their talk at six in the evening until six the next morning, he'd done nothing but think also about what Bianca's grandfather had said to him. Larkin knew he was right and he cussed himself for not using some

404

sweet persuasion, as old Kane had called it.

Always when he'd held her in his arms and kissed her, she had responded to the fires of passion their love-making could ignite. It was one of the things Larkin adored about her. She was a hot-blooded, passionate woman who did not try to conceal the wild desires sparking within her.

By the time the clock was striking seven-thirty in the main house's kitchen, Larkin was hastily gulping down the last of the coffee in his cup and heading for the barn. Raven was saddled and ready to ride in a short time. He was heading for Rancho Río.

When he got to the halfway point along the trail, he halted the fast pace he was riding. There on the high slope of ground he sat on Raven. He felt the need to think about things before he went the rest of the way.

Suddenly, it dawned on him that this was the exact spot where he had been sitting astraddle Raven that spring afternoon when he spied the beautiful Bianca being chased by the Mexican.

He relived every second of that afternoon. Everything in his life had changed for him after that. From that moment to this day, he had felt very possessive and protective of her. She was his woman and he wanted no other man to have her.

Like a bolt of lightning suddenly striking, his green eyes flashed with excitement when he saw Rojo come galloping down in the valley with Bianca in the saddle, her golden hair flowing back from her face. She was coming to him, for she was headed straight for the Circle K Ranch. He had to believe that this was her reason for riding this way.

He spurred Raven into motion and they rode down

off the high slope.

As fine a Thoroughbred as Rojo was, Larkin had always known that Raven could outrun him if he was urged to do so. Larkin was urging him to do just that right now. A grin came to Larkin's face, for he saw that he was narrowing the distance dividing them. In another few minutes he would be overtaking her, he figured.

Bianca's ears heard the sound of pounding hooves echoing behind her, and for a moment a panic struck at her until she turned around to see that it was Larkin and Raven in pursuit.

All fear left her then and a slow smile came to her face. She was pleased that they were going to meet out here on the countryside and not at the Circle K.

She was tempted for one fleeting second to yank up on the reins to slow down Rojo's pace, but she didn't. She knew that Larkin was catching up with her even though she did not turn around to see how close he was or how fast he was gaining on her.

There was a wild excitement churning within her by the time Larkin caught up with her and she had only to see the green fire sparking in his eyes to know that he was feeling the same way.

"You were coming to me, weren't you, Bianca? Tell me you were," he asked her as he moved Raven nearer to Rojo.

An impish smile was on her face. "I *was* coming to you, Larkin, and as you can see, the ring is back on my finger," she assured him.

He took her hand in his and raised it to his lips. As he kissed her hand, he said in a deep husky voice laced with the deep affection and love he felt for her, "Let's never let stubborn pride get in the way of our love."

She said not a word as she leaned over so he could kiss her. Larkin was more than eager to oblige her and his hands clutched her waist but could not enclose her as he would have yearned to do.

When his lips finally released hers, he gave out a moan of pleasure. "Oh, God, Bianca—I've missed you and those sweet lips."

"And I've been very lonely without you, Larkin. Can we get married sooner than we planned? I don't think I want to wait that long," she breathlessly sighed.

"Nor do I," he agreed. "Nor do I want to take you back to the Circle K or Rancho Río."

"I don't want that, either. But what are we to do?" she asked him. Suddenly, Bianca's face was glowing with excitement as she thought of the perfect place. She had not been there since she was ten years old. In fact, she and Estaban, who was almost fourteen then, had received a spanking from their father for wandering so far away from the house.

A devious grin creased her face as she told Larkin, "Follow me. I know where we can be alone." He allowed her to lead the way as they rode back in the direction of Rancho Río.

But she abruptly left the trail that would have led them up to the long drive to go into Rancho Río and went to the north side of the trail. They began to climb up the sloping ground of a hillside.

"I hope you know where we're going, Bianca Moreno, because I sure don't." He did not know if they were on Moreno land now or not.

She laughed. "I know exactly where I'm going, Larkin. Trust me!"

"Oh, I do, *chiquita*," he also laughed as he continued to follow her up the hillside.

Finally she yanked up on the reins as she came to the overhanging ledge on the cliff. Surrounding the spot was a thick growth of underbrush and trees. A massive formation of rock extended out over the cliff like the roof of a house. Sides of the hillside surrounded the spot. Bianca explained to Larkin that she and Estaban had wandered up here. "We thought we'd discovered a cave, but it wasn't. But it *is* secluded and we can be alone as we want to be," she smiled up as him as he helped her down from Rojo.

"Looks like heaven to me, *chiquita*."

"I hoped that you might think that, Larkin. I haven't been back here since the day that my brother and I came here, and I'll never forget how a terrible storm struck so we had to stay here. When my father and some of his men came upon us huddled from the wind and the rain, we were two scared kids and my father was one mad man, for they'd been searching the countryside for almost two hours."

By now, they were walking under the ledge and to the back of the hillside. It was the perfect secluded haven for them to be alone with each other.

Larkin took off his jacket and spread it out on the ground before he lowered her down to sit there. His eyes danced over her face as he sunk down beside her. "Can you be ready for us to get married in a week, Bianca? I can't wait three more weeks without you being my wife. I'm an impatient man."

Her arms reached up to encircle his neck and there was an impassioned look on her face as she told him, "And I am an impatient lady, Larkin. Shall we plan on a week from today?"

"And that is going to be a long, long time," he declared as he took her into his strong arms to kiss and hold her.

Bianca found herself immediately consumed by a wildfire of passion that mounted and spread over her!

Fifty-six

The hillside enclosed them from the brisk autumn breeze and Larkin's heated body covered Bianca as she lay on his jacket on the ground. His sensuous lips flamed her where they touched and caressed. His firm, muscled thighs closed around her as he burrowed himself between her thighs. The liquid heat of his body flowed over her.

She arched her body closer and closer to him to absorb all the fire of his passion. He filled her with all his love and felt the frenzied undulating of her satiny body against him. He knew that his passion was mounting to lofty heights. Soon they were to soar to that peak together.

"Let's get dressed, *chiquita*," he said as they both slowly descended back to the world of reality. "I want nothing delaying our wedding. I'm more impatient than ever now," he grinned down at her.

Both of them scrambled around to get their clothes back on and Larkin insisted that she throw his jacket around her shoulders. They walked toward their horses with Larkin's arm snaked around Bianca's waist. She now felt whole again with him close to her side.

"There's nothing to keep me here at Circle K now, Bianca. I may leave so I can get busy getting Happy Valley Ranch ready for my bride's arrival."

She looked surprised but he quickly soothed her by saying, "Nothing will keep me from getting here to keep that wedding date with you, Bianca Moreno. My only reason for coming here now was that I was afraid I had lost you and I was determined I wasn't going to allow that to happen. Told your grandfather that I'd hog-tie you if I had to."

She laughed softly as they rode back to Rancho Río.

Tony and Amanda saw them coming through the courtyard gate together holding hands and they both knew the lovers' quarrel had been swept away. "Oh, Tony, there will be a wedding after all," Amanda exclaimed.

"Never had any doubt about it really!" he declared.

When Bianca and Larkin joined her parents in the parlor the first thing they told them was that they wanted the wedding to take place a couple of weeks earlier than they'd planned. It was impossible for Tony or Amanda to keep amused expressions from coming to their faces as they exchanged glances.

"Whatever the two of you wish, then that is the way it will be. The only problem may be getting the news to Estaban and your great-grandfather in time to get here," Amanda told her daughter.

"Oh, thank you Mother. I know it's very short notice, but Larkin and I want nothing grand—just a simple wedding."

"We understand, Bianca," her father assured her. "We should, for it was a very simple wedding your mother

411

and I had and no marriage could be happier than ours."

Bianca rushed over to embrace her parents and thank them again for being so understanding.

Larkin thanked them, too. "I've told Bianca that I will be leaving the Circle K this afternoon to get back to Happy Valley." A twinkle was in his eyes as he told Señor Moreno, "After all, the bridegroom has some plans to make, too, for such a special occasion."

"Well, you do whatever you've got to do, Larkin, and we'll have everything ready when you arrive back in Gonzales County. Until you can take over this daughter of ours we'll do it for you," Tony lightheartedly jested.

When Larkin prepared to leave, Bianca did not feel sad, for she was flooded with such overwhelming happiness this afternoon.

She'd walked out to the hitching post with him and he'd given her a farewell kiss before mounting up on Raven. His green eyes had a teasing look in them when he warned her, "Now, keep that ring on your dainty finger day and night, Bianca Moreno!"

She smiled and waved as he spurred Raven into a fast gallop.

Larkin did not linger long after he arrived back at the Circle K. As soon as he gathered up his gear in the guest bedroom, he was rushed back downstairs to say goodbye to Mark Kane.

There was a gleam of excitement in Kane's eyes. "It's a wedding on the tenth of December, eh?"

"Yes, sir—that is the day!"

They shook hands and as Larkin jauntily walked out

the door, Mark knew he was one happy fellow.

He sat back down in the chair to reflect for a while and there was no denying that Rick Larkin had played a very important role in his life. A year ago he had not even known the young man and yet, in a short span of time, he'd become very fond of him. He had Larkin to thank for the improvement in his health. A year ago he was wasting away in that damned rocking chair, but Larkin had encouraged him to get out of it and now he was able to ride again with a little help.

A year ago, Bianca had not known him and now she was marrying him. Kane could not forget that this man had saved his beautiful granddaughter from a fate worse than death.

There was no question that Rick Larkin had had a tremendous impact on all of their lives!

Larkin rode up to his ranch before the sun was setting that late afternoon. As soon as he got Raven quartered in the barn, he made for the house to tell Ola his good news.

"Oh, mercy, Mr. Larkin," she said excitedly. "I've got to get busy tomorrow. We'll want the house to look perfect for her."

"Now, you don't go overdoing yourself, Ola. We'll be arriving late in the afternoon after our wedding, so you don't have to have a feast prepared. Just one of your good tasty dinners will be fine."

"But I want your new bride to have a grand welcome," Ola told him. "Oh, Mr. Larkin, what a wonderful holiday season Happy Valley will enjoy this year!"

* * *

In the next two days, Larkin was to find Ola was worth her weight in gold. She suggested numerous things that needed to be adjusted in the bedroom to be shared by his bride. He would not have thought about having the huge armoire brought in from one of the other bedrooms to provide a place to store his bride's gowns.

When Larkin had taken over the bedroom and office that had been Fred Compton's, the earthy colors dominating the room had seemed all right, but Ola told him a pretty lady would feel much happier surrounded by soft pastels. So she and Larkin made a trip into town for her to purchase the materials to make it softer and more feminine. It also gave Larkin a chance to purchase himself a new shirt and pair of gray trousers to wear with the only coat he owned.

Since he had a lot of time to spare while Ola made all her purchases in the mercantile, Larkin gave way to the first shopping spree of his life. He told himself that he was not a poor man anymore, so he might as well enjoy some of the luxury he could now afford.

Ola had been the one to prompt buying the gifts he ended up purchasing for Bianca, but he also purchased a gift for Ola herself and for Miles Golden.

By the time he was returning to the store to see if Ola was through making her purchases, his own arms were ladened with so many packages that he could hardly see where he was walking.

By the time he was helping Ola into the flat-bedded wagon, she saw that he had not exactly been idle. "My goodness, Mr. Larkin—did you buy out the whole town?" she smiled.

"Just about, Ola! Let's get home before I end up doing just that."

Ola worked diligently to get the curtains and coverlet made. Larkin's male eyes could appreciate the transition of the very masculine bedroom and quarters by the time the ruffled curtains were made and hung. He knew that she was working late into the night, but he also knew that there was no way to stop her so he said nothing.

The next day she had the coverlet completed and all the old curtains and coverlet taken away to be replaced by those of soft pale pinks and greens. While Larkin was out on the range with Miles, she had had the young Mexican boy who did chores around the barn help her move the small dressing table into the bedroom and the stool was also recovered in the soft pastels.

Proudly, she took Larkin to see the room. "I think your bride will feel more comfortable in here now."

"Ola, you are a jewel! Now will you please slow down?" he gently admonished her.

"Yes, sir—I will now," she smiled. "Let us just say that it was my wedding present to you and your bride. I wanted to do it, Mr. Larkin. You've been awfully nice to me, and I was so happy you wanted me to stay when you took over here. I could have been let go."

"Oh, Ola, I don't know what this place would do without you!" Larkin told her, giving her a pat on her shoulders.

An affectionate smile came to her face. "You see, Mr. Larkin, that is what I'm talking about. You're a

415

good, kind-hearted person. Mr. Compton knew what he was doing when he left his ranch to you."

A serious look came to Larkin's face. "I want to think that, Ola. This ranch means everything to me. It's the place my sons and daughters will live. They will grow up to love this country as Bianca and I do.

"Ah, it is a good life you'll have, Mr. Larkin," she declared.

Larkin believed that she was right!

Fifty-seven

Amanda Moreno had worked to give a festive air to her home for the wedding of her daughter and the holiday season rapidly approaching. Garlands of greenery were wound around the bannister railings of the stairway. The traditional wreaths of greenery and red berries hung on doors and archways. Wreaths of chiles were also placed around the house, depicting the Mexican traditions of Tony's family. Garlands were draped across the mantel in the parlor and candlelight gleamed brilliantly in the elegant room.

Everything was exactly as Bianca wished it to be. Her great-grandfather and brother arrived in time to see her being married to Rick Larkin and Jeff and his wife, Mona, along with their daughter, Amanda, were also witnesses to the ceremony.

It was a very emotional affair for Mark Kane, and he could not restrain a mist coming to his eyes as he viewed his beautiful granddaughter looking like a princess in her white satin gown adorned with lace and seed pearls. A year ago he would never have expected to live to see Bianca being married.

His only regret was that his dear Jenny could not have been sitting here beside him today. That would have made everything perfect!

He also knew that he had done the right thing when he'd had his friend and lawyer, Clint, draw up a new will leaving the Circle K to Bianca, for he knew that she and Larkin would run his beloved ranch as he would want it run.

He sat there admiring the two young people standing there side by side. What a handsome pair they were and what beautiful children they would sire! Damn, if he wasn't going to have to stay around a little longer now just to see them, he vowed to himself!

The gathering reminded Kane of Amanda's wedding day; she and Tony had insisted on the same kind of simple wedding in their impatience to be married.

He and Jenny had obliged them just as Tony and Amanda had done today with their own daughter. He had no doubt that his grandson's wedding a month from now would be a more elaborate affair.

When the ceremony was over, Bianca came to her grandfather's side. "You are going to come to visit me at Happy Valley?" she smiled down at him.

"You just try to keep me away!"

Larkin found himself in the corner of the parlor with Mona Kane. Her husband had taken charge of their young daughter to move into the dining room.

Always the gentle lady, Mona voiced to him her wishes for happiness for him and Bianca. "You have to be a very special young man, Larkin, to have caught Bianca's fancy. But while we have this moment alone, I must ask you something that has puzzled me since the first moment I saw you."

"What is it, Señora Kane?"

"Are you the one who sent me the money? I will forever let it be our secret, but I must know," she said as her eyes looked into his.

His green eyes scrutinized her face for a moment.

"Remember, Señora Kane, that you said it would be our secret and I will trust you. Yes, it was me. I had my reasons. You see, Señora Kane, I am putting my trust and faith in you, for I believe you to be a very fine lady. I feel very proud to know that you are my aunt. You see, I am the son of Derek, your brother. I came to Gonzales County to get the cache of money he had hidden on the Big D. I found it, but by that time I realized I didn't want it, for I had come to care too much for the people at Rancho Río and Circle K. I knew it was money stolen from a good man like your father, David Lawson. I wanted no part of it, so I felt that you should have it. I must tell you, Señora Kane, I had a very wonderful mother."

"She must have been, for your ways are not like Derek's," Mona told him.

His hand went out to take hers. "Shall we keep this our little secret, Señora Kane, and someday we shall share it with the family? I think all wrongs have been righted."

Mona was thinking what a remarkable man Bianca had chosen for herself. "I shall share this secret with you, and may I say that I'm very honored to be your aunt, Larkin." She gave him a very warm smile as her hand clasped his arm and he bent down to give her a gentle kiss on the cheek. "Thank you, Tía Mona," he whispered.

Amanda's observing eyes had noticed Larkin and Mona in the corner and it was obvious that Larkin had her charmed tonight. This pleased her, but she turned her attention back to her other guests and the wedding lunch to be served immediately now that the ceremony was over. The young couple was eager to leave Rancho

Río so they could start for Happy Valley. Their travel would not be as fast going in the brand-new buggy Tony had given them as a wedding gift as if they were riding Rojo and Raven, who would be tied to the back of the buggy.

The dining room was as festive-looking as the parlor and glowed with candlelight even though it was midday. A light but delectable meal was served and Celia had baked a wedding cake for the young couple.

When the lunch was over, Bianca had swiftly mounted the back stairs leaving Larkin with the guests, for he had no plans to change his clothes. Estaban had quietly left the house to carry out his mother's request to take the garland the servants had made to drape around the newlyweds' buggy.

When she saw that everyone was very busy roaming around the parlor and enjoying glasses of champagne, Amanda could not resist the urge to slip upstairs for a brief moment alone with her daughter before she left to go to her new home and her new life. She felt that there was going to be a terrible void at Rancho Río when Bianca left.

Bianca opened the bedroom door and invited her in. "I was hoping to have a moment alone with you, Mother. You gave me a most wonderful wedding I shall always remember and I thank you from the bottom of my heart."

Her daughter looked very striking in her soft light-wool ensemble in a rich gold color. The bobbed jacket matched the gown and had a black velvet collar. Her bonnet was the same shade with a band and streamers of black velvet ribbon.

Amanda appraised her. "You look quite fetching,

Bianca Larkin," she declared.

"Oh, goodness, I'm going to have to get used to that," she laughed. "Don't tell my husband, but it will seem strange for a little while."

"I remember how I felt, but I remember what my father told me on my wedding day, so I shall say it to you, dear. You will always be Bianca Moreno, only now you will be Bianca Moreno Larkin."

More than ever, Bianca realized how lucky she'd been to have a mother like Amanda and a father like Tony.

As they went down the hallway together, Amanda suggested that she and Larkin come back for Christmas. Bianca promised her that they would certainly try.

Their moments of privacy were over, for the guests were assembled at the base of the stairway. There were the farewells to say to all of them and suddenly Bianca found herself in the garland-bedecked buggy with her new husband sitting beside her. The high-stepping bay was beginning to trot down the drive.

Larkin set him at a smooth pace as they rolled along the dirt road. His green eyes kept darting over to look at Bianca and he had to keep pinching himself to believe that she was now truly his wife.

"What—why do you keep looking at me that way, Rick Larkin?" she giggled. "Is my bonnet on crooked?"

"Your bonnet is perfect, *chiquita!* I just have to assure myself that this is not a dream and you are my wife, Bianca Moreno."

"The name is Bianca Larkin, señor," she said, a sly smile on her face.

Larkin reached out to pull her closer to him. "And don't you ever forget that, señora."

They both gave out a lighthearted laugh as their

buggy rolled closer and closer to Happy Valley Ranch.

By the time they pulled in under the archway at Larkin's ranch the sun was getting low in the sky and Larkin had already tucked the buggy blanket over Bianca's lap. Bianca had to confess to him that she was happy for the sight of the house just a short distance away. The excitement of the wedding and the journey from Rancho Río to Happy Valley had made it a long day and last night she had slept only a few hours.

Ola had been fidgeting for a couple of hours awaiting the newlyweds' arrival. When the air had turned cooler in the late afternoon, she'd had young Pedro bring in some logs so she could start the fireplace in the parlor and Larkin's bedroom.

A short time later when the buggy came up the drive, Larkin and Bianca were greeted by Miles and six of the men. Larkin introduced her around and Miles presented her with a giant wreath of pine branches and cones to be hung on their front door. Pedro rushed up with a wreath of dried red chiles he'd made.

Bianca graciously thanked them for their kindness before Larkin rushed her on into the warm, cozy parlor where she met Ola. Then he left her to go attend to the horses and get her valises. Ola thought she was an absolutely beautiful creature as she stood by the fireplace to warm herself and asked if she might fix her a pot of hot tea.

"I'm not a tea drinker, Ola, but I'd sure take a cup of hot coffee if you have some made," Bianca told her.

"Oh, sure do, señora. Always have the coffeepot on around here," she said as she rushed out of the parlor.

In a few short minutes Bianca was savoring the steaming hot coffee Ola had brought her while she waited for Larkin to return to the house and Ola had left to rush to her kitchen. Already, she had to say she liked Mr. Larkin's bride very much. She might be a wealthy rancher's daughter, but she wasn't the snotty sort.

When Larkin came back into the house he found his pretty bride making herself very much at home with her slippers removed and her stocking feet warming by the fireplace. She had removed her jacket and her bonnet.

"Well, *chiquita*—you look very relaxed," he grinned.

She had to admit that she was so very comfortable that she was reluctant to move to go to their bedroom so she might refresh herself before dinner, but she followed him down the hall. Such an overwhelming serenity swept over her as she entered the bedroom in the pleasing pastels. She had not expected Larkin's bedroom to look like this.

"Ola did this for you," he quickly informed her. "She wanted you to feel comfortable. It was her wedding gift to you."

"Oh, Larkin—what a nice lady she is!" Bianca was very affected by all the effort she'd gone to.

"She will be happy to know that you're so pleased, Bianca. Now I'll leave you to settle in and get refreshed before dinner."

As he walked out the door, she smiled as she thought to herself that she had only the need to refresh herself, for she already felt settled in.

She knew she was at home here at Happy Valley! No bride could have been happier than Bianca this December evening.

Fifty-eight

Ola had prepared a very delicious dinner for them and they sat in the dining room enjoying the tasty food and sipping on a glass of fine wine which Fred Compton had stored over the years in his cellar.

After dinner, Bianca had confessed to him that she had eaten too much of Ola's good food, for the waistline of her gown was too tight. Larkin urged her to go get into something more comfortable.

That was all he had to say for her to relieve herself of the snug-fitting gold gown. As she was slipping out of the gown and undergarments, which also felt too snug, she felt a giddy feeling from the three glasses of wine she'd drunk during dinner. But this was silly, she told herself, for she had drunk three or four glasses of wine before and during dinner many a night at Rancho Río without this effect.

But by the time she had put on her coral-colored diaphanous nightgown and the satin wrapper of the same color trimmed with delicate ecru lace, she could not deny that she was feeling giddy. It didn't matter if she was a little tipsy, for this was her wedding night and she was with her husband, she told herself as she sat down on the stool at the dressing table to brush out her long thick hair and dab some toilet water at her throat and behind her ears.

Larkin had made himself comfortable, too. After he'd placed another log on the fire he had removed his boots and lit up a cigarette.

Bianca came to sit beside him and the two of them talked about the glorious day they'd had.

Long ago, Ola had gone to the privacy of her own room, and Larkin had dimmed all the lamps in the parlor except for one. He told Bianca about her father's gift to him of a bottle of his favorite brandy and offered her a glass of it.

He didn't detect by the sound of her soft voice that she had no need of the brandy she was sipping now. "Larkin, I think we were meant to be lovers, don't you?" she softly cooed.

"No question about it, *chiquita!*"

The dancing flames of the logs burning had a hypnotic effect on her as she continued to sip her brandy. She had rested her head against Larkin's chest.

Never had he known such happiness as he did tonight as he sat in his own house snuggling with the beautiful woman who was his wife. He felt the need to tell her this and he didn't know how long he had talked before he suddenly noticed that the glass she was holding was tilted and at the point of slipping from her hand. As he took it, he realized that his beautiful bride was sleeping quite soundly with her head resting against his chest.

She was not aware when his arms scooped her up and carried her to their bedroom. Gently he placed her in the bed and did not attempt to take off the wrapper as he pulled the coverlet over her. He dimmed the lamp in the room and returned to the parlor to dim the lamp there.

While he was undressing in the dark bedroom, a devious twinkle came to his green eyes, for in the years to come they would laugh about how she'd fallen asleep on their wedding night. Larkin knew they would have a lifetime to share the passion they both knew was theirs.

But it was very disturbing to Bianca the next morning when she finally awakened at midday and could not remember Larkin carrying her to their bed.

"Larkin, I'll kill you if you ever tell anyone I fell asleep on our wedding night!" she vowed to him.

"Ah, Bianca—we have the rest of our lives for wedding nights, but right now, you delightful little distraction, I've got to leave you to attend to ranch business."

Bianca watched him leave the room and knew she had herself a rare man. By the time she'd spent three more days at Happy Valley Ranch, she was more convinced of this. During the day, he was a very hard working rancher, but at night he was an ardent lover, fulfilling her wildest desires.

After she had been Larkin's wife for one week, she faced the reality that she was also pregnant with his child. She was besieged by nausea. For a while Ola did not say anything to her but finally she told the young lady that it was nothing to fret about, that it would pass in a few weeks."

"Oh, Ola—I don't feel like traveling back to Rancho Río for Christmas as I promised Mother I would," Bianca sighed.

"And you shouldn't. But this is not the time for you to worry or get yourself upset over the likes of that."

Bianca was realizing more and more what Ola meant

426

to her and how much she relied on her and her sage advice. What she had not realized was that her husband had already suspected that she was pregnant, for his hands knew every curve of her sensuous body so well and now he was certain about it. She was carrying his child when they'd made love on the cliff and before they'd married. He questioned if she had realized it, though.

He had felt sorry for her when she'd gone through the spells of nausea and in hopes of brightening her spirits he and Miles had gone out to cut a huge eight-foot fir tree to put in their parlor for the holiday season.

That night she was like an excited child as he and Ola helped her decorate the beautiful tree. Ola was as excited as his wife, for she was thinking that this time next year there would be a wee tot here in the parlor with them.

Without consulting Bianca, Larkin sent one of his hired hands to Rancho Río and Circle K to invite the Morenos and Mark Kane to come to Happy Valley for Christmas. He could not imagine a nicer gift he could give to her.

He never found her more adorable than the evening she left the dining table quite suddenly and confessed to him, "Ola swears I'm pregnant, Larkin!"

"Well, Ola is right. And I've known about it for a while, *chiquita,* and that is why we won't be leaving next week for Rancho Río. You don't need to be traveling when you're feeling so uncomfortable."

Bianca could not argue with him about that so she said no more.

The next seven days Bianca and Ola had the house

427

looking very festive and Ola had spent a lot of extra time baking pies and cakes. Larkin and Miles had gone hunting for wild turkey in the woods bordering the south side of the property and they shot a turkey for Miles's table as well as Larkin's.

By now, Bianca did not give way to the sieges of nausea, for Ola had eased her fears. She accepted them and went on about her day.

Now that she had accepted that this was a normal fact of pregnancy, she was also ready to accept the fact that her clothing and her gowns were becoming more uncomfortable, so she began to let out the seams. She had also come to the conclusion that she was two months pregnant when she and Larkin had gotten married. Why had she not realized that this was a possibility before? she wondered.

But it didn't matter that their baby would arrive months earlier than it should have if one was counting the days from their wedding day. Neither she nor Larkin were conventional people who lived by the rules of others and perhaps that was the thing that had attracted them to each other initially.

On the eve of Christmas, just as twilight was beginning to shroud the countryside and lamps were blazing in the ranch house at Happy Valley Ranch, a carriage rolled into the drive under the archway. Bianca had seen to the lighting of the candles in the parlor and dining room in the same way she'd observed her mother doing it at Rancho Río. She was following her mother's traditions.

Tonight they were having a fine beefsteak, but tomorrow they would be having the roast turkey that Larkin had shot in the woods.

She roamed around the house that she was coming to love more and more to give it a final inspection to see that everything was perfect.

When Larkin came into the parlor to join her, she thought he looked so very handsome with the green silk scarf tied around his neck and his white shirt opened at the neck. She confessed to him that she had had to let out another seam in the gown she was wearing tonight.

The two of them stood in their parlor with the logs flaming and cracking in the fireplace admiring the beauty of the tree. Suddenly there was a rap on the door. Larkin released his arm from around her waist. He was hoping it was the guests he was anticipating to come this evening.

He'd secretly prepared Ola that there could be three extra guests for dinner that evening and he wanted it to be a surprise for his wife. She'd promised not to let the señora know a thing.

He was not to be disappointed when he opened the door, for it was Señor and Señora Moreno standing there with Mark Kane. He warmly invited them into the parlor and Bianca gave out a shriek of delight when she saw them. She rushed to give them a warm embrace. As she was hugging her grandfather she noticed the specks of white on his black wide-brimmed black hat.

It turned out to be the most wonderful Christmas Bianca had ever had. She adored Larkin for making it all happen. The snow that fell that night was gone by the next night and their guests departed the morning after Christmas Day to return to Gonzales County. All of them were convinced that their beloved Bianca was very happy and destined to live a wonderful life at Happy Valley.

Neither Bianca nor Larkin realized that they had started a new tradition that would continue for the years to follow at Happy Valley. The Morenos and Mark Kane came back again and again to share the holiday season at Happy Valley Ranch with Bianca, her husband, and their family.

Ola felt sure that Mr. Compton, wherever he was, had to be smiling and happy, knowing how much his home and land was loved by the two young people raising their fine family there. With each year that passed their devotion and love to each other grew deeper and stronger.

Bianca found the serene contentment and bliss she'd anticipated as the wife of Rick Larkin as the two of them rode side by side over their land on their fine stallions, Rojo and Raven.

She had everything a woman could possibly want to make her happy. Larkin had tamed her reckless, restless heart forever!

DANA RANSOM'S RED-HOT HEARTFIRES!

ALEXANDRA'S ECSTASY   **(2773, $3.75)**

Alexandra had known Tucker for all her seventeen years, but all at once she realized her childhood friend was the man capable of tempting her to leave innocence behind!

LIAR'S PROMISE   **(2881, $4.25)**

Kathryn Mallory's sincere questions about her father's ship to the disreputable Captain Brady Rogan were met with mocking indifference. Then he noticed her trim waist, angelic face and Kathryn won the wrong kind of attention!

LOVE'S GLORIOUS GAMBLE   **(2497, $3.75)**

Nothing could match the true thrill that coursed through Gloria Daniels when she first spotted the gambler, Sterling Caulder. Experiencing his embrace, feeling his lips against hers would be a risk, but she was willing to chance it all!

WILD, SAVAGE LOVE   **(3055, $4.25)**

Evangeline, set free from Indians, discovered liberty had its price to pay when her uncle sold her into marriage to Royce Tanner. Dreaming of her return to the people she loved, she vowed never to submit to her husband's caress.

WILD WYOMING LOVE   **(3427, $4.25)**

Lucille Blessing had no time for the new marshal Sam Zachary. His mocking and arrogant manner grated her nerves, yet she longed to ease the tension she knew he held inside. She knew that if he wanted her, she could never say no!